BLOOD BROTHERS

HEATHER ATKINSON

Boldwood

First published in Great Britain in 2020 by Boldwood Books Ltd.

A CIP catalogue record for this book is available from the British Library.

Paperback ISBN 978-1-80048-265-4

Large Print ISBN 978-1-80048-261-6

Ebook ISBN 978-1-80048-259-3

Kindle ISBN 978-1-80048-260-9

Audio CD ISBN 978-1-80048-266-1

MP3 CD ISBN 978-1-80048-263-0

Digital audio download ISBN 978-1-80048-258-6

Boldwood Books Ltd
23 Bowerdean Street
London SW6 3TN
www.boldwoodbooks.com

This book is dedicated to my lovely husband Paul, my beautiful daughters Charlotte and Sophie, my sister Suzy, niece and nephew Mia and Jack and my mother Stephanie. Also to my father, Tony, who is missed every single day.
It is also dedicated to my granddad, Jim. Watching him writing in his study when I was a child encouraged my own love of writing.

1

'Would you look at that?' said Pete, gesturing to the night sky with his can of lager, slopping it everywhere.

'Hey, watch it, you arsehole,' grumbled Stevie. 'Look what you've done to my trackie top.'

'Oh, aye, sorry about that pal, but would you look at that?'

'Look at what?' said Stevie, ineffectually swiping at his sleeve in a vain attempt to dry it.

'The stars.'

'What about them?'

'Well I mean, they're so fucking sparkly.' He waved his arms with such enthusiasm he almost fell off the garden wall he was perched on.

'Aye, so?'

'They're bloody beautiful.' He scowled at his friend when he realised he was more concerned with his damp sleeve than the celestial bodies. 'Oy, you're no' even lookin'.'

'Because I'm trying to dry my sleeve.'

'Are you still banging on about your shitey top? I'm sick of hearing about it.'

'Keeley only bought it for me yesterday. She'll fucking kill me.'

'If she gie's you any snash tell her to shut her fat hole.'

'Oh, aye, like I'd dae that. Do you think I've got a death wish? But don't worry, I'll be sure to tell her it was your fault.'

Pete swallowed hard at the prospect of being in that harridan's bad books. 'Blame it on one of the weans. She'll no' murder them.'

'No, she'll grind my tackle into the dust instead for giving her them. She's always blaming me for them being wee bastards.'

'You want to put your foot down with that one, pal. You sound like a right fucking poof.'

Stevie slammed his can of lager down on the pavement so forcefully he slopped more of it over himself. 'That's it, you prick, no one calls me a fucking poof. Stand up so I can gie' you a severe doin'.'

The front door of the house opposite opened, casting light onto the litter-strewn pavement.

'Keep the fucking noise down, you dobbers,' yelled a tall stocky man in a beige dressing gown. 'Unlike you lazy sods I have to get up for work in the morning.'

Pete and Stevie turned their antagonism off each other and onto him.

'Oh, aye,' said Pete. 'You wantin' some, big man?'

'I'll smash you into the fucking tarmac, Pete Williamson. Everyone around here is sick of you. I'll...'

A noise down the road drew all their attention. The man in the dressing gown took one look at the approaching chaos and ran back inside as quickly as his slippers would allow, slamming the door shut behind him.

Pete and Stevie turned to look as a gang of youths tumbled towards them amid punches, kicks and cries of pain. Picking up their cans of lager they stepped over the small garden wall, which barely came up to their knees, as though it could protect them from the carnage.

Out of the ten men – whose ages ranged from late teens to early twenties – four were gaining the upper hand, either sending their opponents running or knocking them to the ground. They'd formed a circle in the melee, standing back to back so no one could sneak up on them.

Eventually their opponents realised they weren't going to win and fled, dragging their injured friends along with them. The night air became still once more, only the sound of running footsteps audible.

Pete and Stevie swallowed hard when the four men turned to look their way.

'Pete, is that you?' said one of the men, jogging up to him while the other three remained where they were, standing in the middle of the road.

'Aye, it's me, Jamie. Er, how are you?'

'I'm no' bad, thanks. Looks like you've been wiring into the lager again,' he replied. Jamie was young, in his early twenties, but his eyes, which were hard obsidian flints, said he'd already lived a lifetime. His frame was tall and wiry, but he was renowned on the estate for his physical strength. Jamie's face would have been handsome, with sharp cheekbones, aquiline nose and full lips, had his gaze not been so full of threat. From his right hand dangled a thick bike chain, the blood dripping from it visible in the light cast from the streetlamp. 'You must be good and pissed, Pete,' he added. 'That'll affect your memory.'

'Aye, it does, every time. I'll wake up in the morning and I won't remember a thing about tonight.'

Jamie nodded and turned his intimidating gaze on Stevie, who took a step back. 'Does it affect your memory, too?'

'Every time,' Stevie hastened to assure him. 'I was on the vodka earlier and that always goes straight to my eyes. I cannae even see who I'm talking to right now, you're just a blur.'

'Good,' he replied in a calm voice.

Jamie glanced back over his shoulder at his three friends, who were watching. Stevie noted how their knuckles were stained with blood. When his three friends nodded, Jamie looked back at Pete and Stevie. 'You should go home. It's supposed to rain tonight.'

'Is it?' said Pete. 'I didnae know that. Thanks for the warning, pal.'

With one hard nod Jamie returned to his friends and the four of them casually sauntered off down the street.

Only when they'd turned the corner and vanished from view did Stevie release the breath he'd been holding. 'Thank God for that. Right, I'm off home.'

'What will Keeley say about your top?'

'I don't care. Even she's less scary than the Blood Brothers,' he called back before jogging off in the opposite direction to which the four youths had gone.

'Poof,' Pete muttered under his breath before hastily unlocking his front door, stepping inside and slamming it shut behind him.

* * *

Jamie smiled as he listened to his friends eagerly discussing their latest fight.

'Did you see me stick the heid on Finn Atkins?' grinned Gary, the most rotund of their group, his mop of blond hair flopping into his blue eyes, which were deep-set into a permanently flushed face. 'A wanker with a wanky name.'

'Aye, he broke like a blade of grass,' laughed Digger, who had earned his nickname by working out incessantly until he was the size and strength of one of the machines. 'Did you see me flip over Davey Saunders? He proper shite his pants.'

'I'm no' surprised,' said Logan, the fourth member of their group. Tall and athletic with curly light brown hair, he was the quietest of their band, and preferred to think a move through before making it, while the other three charged in headlong with little thought for the consequences. Logan's cool head had stopped them from making plenty of daft mistakes in the past when inexperience and the invincibility of youth won out over common sense. Out of his three best friends, Logan was the one Jamie admired the most.

'What do you think, Jamie?' said Logan. 'Do you think we saw off the Lawsons permanently?'

'Probably not, but we took them out of action for a while, especially after Digger threw John Lawson into his younger brother.'

Digger grinned and flexed his muscles. 'That's the last time those wee fuds will call me a steroid-pumped donkey.'

'They will be back,' glowered Jamie. 'But we just gave ourselves some breathing space.'

The Blood Brothers, as their group was known locally, turned the corner onto a darker street, passing rows of small new-build houses, each with a strip of grass out front and a freshly painted fence. The shiny new veneer was thin, though, because all the litter and broken-down furniture that had graced the gardens of the old houses had once again congregated outside the new.

'I wish I was in one of these,' said Logan wistfully.

'No, you don't,' muttered Gary. 'You cannae keep the heat in and the pipes keep getting blocked. They're fucking bodge jobs.'

'At least everything's all new. No' like our old place.'

'Your place might be old but everything works. My gran got water fired straight up her when she used the cludgy and it backfired. It's not fucking funny,' he added when they all doubled over with laughter. 'She was in hospital for two days with shock.'

'Aye, it is,' grinned Digger, wiping away tears of laughter. 'It'll do that cranky old cow some good.'

'Keep the noise down,' Jamie told them. 'We don't want anyone looking out their windows and seeing us after the Lawsons have just been attacked.'

'No one around here would grass to the police,' said Gary.

'You never know. Just take it easy.'

They all quietened down at his word. Jamie was the undoubted leader of their group. He always had been, ever since they were little children battling the bullies at school. He'd safely steered them through some choppy waters, so they always knew he was talking sense.

Gary was the first to leave, saying goodnight before quietly entering his house. Digger, who lived just around the corner, was next, although his house was in the older section of the scheme. At the bottom of Digger's road Jamie and Logan turned left onto the next street and the latter sighed.

'What is it?' said Jamie.

'My da's still up,' he muttered, indicating the light on in the downstairs living room.

'So?'

'He'll want to know how we got on with the Lawsons.'

'So what? You can tell him we kicked their heids in.'

'It's never that simple. He'll want every little detail and he'll find something to bitch about, he always does.'

'Want me to come in with you? We can take his shite together.'

'Aye, thanks Jamie.'

'No worries. Come on.'

Logan opened the door and they stepped inside the small stuffy house. Logan's house – like Digger's and Jamie's – was one of the original houses on the scheme, built in the fifties, every room poky. At least they were easier to heat than the new houses.

Dave McVitie sat in the armchair in front of the telly, a can of lager in one hand, the remote control for the television in the other. A plate of biscuits was perched on his belly, so pendulous it resembled a shelf when he sat down.

'All right, son,' he said when they walked in, his eyes glued to the television. 'Did you have a good evening?'

'No' bad. We beat the Lawsons.'

'Really?' he beamed, finally deigning to drag his eyes off the telly and onto them.

'Aye.' Logan glanced at Jamie, who nodded encouragingly.

Dave listened, enraptured, as his son related every detail of the fight. When Logan finally reached the end of his tale, Dave leaned back in his chair, lost in thought.

Jamie glanced questioningly at Logan, who shrugged.

'You did good, boys,' Dave eventually said, making this pronouncement as though he were a general praising his troops. 'If you don't defend your turf all the wee cockroaches will start taking the piss. You have to stomp on them before they infest the whole fucking scheme.'

'There were more of them this time,' said Jamie. 'Seven to our four.'

'And next time they'll come in an even bigger pack.'

'They won't come back, not after the kicking we gave them.'

'They'll be back, mark my words.'

Jamie and Logan glanced at each other.

'Right,' said Jamie, breaking the silence. 'I'll be off.'

'Why don't you stay for a drink?' said Dave, picking up an unopened can of lager off the floor and holding it out to him. 'Celebrate your victory.'

'I can't. My maw will go apeshit if I'm late.'

'Jackie's still fighting the world, is she?'

'She always will, she enjoys it.' Knowing filled his dark eyes. 'And she always wins.'

Dave cleared his throat, jowly face turning red. He'd gone up against Jackie Gray several times and lost. 'Go on, get off then before she spanks your wee arse.'

'See you later,' said Jamie as he left, glancing at his friend, amusement dancing in both their eyes.

Dave didn't speak until Jamie had gone. 'Did you get it, boy?' he asked his son.

'Aye, I did,' replied Logan, pulling a phone out of his jeans pocket and holding it out to him.

Dave snatched it from him with sweaty hands. 'From John Lawson?'

Logan nodded. 'Aye.'

'And your friends know nothing about it?'

'Nothing, not even Jamie.'

Dave swiped at the screen, smearing grease from the crisps he'd been eating across it. 'I hate these bastard things, I can never work them,' he muttered, thrusting the phone back at his son.

Logan took the phone from him, jabbed at the screen and sighed. 'It needs a passcode to unlock it.'

'Oh, that's fucking marvellous. All the information we need to finally get out of this shithole is on that phone and we can't even get to it.'

'Leave it with me, I know someone who might be able to help. I really think we should bring Jamie and the others in on this, though.'

'No,' snapped Dave. 'That's just more people to share the proceeds with. We keep this to ourselves. Do you understand, boy?'

Logan sighed and nodded.

'Good. Now stick some grub on, I'm starving.'

'It's nearly one o'clock in the morning and I'm knackered.'

'Then get on with it so you can piss off to bed. And don't burn the bloody bacon,' Dave called after him as he slunk into the tiny kitchen, which was nothing more than a worktop lining one wall with a fridge and a cooker on the other. After his mother had died four years ago, Logan had shouldered the burden of the majority of the cooking and cleaning, usually because his dad was too bone idle, although he did sometimes cook if he wanted a curry. The one time Logan had made curry he'd purposefully put far too much chilli powder in it and his dad had spent the rest of the day glued to the toilet.

He shut the door behind him and stared at the phone in his hands. It was tempting to smash it to bits. He had the feeling it was only going to cause even more trouble than they already had to deal with on a daily basis but his dad had the scent of easy cash in his nostrils and from experience Logan knew he would never let it go. If only his dad hadn't gone drinking down the pub and learnt about a robbery with a big payoff the Lawsons were planning. He had the horrible feeling they were way out of their depth.

* * *

The streets of Gallowburn were never silent, no matter the time of day or night. Whether it was a dog barking, a drunk singing out of tune or bored neds smashing windows, there was always noise.

Jamie passed a house where a couple screamed at each other so loudly it was audible on the street. There was a loud smash, followed by the man's yells. Jamie continued on his way. This was an everyday occurrence here, all part of the endless Gallowburn symphony. In the older part of the estate the lighting was poor, vandals having smashed the majority of the streetlights. Every time the council repaired them they were broken again almost immediately, so they'd given up, deciding to give the residents what they wanted, which seemed to be darkness.

Glancing up an alley he saw two shadowy figures, which melded into the night when they realised they'd been spotted. Drug dealing was rife on the estate, mainly with the young men who had nothing better to do, stuffing what little money they had up their nose or injecting it into their veins.

He passed rows of squat, pebble-dashed houses, each with a long spit of garden leading from the front door to the decaying fence. Some of the residents took pride in their homes, their gardens neat, adorned with flower baskets and gnomes and – in one case that had become the local joke – a fountain in the shape of a life-size Grecian woman holding an urn spurting water. The rest of the gardens contained broken plastic slides, cockeyed trampolines and weeds so high the local cats vanished when they jumped into them.

Jamie slid his hand inside his jacket, fingers closing around the bike chain. They'd beaten the Lawsons tonight but that family were cockroaches and could choose to get their own back while he was alone.

It was a relief when he reached his street. He could hear the shouting emanating from his house as soon as he turned the corner. His front door opened and a startled-looking man scuttled down the path, shoes in one hand, jacket in the other. A buxom blonde with beefy forearms chased him down the path, hurling insults at him and slapping him about the head.

'Go on, piss off, you manky wee jobby,' she yelled after him. 'You come into my home thinking you can gie' me a load of shite in my own living room. Well, you're about to feel the wrath, you fucking fanny.'

Jamie grinned as the terrified man raced past him out the garden gate and disappeared down the street, not even daring to stop to put on his shoes.

'I take it your date didn't go well, then?' he asked his mum.

'No, it did not,' replied Jackie. 'It started off well enough, he took me out to a decent restaurant, but in typical man fashion he thought he was gonnae get a reward for buying me scampi and chips, the miserable wee scrotum.' She took a deep calming breath, brushing her wispy blonde hair out of her eyes. 'I'm considering going gay. At least I might find someone whose feet don't stink and who tidies up after themselves. Why is it every man I meet is a dirty bastard?'

'From what I've found women are just as much hard work.'

'Probably. I couldn't stand another gobby cow like me.'

Jamie grinned and linked his arm through hers. 'Come on, Maw, let's grab a brew.'

'Okay, sweetheart,' she smiled, the last of her annoyance vanishing.

Jackie Gray's temper was phenomenal but fortunately it was also fleeting and rarely bestowed upon her children. They only felt her wrath when they'd seriously messed up.

They stepped into the light and warmth of their small but impeccably clean home. Jamie was very grateful for his mum's housekeeping skills, she took all the work upon herself. He knew how lucky he was in comparison to Logan and Gary. Digger's mum, though, was just as conscientious as his own.

Jackie's eyes widened when she saw the state of her son's knuckles.

'Oh, Jesus,' she said, grabbing his left hand and pulling it towards her to examine it. 'You've been fighting again, haven't you?'

'It was nothing,' he mumbled, pulling his hand out of her grip.

'Don't give me that old shite. What happened?'

He sighed, knowing she wouldn't stop until he'd told her everything. 'It was the Lawsons. They needed putting in their fucking place.'

'For God's sake, Jamie, don't we have enough on our plates without you starting World War III? That lot have more bloody cousins than the royal family. They'll come back with bigger numbers, then where will you be?'

'They won't, not after what we did to them.'

She grabbed him by both shoulders, fingers digging into his skin, green eyes wide and pain-filled. Jackie was stocky, she didn't look after her health and her hard life was etched into her face, but her eyes were beautiful, full of life and spirit. 'Please don't tell me you used a knife, Jamie. Don't you fucking tell me that.'

'Ow, Maw, that hurts.'

'Sorry,' she said, taking a deep breath and releasing him.

'Course I didn't use a blade, you know I don't carry one.'

'What about Digger? I know all about his fetish for the old razor gangs.'

'He wasn't carrying either, none of us were and neither were the Lawsons. We just used fists and feet. Although I did have my bike chain.' He knew he'd get away with that because he'd used one for years, he was famous for it.

Jackie nodded and ran a shaky hand down her face. 'That's all right then.' Her fear of knives was deeply ingrained. Fifteen years ago she'd seen her younger brother stabbed to death in the street in a stupid argument over a packet of cigarettes. His killer was serving life in Barlinnie but the trauma had never left her. She could cope with the fact that her son got into regular fights, on this estate it was vital you could take care of yourself, otherwise you became a target. But she was terrified her son would one day share his uncle's fate, or his attacker's.

Jamie wrapped an arm around her. 'You know I wouldn't do anything like that.'

'You'd better mean that, Jamie.'

'I do, honest.'

'Good.' She shoved down her fear and forced a smile. 'If you weren't here who'd unblock the toilet?'

'It's good to be needed,' he grinned.

The humour fled from Jackie's eyes. 'Was this fight down to that fat lazy bastard Dave McVitie?'

'Well, we did get his opinion about the hassle we've been getting from the Lawsons.'

'And let me guess – the moron told you to kick seven bells out of them before they did the same to you?'

'Aye,' he sighed. 'He did.'

'Violence is his answer to everything. He booted his postie in the baws because he creased one of his letters and he got fired from his job at the factory for stuffing his boss into a locker. That's why he's no' had a job for the last five years, so he just sits around at home like the slug he is, getting poor Logan to run around after him. You and your friends treat him like he's bloody Wellington when actually he's a thick useless lump of lard who keeps his brains in his fat arse.'

'He's given us useful tips.'

'If he has it's only by accident. I went to school with the prick. He was thick then, too. He thought New Zealand was the capital of Australia.'

Jamie chuckled and shook his head.

'You've got to stop treating him like he's Lord God Almighty. You're only setting yourself up for a fall.'

'We don't listen to everything he says,' mumbled Jamie.

'You shouldn't listen to *anything* he says. Bugger, Charlie's awake now,' she said when there came the sound of someone calling her from upstairs.

Jamie was incredibly grateful to his younger brother for interrupting. 'You see to him and I'll stick the kettle on.'

'Okay, thanks love,' she said. 'You're a good boy, Jamie, despite what you'd have everyone believe. And don't forget to clean your bike chain.'

'I won't.'

He smiled as he watched her head upstairs to tend to her youngest child. They were a one parent family too, like Logan's. Eight years ago, his alcoholic father had run off with what little money they had, as well as everything they possessed that was worth a few quid, which wasn't much. They hadn't seen or heard from him since. None of them were particularly devastated by this, in fact they'd been significantly better off without him as he'd drunk what money they got. Not only did they have a bit more cash now, but they weren't disturbed by his drunken ravings or perpetual sweaty odour.

After setting the kettle to boil, Jamie filled the sink with hot soapy water and began scrubbing his bike chain, the clear water turning pink. When he was sure he'd got all the blood off, he set it down outside the kitchen door to dry.

Jackie returned downstairs just as Jamie was pouring out the tea.

'Is Charlie okay?' he asked her.

'Fine. He had a nightmare about that creepy wee cow out of that film, you know, that lassie with her hair covering her face.'

Jamie puzzled over this statement before realisation struck. 'Oh, you mean *The Ring*, the horror film?'

'Aye. I don't know what the fuss is all about. If she'd been my kid I'd have slapped the spooky right out of her.'

'I think the plot's a little more complicated than anti-social behaviour,' said Jamie wryly.

'I'll never let Sarah bloody McCulloch babysit again. Fancy letting a ten-year-old watch a film like that.'

'She's always been a daft bint. Here you go, Maw,' he said, handing her a mug of tea.

'Ta,' she said, taking it from him. She winced at the sight of his hands. 'What will Malcolm say about those cuts when you go into work tomorrow?'

'I don't care. I hate that bloody shop.'

'It's a job, Jamie, and there's precious few of those about, especially in Gallowburn, so don't mess it up.'

'I won't,' he mumbled. 'But I won't be doing crap like that for the rest of my life. One day I'll be somebody.'

'I know you will, son. If anyone can make it, you can.'

Jamie positively beamed at his mum; she'd always had faith in him. His smile was seldom seen, his hard face and dark eyes rarely displaying any good humour, but he always had a ready smile for his mum, who would fight Satan himself to defend her children.

Jackie poured some of the hot water from the kettle into a bowl, added a bit of cold and used it to bathe his hands.

'At least you haven't come home with a tooth sticking out of your knuckles this time,' she said.

'Ian Rushmore's still got the gap in his teeth,' he replied, dark eyes flashing with pleasure at the memory of punching that walloper in the face. 'He's too lazy to bother going to the dentist.'

'More like he can't afford it, his family's skint.'

Jamie shrugged. 'Not my problem.'

Jackie tutted as she applied antiseptic cream to his cuts. 'Just try and stay out of trouble for a while, please Jamie?'

'I'll do my best but we have to defend ourselves. If we hadn't done what we did tonight the Lawsons would have taken over.'

'Taken over what? You don't own this scheme.'

'The north side of the estate is still our territory and if we'd backed down those animals would have made all our lives a misery. They should stay on the south side, where they belong.'

'South side,' muttered Jackie. 'We're not in bloody Los Angeles. You all need more to occupy your time, then you wouldn't be fighting every five minutes. Too much spare time and too much testosterone.'

'You're probably right, Maw,' he smiled.

Jackie couldn't help but smile back when her son's eyes twinkled. He was so serious all the time that it was a relief to see. 'There,' she said when she'd finished tending to his hands. 'They shouldn't get infected. Now get yourself to bed, you've got to be up for work in five hours.'

'No problem. You know I don't need much sleep.'

'It's a good job with the hours you keep. Away you go, then, and don't wake Charlie.'

'I won't.' He kissed her cheek. 'Night, Maw.'

'Night, sweetheart.'

Jackie watched him go, worry niggling at her. She'd always known Jamie would wind up getting involved with the local gang culture, he'd come out of the womb fighting, but she could see the effect it was having on him. She was afraid one day he'd retreat from her entirely.

It was all that silly sod Dave McVitie's fault, acting Fagin with the boys, thinking he was some great leader. Well she'd be having words with that bastard tomorrow. The General was going to find himself being demoted.

Jackie's eyes narrowed with pleasure at the thought.

2

Jamie ambled down the garden path miserably, backpack slung over one shoulder. Logan sat in his car at the kerb, waiting for him. His friend drove a beige Dacia Logan MCV, the name proudly emblazoned across the back. Logan always joked it was the closest he'd ever get to having a private registration. As the shop Jamie worked at was barely a five-minute walk from Logan's work in the neighbouring suburb of Baillieston, he gave him a lift in each morning.

'Come on, shift your arse,' Logan called to him through the open window. 'I've got to be at work soon.' He worked in a call centre for a mobile phone provider and loathed his job as much as Jamie loathed his.

Jamie tossed his bag into the backseat and climbed into the front with his friend.

'Christ, you look miserable,' said Logan as he set off down the street. 'What's up with you?'

'I hate my job. It's shit.'

'I feel your pain. I hate working at the call centre.'

'Yeah, but you're part-time. I'm stuck in that craphole forty hours a week.'

'It's only temporary. One day you'll have so much cash you won't need to work.'

'Oh, aye, a lottery win I suppose?'

'You never know. We're small time now but one day we could be big.'

'You mean the Blood Brothers?'

'Aye, how no'?'

'Because all we do is scrap with arseholes. We're no' a Columbian drug cartel.'

'I don't necessarily mean drugs. That shite's dangerous. Too many people get done in arguing about who's got the right to deal around here. There are other ways,' trailed off Logan, thinking of the phone he'd taken off John Lawson, which was in his pocket.

'Like what?'

'I don't know but we'll figure something out.'

'If anyone can, you can, pal.'

'I cannae do it alone. We'll do it together.'

'Sooner rather than later,' he sighed. 'Anyway, my maw saw the cuts on my hands from last night and she's blaming your da' for it.'

'Good. I hope she kicks the crap out of him again.'

Jamie frowned at his friend. 'Something wrong?'

'He made me cook him a fry up last night at one o'clock in the morning.'

'You should have told him to piss off, he cannae gie' you a whack any more.'

'I know, but he's my da'.'

'Is that all that's bothering you?' frowned Jamie. He'd known Logan his entire life so he could tell he wasn't giving him the whole truth.

John Lawson's phone felt to be burning a hole in his pocket. 'No, nothing. Ignore me, I'm tired after last night. I didnae get to bed until about three.'

Jamie wasn't convinced by this excuse but he decided to let it drop. Logan would tell him when he was ready.

The rest of the journey passed in silence, Logan lost in thoughts about the phone and Jamie dreading the day ahead while staring out of the window at the Gallowburn whizzing by, which in his opinion was when it looked most attractive. Gallowburn had started out as a housing estate but over the six decades of its existence it had evolved into so much more and now was a suburb of Glasgow in its own right, twelve kilometres square. Containing shops, cafés, offices and even a couple of factories, all circling the scheme, it sat squat and sinister in the centre of the retail district.

Logan dropped him off outside the shop where he'd worked for the last seven months. Jamie stared up at its tattered, peeling frontage, lip curling at the tacky crap in the window – cheap make-up, a wide selection of hideous ornaments, unheard of brands of cat food and toilet seats. Surprisingly the shop did pretty well, it was amazing what utter shite people were willing to buy, but that didn't stop the owner Malcolm from being a miserly bastard. He'd only hired Jamie because his wife had busted her knee carrying too many boxes and had been unable to work since. Now he piled the weight of all those boxes onto Jamie's wiry shoulders. The only plus side to his job was that it had made him physically strong and he'd developed muscles where none had existed before.

When he saw Malcolm frowning at him through the window and pointing at his watch he sighed again, shoulders slumped as he headed inside. He was fucked if this was going to be his life for much longer.

'What were you doing dawdling out there on the pavement?' demanded Malcolm. With his thin lanky body, stooped shoulders and mass of wiry hair he looked like a praying mantis with the head of a llama. He was the weirdest-looking individual Jamie had ever seen.

'I had a rough night last night,' muttered Jamie.

Malcolm frowned at his knuckles. 'So I see. Can't say I'm surprised, living on that scheme. Every single day must be a fight.'

'Something like that.'

'Well don't just stand there, we've got a lot to do today. We're swapping the air fresheners over with the toilet cleaners. It'll gie' the shop a whole new lease of life.'

'Thrilling,' said Jamie flatly, Malcolm's enthusiasm for the task only making the situation even more depressing.

He headed into the tiny room at the back of the shop where he dumped his bag and coat and donned the dreaded dark blue overall Malcolm insisted he wear, which fastened up at the front, hung down to his knees and was three sizes too big.

Jamie had to clear the air fresheners off the shelf while Malcolm tackled the toilet cleaners with gusto. Jamie thought it pathetic that this shop was the older man's entire world and where he was happiest. He'd rather shoot himself in the head than live like that.

Once everything was off the shelves, Malcolm received a phone call from his wife demanding to know where he was as he was supposed to take her to hospital for an appointment about her knee.

'Are you sure you'll be okay on your own?' Malcolm asked Jamie anxiously once he'd hung up, ears buzzing from the tongue-lashing he'd been given.

'I'll be fine, don't worry,' Jamie replied, delighted at the prospect of being rid of him for a while. 'You'd better get going, Linda needs you.'

'Aye, but what if you get two or three customers in the shop at once?'

'I can cope. You'd better go before she misses her appointment. With the NHS the way it is she might have a long wait for another and that will piss her off even more.'

This decided him. 'Aye, you're right. She already blames me for busting her knee in the first place, I don't want to make it worse. Carry on putting all this back on the shelves.'

'I'm on it, don't worry.'

Reluctantly Malcolm left, continually looking back over his shoulder, as though he was anxious Jamie would burn the entire place down in his absence.

'Thank God for that,' muttered Jamie when he'd gone. He decided to sod the air fresheners and toilet cleaners and wandered into the back room to make a brew.

He'd only just switched on the kettle when he heard the bell go, indicating they had a customer.

'For fuck's sake,' he muttered, heading back into the shop.

For once it didn't smell like candles and mustiness, the usual stink overpowered by the pleasing scent of coconut, sending a craving for sun and sand surging through him. He'd never been abroad and his mum hadn't been able to afford a holiday in years.

The scent emanated from a customer standing at the shelves that held the vape refills. However, this wasn't the shop's usual customer. Long blonde glossy hair hung down her back. Her cream blouse and short dusky pink skirt clung to a voluptuous body. The high heels were expensive and the handbag slung over her shoulder was undoubtedly designer. However, the most notable thing about her was the fact that she was stuffing the vape refills into her handbag as though her life depended on it. He might loathe the shop but he refused to let anyone take the piss while he was in charge.

'Oy,' he said. 'What the fuck do you think you're...'

Jamie trailed off when the customer turned around. Wide blue eyes looked back out of a delicately beautiful face, the skin flawless, lips painted ruby red.

Those lovely lips crooked into a smile, derision filling her eyes as she looked him up and down. 'Nice jacket. How many of you are in there?'

'Just me,' he murmured. He'd never seen anyone so beautiful or classy before.

'Looks like you could get three people in that jacket, which could be a lot of fun.'

With that she turned her back on him and shoved more refills into her bag.

'What are you doing?' he said.

'I saw that llama leave so I thought I'd take my chance.'

'Chance to do what?'

'Duh, nick these of course,' she said, holding out a handful of refills before stuffing those into her bag too.

'Why do you want all those? Are you going to sell them?'

'Er, no. I'm trying to quit smoking. Are you thick or something?'

Jamie's pride shook him out of his shock. 'Don't talk to me like that, you cheeky cow.'

'Cheeky cow, am I?' she replied, unconcerned. 'You're probably right. That's what everyone else says I am but I always have my reasons.'

'You look coined up, you can pay for them.'

'But I don't want to pay for them. I came in here yesterday for a couple of these and that scrawny prick who just left short-changed me. When I told him what he'd done he went mental at me and told me to piss off.'

'Oh, aye?' said Jamie, folding his arms across his chest. 'And how did you tell him?'

'I asked him if his maw kicked him in the eyes with her hooves when she spat him out of her fanny.'

Jamie forced himself not to laugh. He'd had to restrain himself many times from calling that walloper names. 'I'm no' surprised he chucked you out. If you'd said that to me I would have thrown you through the window.'

'Oh really?' she laughed, eyeing his skinny frame.

'I'm a lot stronger than I look.'

'I'll bet you are. You've got beautiful eyes, all dark and threatening.' She spotted the cuts on his hands and smiled. 'Someone's been up to something naughty. I like that.'

'You do?'

'I do. You're dangerous, aren't you? Actually, that name suits you,' she said before taking another handful of refills.

'Oy,' he said, snatching them from her. 'You're no' taking the piss while I'm in charge. You'll put the lot back.'

She hitched her handbag up her shoulder. 'Make me, Dangerous.'

'Don't think I won't just because you're a woman.'

'Go on then... oy!' she exclaimed when he wrenched the bag off her shoulder. 'Give that back.'

'No,' he retorted, tipping the contents out all over the countertop. 'Looks like the painters are in,' he grinned when a box of tampons fell out last, landing on the heap of vape refills.

'That's none of your business,' she snarled, snatching it up.

'How much were you short-changed by?'

'What do you care?'

'Just answer the question.'

She huffed. 'Four quid.'

'All right, you can take one refill. They're three ninety-nine, so that's most of it back.'

'What are you doing?' she said when he rooted around in his jeans pocket.

'Getting you the penny. Then you're all squared up.'

'You can stick your penny right up your skinny little arse.'

'The clothes and handbag are classy. It's a shame your gob spoils them.'

'You cheeky little sod,' she hissed, snatching up one of the refills and stalking to the door. 'You've not heard the last of this.'

'Going to get your rich daddy to gie' me a spanking, are you, Princess?'

'I'm perfectly capable of spanking your arse myself. Your bum will be black and blue by the time I'm done.'

'I'm game if you are, Princess.'

With a growl of rage, she stamped her high-heeled foot and flounced out, slamming the door shut behind her.

Jamie stood at the window to watch her storm across the road towards a convertible light blue BMW. Just as he thought, coined up. She jumped in and slammed the door shut. When she saw him watching her she gave him the V-sign, started the engine and sped off down the street, forcing an elderly man crossing the road to reel backwards. With a screech of tyres she disappeared around the corner and was gone.

'Well, that livened up the day,' Jamie murmured to himself. Even though she was obviously nuts he wished she'd come back. She might make the day go quicker.

He slinked over to the pile of vape refills and began neatly stacking them back on the shelf. The annoyance of her adding to his workload was tempered by the sweet aroma of coconut she'd left behind.

* * *

As Jackie walked her younger son Charlie to school her mood darkened with each step. Dave fucking McVitie was leading her son down a path to self-destruction and she was buggered if she was going to allow it. Jamie had a good head on his shoulders, he had a chance to make something of himself and that lard arse was not going to steal that from him. Well, as soon as she'd dropped Charlie off she was going to see Dave and ensure he never went near her eldest boy again.

'Maw,' said a voice, disturbing her thoughts. 'Maw.'

Jackie shook herself out of it and smiled down at the little dark-haired boy gazing up at her. He had dark eyes just like his older brother but, whereas Jamie's were always hard and brooding, Charlie's were wide and soft. Even though he was being raised on the Gallowburn he was still naïve and gentle, the opposite of his brother. Jackie had never intended to have a second child, especially not with Jason, her violent drunken bastard of a husband. He'd inflicted enough misery on one child and she was buggered if she was going to let him do it to a second. When she'd found out she was pregnant again she had intended to get an abortion without telling Jason. She'd even walked into the clinic but she'd been unable to go through with it and it was the best decision she'd ever made. That day she resolved Jason would never lay a hand on herself or Jamie ever again and he would

certainly not touch the new baby. She'd passed this message onto Jason
by waiting until he was in a drunken stupor on the couch, straddling
him and holding a butcher's knife to his throat. After breaking the
news about her pregnancy she made it very clear that if he thought he
could continue to abuse them all then she would slit him open from
his tiny privates to his big empty head and laugh while she did it. Even
now the memory of the fear in his eyes made her smile. The pathetic
bastard had even wet himself. She'd made him clean the piss out of the
cushions, standing over him brandishing the knife while he'd frantically scrubbed, casting fearful glances at her over his shoulder. For
years she'd lived in terror of him and in that moment she'd learnt that
he was actually an incredibly weak excuse for a man, only able to feel
powerful when he was bullying others. From that day on she'd never
taken any shit off anybody ever again. The doormat had died that day
and good bloody riddance. Jason had pissed off when Charlie was two
and good bloody riddance to that too. Now Dave McVitie thought he
could control her son just like Jason had tried to. Well, he was about to
get a harsh life lesson.

She kissed Charlie goodbye and watched him meet up with one of
his friends as he walked inside the school. Last year a couple of boys in
his class thought they could start bullying him but after what Jamie
had done to their older brothers they hadn't gone near him since.
Neither had any of the other bullies in the school, for that matter. It
was one less thing to worry about.

Only once Charlie was safely inside the building did she head back
the way she'd come, her anger growing with every step. When Tricia, a
good friend of hers, attempted to stop her to chat she brushed her off
with a curt apology. Tricia didn't argue, she knew better than to mess
with Jackie Gray when she was in one of her moods. Jackie was always
wondering where Jamie got his temper from. She was the only one
who failed to realise he'd inherited it from her.

Jackie banged both fists on Dave McVitie's peeling front door,
breathing furiously. When there was no answer she banged on it again

and gave it a kick for good measure, but still nothing. Movement to her left caught her eye and she spied Dave's sweaty moon face peering at her through the window. When he realised he'd been spotted his eyes widened and he ducked out of sight.

'I know you're in there, you spineless jobby,' she yelled. 'Open the door and face me like a man.'

Still there was no response. She tried the door handle but it refused to open and she grunted with rage. 'You're no' corrupting my boy, do you hear me, Dave McVitie? I'll see you dead before I let him turn out like you. This isn't over,' she added, giving the door another hard kick, chipping off more of the decaying red paintwork before stomping down the path, pausing to kick over the disintegrating wishing well in the middle of the garden.

She stormed down the street, still full of rage and the need for righteous justice. Once she was out of sight of the McVitie homestead she darted around the corner of the house on the end and headed down the back street. When Dave's back gate opened she pressed herself against the wall. Sure enough the fat sweaty lump emerged wrapped in a grey anorak. As he was concentrating so hard on trying to close the gate as quietly as possible, he failed to see her standing there. If Jackie hadn't been so angry she would have found it funny.

She stuck out her foot and he went flying, landing face down on the cobbles. Before he could rise, she planted her foot in between his shoulder blades, pinning him to the ground.

'Jackie, that's got to be you,' he cried as he ineffectually thrashed.

'Damn right it's me, Davey boy.'

'What the fuck are you doing? Have you finally lost the plot?'

'My boy got into another fight last night and it's all your fault.'

'It was nothing to do with me.'

'Don't lie to me, you arsehole. You told him and his friends to defend their territory by attacking the Lawsons, didn't you?'

'No, I didn't, I swear to God.'

'One day, Dave McVitie, you'll be struck by lightning for the number of lies you tell in God's name. You'll be fried like the fat piggy you are,' she said, pressing down harder with her foot.

'They do have minds of their own, you know,' he said, flopping about on his belly but Jackie's foot was immovable. 'If you want someone to blame for that fight, blame the boys, no' me.'

'I know what you're up to, acting the Fagin with them.'

'What's a Fagin?'

'You never did like to read, did you, Davey? Fagin is a character out of *Oliver Twist* by Charles Dickens who runs a gang of thieving weans.'

'The boys are no' thieving weans. They're grown men but you cannae accept it because you want to keep your boy a baby. Now, are you gonnae let me up, you mad cow?'

'Not yet,' she said, pressing harder.

'Ow,' he cried. 'That fucking hurts.'

'Good. Now listen to me, Dave McVitie. You stay away from my boy. If I find out that you've been giving him more of your shite advice I'll come back and take your wee willie winkie right off. Do you understand me?'

'Aye, aye, I understand,' he cried. 'Can I get up now?'

Jackie removed her foot. 'On you go, then.'

Slowly Dave pushed himself up onto all fours, wincing at the ache in his lower back. It took him another minute to drag himself to his feet. He was appalled to see a crowd had gathered at the end of the street to watch his disgrace. Anger sparked through him and he took an aggressive step towards Jackie. 'See you, Jackie Gray, you've gone too far.'

'Oh aye, fat boy, and what are you gonnae do about it?'

'I'm gonnae gie' you the hiding you've been asking for for a long time.'

Jackie delved into her handbag and produced a bike chain, holding it by one end so he could see the length and viciousness of it. Just the sight of it made him turn white.

'This is my Jamie's,' she said. 'It's his favourite weapon and that's all thanks to you. I believe you recommended it to him? Well it's about to have another victim. Brace yourself, Davey boy,' she said, drawing it back. 'This is gonnae hurt.'

'Just calm down, hen,' cried Dave, holding out his hands and stumbling backwards.

'Don't tell me to calm down,' she yelled, lashing out with the chain and missing, just brushing Dave's right arm. 'Stand still, you coward, and take what's coming to you.'

'Help, she's gone aff her nut,' cried Dave, running away.

'Get back here, you wobbly fucking jelly,' she bellowed, making chase.

She slowed to a halt when Dave vanished around the corner, running faster than he'd ever moved in his life. While the assembled crowd burst out laughing, Jackie glared after his retreating form. She'd put the shits right up him, but she knew it wasn't enough to stop him from negatively influencing her boy. Back to the drawing board. She needed to come up with something that would keep him away permanently.

Malcolm returned to the shop two hours later and sent Jamie out for an early lunch. Fortunately, he had the vape refills, air fresheners and toilet cleaners alike stacked back on the shelves, so Malcolm didn't give him a hard time.

Jamie bought a sandwich, a packet of crisps and a can of Irn Bru from the bakery down the road and ambled through the shopping precinct as he ate. Despite the springtime chill hanging in the air he wanted to be outside to get the musty smell of the shop out of his nostrils. Malcolm could easily afford to have the place renovated and make it look like it didn't belong in a third world country but he was too bloody tight.

'All right, Dangerous,' said a sultry voice.

A frowning Jamie spun on his heel to see the mad blonde from the shop leaning against her BMW, which was parked at the kerb.

'Oh God,' he said. 'No' you again.'

'I was hoping to bump into you. I knew the llama would have to let you out at some point.'

'Have you been hanging around here waiting for me?'

'I have.'

'That's a bit weird.'

'I didn't have anything else to do.'

'No work for you, eh, Princess?'

'Something like that. Let's go shopping.'

'I don't want to go shopping.'

'I don't care because you're going,' she said, linking her arm through his.

Jamie was so shocked he didn't protest and allowed himself to be half-led, half-dragged down the street. 'You're aff your heid,' he told her.

'I just know what I want and I always get it,' she replied.

'You're no' getting me,' he said, shrugging his arm free.

She grabbed hold of his arm again and hung on tighter. 'You're so tense, you need to unwind. Come on, it'll be fun.'

For the first time in his life Jamie had no idea what to do, he'd never encountered anyone like her before and the next thing he knew she'd pulled him into a shop selling make-up, toiletries and perfume.

'Christ, I hope no one I know sees me in here,' he muttered.

'Don't worry, you can tell them you were buying your girlfriend a present.'

'I don't have a girlfriend.'

'You do now.'

'What, you? You must be joking.'

'Why not? What's wrong with me?' she said, glancing around before slipping a blusher brush into her handbag.

'Put that back right now,' he hissed at her.

'What's your problem?'

'You're gonnae get us both lifted,' he whispered, looking around to see if they were being watched but the two assistants were deep in conversation.

'Relax, will you? I spend a lot of money in this shop, so I'm entitled to a freebie now and then.'

'That's two freebies,' he glowered when a mascara wand joined the blusher brush in her handbag.

'If you don't keep your voice down I'll tell them you're a shoplifter.'

'I haven't nicked anything.'

'Then how did that lipstick get in your pocket?'

Jamie's eyes widened when he touched his left jacket pocket and felt a lump there. 'How the hell did you do that?'

'I'm good, aren't I?' she smiled.

'Don't you dare nick that too,' he whispered when she picked up a bottle of make-up remover.

'I don't intend to. This is what I came in for.'

He sighed with relief when she walked towards the till, marvelling at her nerve as she beamed at the two assistants, who smiled back at her. While the madwoman wasn't looking he took the lipstick out of his pocket and dumped it back on the shelf.

Keeping his head down, he headed out of the shop and walked away as fast as his long-legged stride would take him. It was tempting to break into a run but he thought that might look suspicious. He sighed when he heard high heels hurrying to catch up.

'Oy!' she called after him. 'Where are you going?'

'Away from you,' he retorted. 'You're mental.'

She quickly caught him up, which was a miracle given how high her heels were. 'I get bored easily,' she said. 'That's all.'

'You're no' dragging me into your games, Princess.'

'My name is Allegra,' she retorted.

Jamie sniggered. 'After the car? Were you conceived in a Vauxhall?'

'No one in my family would be seen dead in a Vauxhall. What's your name, Dangerous?'

'I'm not telling you.'

'You don't need to. I already know it's Jamie.'

He came to a halt and rounded on her. 'How do you know that?'

'I was passing the shop where you work a few days ago and I saw you in there. I thought *wow, he's incredible*. So I asked the woman who works in the shop next to yours selling all that knitted crap about you and she was very happy to oblige, for a few quid. When I went in for the vape it was to talk to you but you weren't there. That dumb llama was, though,' she frowned.

'You think I'm incredible?' he said with a suspicious frown.

'I do,' she said, holding her head high.

'Why?'

'You look like a young Robert De Niro. He's my favourite actor,' she said with a dreamy sigh. 'Even though he's seventy-six he's still sexy, don't you think?'

'Funnily enough, no,' he retorted.

'Plus, you're dangerous,' she purred. 'And that's what I like.'

Suspicion filled his hard eyes. 'Gary put you up to this, didn't he? This is just the sort of wind-up he loves to pull.'

'Who's Gary? Ooh, do you have a brother?' she replied, attempting to slide her arms around his neck.

He took her by the shoulders and gently pushed her away. 'You can tell that fat dick nice try but I'm no' falling for it.'

'I'm not kidding.'

'Aye, right,' he said as he walked away, leaving her standing on the pavement.

'This isn't over,' she called after him.

'Yes, it is,' he called back over his shoulder, leaving her to stomp her high heel in anger.

3

Logan had been so consumed with thoughts about the phone he'd nicked off John Lawson that he accidentally hung up on two callers and mixed up two accounts. As he was usually such a conscientious worker his manager let him off with a gentle warning but he had to get his act together. As much as he hated his job, he needed it.

Finally lunchtime came around and he hurried out of the building to his car. He drove to his friend Mark's house, which was barely ten minutes from the call centre. The route took him past Jamie's place of work and he saw his friend arguing with a rather stunning blonde on the pavement. He was tempted to stop and find out what was going on but the phone was his most pressing matter. He just hoped Mark could help him access it and that John hadn't reported it stolen. As it was a cheap pay-as-you-go model containing sensitive information he guessed John wouldn't want anyone finding out about it, he would be much more likely to try and retrieve it himself, which worried him, especially as his dad had said he couldn't tell his friends. Without their back-up, he'd be vulnerable.

He arrived at Mark's house, which was even smaller and more depressing than his own. He got out of the car to the sound of barking.

'Oh, great,' he muttered when he saw Mark's white Akita, Stalin, at the window, teeth bared and growling at him. 'That bastard hates me.'

As he approached the front door Stalin started barking, bright blue eyes diabolical.

'Shut the fuck up,' he heard a voice yell from inside. Immediately the barking ceased.

The door was yanked open and Logan grimaced.

'Jesus, Mark, put on some pants.'

His friend scratched his bare chest, fag hanging out of his mouth, naked white chicken legs sticking out of his black and white spotted boxer shorts. 'What do you think you're doing coming round here so early?'

'Early? It's quarter to one.'

'In the day?'

'Well... yeah,' frowned Logan. 'Why do you think it's daylight?'

Mark took the cigarette out of his mouth and dragged a hand through his ruffled dark hair. 'What do you want?'

Logan took the phone out of his pocket. 'I need you to unlock this for me.'

'You got the cash?'

He nodded.

'How much?'

'Twenty quid.'

'You got me out of bed for twenty fucking quid?'

'Oh, come on, Mark, I've seen you do it before. It only takes you five minutes.'

'Suppose. All right, come on in then.'

Logan entered and closed the door behind him. Stalin bounded into the hallway, making him back up against the door in fear as the dog growled at him.

'Stalin. Kitchen. Now!' yelled Mark.

The dog gave Logan one last glower before slinking off into the kitchen, leaving him to breathe a sigh of relief.

He followed Mark upstairs to a bedroom that contained only a single bed and a desk holding a laptop. As there wasn't enough room to get a chair between the bed and the desk they both perched on the edge of the bed. Mark switched on the computer and Logan held the phone out to him.

'Is it nicked?' Mark asked him.

Logan nodded.

'Then I'm no' touching it. Connect it to this,' he said, picking up a data cable, which was plugged into the side of the laptop.

Logan connected it and sat back to watch his friend work. Mark was the laziest bastard he knew, but his tech knowledge was phenomenal and he made a good living doing jobs for people who liked to keep their activities quiet. Best of all, he never asked for details. As far as he was concerned, where the items he worked on had come from was none of his business.

Stalin nudged open the door with his nose and launched himself at Logan, knocking him back onto the bed and pinning him down. When Stalin's jaws clamped down on his arm Logan released a cry of terror, even though the dog's teeth thankfully didn't break the skin.

'Relax, he's only playing,' Mark told a frantically writhing Logan, not taking his eyes off the screen. 'He won't hurt you.'

'Get him off me, man,' he cried, trying to bring up his legs so he could push Stalin away with his feet, but the dog was giving him no respite.

'He'll get bored in a minute and bugger off back downstairs.'

'Taking my arm with him,' Logan exclaimed.

'For Christ's sake, he's only messing. Have you never had a dog?'

'No, I don't like them. Get him off me, Mark. Now.'

Mark tutted. 'Fine. Stalin, piss off into the kitchen.'

The dog immediately released Logan and happily bounded out of the room, pleased he'd asserted dominance over the newcomer.

Logan slowly sat up, dazed and shaken. He examined his arm but there was no damage. His jacket, however, was a different matter.

'There's teeth marks in my sleeve and he's covered me in slabbers.' He sniffed at the drool staining his jacket and grimaced. 'Jesus, his breath stinks. What do you feed him?'

'Whiny wee babies like you, that's what,' said Mark.

'I smell and I've got to go back to work.'

'Not my problem. Right, all done. You can take your phone.'

'Nice one,' said Logan, removing the data cable and picking up the phone. He swiped at the screen and smiled when the home screen popped up.

'Gimme the cash,' said Mark.

Logan pulled the twenty pound note out of his pocket and dumped it in his hand. 'Cheers, pal.'

Logan followed Mark downstairs, refusing to go first in case Stalin was lurking at the bottom, which he was. When he saw his master was leading the way Logan could swear he looked disappointed.

'Thanks Mark, I really appreciate it. You can go back to bed.'

'No, I'm up now. I may as well have some breakfast,' he sighed as though terribly put-upon.

'I've got to get back to work. See you around.'

'Aye, bye.'

Just as Logan was going out the door, Stalin made one last lunge for him, Mark making no effort to restrain the dog. Logan staggered out backwards, stumbling down the single step into the garden, yanking the door shut before Stalin could follow. He frowned when he heard Mark's laughter on the other side of the door.

Logan sniffed his arm again and winced. He was honking, which wasn't a good thing to be when you worked in a warm office.

He got back in his car to examine the phone. Sure enough, the phone numbers his dad wanted were on there, which he made a note of on his own phone, typing them into his contact list. As he was due back at work in ten minutes there wasn't enough time to examine the rest of the contents; that would have to wait until later.

* * *

Jamie kept watch at the shop window for the rest of the day but the mad woman didn't come back. He wasn't sure whether to be glad or disappointed. She might be off her head but at least she livened things up.

The afternoon passed interminably slowly, although they did have quite a few customers in and out, mainly to escape the rain that came on suddenly in short heavy bursts.

Finally, four o'clock came around and he could leave.

'I want you in at eight o'clock tomorrow morning,' Malcolm called after him. 'I've got a delivery coming I need a hand with.'

Jamie groaned inwardly. 'Are you gonnae pay me extra, then?'

Malcolm's eyes darted about the room in panic. 'Er, no. Tell you what, you can finish an hour early. How's that?'

'Aye, nae bother,' he sighed before leaving.

He stepped outside, letting the door swing shut behind him, which never failed to annoy Malcolm. He headed down the street towards the bus stop.

As he rounded the corner he came to a halt.

'Oh, shit,' he said.

John Lawson and three of his cousins were standing at the bus stop and judging by the way they were glaring at him they weren't waiting for a bus. One of them he could easily have taken on, probably even two, but not four of the bastards. Neither did he have a weapon on him, unless he counted his house key.

'One of youse nicked my phone,' announced John in his reedy nasal voice. 'And I want it back.'

'No we didn't, you lying bastard,' retorted Jamie. 'You must have lost it.'

'Don't fucking lie,' said John as the four of them advanced on him.

'I'm no' lying, you prick. Why don't you ask that lot of inbred tossers,' he added, nodding at John's cousins.

'That's fucking it,' yelled John. 'Get him.'

When the four of them rushed him, Jamie ran back up the road, wondering where the hell he should go. If he took this fight to Malcolm's shop he'd sack him and what his mum would do to him if he lost his job would be ten times worse than anything the Lawsons could dream up.

Instead he tore down the street, heading towards the precinct. Jamie was a fast runner, but glancing over his shoulder he saw that the Lawsons were gaining on him. He darted across the road, there was the screech of tyres followed by a thud. Looking round he saw a light blue convertible BMW stopped in the middle of the road and John Lawson lying on the ground before it, groaning.

The front passenger door was flung open to reveal Allegra.

'Get in,' she yelled at him.

Deciding she was marginally safer than the Lawsons' wrath, he dived into the car and pulled the door shut. Allegra slammed her foot down on the accelerator, dodging around John, who was struggling to his feet with the help of his friends.

'I can't believe you ran him over,' said Jamie, gripping onto the door as she negotiated a corner at speed.

'I didn't, I just gave him a little nudge with the bumper.' Her face split into a grin. 'I knew you were dangerous. Why were they chasing you?'

'The one you hit thinks I nicked his phone.'

'Did you?'

'No. I've got my own phone. I don't need his.'

'Okay, take it easy. I didn't mean to insult you.'

'Did you nick this motor, too?'

'No. It was a birthday present from my father.'

'Oh, aye, how old are you?'

'Never ask a lady that question.'

'Thanks for the tip but you're no' a lady. How old are you?'

'Twenty,' she sighed.

'I got a DVD and a pair of socks for my twentieth.'

'There's nothing wrong with that. So where am I dropping you off?'

Jamie took in the car and Allegra's expensive clothes, even though as yet he wasn't convinced that she hadn't nicked them all, and shame rose inside him. What would she think when she saw his street? 'You can drop me off at the bus station. I can get home from there.'

'Don't be stupid, that shower might find you. I'll take you home. Now where is it?'

'I thought you'd already know. You seem to know everything else about me.'

She pressed a button on the dashboard and there was an alarming clunk as the doors were locked.

'Unlock the doors,' he told her.

'I'm not pulling over until you tell me where you live. I've got a full tank of petrol, which gives me about four hundred and fifty miles. How do you fancy a trip to London?'

'No,' he exclaimed. From his brief experience of her he knew she'd be perfectly willing to drive down south. He sighed. 'I live on the Gallowburn scheme.'

'There we go, that wasn't so hard, was it? Or do you not want me to know where you live?'

'You drag me into a shop and start nicking stuff, you run someone over and then you kidnap me. Bloody right I don't want you knowing where I live, and what the hell were you doing on that street anyway? Were you waiting for me to come out of work?'

'Yes.'

'Why?' he exclaimed.

'Because I like you and I wanted to see you again.'

'Don't you have anything better to do?'

'No, not really. My life's so boring,' she sighed, pulling onto the strip of motorway that would take them to Gallowburn. 'You're the first interesting person I've met in ages. Come on, admit it – I made your day brighter.'

'I'm no' so sure about that, but you did make it a lot less boring.'

'That's not so bad, is it?'

'Suppose not.'

'That's the nicest thing you've ever said to me, Dangerous,' she smiled.

'My name's Jamie,' he sighed.

'I prefer Dangerous. It suits those eyes of yours.'

'Will you stop banging on about my eyes?'

'Why not? Can't take a compliment?'

'I'm no' used to them, apart from my maw.'

'Aww, sweet.' Her blue eyes flickered. 'My mum died five years ago.'

'Oh,' he mumbled. 'Sorry.'

'Why, did you kill her?'

'No,' he exclaimed.

'Then why are you sorry?'

'I have no idea,' he sighed, relieved to see the sign indicating the turn-off to Gallowburn.

The pain vanished from her eyes. 'Why do they call it Gallowburn?'

'Because they used to hang criminals next to the stream that runs through the middle of the scheme. The original hanging tree is still there, which they used until they built a permanent gallows.'

'I'd love to see that. I enjoy a good bloody history.'

'Cannae say I'm surprised. We call that part of the scheme the Gallows. Turn left here.'

She indicated and turned into Jamie's street.

'For a psycho you're a pretty good driver,' he commented.

'I find it very calming.'

'What number's yours?' she said.

'Eighteen,' he muttered. He'd grown up with these streets and they'd never really bothered him before, but he regarded all the litter, the furniture dumped in gardens and burst bin bags spewing rotting food onto the streets with fresh eyes. It made him feel ashamed because Allegra with her ridiculous name, fancy car, clothes, handbag and completely unique outlook on life had made him realise there was a whole world outside Gallowburn.

Allegra parked the car outside his house and peered out of the window. 'Cute. How many of you live in there?'

'Just me, my maw and my brother.'

Her eyes lit up. 'So, you do have a brother. What's he like?'

'Just like me but ten years old.'

'Oh. Never mind, you can't have everything,' she said, unlocking the doors and flinging off her seatbelt.

'Why have you taken off your seatbelt?'

'Because I want to meet your family,' she replied before opening the door and climbing out.

'What? No you're fucking not... ow,' he groaned when he tried to get out of the car without removing his own seatbelt. By the time he'd managed to throw it off and get out, Allegra had already pushed open the front door and stepped inside.

'Oy, you cannae just walk in,' he called.

He practically ran inside to find Allegra already talking to his mother.

'Maw,' he said breathlessly. 'I'm sorry about her barging in but she's a loon.'

'You can't be talking about this beautiful girl,' said Jackie, smiling approvingly at Allegra.

'Aye, I am.'

'Don't be so rude to our guest.'

'Guest?' he exclaimed. 'Maw, you don't know what she's like. She's a shoplifter, she ran over John Lawson and she kidnapped me.'

Jackie chuckled. 'I do apologise for my son, Allegra, but he's always had a vivid imagination.'

'That's quite all right, Jackie,' she politely replied while Jamie gaped at them both.

'So, are you two dating?'

'Yes,' she beamed.

'We're bloody not,' interjected Jamie.

'How nice,' Jackie told Allegra, ignoring her son. 'Is it true you ran over John Lawson?'

'Not strictly. I just bumped him a little bit with my car. He was waiting for Jamie after work with three of his friends.'

'Oh Christ,' she sighed. 'Jamie, didn't I tell you not to listen to Dave McVitie? This lovely lassie saves your arse and all you can do is insult her.'

'Because she's insane!' he exclaimed. 'Why won't you listen to me?'

'I repeat, do not be rude to our guest.' She frowned at her son, who decided it would be wise to remain silent. Jackie turned her attention back to Allegra. 'Would you like to stay for tea? It's only sausage and mash but I make a cracking mash.'

'That would be lovely, Jackie, thank you.'

'Great. Take a seat, it won't be long. Cuppa?'

'I don't drink caffeine. A glass of water would be lovely, though, thanks.'

'Coming right up.' Jackie pointed a digit at her son. 'You'll stay right there and keep Allegra company.'

'But I said I'd go round to Gary's.'

'Gary can wait, you see him every day. Now, talk to Allegra,' she said, scowling at him with warning in her eyes before heading into the kitchen.

Jamie sighed and slumped onto the couch.

'I like your mum,' smiled Allegra, sitting beside him. 'She's feisty. It must be where you get it from,' she purred, resting her hand on his knee.

He brushed her hand away. 'Don't do that.'

'Why not? I'm beautiful, you should be all over me.'

'Someone's up their own arse.'

'I'm just stating a fact. Men are usually all over me, so why aren't you?'

'Because I don't like going out with mincey-heids. You're off your bloody rocker.'

'I am not. I'm just not full of the fear that everyone else carries around inside them. I wanted the blusher brush and mascara so I took them. I wanted to protect you from that idiot in town, so I hit him with my car.' Her hand returned to his knee and she leaned into him. 'And I want you,' she breathed.

'You gonnae run me over too if I turn you down?'

'Who knows?' she said with a twinkle in her eye.

Jamie was torn between amusement and fury. 'You know, people around here are feared of me.'

'Really?' she said, leaning in even closer. 'Do tell.'

'The north of this estate belongs to me and my pals. We rule it and anyone who steps out of line gets a fucking pasting. Know what my favourite weapon is?'

'No,' she said, voice practically a whisper.

'A bike chain. It's fucking nasty when you know how to use one properly. It looks like it's rusty but it's no' because of that. It's because of all the blood on it. You mess with me, sweetheart, you're getting in deep.'

Allegra stared into his eyes, the muscles in his face taut. Her own eyes were wide and her skin was pale and Jamie thought she was finally going to run out screaming.

Instead she grabbed his face with both hands and kissed him. Jamie released a startled cry, which was muffled by her lips. He could have pushed her away but his mum had schooled him never to lay hands on a woman after what she'd been through with their dad and he found that teaching impossible to break.

Finally, Allegra released him. 'You are so sexy, Dangerous.'

'Did you no' hear what I said?'

'I heard perfectly and you're everything I thought you would be. I'd no idea about the bike chain though, that's even better.'

'That's it,' he said, leaping to his feet. 'I'm out of here.'

Before he could make for the door his mum called, 'Tea's ready,' from the kitchen. If he left now she'd make him suffer for weeks by cooking him nothing but corned beef hash, which he hated.

'Come on, Dangerous,' said Allegra, taking his hand and pulling him towards the kitchen. 'Your Princess is hungry.'

'Oh, God,' he said, rolling his eyes.

* * *

Allegra stayed for two hours before finally declaring it was time for her to go home. Surprisingly she got on very well with Jackie, although the two women were poles apart, and Charlie positively adored their visitor, blushing whenever she looked his way. Jamie, however, spent the time looking at his watch, yawning and impatiently tapping his foot.

Jackie made him walk Allegra out to her car, which had remained unmolested thanks to his reputation on the estate. No one messed with anything to do with the Gray family.

'Well, thanks for a lovely evening,' smiled Allegra. 'I really enjoyed myself.'

Jamie looked back over his shoulder and huffed to see his mother standing in the doorway, warning written all over her face.

He turned back to face Allegra. 'Aye, it was... different.'

'Want to go out somewhere tomorrow?'

'With you?'

'Well, I don't mean with him,' she replied, pointing to a drunk staggering down the street, the sound of clanking bottles emanating from the blue plastic carrier bag hanging from his hand.

'He'd love to, Allegra,' called Jackie.

'How the hell did you hear that from all the way over there?' Jamie demanded of his mother.

'I'm blessed with excellent hearing,' she replied. 'It runs in the family.'

'Jesus,' he muttered.

'I'll pick you up at seven then,' said Allegra, opening the car door. 'See you tomorrow, Dangerous,' she winked.

He tensed, preparing to leap out of the way in case she decided to kiss him again but to his surprise she got in the car and drove off, not even bothering to look back at him.

'That's no' a woman,' he murmured to himself. 'That's a fucking plague.' He slouched up the garden path, frowning at his mum, who was still standing in the doorway, smiling. 'What did you do that for? Now I'll never get rid of her.'

'That girl's just what you need, trust me.'

'I need her like I need a horrible skin condition. At least that would be less annoying.'

'She might surprise you.'

'No' in a good way. Can I go to Gary's now?'

'Aye,' she sighed. 'Away you go, but be careful, the Lawsons will still be gunning for you.' She held his bike chain out to him. 'Take this.'

'Finally,' he muttered, taking the chain from her and slinking away, shoving the bike chain into his jacket pocket as he went.

4

'It's about bloody time you were home,' Dave told Logan the minute he came through the door.

'I'm back at the time I normally would be,' he replied.

'Did you get the phone unlocked?'

'Aye, I did,' he said, producing it from his pocket and holding it out to him.

Dave snatched the phone from his hand and recoiled back into his armchair. 'Jeezo, you stink.'

'It's no' my fault, it's Stalin's.'

'I thought he died in the fifties.'

'I don't mean the leader of the Soviet Union, I'm talking about my friend's dog. He attacked my arm and drooled all over me.'

'I think he licked his arse before he did it,' frowned Dave, wafting his hand before his nose.

Logan noted the bruise to the side of his face. 'What happened to you?'

'Oh, nothing,' he mumbled, casting his eyes to the floor. 'I... had an accident.'

'Really? Or did Jackie Gray get hold of you again?'

His head snapped up. 'The woman's insane. I could have easily taken her down but you know me, I don't hit women.'

'Aye, course you don't, Da,' said Logan, knowing in his eyes as he shrugged off his jacket.

'Have you looked through this phone?'

'Only the numbers in the contact list, nothing else. I didn't have time.'

'Does it have what we want?'

'Aye, it does.'

'Great. Maybe John's got some embarrassing photos on here, too?' said Dave, eagerly flicking through them. In truth, John Lawson's girlfriend was a proper stunner and he was hoping to find some photos of her in the nude. 'What a fucking fairy,' he scowled at the phone as Logan vanished into the kitchen to stick his jacket in the washing machine. 'They're all of his bloody cat.'

He continued to flick through the images, sick of the sight of the ball of black and white fur.

'Jesus H. Christ,' he cried, throwing the phone to the floor.

Logan dashed back into the room. 'What is it?'

Dave just pointed at the phone, face white with fright.

Logan picked it up and frowned. 'What am I looking at?' Realisation struck and he threw it onto the couch. 'Oh my God, that bloke's deid.'

'Looks like he was stabbed,' replied Dave, looking at the photo again, his voice practically a whisper. 'Repeatedly.'

'Why the hell would John have a photo of a deid body on his phone?'

'Because he made it deid, that's why,' said Dave, glad when his voice sounded stronger.

'It might not be,' said Logan, the logical, reasonable side of himself coming to the fore. 'It could be a still shot from a TV programme.'

'Oh aye? If it is from the telly then why is John in the photo too? Who is he, Al bloody Pacino?'

Tentatively Logan picked up the phone again, attempting to look at it side-on so he wouldn't be subjected to the full horror again. His dad was right, John was in the photo. He'd been so horrified by the look on the victim's face and all the blood and gore that he'd failed to notice him before. 'This can't be right. John's no' a killer, he's just a bully boy, into petty stuff.'

'Well, it looks like he's graduated.'

'This doesn't make sense. If he did kill someone why would he take a photo of himself with the victim? This image could send him to prison.'

'To prove he'd done it to whoever wanted that poor bastard deid.'

'Nah, I don't buy it. I hate John Lawson but I don't believe he's capable of this. Besides, there's been no reports of any deid bodies turning up.'

'Maybe he didn't kill them locally? All that photo shows is some woodland in the dark, it could be anywhere.'

Logan tapped at the screen. 'It was taken two weeks ago. I'll see if there's been any reports of deid bodies being found anywhere in the country in the last couple of weeks. If not, then we can put this down to some prank he was playing, agreed?'

'Fine by me, son. I want to forget all about it.'

Logan frantically stabbed at his phone. No articles popped up that tallied with what was in the photo. 'I can't find anything,' he said, the relief audible in his voice. 'For all we know that's just make-up, a joke, nothing more.'

'Or maybe the body's not been found yet?' said Dave grimly.

Logan wished even more that he'd left that fucking phone in John Lawson's pocket. Once again one of his dad's hare-brained schemes was coming back to bite them on the arse.

* * *

'Where've you been?' said Gary when he opened his front door to Jamie. 'You were supposed to be here over an hour ago.'

Jamie stepped inside and closed the door behind him. Gary's house might have been one of the new builds but it was no bigger than his own house, although it did have nice magnolia paintwork and cream carpets. Those carpets, however, were already scuffed and torn in places. Gary's parents were both alcoholics and spent all their time and money down the local boozer. As always their son was home alone, his two older siblings having moved out the second they got the chance, which was fine by him, he loved having the run of the place. His house-keeping skills were no better than his parents' and an underlying smell of unwashed clothes and stale food permanently pervaded the place.

'Some bloody mad woman's latched onto me,' said Jamie. 'She took me shoplifting and hit John Lawson with her car.'

'You fucking what?' exclaimed Gary, sandy eyebrows shooting up. He swallowed hard when he caught sight of Jamie's expression. 'Something wrong, pal?'

'Aye, there's something wrong. Did you nick John Lawson's phone?'

'Why would I want to nick anything off that dickhead? Everyone knows his house is full of fleas.'

'Mobile phones can't catch fleas.' Jamie took an aggressive step towards him, causing him to take one backwards. 'Did you take it?'

'No, I did not. I was too busy smashing his brother's face in to nick anything. Why, what's this about?'

Jamie studied his friend carefully before replying. Gary was a crap liar, he always went way over the top with his denials but now he looked genuinely confused. 'I believe you.'

'Good,' said Gary, releasing a small exhale of relief. They might be best friends but Jamie wouldn't hesitate to give him a walloping if he thought he deserved it, it certainly wouldn't be the first time. 'So, what's all this about John Lawson and mad women?'

With a weary sigh Jamie related the entire episode. When he'd finished, Gary chuckled.

'Wow, Allegra sounds like a real firecracker.'

'More like an out-of-control bonfire.'

'Aye, but just imagine what she'd be like in the sack.'

'I don't want to, it's too scary.'

'Jamie Gray scared of a wee lassie. I never thought I'd see the day.' His eyes widened when Jamie grabbed him by the front of the jumper and yanked him towards him. 'Take it easy mate, I was only having a joke. You know me.'

'Sometimes joking can get you into trouble,' he said before releasing him.

'We need to find out what John Lawson's on about though,' said Gary, straightening his jumper. 'He could try to attack you again.'

'I've no idea what he's on about. I never touched his phone.'

'Maybe it was Digger or Logan?'

'No way was it Logan, but it's something Digger would do.'

'You wantin' to pay him a visit?'

'Aye, I do. Let's move.'

Gary grabbed his coat and followed him out the door, relieved he was no longer a focus for his friend's anger.

* * *

Allegra quietly closed the front door behind her and attempted to tiptoe to the staircase. It was a grand staircase, the sort of staircase movie stars descended wearing gowns of silk and satin, a cigarette holder elegantly clasped between two slender fingers. The floor was polished marble, the large chandelier hanging from the ceiling reflecting dazzlingly off it. Most people would kill to live in a house like this but to Allegra it was a prison.

She slipped off her high heels so she could move more stealthily but as she reached the bottom step an angry voice from the lounge echoed towards her.

'Allegra, is that you?'

She sighed and hung her head. 'Yes, Father, it's me.'

'Where the hell have you been?'

With her shoulders slumped resignedly, she walked across the cool marble floor and entered the large lounge, which was tastefully decorated in a baroque style with expensive Louis XV-style furniture, brocade and silk curtains, gilt edged chairs with curved legs and a marble fireplace. The effect could have been tacky, but her mother had had excellent taste and the effect was stunning. She couldn't enjoy the beauty her mother had left everywhere because she was dead and gone, run off the road by persons unknown. Allegra had the horrible feeling the big bull of a man standing by the fireplace clutching a glass of whisky was responsible.

'Out with it, girl,' snarled Cameron Abernethy.

'I've been with a friend.'

'What friend?'

'You don't know him.'

'Him? Is this another boyfriend?'

'Not as such.'

'What's that supposed to mean?'

'I've only just met him.'

Her father slammed his glass down on the fireplace so hard Allegra was amazed it didn't smash and he stalked up to her. Although he'd never played a sport in his life he looked like the rugby player from someone's worst nightmare with his massive rounded shoulders, shaved head, flat nose and fierce blue eyes. His legs were like tree trunks and his thick arms could throttle a rhino.

'What's his name?' he demanded.

'Adam... Granger,' she replied, giving him the first name that popped into her head.

'Is he from a good family?'

'Er, yes.'

His body relaxed. 'Good. As long as you're not slumming it again with another scrag-end from one of those dodgy estates.'

'No, Father. I know you don't like it when I do that,' she said, hanging her head.

'Good.'

She flinched when he touched her chin, tilting her face up to his. 'Just obey me and I'll look after you, Allegra.'

'I will.'

He ran his thumb along her jawline, making her wince. 'All right. Give your dad a kiss.'

She screwed her eyes tight shut as she went up on her tiptoes to plant a reluctant kiss on his stubbly cheek.

'That's my girl,' he breathed in her ear.

Allegra forced herself not to shake or even move, the silence stretching out endlessly, taunting her.

Finally, he turned from her and picked up his glass. 'You can go to your room.'

She nodded and walked to the door, quietly closing it behind her. Once she was out of his sight she ran to the stairs and dashed up them, not stopping until she was safely in her bedroom. After closing the door and locking it, she jammed a chair under the handle for good measure. On unsteady feet she tottered towards her super king-sized bed and collapsed onto it, tears rolling down her face.

Removing her jacket, she rolled up the sleeves of her blouse, opened up the drawer of her bedside cabinet and took out a small knife. She dragged the blade across her forearm, managing to find a gap between two old wounds, watching in fascination as the blood welled up and slowly trickled down her skin.

She sighed with relief, the pain easing the fear that kept her body permanently wrapped up in knots.

After stopping the blood flow, applying antiseptic cream and dressing the wound, she lay back on the bed and curled up into the foetal position, silent tears rolling down her face.

* * *

'I didn't nick any phone,' exclaimed Digger. 'I swear to God.'

Despite his friend's superior size, Jamie had easily managed to pin him up against the wall of his own bedroom, Digger able to feel the power running through Jamie's wiry arms, every muscle hard as rock. Even with all the steroids, protein shakes and weights, he still couldn't compete.

'You didn't nick it and Gary says he didn't, which means it was Logan. Do you expect me to believe that?' he yelled, showering Digger's face with spittle.

'I don't know who nicked it, Jamie. All I know is it wasnae me.'

'John Lawson and his pals were gonnae dae me in because of that fucking phone and I'm gonnae find out who did take it and when I do I'll shove it right up their arse.'

'It wasnae me. Search my room if you don't believe me.'

'If you did take it you'd have moved it on by now.'

'But I didn't,' he replied, shooting Gary a pleading look.

'I think he's telling the truth,' said Gary, standing at the back of the room, well out of harm's way.

Jamie studied Digger hard, causing sweat to pop out on his forehead.

'All right,' Jamie eventually said, releasing him. 'I believe you. Sorry, pal.'

'It's okay,' said Digger, running a hand through his hair, hoping he didn't look as agitated as he felt. Jamie could be fucking terrifying when he wanted to be.

Gary was put out that he hadn't got an apology after being unjustly accused, but decided against mentioning it. 'That only leaves Logan.'

'No way was it him,' said Jamie.

'It's only fair we check.'

Jamie was starting to feel a bit guilty about roughing up two of his best friends, so he nodded. 'Aye, you're right. Let's head over there now.'

'He probably didn't take it,' said Digger. 'John could have just dropped it somewhere and not realised or maybe one of his dodgy pals nicked it.'

'More than likely,' said Gary. 'You know Kerry, who used to go out with John?'

'Aye,' Jamie and Digger said in unison.

'She told me he dropped his car keys down the cludgy in the pub and he made Tom Marshall go down a manhole under the road outside to look for them and he saw a rat the size of an Alsatian and it chased him and bit him and he came out of the drain all shaking and sweating and foaming at the mouth. He had to have an injection at the hospital in his arse cheek and he couldn't sit down for three days and he became addicted to cheese.' When Gary got into a story he became breathless and talked so fast it became difficult to follow him. Sentence structure also went right out the window.

'You just made all that up, didn't you?' said Digger.

'No, that's what Kerry told me, swear to God.'

'Then she was having you on. She spends half her life on crack. She's the one who probably sees rats the size of Alsatians running about, as well as dragons and leprechauns.'

'I'm off out, Maw,' Digger told her as they tramped through the living room to the door.

'Okay, love,' said the plump, sweet-faced woman, dragging her eyes off the film she was watching. 'Let me know if you're going to be out late.'

'Maw, I'm twenty-one,' he blushed.

'You're still my baby and you always will be, even when you're fifty.'

'Don't worry, Mrs Barrie,' grinned Gary. 'We'll change his wee nappy if he dirties it.'

Digger grabbed him by the back of the jacket and propelled him out the front door. Jamie gave Mrs Barrie a polite smile before following them.

'Stay alert,' Jamie told his friends as they headed down the street. 'The Lawsons will be back on the estate and they'll still be gunning for us.' His phone rang and he pulled it out of his pocket. 'All right, Maw?'

'Get your arse back here pronto. The Lawsons are outside the house.'

'Jesus, we're on our way,' he said, breaking into a run, the others following.

The noise was audible before they'd even rounded the corner onto Jamie's street. Jackie was in the garden, swinging a frying pan at John's head. He managed to avoid the blow and retreated back a few paces towards the gate, limping on his left leg, which had already been injured by Allegra's bumper.

'Oy, you fucking dobbers,' yelled Jamie. 'It's me you want. Leave my maw alone.'

'Run, Jamie,' Jackie called to him. 'I can take care of these arseholes.'

'It's all right, Maw. Get back inside and see to Charlie, we'll deal with this lot,' Jamie said, taking the bike chain out of his pocket and swinging it.

'I'm going nowhere,' replied Jackie, swinging the pan at John again and missing.

'Gie' me my phone back Jamie,' called John. 'Your girlfriend and her car are no' here to save you now.'

'How many fucking times, you prick? I havenae got it.'

'If not you, then it's one of your friends. It went missing during our fight last night.'

'Why don't you ask that bunch of inbred freaks?' he retorted, nodding at John's five friends. 'It would be much easier for them to nick it off you and what a perfect time to do it, right around the time of the fight when you're more likely to blame us.'

Clearly John hadn't thought of this because his eyes flicked from side to side and he turned to frown at his friends over his shoulder. 'No,' he eventually said, turning back to face Jamie. 'It's one of you lot. Now give it back.'

'We don't fucking have it!' Jamie exclaimed again. 'Feel free to come and search us.' He swung the bike chain again. 'If you dare.'

'Oh, I dare,' said John, producing a large knife.

There was a cry of distress from the direction of Jackie, who had ignored her son's advice to go back inside. She slammed the pan into John's hand, making him scream. The knife fell to the ground and she snatched it up and dragged the blade along the ground, snapping it. 'You nasty little bastard,' she cried, bringing the pan down on the middle of John's back, knocking him to the ground. 'You think you can threaten my son with a knife? I'll kill you.'

John's friends had to rescue him, dragging him out of the garden and out of harm's way. Even then she kept swinging the pan, forcing them to run down the street, making Digger and Gary laugh out loud.

'You just keep getting your arse kicked by women, don't you, John?' Jamie yelled after him as he retreated cradling his injured hand. 'If you bother us again we'll set Digger's wee sister on you.'

He jogged into the garden to hug his mum, who shook in his arms. 'You were awesome, Maw. You okay?'

'Aye, I'm fine, son. It was the knife, it sent me demented.'

'Good thing, too. They won't be back.'

'Don't be naïve, of course they will. All right, boys?' she said when Gary and Digger followed Jamie into the garden.

'Yes, Mrs Gray,' said Digger. 'That was amazing. You're lethal with a frying pan.'

'I've had to be,' she said with a wry smile. 'John really wants his phone back.'

'Maybe he's got something embarrassing on it?' said Gary. 'He could have filmed himself dancing around his bathroom with his cock hanging oot of his maw's undies while singing along to ABBA.'

'Lovely Gary, you always make me laugh,' smiled Jackie. 'Do you want to come in, lads?'

'Logan,' said Jamie, eyes widening. 'We need to get over there. They might try him next. Get inside, Maw, and keep the doors locked,' he told her before tearing off after his friends.

* * *

Dave and Logan were sitting in silence, staring at John Lawson's phone, which lay on the coffee table looking sinister.

'So, what do we do, Da?' said Logan.

'We've got the phone numbers we wanted. Let's get rid of it.'

'But that photo could be proof of a crime.'

'Or it could be some stupid prank John pulled.'

'We have to take it to the police.'

'No fucking way. I've never gone to the police in my life.'

'This is murder, Da, it's serious.'

'We don't know that it is murder. That could all be make-up.'

'If it is then it was done by someone who makes Hollywood films and there's none of those in Gallowburn.'

'All right, take it to the police and when they ask how you got the phone you can tell them you beat the crap out of John Lawson and stole it so you could get the phone numbers he's using to set up a robbery because we want to do the robbery instead.'

'All right, maybe not.'

'We've no choice but to get rid of it.'

They jumped out of their seats when there was a bang at the front door.

'What the hell is that?' said Dave.

'Open up, McVitie, I know you're in there,' yelled a voice.

'Oh, Christ,' said Logan. 'It's John Lawson.'

Dave paled. 'Stay where you are and stay quiet. Hopefully he'll go away.'

'I don't think it'll be that easy.'

'You locked the front door?'

Logan nodded.

'Good. Then he cannae get in.'

The door started to violently shake in its frame, accompanied by loud bangs.

'They're trying to kick the door down,' said Logan.

'If you've got my phone, Logan, you'd better give it back,' yelled John.

Logan shot his dad an accusing look, and he had the grace to look ashamed.

'Maybe we should just give it him back?' said Dave resignedly.

'We can't,' replied Logan. 'When he sees it's been unlocked he'll know we went through everything on it and that we saw that photo. What if he kills us too to keep us quiet?'

'Oh, shite,' rasped Dave.

'You heard him – he said *if* I have his phone. He doesn't know for sure. All we can do is front it out and pretend we don't know what he's talking about.'

'You're right, we've no choice.'

When his dad glanced at the stairs, Logan frowned. 'Don't even think of hiding upstairs and leaving me to face the music.'

'I wouldnae do that,' he retorted, blushing. Determined to do something right for the first time in his life, he hauled himself to his feet and stood tall and proud. 'Come on, son, we can do this. Let's put on a show for him.'

Logan nodded and rose too. 'Aye, Da, we can.'

Dave strode to the door and pulled it open, just in time too because the wood was on the verge of splintering.

'What the hell are you noisy rabble wantin'?' he yelled at John and his friends. 'Look what you've done to my door,' he added, indicating all the scuffmarks.

'I want my phone back,' snarled John, who looked like he was on the verge of a breakdown with his sweaty face and wild eyes. For a reason Dave didn't understand, his right hand was bruised and swollen and he cradled it to his chest.

'Well, it's no' here.'

'Aye, it is. Either he nicked it,' said John, gesturing to Logan standing by his dad's side in the doorway, 'or it was one of his dickhead friends.'

'Oh aye? You asked the others then? Is that why your hand's all fucked up?'

'I did ask them actually, smart arse, and they denied it but they didnae touch my hand. I was in a knife fight with ten, no, twelve roasters. Fucked them right up, I did. This is the only injury I got. They're all in hospital right now.'

'Aye, twelve roasters. Course you did. We havenae got your phone so you can bugger off out of it and you're buying me a new door. Look at what you've done to it.'

'Piss off, I'm no' buying you a new door. The paint was the only thing holding it together before we even arrived.' He looked to Logan. 'You've got it, haven't you? Admit it.'

'No, I haven't,' replied Logan. 'Get lost, John, you're making a tit of yourself and you woke up all our neighbours.'

John wilted slightly when he glanced around and saw all the immediate neighbours out on their doorsteps, frowning at him. He wilted even more when Jamie, Gary and Digger tore down the street towards them.

'You really don't have it?' said John, turning back to Logan.

'Really, I don't. You're barking up the wrong tree.'

John, just like Jamie, thought Logan the least likely of the Blood Brothers to have the phone as he wasn't known for nicking from people. It must have been one of the other three but it was time to go, there were too many witnesses. Besides, he wanted to get to hospital. His hand fucking hurt and it was still swelling. 'All right Logan, I believe you.'

Logan just nodded, although inwardly he sighed with relief.

John and his friends turned to face the other three Blood Brothers when they tore into the garden. 'Take it easy,' he told them. 'We're going, for now, but I want my phone back and soon. If you've sold it then get it back. If you don't then things are going to get really fucking bloody.'

'For Christ's sake, how many times?' yelled Jamie. 'We haven't got your fucking phone, so piss off.'

The agony in his hand encouraged John to wrap things up. 'This isn't over, Jamie, I promise you that.'

They watched John and his friends leave, throwing threats and insults over their shoulders as they went.

'You okay?' Jamie asked Logan and Dave.

'Aye, we're fine,' replied the latter. 'You turned up just in time.'

'He really wants that phone fucking badly,' said Gary. 'Why does he no' just get another one? It's just some shitty pay-as-you-go, I saw him on it in the pub. It's no' worth all the rammy he's been kicking up.'

Logan and Dave glanced at each other.

'Which of you lads messed up his hand?' said Dave.

'None of us,' replied Jamie. 'That was my maw.'

Just the mention of Jackie Gray brought that morning screaming back. 'He's lucky that's all she did to him. Well, thanks a lot, lads. You can get yourselves off home now.'

'But we need to decide what we're gonnae do about the Lawsons,' said Jamie.

'They won't be back tonight,' Dave replied, conscious of John Lawson's phone still lying on the coffee table. No way did he want them coming inside and seeing it. 'It's Saturday tomorrow, so none of you have got work. Come round in the morning, not too early. Logan can make you all breakfast,' he added, earning himself a glower from his son.

'Aye, all right, Mr McVitie,' said Jamie, to his relief. 'See you tomorrow, then.'

Dave and Logan hastily stepped back inside, slamming the door shut and locking it.

'I really think we should tell them what's going on,' said Logan. 'It's not fair that they're being threatened and they don't even know why. They didn't even ask me if I'd taken the phone because they know it's not the sort of thing I usually do.'

'You can't, son. Like I said, it'll mean we get a smaller cut when we do that robbery.'

'Should we even do it? If that photo is real then God knows what John's involved in. We could walk in there and end up like that deid body.'

Dave's natural cowardice came rushing to the surface. 'That's a good point. We need to tackle this carefully.'

'So, we're going to tell the others?'

'Let me think about it. I always like to sleep on a decision. Get yerself to bed boy, you're gonnae need your rest. I have the feeling things are gonnae get tougher.'

5

The next morning Logan found himself stuck in the kitchen cooking breakfast for his dad and his friends while they laughed and joked in the living room.

Jamie spotted his friend's glum face through the open kitchen door and decided to help.

'Need a hand, pal?' Jamie asked him.

'Aye, please,' replied Logan. 'You can set the plates out and butter the toast when it pops.'

'On it,' said Jamie, opening a cupboard door and taking out five plates. 'You okay?'

'No. I'm pissed off being used as a glorified servant.'

'Have a word with your da, then. You're no' a wean any more. It's no' like you don't pay your way either.'

'I know, I really need to have it out with him but now doesn't feel like the time, we've got so much going on. The last thing I need is him kicking off.'

'No need to worry. If he does I can get my maw to have a word with him. She's the one who gave him those bruises.'

'So I believe, although he'd never admit it.'

'He never does,' said Jamie, taking the toast out of the toaster when it popped. 'I've got a date with the madwoman tonight.'

'Not Twitchy Tina again? She's so paranoid she thinks MI5 spies on her when she's on the cludgy.'

'God, no, although she'd probably be an improvement. No, this is some mental case who came into the shop.'

He then explained about his encounter with Allegra. When he'd finished, Logan burst out laughing.

'She actually ran over John Lawson?' said Logan, thinking she must be the woman he saw his friend arguing with near his work.

'Well, more hit him than ran over him.'

'I don't know what you're worried about, she sounds pretty awesome.'

'She is not, she's aff her heid and for some reason she thinks I'm amazing. She has a huge crush on me.'

'Maybe you're right, she is nuts,' grinned Logan.

'Fucking hilarious. She's a headache I don't need with all the shite we've got going on but my maw's making me take her out.'

'You're telling me to stand up to my da when you need to do the same with your maw.'

'There's a difference – my maw's way scarier than your da.'

'True. Well, you can go out with her tonight and tell Jackie it didn't work out, then you'll never have to see her again.'

'It'll no' be that easy, you don't know what Allegra's like.'

'Allegra?' he spluttered. 'That's her name?'

'Aye. She's a posh bird and she never gives up.'

'Then you'll have to put her off you.'

'I'm no' sure that's possible.'

'You could tell her you've already got a girlfriend.'

'Too late. I already told her I haven't.'

'Then tell her you're gay.'

'Piss off, Logan,' he retorted, making his friend chuckle.

'Just go out with the lassie. You never know, you might end up liking her and then problem solved. Anyone who hits John Lawson with their car has got to have some good points.'

'She doesnae, apart from her tits. They're pretty nice.'

'So you've had the wrappers off her already?'

'God, no, I just mean they look pretty good through her clothes but no' good enough to go out with her. Nothing's worth that nightmare.'

'Then I don't know what to suggest. Anyway, grub's up.'

Between them they dished up the food and carried the steaming plates into the front room.

'Smells good,' grinned Dave, clapping his hands together with anticipation.

Once they were all settled with their food and a cup of tea each, they could finally discuss the Lawson problem. Dave had already told Logan he didn't want the rest of the Blood Brothers to know about the phone, despite his son's protests. The phone in question was safely stashed in a drawer in Dave's bedroom.

'John Lawson's never gonnae stop until he finds his phone,' opened Jamie. 'And as we don't have it we'll have to make him stop.'

'By beating the shite out of him again,' said Digger with an evil smile.

'Or we could point him in the direction of someone else,' announced Dave, smiling when they all looked his way.

Logan frowned. His dad had mentioned nothing of this idea to him.

'How do you mean?' said Gary before shoving half a sausage into his mouth.

'I mean spread it about that someone else nicked his phone,' replied Dave. 'Someone we don't like. He'll go after them and beat the shite out of them, or John will get the shite beaten out of him. Either way, it gets him off our backs.'

'That's a great idea,' said Jamie.

Logan hated his dad's plan, it would only get innocent people hurt, if there was an innocent person left in Gallowburn. 'I don't know, Da,' he said. 'That'll only make things more complicated.'

'Can you think of a better way to get him off our backs?' Triumph lit up Dave's piggy eyes when his son failed to reply. 'Didn't think so.'

'Give me a couple of days and I'll come up with something.'

'We don't have a couple of days. The Lawsons could come back at any time.'

'I like the idea,' said Digger.

'Me too,' said Gary.

'But someone innocent could get hurt,' said Logan. 'And that's no' fair.'

'Life's no' fair,' announced Dave sagely. 'So, who should we pin the blame on?'

'John's first cousin Mike,' said Jamie. 'They've already had a falling out over some bird, so it wouldn't take much to make John think he'd stolen from him.'

'No' bad,' said Dave with a nod.

While Digger and Gary came up with the names of more poor sods they could throw under the bus, Logan was ready for tearing his hair out. All these people they were discussing were people who were more than capable of causing a lot of trouble themselves. He had to stop this insanity before someone got seriously hurt over a poxy mobile phone.

'You're being very quiet,' Jamie told him.

'Because I hate this plan,' replied Logan. 'It'll make everything worse.'

While the others brushed aside his objections, Jamie listened to him seriously. Logan had stopped him from doing something stupid so many times in the past and he knew he should listen to him now. 'What makes you so sure?'

'Because you're gonnae end up with John Lawson running about twatting people left, right and centre. Then it'll come out that we put those rumours about and all those people will come after us for revenge. So, as well as the Lawsons, we'll have half the scheme gunning for us.'

'Christ, you're right,' said Jamie. 'We need to handle this in-house. We cannae let anyone else get involved.'

'No one will trace the rumour back to us,' said Dave with a dismissive wave.

'By now everyone in Gallowburn will know about the rammy last night between us and the Lawsons. If any rumour starts it'll be obvious where it came from.'

'And it'll make us look like a bunch of poofs who are trying to take the heat off ourselves by blaming someone else,' said Digger, a blob of ketchup on his strong dimpled chin. 'Maybe you're right, Logan, and this isn't the way to go.'

'I'm no' looking like a poof,' said Gary, stuffing a heap of baked beans into his mouth and proceeding to chew with his mouth open, making Logan grimace.

'How no'?' said Digger. 'You don't seem bothered about it the rest of the time.'

'You cheeky bastard. If I wasn't eating I'd take you outside and give you a kicking. But my slice is more important,' he replied, cutting into the square slab of sausage meat.

'We need to come up with another way,' said Jamie.

'We don't have another way,' retorted Dave.

'Then we'll have to think of one.'

Dave could see all the boys were now against his grand plan, so he decided not to push it. The victorious look his son shot him irritated him.

'Maybe we should just beat the ever-living shite out of John?' suggested Gary. 'Put him in hospital for a couple of weeks. Pissing in a bottle and being fed baby food will make him forget all about his stupid phone.'

'But we'll still have the rest of the Lawsons gunning for us,' said Jamie. 'Christ, I'd love to get hold of that phone. There must be something really tasty on it for John to go to so much trouble to get it back.'

'Like I said last night,' said Digger between mouthfuls of food. 'Embarrassing footage.'

'You're probably right. Just think what we could do with that.'

'Put it all over the internet,' grinned Gary. 'His rep around here would be ruined. He'd probably have to leave the scheme and we could take over the south side, finally.'

'That would be fucking sweet,' said Jamie. 'I'm just glad his older brother Craig's in prison. If he was thrown into the mix things would get really fucking dangerous.'

'He was done for GBH, wasn't he?' said Digger.

'Aye. He got five years. He's only got another eight or nine months to do. He's a proper psycho but he's smart too.'

'Unlike John,' Gary chuckled to himself.

Logan caught his dad glowering at him. Clearly he was pissed off with him and if he didn't come up with a solution to their dilemma he'd never stop banging on about it. Plus his dad wasn't above giving him a clump now and then.

'Maybe there's another way,' said Logan, drawing their attention back to himself.

'What's that?' said Jamie, always eager to hear one of Logan's ideas – in his opinion he was the most intelligent member of their group.

Logan hated the confidence in his friend's eyes that his plan would get them out of the shit. Jamie had no idea it was his fault they were in this mess in the first place. When would he learn not to listen to his dad? 'John wants his phone back so we'll give it to him.' He enjoyed the panic that lit up his dad's eyes.

'But we don't have it,' said a puzzled Digger.

'You said you saw him in the pub on his phone.'

'Aye, I did.'

'Can you describe it?'

'It was a black Nokia 1 Plus.'

'We buy the same model and get someone to give it him back. They can say they found it on the street.'

'Surely he'll know it's not his phone?' said Jamie. 'None of his stuff would be on it for a start.'

'Someone picked it up and did a factory reset.'

'Why would someone reset his phone than leave it in the street?' said Gary. 'That makes no sense. John's thick but not even he's stupid enough to fall for that one.'

'Aye, it's a wee bit thin, pal,' said Jamie. 'I mean, everyone knows their own phone, don't they?'

'I don't know,' sighed Logan, dragging his hands through his hair.

'Look,' said Dave. 'John's vulnerable after Jackie messed up his hand. Just beat the crap out of him and tell him that if he doesn't let this drop you'll beat the crap out of his family too, but you'll go heavy duty on them – hammers, crowbars, baseball bats, the works.'

Logan wondered if he was the only one who'd noticed his use of the word *you.*

'That will only start a war,' said Logan. 'We might be the better fighters but there's more of them than us.'

'Well it's better than your crap idea of buying the tosser a new phone.'

'At least my plan won't lead to blood in the streets.'

'Aye, it will,' retorted Dave. 'As soon as John realises it's no' his phone, which will take him about three seconds.'

It suddenly occurred to Jamie that Allegra might actually be useful, although as yet he wasn't quite sure how. 'I've got an idea,' he said, causing them all to look his way.

'What's that, Jamie?' said Dave.

'I've got a... er... friend who might be able to help, but I need to talk to her first.'

'Her?' said a nervous Dave. 'You don't mean your maw, do you?'

'No, course not,' he replied, making Dave sigh with relief.

'No' the mad woman?' said Gary with a mischievous smile.

'Aye. She's a weapon of mass destruction all on her own. I bet she can help. She'll probably enjoy it, too.'

'You gonnae ask her when you're on your date tonight?'

'Aye.' His dark eyes narrowed. 'What of it?'

'Nothing,' Gary grinned, shovelling the last of his food into his mouth. 'Bloody hell, Logan, that was pure gallus. You'll make someone a very pretty wife one day.'

'Piss off, Gary,' he muttered.

* * *

To their surprise, the Blood Brothers heard nothing from the Lawsons for the rest of the day. Gary and Digger were convinced it was because they'd realised they'd been outclassed and outmanoeuvred, so they'd decided to drop the whole thing. Jamie and Logan thought it was just the calm before the storm.

Jackie watched her son carefully from the moment he came home at five o'clock that afternoon to make sure he couldn't escape before Allegra arrived for their date.

'You don't need to watch me every second,' he told her. 'I'm no' gonnae do a runner.'

'I'm not so sure about that. The lassie will be here in half an hour. Why don't you go and get changed?'

'I don't need to get changed. I'm fine as I am.'

'You've been in those clothes all day.'

'So?'

'When you had a date with Sarah Tierney you spent two hours getting ready.'

'Allegra won't care what I'm wearing.'

'Well, I do and you're no' taking that lassie out in trackie bottoms and a T-shirt. Go and take a shower and get changed right now and put on your best clothes. Allegra's got class and you're no' going out with her looking like a scruff.'

'Fine,' he muttered, dragging himself up off the couch.

'And don't just run the water,' she called after him as he stomped upstairs. 'I'll know if you do.' She turned her attention to Charlie, who was grinning to himself. 'I don't know what you're looking so smug about. Get yourself upstairs and tidy your room.'

'But I want to see Allegra.'

'Then you'd better hurry and get it done before she arrives.'

Charlie leapt up off the couch and sped upstairs, making her smile. If only Jamie was as keen on that girl as his younger brother was.

Jackie tidied up the living room, happily humming to herself, praying the girl steered her son onto a positive path. If anyone had the strength of character to do that, Jackie thought it might well be Allegra.

Jamie returned downstairs just before Allegra was due to arrive, still sulking, but at least he looked much more presentable with his hair freshly washed, wearing his black trousers and a deep red shirt.

'Much better,' smiled Jackie.

'Whatever,' he muttered. 'Oh God,' he added when the doorbell rang. 'She's early. That's just typical of her.'

Jackie hurried to answer the door, missing Jamie ducking into the kitchen. 'Allegra,' she beamed. 'My, you look beautiful, hen. Come away in.'

'Thanks, Jackie,' she smiled, stepping inside.

Jamie took a few deep breaths, psyching himself up to face the force of nature he would have to deal with all evening.

He stepped into the living room and gaped at the vision talking to his mother. Allegra's blonde hair streamed down her shoulders, her curvy body encased in smart black trousers and high-heeled boots. Her smooth white midriff was bare, a light purple halter neck top encasing her breasts. A long black knee-length jacket completed the look. Despite all the bare skin, the effect was cool and sophisticated. She barely wore any make-up, just a kiss of light pink on her lips and a hint of grey shadow around her eyes, giving them a smoky look.

'Hi, Jamie,' she smiled, brimming over with confidence and enthusiasm, as usual. 'You look good.'

'Thanks.'

'Doesn't she look lovely, Jamie?' said Jackie, warning in her voice when her son continued to stare at their visitor.

'Aye,' he replied. 'Very.'

Charlie charged downstairs and into the living room, coming to a sudden halt. 'You look really pretty, Allegra,' he blushed.

'Thank you, Charlie. You look handsome,' she replied, making him blush deeper. She looked back at Jamie. 'It runs in the family,' she winked at him.

'If it does, it didn't come from their ugly sod of a father,' said Jackie. 'So where are you two lovebirds off to, then?' she added, earning herself a withering look from Jamie.

'I don't know,' said Allegra. 'Where's good to go around here?'

'You want to hang around Gallowburn?' exclaimed Jamie.

'Why not? It's your home.'

'Because it's a shitehole,' piped up Charlie, looking down at the floor when his mum glared at him.

'There must be somewhere around here you like to go?' said Allegra. 'What about your local pub?'

'It's very... earthy,' said Jackie. 'Why don't you take Allegra for a nice meal, Jamie?'

'Nice meal, here?' he replied. 'There's only the kebab house or the burger bar and they've both been investigated by Environmental Health.'

'There's Di Giorgio's. Arthur took me there on our date. It was very nice. I had scampi in a basket.'

'Scampi in a basket?' smiled Allegra. 'How seventies. I love the seventies. Let's go there,' she said with all the excitement as though they'd suggested a trip to Florida.

'If you want,' said Jamie.

'We haven't got a reservation. Is it necessary to book?'

'No, not at all,' replied Jackie when Jamie snorted with laughter. 'They've always got tables.'

'I wonder why,' he muttered.

'Well, on you go, you two,' said Jackie, to Charlie's disappointment. 'You don't want to spend your date hanging around here.'

'I promise not to keep him out too late, Jackie,' said Allegra.

'You can keep him as long as you like, hen,' she replied, making Jamie frown. 'And have fun. Don't do anything I wouldn't do, which leaves the field wide open.'

Allegra roared with laughter.

'Finally, someone who appreciates my sense of humour,' grinned Jackie. 'Well, away you go then and enjoy yourselves.'

'We will,' smiled Allegra. She winked at Charlie. 'See you later, handsome.'

He turned positively crimson and released a nervous giggle.

As Jamie slinked past his mother, she slipped him thirty pounds.

'Treat that lassie nice,' she whispered when he gave her a questioning look.

He nodded and slid the money into his trouser pocket. This showed how much Jackie thought of Allegra because they didn't have much spare cash.

They got into Allegra's BMW, Jamie sliding down in his seat when he spotted all the neighbours peering out of their windows at them.

'So, where's this restaurant, then?' Allegra asked him as she pulled on her seatbelt.

'Not far,' he replied. 'Turn left at the end of the street. It's only three streets away.'

'Exciting. I've never eaten there before.'

'Don't get carried away. It's just a glorified café run by a proper walloper.'

'Is it cosy and intimate?'

'It's pretty dark if that's what you mean because the owner's a stingy git who uses cheap lightbulbs.'

'Even better,' she said, patting his knee. 'I've not been able to stop thinking about when you kissed me.'

'I didn't kiss you. You kissed me.'

'You were so passionate,' she continued, her hand sliding higher up his thigh. 'It got me so hot.'

'All right, take it easy,' he replied. 'You don't want to boil over.'

'I'm making no promises,' she said with another wink.

'Turn right here,' he told her, relieved when she had to remove her hand to change gear.

'Have you been thinking about me?'

'Constantly,' he said flatly.

'I knew it,' she smiled. 'You should wear shirts and shower more often, you look great.'

'I shower every day, you cheeky cow.'

'Really? I stand corrected.'

'Are you saying I smell?'

'No, not at all. Come to think of it, it was probably the smell of the shop, not you.'

'Aye, it's the smell of the shop. It always stinks, in more ways than one.'

'Yes, it's the shop,' she said, lips twitching, making him glower.

'Here we are,' he said, relieved.

Allegra parked her car in a space right outside the restaurant, which sat in the middle of a row of three units, a barber on the left and a convenience store on the right.

Shame once again washed over Jamie as he regarded the faded signage and litter-strewn pavement. Allegra was probably used to five-star restaurants that served champagne and lobster. Now she was going to have scampi in a basket with lukewarm chips and cheap plonk.

'Aww, it's cute,' she said, getting out of the car.

'Cute?' he said, climbing out too and slamming the door shut.

'Yes. I like it,' she announced, purposefully striding to the door, Jamie hurrying to catch up.

She walked inside the restaurant and let the door swing shut, almost smacking him in the face.

They were greeted by the restaurant owner. Superficially he looked

Italian with his slicked-back black hair and dark eyes, although he was
no more Italian than deep fried Mars bars.

'Jamie,' he said in his over-the-top fake Italian accent, heartily
shaking his hand. 'It is so good to see you.'

'Aye, you too, Gerry.'

Gerry looked to Allegra. 'Who is this beautiful lady?' he smiled,
eagerly looking her up and down.

'Allegra, Gerry,' said Jamie. 'Gerry, Allegra.'

'I have a beautiful table for a beautiful lady,' said Gerry, his accent
becoming even more flamboyant, ushering them to a table for two by
the window and pulling out a chair for her.

'Thank you,' she said, taking a seat. 'Lovely,' she added, when he lit
the candle in the middle of the table with a flourish.

Jamie rolled his eyes and slid into the chair opposite her. Gerry
failed to pull out his chair for him as he was too busy staring down
Allegra's cleavage, which she either didn't notice or pretended not to.

'I hear you do a great scampi in a basket?' Allegra asked Gerry.

'We do,' he replied. 'The best in Glasgow.'

'I'll have that, please.'

'Excellent choice, signorina. Jamie?'

'The same please. And a pint of lager.'

'Wine for the beautiful signorina?'

'No thanks, I'm driving,' replied Allegra. 'I'll have tonic water with
ice and a thinly cut slice of lemon.'

'A wonderful choice,' said Gerry. 'I shall fetch them immediately.'

'He's not really Italian,' Jamie told her when he'd gone.

'I know. If the terrible accent wasn't enough of a giveaway, he didn't
know that my name's Italian. Great service, though.'

'It's not usually this good. I think it's more to do with you.'

'Me, why?'

'Because you're...'

'What?' she said when he trailed off.

'You look good,' he mumbled.

'I do?' she said, leaning in closer. 'What looks good about me?'

'Dunno,' he blushed. 'Just... everything.'

'And what's your favourite part of my everything?' she purred.

Jamie felt himself turn even redder. It wasn't like he was inexperienced with women. Being leader of the Blood Brothers meant he was never short of offers, but Allegra so confused and surprised him that he never knew what to say. 'I like everything, okay? I'm not pointing out bits of you.'

'So, you're a man of broad tastes. Even better.'

He jumped when her hand slid right up his inner thigh, causing him to bang his knee on the underside of the table.

'My,' she said. 'Someone's feeling frisky.'

'You're the frisky one,' he retorted.

She rested her elbows on the table, supporting her chin with her hand. 'Tell me about yourself, Dangerous.'

He shrugged. 'What do you want to know?'

'Everything.'

'What's everything?'

'Everything as in the traditional meaning of the word – childhood, likes and dislikes, the lot.'

Jamie, never comfortable talking about himself, decided to turn the conversation around. 'My life's been pretty boring. Why don't you tell me everything about yourself instead?'

She huffed out a breath and leaned back in her chair, the heel of one shoe tapping a staccato on the tiled floor. 'What do you want to know, Dangerous? About my father, who is the wealthiest man in the entire city, as well as a violent, bullying psychopath who I live in constant terror of? About how I think he murdered my sweet gentle mother but no one's willing to do anything about it because everyone's scared of him? Or would you like to know that I'm afraid that one day he'll kill me just like he killed her?'

Jamie stared at her, dumbstruck. At first he thought this was some sort of twisted joke and that at any moment she'd break into that carefree smile. In fact, he longed to see that smile because it would mean all that stuff she'd just said was untrue and he wouldn't have to deal with it. He gazed into her deep blue eyes and finally recognised the pain and fear there, telling him she was being entirely truthful.

Fortunately, he was saved from replying by Gerry placing their drinks before them.

'Pint of lager for the signor,' he smiled, slopping some of the lager onto the red and white checked tablecloth. 'And tonic water for the beautiful signorina.'

Jamie watched Allegra shove all her pain back down inside herself.

'Thank you, Gerry,' she said, summoning her cheerful smile.

'You are very welcome.'

When another couple walked through the door Gerry moved to greet them, leaving Jamie and Allegra alone.

'Wow,' said Jamie. 'Was all that true?'

'Why would I make up something like that?' she replied.

'Dunno. You do keep surprising me.'

'You're right, I do. Anyway, that's enough about me.' The sultry look returned. 'I want to know all about you.'

Once again she'd disorientated him, made him feel as though he didn't know up from down. He'd been Allegra'd. Yes, that was the perfect word for it. Well, he was going to give as good as he got.

'My dad was a violent drunken bastard who beat up me and my maw for years and stole all our money. When my maw found out she was pregnant with Charlie she threatened my da with a knife and he never touched her again. Life got a hell of a lot better after that. He ran out on us eight years ago and we haven't seen him since. End of story.'

'Come now, there's much more to your life than that.'

'Not really.'

'What about your little gang, the Blood Brothers?'

'What about us?'

'How did you get together?'

'We've known each other since primary school. Other kids tried to bully us, so we fought back. A few years ago we kicked out some twat of a gang that had taken over the north side of the scheme. They were terrorising the old yins, attacking the lassies. We look after the place now.'

'So, do you do much terrorising?'

'No. But we do protect.'

'And have you been protecting your scheme by fighting that idiot I hit with my car?'

'Aye, we have. They own the south side but not for long.'

'Ooh, I love that dark glower of yours,' she breathed. 'It's so sexy.'

He was saved once again by Gerry, who plonked their scampi baskets before them.

'Enjoy your meals,' he told them in his exaggerated accent.

'I'm sure it'll be lovely,' said Allegra.

Gerry beamed at her before turning to attend to the only other table.

'Great,' she said, picking up her knife and fork and daintily cutting into a piece of breaded scampi. Jamie, however, tore into his. He was used to having his tea earlier than this.

'Slow down before you choke,' Allegra told him.

'Hungry,' he mumbled between mouthfuls.

'So I see. You're a man of large appetites. I like that.'

'You like a lot of things.'

'Life is for living.'

'I bet you live it to the full.'

'As much as I can.'

Despite her earlier flirtatious comments, she seemed a little subdued after revealing the truth about her home life.

'Why would you tell me all that stuff when we hardly know each other?' he said, still suspicious.

'I don't know,' she sighed. 'I think I needed to get it off my chest.'

He studied her carefully, making sure she wasn't taking the piss out of him. The sadness in her eyes and the way her shoulders slumped, all the life and vivacity draining out of her told him she wasn't. 'Have you told the police?'

'How can I? My father owns most of them.'

'There must be someone you can talk to.'

'There's no one willing to go up against him. The people he doesn't own either through threats or blackmail are terrified of him.'

'No one's untouchable.'

'Actually, they are, if they have enough power and wealth and are completely psychotic.'

'Can't you just leave?'

'He's already told me if I do he'll kill me. He has the resources to find me, too. No matter where I went, he'd always find me.'

'Have you got any brothers or sisters?'

'An older brother but he's almost as bad as my father.'

'Your dad's really the richest man in the city?'

'Yep,' she sighed, this fact seeming to make her miserable.

'What would he say if he saw you in this shitey restaurant with me?'

'He'd go ballistic, to say the least, but he won't find out. He's too busy to notice where I go. Workaholic isn't the word. He wants me to marry a man from a good family, someone rich and connected, but I can't stand all those tossers. He's set me up with lots of them and they're all deathly dull. They've been so sheltered all they can talk about is politics, the news or cricket. I much prefer men like you. You're much more interesting.'

'You mean a bit of rough?'

'No. I mean real men living in the real world. You've done things.'

'I've spent my life on this estate. I've never been abroad. The furthest I've travelled is Saltcoats for a holiday and that was years ago. I don't even have a car.'

'So what? You've had to fight to survive. Life isn't about how much money you have or what car you drive, or having holidays in the Bahamas. It's about getting out there and doing stuff, having real experiences. If any of those sad silver spoon cabbages were chased down the street by a gang out for their blood they'd curl up in a corner and cry. They couldn't handle stuff like that. Then there's your mother, struggling to raise her sons alone. That takes a hell of a lot of guts and strength. I know women who fall apart if their manicurist can't fit them in. They're all so pathetic I can't stand it.' Allegra frowned down at her food. 'Your family's a real family. You love each other, that's so clear. You've no idea how lucky you are. I'd give everything I have to know what that's like.'

Jamie wished his mum was here right now, she'd know exactly what to say. He was useless at deep emotional conversations. At least what Allegra had told him explained why she was completely nuts.

'How is your food, beautiful lady?' Gerry asked them, suddenly appearing at the side of their table.

Jamie watched as once again Allegra stuffed all that pain deep down inside herself and became the confident, carefree – if slightly unhinged – woman who left her mark wherever she went.

'It's lovely, thank you,' she smiled up at him. 'The best scampi I've ever had.'

'I knew you'd like it,' he beamed. 'You are so obviously a lady of great taste and sophistication.' He looked to Jamie. 'Where did you find this dream?'

'I didn't,' he replied. 'She found me.'

'It's true, I did,' she said, patting Jamie's right hand, which gripped his fork in a way his mum was always telling him off for. She said the way he held it made him look like he was contemplating stabbing someone with it.

'You're a lucky man, Jamie,' said Gerry before trotting off again when the chef bellowed for someone to collect the waiting food.

Jamie wondered if now was the time to broach the subject of John Lawson. He wasn't yet sure how Allegra could help, but he felt certain anyone capable of causing as much chaos as she was would be able to do something. 'I saw the bloke you hit with your car yesterday.'

'Oh yes?' she said casually. 'How is he?'

'Limping,' he replied.

'Good,' she grinned.

'He attacked my maw.'

She slammed down her knife and fork and frowned. 'The bastard. Did he hurt her?'

'Course not. She's made of metal is my maw. She smashed his hand in with a frying pan when he pulled a knife.'

'Good old Jackie,' she smiled. 'I can just imagine her doing that. So, you get your street smarts and toughness from her, then?'

'Aye. It certainly didn't come from my da, who was a useless, spineless piece of shit.'

'So this John is still looking for his phone, then?'

'Aye, he is, and he won't believe we don't have it. He's off his nut. We cannae get him off our backs.'

'I'm sure you're more than capable of making him.'

'We are but it'll take some drastic action.'

Allegra appeared thoughtful as she sipped her tonic water. 'I want to help you get the sod. I hate to think of him hurting Jackie.'

Jamie smiled. With a firecracker like her on their side how could they possibly fail? 'Have you got something in mind?'

'Not yet, but I will.'

Gerry stopped by their table again, swept up their empty baskets and asked if they wanted dessert. Allegra ordered a fruit salad and Jamie a tiramisu. As he wanted to keep her sweet, Jamie told her more about his life, relating some of the scrapes he and his friends had got into, some of which were funny and made her laugh. It was a relief that the sadness he'd seen in her earlier had retreated and she appeared to be genuinely enjoying herself. He thought some of the hostility he'd felt towards her was due to the fact that he thought she wasn't really interested in him and all this was some spoilt rich girl's idea of a prank, but he was swiftly beginning to realise he'd never met anyone more genuine than her. This beautiful, wealthy woman actually wanted to spend time with him. He could take her to the crappiest dive in

Gallowburn and it wouldn't bother her. She might be rich but she wasn't a snob and she could feel at home anywhere. That still didn't change the fact that she was as mad as a box of frogs but he felt a little more relaxed with her now he was sure she wasn't taking the piss out of him.

'Do you want to go to the pub?' he asked her after he'd paid the bill. She hadn't objected to him paying, knowing he would have taken it as a personal affront.

'Sounds good, Dangerous, although I won't be able to have a drink.'

'You could leave your car at mine and get a taxi back.'

'I'd better not. Don't pout in that sexy way at me,' she smiled when his eyes flashed. 'I know my car would be safe at your house but my father would be angry if I went home without it.'

'Oh, I see,' he replied, not wanting to be responsible for pissing off that lunatic. 'Let's go, then.'

They said goodbye to Gerry and it took them a full five minutes to get out of the door because he was so busy repeatedly kissing Allegra's hand and bestowing compliments upon her about her beauty and grace. He only relinquished her because the chef's voice echoed through the restaurant that if he didn't come and collect the food waiting to go out pronto he'd come out there and ram his fish slice up his arse.

Allegra was so deep in thought she didn't even bother to molest Jamie as she drove them to the pub.

'You okay?' he asked her.

'Fine,' she replied. 'I'm trying to think of a way to get that bastard off your back.'

'My pals will be in the pub. We can talk it over with them.'

'Ooh, so I get to meet the rest of the Blood Brothers, do I?'

'Aye, you do.'

'Great. Are they all like you?'

'No. We're all pretty different actually.'

'Then this is going to be very interesting,' she smiled.

6

Allegra parked her car on the street outside the front of the pub and they walked inside together. When she took Jamie's hand he opened his mouth to object, promptly shutting it again when he remembered he needed her onside.

The Bonnie Brae was a hugely misleading name for the squat rectangular building with its barred windows. The pebble-dash coating the exterior was so sharp many a drunk person staggering out the worse for wear had grazed their hands and other parts of their anatomy on it. Inside, the walls were still stained nicotine yellow from catering to heavy smokers for years. The landlord and landlady – a formidable husband and wife team – enforced the countrywide smoking ban with glee, throwing out any rulebreakers by the scruff of the neck. Now no one dared spark up inside, but the owners had never bothered to redecorate. The bar was chipped and stained, covered in ring marks of varying size and age. The pub was all one room, no cosy intimate nooks leading off it, and the floor was wooden; consequently the noise level ensured a private chat was never possible. There was a single room behind the bar where those who really didn't want their nefarious conversations being overheard could go to talk, and the pub's customers couldn't exactly be called law-abiding.

Jamie and Allegra walked in to find the pub was busy and loud, as always. He spotted his friends at a table in the corner. When they saw who was holding his hand they all stopped talking to gape at her.

'Hello,' Allegra smiled at them all, completely unfazed by the attention.

'Who's your lovely friend, Jamie?' smiled the landlord, a leviathan of a man, shirt straining to contain his pendulous belly. His face was permanently flushed red and his thinning black hair badly dyed. Beside him was his wife, a stick-thin scarecrow of a woman, deep lines etched into her face. Despite her slight build she was more feared than her huge husband, mainly because in any fight she went straight for the genitals. One particular customer had never walked the same way again after she'd chucked him out for complaining that the lager was flat.

'Allegra,' said Jamie. 'This is Eric and his wife Deirdre. They own this pub.'

'Allegra,' smiled Deirdre. 'What an unusual name.'

'Were you named after the car?' rumbled Eric in his deep voice.

'No,' she smiled. 'It's Italian, it means joyful.'

'The car,' said Deirdre, shaking her head at her husband. 'You fud.'

'It was a fair guess,' he replied. 'I know a bloke who named his son Enzo after the Ferrari.'

'Aye, and he owns a fucking Skoda.' She looked back at Allegra. 'What can I get you to drink, hen?'

'Tonic water with ice and lemon please. I'm driving.'

'Aww, that's such a shame. Jamie, you tight wee sod, you can get the lassie a taxi so she can have a swally.'

'Hey, I've already offered,' he replied, holding up his hands. 'But she wants to drive home.'

'It's true, I do,' said Allegra. 'He's been the perfect gentleman all evening.'

'Really?' said Deirdre. 'Jamie Gray a gentleman?'

Allegra smiled and nodded.

'Well, wonders will never cease. Pint, Jamie?'

'Aye, please.'

'You and your lady take a seat. Eric will bring them over.'

'Thanks,' he said. Allegra hadn't relinquished his hand yet and he was starting to get a sweaty palm.

'Where are your friends?' Allegra asked him, scanning the room.

'Over there,' he replied with a nod of the head.

'Fabulous. Let's join them.'

He wanted to maintain his usual cool swagger but she pulled him along with such violence he was forced to hurry after her. The woman was freakishly strong but he'd heard lunatics had much more strength than normal people.

'Bloody hell, Jamie, who's this?' said Gary, eyes lighting up. 'She can't be the date you told us about.'

'Aye, this is Allegra,' he mumbled.

They stared at her with their mouths hanging open.

'Hello, boys,' she smiled in her usual friendly manner.

'Where'd you find this angel?' Digger asked Jamie.

'Oh, I found him,' she replied, pressing a hand to Jamie's chest. 'I saw him in the shop and thought *wow*.'

'Really?' frowned Digger.

She smiled and nodded. 'Aren't you going to introduce me then, Jamie?'

'Aye. Allegra, this is Gary, Digger and Logan.'

'Nice to meet you, boys,' she replied.

'You too, doll,' said Gary. He patted the empty chair beside him. 'Why don't you park your pretty wee self next to me.'

'So kind,' she smiled, sitting beside him, placing her handbag on the floor between her feet.

As Jamie sat beside her, he cringed when he saw she'd put her expensive leather bag down in a sticky patch, the residue of some old spilled beer. He couldn't help but grin when his friends stared at her like she was something from another dimension, which he supposed she was. Even Eric blushed when she gave him one of her radiant smiles as he placed their drinks before them. Head bowed, he hurried back to the bar before his wife noticed he'd taken a beamer.

'So where did you meet?' Logan asked Allegra.

'In Jamie's shop.'

Logan nodded. This confirmed she was the woman he'd seen his friend arguing with in the street.

'Why do you want a lanky string bean like him, Allegra?' said Digger, flexing his sizeable muscles, which were enhanced by his tight white muscle T-shirt. 'Surely a woman of your class and taste would like someone with more meat on their bones? Someone who can crack open watermelons with their bare hands?'

Jamie opened his mouth to have a go at him for his cheek but Allegra got there first.

'Oh, no,' she said with a wave of the hand. 'That's not my thing. I don't go for men who look like a bag of rocks.'

Gary, who was taking a sip of his lager, snorted and sprayed the liquid across the table while Logan and Jamie hooted with laughter. Digger for his part pouted and folded his arms across his chest.

'Bag of rocks,' spluttered Gary. 'That's fucking priceless.'

'I prefer them leaner,' purred Allegra, leaning into Jamie. 'Wiry and strong.' She wasn't about to tell them that the big muscular look terrified her because it reminded her of her father.

'Well, that's Jamie,' said Logan, smiling at his friend.

'Yeah, he's a bloody rake,' muttered a sulky Digger.

'Shut it, Rocky,' Gary told him, causing him to narrow his eyes at him.

'Are you the one who ran over John Lawson?' Logan asked her.

'I am,' she said proudly.

'Good on you, hen.'

'Thank you. It was fun.'

'I'll bet.'

'So tell me,' she said. 'Why are you called the Blood Brothers?'

'We made a pact when we were all fourteen,' replied Logan. 'A blood pact.'

'Fascinating. How did you seal this pact?'

The four men held out their left hands to reveal scars cutting horizontally into the skin of their palms.

'That is so awesome,' she smiled excitedly. She frowned at Gary's hand. 'Why is yours smaller than theirs?'

It was Digger's turn to burst out laughing. 'Being called a bag of rocks doesn't seem so bad now, does it?'

'It's because I used a smaller knife than them,' he sniffed.

'Why?' she said, genuinely curious.

'It's not the size of the weapon that counts, it's how you use it.'

'That is so true,' she replied, her dazzling smile making him beam and forgive her tactless remark.

Jamie sat back and listened to them chat, glad the onus to make conversation had been taken off him. He wasn't exactly a talker at the best of times. His friends all seemed to be as delighted by Allegra as his mum, brother, Gerry, Deirdre and Eric. Why was he the only one who could see how nuts she was? Perhaps because he was the only one she'd molested and who she'd dragged into her shoplifting activities.

Jamie whipped round in his seat when a finger was jabbed in his back, expecting to see one of the Lawson family. Instead it was a tall, striking-looking brunette. Her T-shirt with the word 'Paris' emblazoned across the front in glittery pink letters was two sizes too small and her black skirt barely covered her bottom. Her face was bright orange, false eyelashes so thick her eyeballs were almost hidden and her eyebrows had been shaved off and drawn back on with black eyeliner. He thought how cheap and ridiculous she looked, which came as quite a shock because only recently he'd lusted after her. They'd slept together a few times but they weren't in a relationship, despite her trying to ensnare him. She liked the status of dating the leader of the Blood Brothers.

'Leanne,' he said flatly. 'What do you want?' He glanced sideways at Allegra to see if she'd noticed Leanne but of course she had and was glaring at her with blatant hostility.

Leanne returned the full force of that hostility. 'Who the hell's this tart?'

'I'd rather be a tart,' said a cool Allegra, 'than an orange bat.'

For the second time that night, Gary spat his lager out across the table. 'A bag of rocks is better than an orange bat,' he grinned at Digger, nudging him with his elbow.

'Jamie is mine,' Leanne told her, jabbing a bright red painted nail at him. 'So back off.'

Allegra got to her feet, enjoying the surprise in Leanne's eyes that she was taller than her. 'Actually, he's mine,' she said. 'We're on a date, so you're the one who should back off.'

'Er, excuse me,' said Jamie. 'I don't belong to anybody.'

'Be quiet,' both women told him before turning their attention back to each other.

'You really think you're something special, don't you, bitch?' Leanne snarled at her. 'With your cheap shoes and knock off clothes.'

'Well, that shows what you know. These shoes are Gucci and this outfit came from Marine Serre.'

'Who the fuck's Marina Serrey?'

'A French fashion designer from Paris. It seems the closest you've got to Paris is that awful T-shirt,' Allegra announced with a curl of the lip.

Leanne's orange hue morphed into violent crimson when Jamie sniggered. 'You fucking cow. I'm gonnae dae you over fae that.'

Leanne drew back her fist but that was as far as she got because Allegra punched her full in the face. She tottered backwards with a startled look before crumpling to the floor.

Leanne's two friends shot to their feet, outraged by this assault on their friend. Jamie leaned back out of the way when Allegra's eyes filled with the wildness that he was growing increasingly familiar with. She snatched Gary's pint glass from his hand, smashed it on the side of the table and waved the vicious jagged shard at the girls, stopping them in their tracks.

'Bring it on if you think you're capable,' yelled Allegra. 'But I promise all the cheap make-up in the world won't hide the mess I'll make of your faces.'

The two girls looked at each other, shook their heads and backed off while the rest of the pub stared at Allegra in amazement.

'I told you,' Jamie whispered to Logan. 'Crazy.'

'You mean magnificent,' he replied, gazing at her in awe. 'Even Deirdre looks like she doesn't want to mess with her,' he added, indicating the landlady, who had remained behind the bar with her husband. Usually with any rammy she was the first in there, but it appeared she wasn't about to make a move.

The door opened and everyone was so caught up in the dramatic scene playing out that they didn't notice the newcomer.

'Oy!' he yelled, grabbing all their attention.

They looked round to see John Lawson limping in, his bandaged right hand cradled in a sling. He was flanked by two friends.

'Who's is that blue BMW outside?'

Allegra whipped round still clutching the jagged glass. 'It's mine,' she yelled. 'What of it?'

John's eyes widened at the sight of the weapon she brandished. He also noticed Leanne staggering to her feet, a hand pressed to her swollen cheek.

'Is she the one who ran you over, John?' one of his friends asked him.

'Aye, that's the cow.'

When the three men started to advance on her, the Blood Brothers shot to their feet and stood in front of her protectively.

Logan noticed how John hung back, looking very wary of Allegra.

Surely such a natural born coward couldn't possibly be capable of murdering someone?

'Oy,' said Deirdre, coming out from behind the bar with Eric. 'There'll be no more fighting in our pub, we've had enough for one night. If you lot want to scrap then you'll go outside and down the street, well away from here.' She wagged a finger in John's face. 'And if you know what's good for you, you'll leave that lassie alone.'

'She ran me over in her car,' he exclaimed, as though she were simple.

'Is that what happened to your hand?'

'No, that was his maw,' he said, pointing at Jamie with his good hand.

'Why don't you tell everyone why my maw hit you with a frying pan?' yelled back Jamie. 'Because you were waving a knife at her.'

'You what?' spat Deirdre, her own volatility rising to the surface. Jackie Gray was one of her best friends.

'I wasn't waving it at her, I was waving it at him,' exclaimed John, pointing at Jamie again.

Deirdre released a snarl and punched him. His eyes rolled up in his head and he toppled backwards, his friends catching him.

'That's the third time he's been beaten by a woman in the last two days,' exclaimed Gary. 'What a fucking jessie.'

The entire pub erupted into laughter. Allegra leaned into Jamie and was delighted when he wrapped an arm around her waist. He thought why not, she'd earned it. The corner of his mouth lifted into a smile when she winked at him.

The laughter went abruptly silent when the door swung open again and in walked a tall, athletic individual in his late twenties with thick brown hair. His narrow green eyes were sharp and predatory as they darted about the room, taking everything in. He would have been handsome had it not been for the coldness radiating off him, he was the type of person who made people shudder if they brushed past him in the street, although they couldn't have said why, other than there was something wrong about him.

'Craig Lawson,' Gary told his friends. 'When the hell did he get out of prison?'

'Who's Craig Lawson?' Allegra asked Jamie.

'John's older brother. He's been in prison for GBH. He almost killed a man who owed him some cash. Rumour is he killed a man in prison too.' He turned his attention to Craig. 'When the hell did you get out?'

'Three weeks ago,' he replied in a voice as hard as stone.

Logan felt sick. That meant he could have killed that man in the photo on John's phone. Craig Lawson would have been more than capable of committing that atrocity.

'That's shocked the shit out of you, hasn't it?' retorted John, all bravado now his brother was here. 'Not so fucking lairy now, are you?'

Craig looked to his brother. 'Which one of them hit you?'

'It wasnae them,' chuckled a drunken old man sat at the end of the bar. 'Deirdre stuck one on him.'

The glare his older brother shot John for his weakness made him hang his head.

'There's been enough violence in this pub for one night,' Eric told them. 'We'll have no more. If you lot want to get stuck in that's your decision, but you do it outside.'

Craig held up his hands. 'We only came in for a quiet drink.'

'Why have we no' seen you before if you got let out three weeks ago?'

'I've been busy,' he replied, his tone indicating it was none of his bloody business.

'Aye, well, it's good you're out. Take a seat at the bar. First pint's on the house.'

'Cheers,' he nodded.

'Just his,' Eric told John. 'No' yours or your wee pals.'

The Lawson brothers sat at the bar, flanked by their friends. When it became apparent they weren't going to attack, the Blood Brothers resumed their seats, along with Allegra. A dazed Leanne was slumped in a corner, being fussed over by her friends.

'The walloper got let out early,' Gary told the table. 'He was supposed to serve another six months.'

'He looks a dangerous man,' said Allegra.

'He is, doll,' said Logan. 'A stone-cold psycho, not a joke like his younger brother.' Christ, he wished he could tell his friends about that photo. Perhaps he should sod what his dad said and tell them anyway? But now certainly wasn't the time or place.

'Where did you learn to punch like that, Allegra?' Digger asked her, deciding to forgive her for calling him a bag of rocks after he'd seen how she fought.

'Finishing school,' she replied with a stunning smile.

'You've got a cracker there, Jamie boy,' Gary told him. 'You want to hang onto her.'

Jamie was reserving judgement on that for now, although he had to admit she'd impressed him.

'Thank you,' smiled Allegra, enjoying the compliments.

'What do you think Craig coming back means for us?' Logan asked Jamie.

'It's not good,' he replied. 'He'll want revenge for what was done to his brother, he'll have to or his family will be a laughing stock on the scheme. Plus, John will have told him about that stupid phone and he'll start bugging us about it too even though we don't have the sodding thing.'

Allegra's sharp eyes spotted Logan's guilty look. When he realised he'd been caught out he hastily looked down at the floor but she decided not to say anything, for now, anyway.

They all glanced at the Lawson brothers, who were swigging pints while glowering at them.

'I've got a bad feeling about this,' said Gary. 'Not that wee fud John but Craig, he's something else. He's one nasty shitebag.'

'I think this is gonnae get worse before it gets better,' said Jamie.

His eyes narrowed when Craig looked at Allegra, eyes roaming up and down her exposed legs before his lips crooked into a sly smile.

'Hey, sweetheart,' Craig called across the room.

Everyone turned to look at him.

'Are you talking to me?' Allegra politely enquired.

'Aye, I am. Park that pretty arse next to me. You don't want to hang around with those losers.'

'I'm very happy where I am, thank you,' she retorted, taking Jamie's hand.

'You don't know what you're missing, doll. I'm a lot more experienced than that young pup.'

Jamie shot to his feet. 'Piss off back to prison, you fucking tosspot.'

Craig, John and his friends leapt up while the Blood Brothers did the same.

Eric and Deirdre raced out from behind the bar again, the latter brandishing a broom. 'I'm warning the lot of you,' she yelled. 'Whoever throws the first punch will get this right up their bellend, I swear to God.'

Craig smiled and held up his hands. 'Point taken, Deirdre.'

'I bet you took plenty of points in prison, didn't you, Craig?' said Jamie. 'Right up your fucking arse.'

Eric grabbed Craig and held him back, turning even redder with the effort as Craig strained against him.

'I think it's time we went, Jamie,' said Allegra. 'I should be getting home anyway. Thank you Deirdre and Eric, you've been very hospitable.'

'You're very welcome, sweetheart,' Deirdre replied with a gracious nod. 'You boys could learn a lot from this lassie.'

'Like how to run people over and smash them in the face with broken glass?' retorted John.

'Shut it, you,' snapped Deirdre, silencing him. She looked back at Allegra. 'Take her home, Jamie. You'd better go with them too, lads,' she told the rest of the Blood Brothers.

Deirdre's dismissal allowed them all to make a dignified exit without bloodshed, the two groups glaring at each other as they passed by. Jamie and Craig in particular locked eyes, battle lines already being drawn. Craig decided to wind him up even more by letting his gaze linger on Allegra's backside. Digger and Gary between them ushered Jamie out the door before he could attack him.

'Fucking wankers,' yelled Jamie once they were outside on the pavement. 'They're gonnae get the kicking of a lifetime.'

'Aye, they will,' said Digger, flexing his muscles to display his rage. 'Cheeky fucking bastards.'

'Craig being released has just made everything ten times more dangerous,' said Logan. 'He's a hell of a lot smarter than John. How do we handle this?'

They all looked to Jamie, who sighed. He had no bloody idea. 'We'll discuss it tomorrow. Allegra needs to get home.'

'Can I give you a lift, boys?' she asked them.

'Aye, that would smashing, doll,' said Gary.

'Lazy bastard,' muttered Digger, even though he was keen to get a look inside that flash motor.

Jamie got in the front with Allegra while the other three squashed into the back.

'Move your fat arse up,' Digger told Gary. 'There's no room for Logan.'

'It's no' me,' he retorted. 'It's you and all your bulging rocks.'

Gary was repaid for his insult by Digger shoving him right up against the door, squashing his face against the glass, providing enough room for the slender Logan to hop in. He closed the door behind him and they set off just as the pub door swung open and Craig Lawson stalked out, watching them go with his unnerving narrow eyes.

'Spooky bastard,' commented Digger as they left him and the pub behind.

'Nice car, Allegra,' said Gary, who'd managed to unpeel his face from the window. 'Small but nice.'

'Thanks,' she replied. 'I like it. It's a nice drive.'

'Brand new, eh?'

'Yes, brand new. So which way am I going?'

They dropped Digger off first followed by Gary, who was unable to resist a cheeky quip about not making the car rock and steaming up the windows. Logan was last, who made a similar innuendo as he climbed out.

'Sorry about them,' Jamie told Allegra when they'd all gone.

'Why?' she replied. 'They're nice.'

'Nice? They're my best pals but nice isn't the word I'd used for them. Except Logan. He's the best.'

'Are you sure none of them have this phone everyone seems to be after?'

'Aye, positive.'

'Maybe you should ask Logan again.'

'Logan?' he frowned. 'He's really no' the type to nick a phone.'

'He was looking pretty guilty about something at the pub when everyone was talking about that phone.'

'Nah, not Logan. No way.'

'Well, it's up to you but I think you're making a mistake not asking him about it.'

Jamie was about to defend his friend again when he hesitated. What if she was right?

'Here you go,' she said, bringing the car to a gentle halt at the pavement. 'Looks like your mum's still up.'

'Do you want to come in for a bit?' he said, feeling he should ask, especially after how solid she'd been that evening.

'I'd love to but I'd better go home.'

He noted the sadness in her eyes. 'Will you be okay?'

'Fine,' she replied, forcing a smile. 'I can look after myself.'

'Aye, I saw that back at the pub.'

'You're not angry at me for hitting that silly bat girl?'

'Course not. It's about time someone put her in her place.'

'So she's an old girlfriend of yours?'

'No, not girlfriend.'

'Have you slept together?'

'A few times, aye. Why, does that make you jealous?' he said when her eyes flashed.

'Yes.'

'Oh,' he replied. He'd expected her to deny it. 'Well, I don't think she'll bother you again.'

'Oh yes? Will you be bothering with her again?'

'Nah. I don't go for big orange bats any more,' he replied, making her smile. When she didn't reply he said, 'Right, I'd better be off then. Will I see you again?'

'Without a doubt,' she replied.

He hesitated before getting out of the car, expecting to be kissed or at the least groped but she seemed too preoccupied for that, staring thoughtfully out of the window.

'See you around, Princess,' he said.

'Yes, you will, Dangerous.'

He got out and closed the door, watching as she drove off without a glance or a wave. The madwoman had done it again, left him feeling disorientated and uncertain. Perhaps she was losing interest in him? Or maybe she thought he should have hammered Craig Lawson in the middle of the pub and the fact he hadn't had reduced him in her eyes.

'Good bloody riddance,' he muttered, shoving his hands into his pockets and slinking up the path to the door. 'Jeezo,' he exclaimed when he opened it to find his mum lurking on the other side. 'What are you doing?'

'I wanted to see how your date went,' said Jackie.

'Fine, I think. Allegra's so unpredictable it's hard to tell.'

'Did you have a nice meal?'

'It was no' bad. She seemed to like it. Gerry was crawling all over her, putting on his bad Italian accent for her.'

'I'm not surprised, she's a beautiful girl. Then where did you go?'

'To the pub.'

'Couldn't you have taken her somewhere nicer?'

'She wanted to meet my pals. She fit in pretty well, actually, everyone seemed to like her. Then Leanne started mouthing off at her.'

'That silly little painted tart? She was jealous because Allegra was with you?'

He nodded, trying not to let on how thrilling it had been having two women fight over him. 'Aye, but Allegra put her in her place. Actually, she put her on her arse.'

'She hit her?'

'Right in the face. It was a cracking punch. You don't want to be on the wrong side of her right hook. When Leanne's friends tried to join in, Allegra smashed Gary's pint glass against the table and threatened them with the jaggy end.'

'Wow, go Allegra,' Jackie smiled.

'I thought you wouldn't approve.'

'Why wouldn't I? Leanne needed sorting out. She seems to think she owns you.'

'Well, she doesn't any more. Then things got complicated.'

Jackie's eyes widened as he told her about Craig Lawson's return.

'Oh, God, Jamie,' she said when he'd finished. 'That lad's a pure psycho. Worst of all he's smart, unlike his younger brother. Oh, I don't like this at all.'

'Don't worry, Maw, it'll be fine,' he said, putting an arm around her shoulders.

'I worry about you so much.'

'I can take care of myself and I've got my pals.'

'From now on you don't go anywhere alone, do you hear me? You always have at least one of your friends with you.'

'Aye, whatever you say, Maw,' he said, just wanting to make her feel better.

She took a deep breath and nodded, stomping down the rising

panic. Craig Lawson had been known to carry a knife. 'Anyway, enough about those wallopers. When are you seeing Allegra again?'

He shrugged. 'I'm no' sure she even wants to see me again. I expected to get molested when she dropped me off but she didnae touch me. She hardly even looked at me but she did say I'll see her again.'

'Oh, Jamie, she was the best thing to happen to you in a long time. Still, it's hardly surprising if you were threatened by the Lawsons and she got in a rammy with your ex on your first date. Honestly, I could swing for that Leanne myself.'

'Never say never. Who knows what Allegra's gonnae dae next?'

* * *

Allegra pulled up the sweeping driveway of her family home and came to a halt just outside the front door. She sat for a few minutes staring at the wheel, attempting to work up the nerve to go inside. If only her home was as warm and welcoming as Jamie's. She'd love to have had a mother like Jackie waiting for her to ask about her day and smother her with maternal warmth. She hadn't experienced anything that could be termed love in years. She was starting to forget what it felt like.

With a resigned sigh she got out of the car and trudged up to the door, unlocking it with her key.

'Jesus,' she gasped when a huge shadow loomed over her.

'What have I told you about swearing?' snarled her father. 'Ladies don't swear.'

'Sorry, Father,' she replied. 'You startled me.'

'Where have you been?'

'Just out.'

'Out where?'

'My friend Veronica's.' Veronica was her best friend and always covered for her when she had a date with a man she knew her father would deem unsuitable. He always called Veronica to double-check and her friend always covered her back.

'You've been seeing a lot of her recently,' he replied, eyes full of suspicion.

'She's my best friend. We like spending time together.'

'So you can talk about shopping and nails and hairstyles, I suppose.' His ugly face twisted into a scowl. 'And men.'

'We talk about lots of things.'

'I bet you talk about men too, don't you?'

'No, not really.'

'I bet you talk about which ones you want to sleep with, which ones are the sexiest.'

Allegra's stomach turned over. He'd been drinking, he reeked of it. His face was bright red and he was so big it felt like he could smash her to pieces with a single blow but it was always his eyes that were the most frightening. He looked insane.

'We don't, Father,' she said weakly.

'I wasted thousands on that finishing school for you. You're a whore, just like your mother was.'

Defiance rose inside her as it always did whenever her beloved mother was unfairly slurred. 'I am not and neither was she.'

She squeaked with fear when he grabbed her by the shoulders and pulled her towards him, fingers digging painfully into her flesh. She attempted to turn her head to escape his hot stinking breath.

'Yes, you are,' he said. 'You're exactly like her in every way. Well, whores always get theirs, just you remember that. Whores always get theirs.'

With that he shoved her and she went sprawling, landing painfully on the hard marble floor.

'Get out of my sight,' he spat.

'Yes, Father,' she breathed with relief, dragging herself to her feet, charging upstairs and racing into her room. As had become her routine years ago she closed and locked the door before shoving a chair under the handle. After kicking off her shoes and jacket she delved into the mini fridge in the corner of her room and took out a bottle of white wine. Thankfully it was a screw cap because she couldn't have coped with a cork as her hands were shaking so badly. She threw the top aside and glugged down some of the wine. She'd polished off half the bottle before she felt calmer, the shaking in her hands easing.

After wiping her eyes on the backs of her hands, she plonked the bottle down on the bedside cabinet, perched on the bed, rolled up her sleeves and took out the knife.

Allegra sighed with relief when she saw the blood bubble up out of the wound she'd sliced into her skin, the fear draining out of her with the ruby red liquid.

She slumped into the pillows, her thoughts turning to Jamie. She'd not said goodbye to him properly because it was only when she'd arrived at his house that she'd realised how late it was and that her father would be pissed off. She'd been so worried about what he'd do that she'd barely said two words to her Dangerous. It occurred to her that she didn't have his phone number either. She'd stop by his house tomorrow and surprise him. He liked surprises.

7

Logan's dad was in bed by the time he got home but he felt recent events were important enough to wake him.

He entered Dave's bedroom, wrinkling his nose at the sweaty stench that hung in the air. His dad only liked to shower a couple of times a week, three at the most if it was a hot summer. Dave was always bemoaning the fact that none of the local women would go out with him. He failed to understand that taking care of his personal hygiene would greatly increase his chances of getting a date.

'Da,' he called from the door. 'Da.'

His voice was drowned out by Dave's warthog-like snoring.

'Oh, great,' muttered Logan.

His dad always slept naked. Logan had no wish to touch his sweaty bare skin, so he picked up the comb off the bedside cabinet and jabbed him in the shoulder with it.

Dave snorted and grunted, eyes rolling open. 'Logan?' he mumbled, peering up at him. 'Why the hell are you poking me with a comb?'

'I was trying to wake you up. We need to talk.'

'Can't it wait until morning?'

'No, it can't. Craig Lawson's been released from prison.'

Dave's eyes widened and he sat bolt upright.

'What's wrong?' said Logan when he groaned and pressed a hand to his forehead.

'I sat up too fast, I've gone dizzy.' He shook his head to clear it. 'How do you know he's been released?'

'Because he was in the pub tonight, he came in with his brother.'

'Oh, Christ. What did he say?'

'Nothing much. He was winding Jamie up about his date.'

'Date, with who?'

'It doesn't matter, but he was trying to rile him into a fight. Da, he was released three weeks ago.'

'If that's true then how come no one's seen him?'

'He said he's been busy. If he was released three weeks ago then that means he could have killed the bloke in the photo.'

Dave's eyes widened. 'Oh... bloody hell.'

'Just think what Craig Lawson would do to get that phone back. We have to dump it somewhere, leave it in the street. We've got the numbers we wanted anyway. John will think it fell out of his pocket, it won't be linked back to us, end of story.'

'But he'll see it's been unlocked.'

'I know, but there's no choice. They'll never be able to prove who took it anyway.'

'Christ, you're right. We have to get rid of the bloody thing.'

Logan could have cried with relief but that wouldn't have done his reputation much good. Dave might be his dad but that wouldn't stop him from telling everyone in the pub that his grown son bawled like a baby. 'It's the right thing to do, Da.'

'I wish you'd never brought the sodding thing into the house.'

Logan's eyebrows shot up with astonishment. 'You told me to nick it.'

'Since when do you listen to me?'

Logan had never experienced such a strong urge to punch someone in his life. 'Put on some clothes,' he exclaimed when his dad clambered out of bed and trundled over to the chest of drawers in the corner of the room.

'You barge into my bedroom, this is what you get,' he muttered, pulling open a drawer and rummaging around in it. 'Put on the light, will you? I cannae see a bloody thing.'

'You can put this on first,' said Logan, tossing him his dressing gown. 'Or you can pay for the therapy I'm gonnae need.'

Dave tutted and pulled on the dressing gown while muttering to himself. 'There, I'm decent now,' he snapped.

'Good,' replied Logan, switching on the light, making them both blink.

'There we go,' said Dave, producing the phone from the drawer and holding it out to his son.

'I don't want it,' said Logan.

'You said you were gonnae drop it somewhere on the pavement.'

'Why don't you do it?'

'Because I didn't nick it.'

'You told me to nick it.'

'We've already had this conversation, boy. Now either you plant it or it goes back in the drawer.'

Logan sighed and snatched it off him. 'I'll do it first thing in the morning. The Lawsons were still at the pub when we left and I don't want to bump into them carrying this.'

'Good thinking. Right, bugger off so I can get back to sleep.'

Logan looked down at the phone in his hand. 'Do you think we're doing the right thing? Maybe we should hand this over to the police? Craig will probably be on parole. This could get him banged up again.'

'Do you really want to get involved in a murder inquiry?'

'Well, no, but that body was a real person with a family who are probably wondering where he is.'

'Maybe. We still don't know if it's a prank or not. Don't forget that could all be fake blood and if we go to the police and Craig and John get lifted then everyone will find out we grassed and our lives will be made a misery. No one on the Gallowburn goes to the police.'

Logan thought his dad was trying to kid himself. They both knew the body in the photo wasn't a fake. Doing nothing about this didn't sit well with him but he was too exhausted to argue. 'Okay, Da,' was all he said.

'Good lad,' replied a relieved Dave. 'Now, if you don't mind, I'm going to back to sleep.'

As his dad started untying his dressing gown, Logan turned and hurried out of the bedroom, flicking off the light as he went.

* * *

Not long after the Blood Brothers had left the pub, Craig left too. He drove his brother's car to Mark Flynn's house. Just as he'd suspected, a light was burning in his living room window.

He banged on the door, his knock followed by barking.

'Shut it, Stalin,' yelled Mark's voice.

The door was yanked open by Mark in stained jeans and a T-shirt. 'What the fuck do you want at this time of night?' When he saw who his visitor was the anger fled from his eyes and the cigarette clenched between his lips drooped. 'Craig. I didnae know you'd been released from the jail.'

'Three weeks ago.'

'You kept that quiet.'

'I had my reasons.' His eyes flicked to the dog standing by Mark's side. 'Fuck off, Stalin.'

The dog whimpered, turned tail and fled into the kitchen. Stalin had once tangled with Craig Lawson and had come off worse.

Mark swallowed hard when Craig's unnerving green eyes fixated on him.

'You're the one everyone comes to with nicked mobile phones,' said Craig.

'Aye, what of it?'

'Have any of the Blood Brothers been by lately?'

He nodded. 'What of it?'

'Which one?'

'Logan McVitie.'

'What did he bring you?'

'A Nokia 1 Plus. He wanted it unlocking.'

'Did you look at anything on the phone?'

'Nah, you know I never dae that and I don't ask questions. I just unlocked it for him and he went on his way.'

Mark took a step back when Craig thrust his face into his, eyes hard and unblinking.

'Maybe you should start asking questions?' hissed Craig. 'It might be better for your health.' He glared at him for another few seconds, satisfied by the fear in Mark's eyes. 'See you around.'

Craig turned and left and Mark slammed the door shut and locked it. Christ, he was glad he wasn't in Logan McVitie's shoes.

* * *

Allegra's words about asking Logan about the phone had played on Jamie's mind all night. He'd repeatedly dismissed what she'd said. Petty thievery just wasn't Logan's style. However, if that was the case, why did he keep coming back to it?

He resolved to ask Logan when they were in his car together the next morning. They would be alone, no one to overhear and Logan would be unable to run away.

'All right, pal?' said Jamie, hopping into the front passenger seat of Logan's Dacia when it pulled up outside his house the next morning.

'Not so bad. You?' replied Logan as he set off.

'Fine.' He turned to study his friend. He looked cool and calm as usual but there were dark shadows around his eyes, as though he'd lain awake all night worrying about something.

'How did you get on with the lovely Allegra after we'd gone?' Logan asked him.

'She dropped me off and said she'd see me later. That was it.'

'Well, that's disappointing. Did you no' even get a good feel up?'

'Nothing. It was the first time since we met that she didn't molest me. She seemed distracted by something.'

'What?'

'Nae idea. God knows what goes through her mad heid.'

'That's a bit harsh.'

'You saw her deck Leanne and smash that pint glass. She's aff her nut.'

'Course she's not. She's lovely. Unique, aye, different to all the other birds but no' mad.'

'You sure about that?'

'Definitely. She's a cracker.'

'Is there only me who thinks she's nuts?'

'Seems so,' he sighed.

Jamie frowned. Logan definitely had something on his mind. 'I wanted to ask you something.'

'What's that?'

'Did you nick John Lawson's phone? Woah,' he added, clinging onto the dashboard when Logan swerved. 'I'll take that as a yes, shall I?'

Logan steered the car to the kerb, pulled on the handbrake and switched off the engine.

'Are you gonnae say something, then?' Jamie asked him when he stared at the steering wheel in silence.

'It's been tearing me apart,' mumbled Logan.

'So you did?' exclaimed Jamie. 'What the fuck did you do that for? Have you any idea of the chaos you've caused?'

'Aye, I have. I'm so sorry, I've really messed up.'

'You lied to me and the others. That's against the rules of the Blood Brothers. We took a blood oath, or have you forgotten?'

'No, I havenae forgotten. It was my da's idea. He overheard the Lawsons were planning a robbery, so he told me to get hold of John's phone because it had the contact numbers he needed.'

'Did it?'

'Aye, it did.'

'And what was he going to do with these numbers?'

'Speak to John's contacts, convince them that John would mess it up and that we'd be better doing the robbery instead. I'm sorry, Jamie,' he hastily added when his friend sighed. 'I know it was a stupid idea and I tried to talk him out of it but he wouldn't listen. You know what he's like when he gets something in his head.'

'Of course it's stupid. If you'd called those blokes they would have thought you were either coppers or tracked you down and kicked the shite out of you both. You should have told your da to piss off.'

'I wish I had, believe me. These last couple of days have been fucking awful.'

'Where's the phone now?'

'Here,' he said, producing it from his pocket. 'With all the trouble it's caused my da told me to dump it somewhere and John would think he'd dropped it.'

'Why haven't you?'

'Because things have got a lot more complicated than a stupid robbery. There's a photo on that phone of John Lawson posing with a deid body.'

'You what?'

'I'll show you,' he said, bringing it up before dumping it screen down on his friend's lap. 'I'm warning you, it's not pretty.'

Jamie turned the phone over and gasped.

'Jeezo, you're right. That guy's deid.' The truth was in the eyes and the unnatural posture of the body. Fucking hell, those eyes were terrible – wide open, staring up at the sky. It was clear whoever it was had died in pain and fear. Jamie chucked the phone onto Logan's lap, not wanting it anywhere near him.

'We thought at first it was a prank and that was all make-up,' said Logan. 'At least, that's what we tried to tell ourselves.'

'That's no' make-up, it's the real deal.'

'It's been tearing me apart,' said Logan, stuffing the phone back into his pocket and dragging his hands through his curls. 'I wanted to take it to the police but my da wouldnae let me, he said we could end up being killed too and people in Gallowburn don't grass. But this is murder, Jamie. Some poor bloke's deid. He might have family wondering where he is.'

'Aye, you're right. This is too big to sit on.'

'It is?' said Logan. He'd expected Jamie to tell him to dump the phone and forget about it. Or maybe he couldn't forget about it either?

'Maybe there's another way to do it. You could send the phone anonymously to the police. John's well known to them so it wouldn't take them long to track him down.'

'Actually, that's a pretty good idea. Do you think I should do that?'

'Aye, I do.'

'The thing is, I didn't think John could do anything like that but this photo was taken two weeks ago after...'

'Craig was released from prison,' replied Jamie.

'That psycho's more than capable of stabbing something to death.'

'I know. My guess is he did it and John was there.'

'Why would John take a selfie with the victim? That makes no sense.'

'Because he's a fucking fanny. Or whoever got them to do it wanted proof it had been done?'

'Maybe, that's if someone got them to do it. They could have just done it off their own backs.'

'Any idea who the deid guy is?'

'No. I looked on the internet for any stories of any bodies being found but nothing.'

'Then it mustn't have been found yet.'

Logan stared out of the window, not wanting to meet Jamie's eyes. 'Are you pissed off at me?'

'Course I am, I'm fucking livid but you're my best pal, so I'm trying to be understanding.'

'If it had been Digger or Gary you would have torn them apart by now.'

'I would. It's worse that you're the one who did this because you're smarter than that. Why didn't you just come to me with this?'

'I wanted to Jamie, really I did, but my da kept convincing me not to. I felt so bad when you were getting hassled for something I'd done but I thought I could take care of it myself.'

'We're Blood Brothers, which means we've always got each other's backs and we never ever lie to each other.'

'I know and I'm so fucking sorry,' Logan said, eyes full of sadness. 'I wouldnae blame you if you kicked me out.'

'I'm no' gonnae dae that. We need your smart brain, Logan, although it's no' been very smart these last few days.'

'No, it's been bloody daft. I promise nothing like this will ever happen again, Jamie.'

'It better not because no more chances. Lies weaken us. Besides, I feel I owe you this chance because you've stopped me from doing so many stupid things in the past. Without you I probably would have been banged up years ago.'

Logan smiled with relief and gratitude when Jamie shook his hand.

'Blood Brothers forever,' smiled Jamie.

Logan smiled back. 'Blood Brothers forever.'

'Bring the photo up again.'

'Why do you want to look at it?' replied Logan, producing the phone from his pocket.

'I don't but it might be a good idea to take a copy, in case the phone gets lost.'

'How will you take a copy?'

'I'll take a photo of it on my own phone...'

Jamie and Logan looked at each other when they heard the roar of an engine. They cried out with surprise when the car was hit from behind with such force Logan bashed his head on the steering wheel. Jamie's seatbelt tightened painfully around him but the violent movement jolted him and he banged his head on the side window. The car was shunted forward several feet amid a screech of metal before coming to a halt with an agonised groan.

Craig Lawson climbed out of the old Mercedes he'd used to ram the Dacia. It was a huge heavy car with a large front end, which had protected him from the worst of the crash. As he'd been prepared for the impact he was unhurt.

He pulled open the driver's door of the Dacia, eyes immediately alighting on the phone in the unconscious Logan's lap. His head rested on the steering wheel, his face covered in blood.

'You cheeky little twat,' said Craig, snatching the phone from him.

Jamie was also unconscious, blood trickling from a cut to the side of his head, so neither man had a clue he was even there.

People had come out of the surrounding houses to see what all the noise was about but Craig paid them no mind. He knew none of them would grass to the police.

After slipping the phone into his jacket pocket he got back in the car and reversed. The front of the car was badly crumpled but at least it was still moving. Fortunately, it didn't have far to go. Soon it would be burning on the patch of wasteland on the edge of the scheme, which was home to many car skeletons. John was in his car further down the street. As he was unable to drive because of his injured hand one of their cousins was in the driver's seat; John sat beside him, back-up in case the Mercedes failed to start.

As Craig drove away John followed. Only once both Lawson brothers were out of sight did those in the surrounding houses rush out to check on Jamie and Logan.

* * *

Jackie was helping Charlie with his school tie when there was a frantic knock at the door.

'All right, take it easy,' she snapped as she went to answer it. 'You'll knock the bloody thing down if you're no' careful.' She pulled open the door to reveal her friend Tricia, who lived further down the street. 'What's up?'

'It's your boy.'

Jackie's blood turned cold. 'What's happened to my son?' she rasped.

'A car ran into Logan's. They're both okay but they'll need a wee trip to hospital. They're just down the road there.'

'Look after Charlie for me,' Jackie called over her shoulder as she pelted down her path, out the gate and tore down the street.

'No worries. I'll take him to school for you,' Tricia called after her.

'Thanks, love.'

Jackie ran as fast as she could, turning cold when she saw the back of Logan's car was crumpled inwards. Both front doors were hanging open and people were kneeling either side, talking to the occupants.

'Jamie,' she cried. 'Where's my boy?'

She ran to the passenger side and shoved the man standing before the door out of the way. Her heart almost stopped at the sight of the blood on Jamie's forehead.

'Jamie, sweetheart, are you okay?'

She wanted to cry with relief when his eyes blinked open and the corner of his mouth cocked into a smile. 'Aye, I'm great, Maw, never felt better.'

'You're bleeding and you're still cheeking me.'

'An ambulance is on its way, Jackie,' said Carol, another neighbour.

She nodded at her before kneeling beside Jamie and taking his hand. 'You'll be okay, son, we'll get you to hospital and you'll be right as rain. Logan, are you okay?'

'What?' he groaned, eyes remaining closed. His nose was a mashed mess.

'What happened?' Jackie asked her son.

'Nae idea,' he murmured.

Realising he wasn't up to being questioned, Jackie looked to Carol.

'A car ran into them from behind,' she told her.

'Whose car? Was it one of the Lawsons?' she pressed when she appeared reluctant to reply.

'It was Craig Lawson,' Carol whispered in her ear.

Jackie's eyes sparked with fury. 'He's going to pay for this.'

'I heard whispers he took something from Logan. He was seen opening Logan's door and snatching whatever it was off him.' Carol was a caring woman but she was also a gossip and her natural nosiness came rushing to the surface. 'Any idea what it could be?'

'No, none,' said Jackie, her mind frantically ticking over. Had this attack been aimed at Logan and Jamie was just unfortunate enough to be in the car at the time?

At the sound of approaching sirens most of the neighbours hurried back indoors. Only a hardy few, including Carol, remained outside. An ambulance along with a police car tore down the street. While the paramedics hurried to attend to the boys, two officers Jackie recognised as veterans who'd worked the scheme for years approached the residents to begin questioning them. The officers appeared resigned to the denials of having witnessed anything. They'd known they wouldn't get anything out of this lot. It was clear Logan wasn't up to being interviewed, so they turned their attention to Jamie, who denied seeing anything, which made sense as the car was hit from behind. The two officers sighed and returned to their car to wait for the boys to be carted off to hospital so they could arrange for the damaged Dacia to be shifted.

'So you're finally here,' Jackie snapped when Dave lurched down the street.

'I came... as fast as I could,' he panted, doubling over.

'I suppose,' she sniffed. 'The only time you run is when you hear the chimes for the ice cream van.'

'Don't start, Jackie,' he told her before ducking down to talk to his son. 'Jesus, what happened to his nose?'

'He hit it on the steering wheel,' one of the paramedics told him.

'Logan, it's your da. Can you hear me? Answer me, Logan.'

'Da,' he breathed.

'Aye, it's me, I'm here. What is it?'

'Don't forget to turn the chip pan off.'

'Eh? Why are you talking about the chip pan? It's no' even on.'

'He's got concussion,' said the paramedic. 'We're taking him to hospital.'

'Jamie too?' said Jackie.

'Aye, both of them.'

'Can I go with you? Jamie's my son.'

'And Logan's my son,' interjected Dave.

'We've got room in the van for you both,' the paramedic replied good-naturedly.

The boys were loaded into the ambulance. Jamie was able to walk, although he was laid back on a stretcher in the ambulance because he was still woozy. Logan, however, was manoeuvred in because he was still semi-conscious. Dave spent the journey looking everywhere except at Jackie, who glared at him from the opposite side of the ambulance. She just knew this shit was something to do with that idiot and his stupid schemes but because of the presence of one of the paramedics, who'd got into the back with them, she was unable to quiz him about it.

On arrival at the hospital the boys were taken through to A&E, leaving Jackie and Dave in the waiting room.

'Shall I get us both a brew?' he asked her.

Before he could escape she grabbed his arm. 'Craig Lawson rammed the back of Logan's car. Have you any idea why he would do that?'

'I've nae idea, except that he's a psycho.'

'Too right he is, but even psychos have reasons for doing things.'

'It's probably all this bad blood between the boys and the Lawsons, you know that.'

'But why not one of their usual fights? Why ram Logan's car? One of the neighbours said they saw Craig open Logan's door and take something from him.' She frowned when Dave turned white. 'You do know something. What is it?'

'I don't know anything.'

As an old lady crossed between them on a Zimmer frame, Dave turned and ran off.

'Coward,' Jackie whispered at his receding figure. She would get to the bottom of this if she had to pull bits off that fat twat to do it.

John Lawson lived with his parents in one of the new houses on the south side of Gallowburn. The four miles between the north and south sides were not enough to prevent frequent bloodshed between the Lawsons and the Blood Brothers. Like the new houses on the north side, the ones on the south were poky, the plumbing didn't work properly and the double-glazing was poorly fitted, meaning the heat went straight out and the cold came straight in. But that didn't stop John and Craig's mother Iza Lawson from being incredibly house-proud. Every surface gleamed, not a speck of dust was permitted to land and the cream carpets were as pristine as the day they were fitted. Even Craig didn't dare object to her insistence that shoes were removed at the door. However, Iza's obsession with cleanliness didn't extend to herself. She could usually be found in a stained T-shirt and leggings, her hair perpetually greasy. Craig got his narrow green cat's eyes and hard hatchet face from her while John was more like his father with his softer dark brown eyes and round face.

'All right, boys?' said Iza in a voice that had deepened because of years of chain-smoking and was reminiscent of car tyres crunching along gravel. 'How'd it go?'

'Good,' said Craig. 'We got what we wanted.'

Iza wasn't sure what her boys had gone to retrieve from the Blood Brothers, she'd long ago learnt not to ask, especially in Craig's case. 'Good,' she nodded. 'Wait, wait,' she shrieked when Craig made a move to sit down. 'You haven't any dirt on you, have you? Or oil from the car?'

'Nothing, Maw, look,' he said, doing a turn so she could examine his clothes.

Iza breathed a sigh of relief. 'Good. John?'

John, his left eye swollen from Deirdre's fist, did the same. Once she was satisfied her boys weren't going to ruin her spotless beige sofa she said, 'Anyone want a brew?'

'Please, Maw,' said John. 'That would be smashing.'

'Aye, please,' said Craig.

She nodded and retreated into the kitchen, closing the door behind her. Whatever her boys were up to now, she wanted no part of it. She'd already heard about Logan McVitie and Jamie Gray being carted off to hospital after Logan's car had been rear-ended.

'I'm so relieved we got the phone back,' said John, sinking back into the couch and dragging the fingers of his good hand through his hair. 'That could have gone bad for us both.'

'Why would it be bad for me?' said Craig, looming over his younger brother. 'You're the only one in the photo. Or would you have grassed on me?'

'No, course not. I'd never do that to you.'

'Good.' Craig grabbed him by the front of his jumper and yanked him towards him. 'Because if you ever did it wouldn't matter that we're brothers. I'm never going back to prison and I don't care what I have to do to stay on the outside.'

'All right, I get the point,' said John, holding up his good hand. 'At least it's over now.'

Craig released him and straightened up. 'Nothing is over. Logan got Mark to unlock that phone. Do you honestly think he's had it all this time and not looked at it?'

'You think they saw that photo?'

Craig nodded. 'I do. They know what you did.'

'But I didn't do anything.'

'If they saw that photo then they think you did. Logan we know for sure and probably Jamie too. That's why Logan had the phone in his hand, he was showing it to him. That fat fud Dave McVitie's probably seen it too. Perhaps all four Blood Brothers know, they share everything with each other.'

John turned pale. 'No, they can't. I mean... if they did surely they would have taken it to the police by now?'

'No one from this scheme takes anything to the police. They were probably going to blackmail you with it.'

'No emails or texts have been sent from this phone since it's been missing, so they couldn't have done.'

Craig snatched it from him, brought up the photo and took out his own phone. He took a photo of John's phone with his own and turned his phone round to show him. There was the photo of John and the body as clear as day, making John wince.

'No emails or texts necessary,' said Craig, deleting the photos from both mobiles.

'What are you doing?' said John when he pocketed the phones.

'Getting rid of them. Or do you really want to keep this phone after everything that's happened?'

'Suppose not,' he mumbled.

'You've fucked things up so badly, John. From now on you leave everything to me.'

'I can help.'

'Really? First you were run over by that Allegra, whose knickers I will get into, by the way. Then you had your hand smashed in by Jackie Gray. To top it all off you were almost knocked out by Deirdre in the pub. You keep getting twatted by women. What fucking use could you possibly be?'

'This is our family's big chance and I want to be a part of it.'

'Then you'd better learn how to take care of yourself or you're fucking out. I mean it, John. So far you've proved to be as useful as a chocolate teapot.'

'Let me prove myself,' he said eagerly. 'Gie' me something to do.'

'Fine. Go and get Maw's messages from the shop. That's all you're fit for.' He raised a derisive eyebrow at his bandaged hand. 'Actually, she'd need to gie' you a hand.'

'I can find out what Jamie and Logan know.'

'We already know what they know and they probably have the proof too. They need to be silenced.'

'Jeezo, Craig, that'll make things ten times worse. We cannae go bumping people off left, right and centre.'

'There are other ways to shut people up, by threatening those they love, for instance.'

'You mean Dave?'

'Even the fleas who live on him don't love that bastard. Jamie Gray loves his maw, though, and his little brother.'

'Aye, he does.'

'If he wants to keep them safe he'll keep his trap shut.'

'I can do that. I'll shit him right up.'

'He'll laugh in your face. The cat's more intimidating than you are,' retorted Craig. 'Leave that with me. We need to play this carefully and you will keep out of it. Understood?'

John sighed and nodded. 'Aye, understood but gie' me something to do, please Craig.'

'All right, then.'

John beamed with delight.

'Go and help Maw with the brews. That's something you might not fuck up.'

John sighed, got to his feet and slunk into the kitchen.

Craig took his place on the couch, glaring at his retreating back. John had allowed the Blood Brothers to get a firm grip on the north side of the estate since he'd been sent to prison.

It was time to take it back.

* * *

'Mrs Gray?' a sweet young nurse asked Jackie, who was sipping coffee from a polystyrene cup in the A&E waiting room. Dave had plucked up the courage to return but he was sat as far from her as possible. Every so often he gave her a sheepish look, which she returned with a ferocious glare.

'Aye, that's me,' she replied. 'How's my boy? Can I see him?'

'He's fine, just a few stitches. I'll take you to see him. This way.'

She glanced back at Dave, who was keeping his gaze firmly on the newspaper in his hands. His cowardice made her blood boil.

Jackie was led into a cubicle where Jamie lay on a bed, a large dressing covering one side of his head. His eyes slowly rolled open when the curtain was whipped aside.

'Hi, Maw,' he said.

'Jamie,' she replied, taking his hand. 'How are you, sweetheart?'

'I've got a cracking headache but that's it. How are you?'

'You're asking about me? I wasn't just in a car crash.'

'We're keeping him in overnight,' said the nurse. 'He's got a wee bit of concussion. He cracked his head a good 'un.'

'But he'll be okay?' said Jackie, eyes full of concern.

'Yes, it's just a precaution. As long as he has a good night he can go home tomorrow. He'll have to keep the stitches in for about five days. His GP can remove them.'

'So he's going to be all right,' said Jackie more to herself than anyone else.

'He's one tough cookie,' said the nurse. 'We're moving him up to the ward soon, so you can stay with him until then.'

'Thank you so much,' said Jackie as the nurse left. She turned back to Jamie. 'Do you remember anything about the crash?'

He frowned. 'I was talking to Logan. The car was stopped. Something hit us from behind. I remember the noise, it was so loud. Then a paramedic was talking to me. You were there.'

'Aye, I was sweetheart. Do you remember anyone else being there, before I got there?'

He frowned. 'There were some of the neighbours, I can't remember exactly who. It's all mixed up. Is Logan okay?'

'I don't know, I've not seen him yet but I'll find out for you.'

'Please, Maw.'

He was struggling to keep his eyes open, the poor lad was exhausted and he'd been through an ordeal, so she decided not to put any pressure on him for now, although she was desperate to find out why Craig Lawson had rear-ended them.

Ten minutes later a porter arrived to wheel him up to the ward, so Jackie left, promising to return at visiting time with an overnight bag for him. She'd bring Charlie to visit too. She asked the nurse about Logan but she couldn't tell her anything as she wasn't family. Dave wasn't in the waiting area, so she surmised he'd been taken through to see his son. She hung about outside the doors to A&E for a bit, hoping to come across Dave but she guessed he'd leave by another way just in case she was waiting for him, so she caught the bus home.

Tricia had taken Charlie to school, leaving her free to pack a bag for Jamie, putting in a packet of his favourite biscuits.

After sorting out Jamie's things, making herself something to eat then having a tidy up, it was almost time to collect Charlie from school, she'd had that long a wait at A&E.

Just as she pulled on her coat to set off there was a knock at the door.

'Allegra,' she beamed, delighted to see her. Perhaps Jamie had been wrong and she wasn't losing interest after all.

'Hi, Jackie. Is Jamie in?'

'Oh, of course, you won't have heard.'

'Heard what? Is he okay?'

'He was in a car accident, he's in hospital.'

'Oh my God,' Allegra said, hands flying to her mouth. 'Is he okay?'

'He's fine. He's got some stitches and concussion but he'll be all right. They're keeping him in tonight. I was just on my way to pick up Charlie from school to take him for a visit.'

'Can I come? I can give you a lift.'

'Oh, that would be smashing, thanks.' The relief at not having to haul a heavy overnight bag and a whiny ten-year-old on a bus was immense. 'You sure you don't mind?'

'No, course not.'

'That's so good of you, Allegra, sweetheart.'

Jackie locked the front door while Allegra put Jamie's bag in the boot. She sank into the front passenger seat, admiring the luxury. 'This is a beautiful car.'

'Thanks,' smiled Allegra. 'I like it.'

'It must have cost you a pretty penny.'

'It was a present from my father.'

'Wow, that was good of him. I wish I could afford to buy my Jamie a car, it would increase his chances of getting a better job but it's all the running costs – tax, insurance, MOT, all that pish. Mine and Jamie's wages between us wouldn't cover it.'

'It's certainly not cheap,' replied Allegra.

'Jamie will be pleased you're gonnae visit him, he said you were a bit distant when you dropped him off last night. He was worried all the rammy at the pub had scared you off.'

'I don't scare easily.'

'I'll bet.'

'I was just a bit... tired last night.'

Jackie glanced sideways at her. She didn't think Allegra was prone to telling lies; in fact she was one of the most painfully honest people she'd ever met, but she knew she wasn't telling her the truth. She decided not to push it, it was none of her business. 'Jamie told me you smacked that Leanne right in the face.'

'I did. She was asking for it.' When they stopped at a red light, Allegra turned to look at her. 'Do you have a problem with that?'

It wasn't said as a challenge, merely with curiosity.

'God, no,' replied Jackie. 'That gobby wee orange cow deserved it. Did you smear her eyebrows across her face at the same time?'

The two women looked at each other and burst out laughing.

8

Jamie lay in bed, wondering if Malcolm would sack him for not turning up at work today. Part of him hoped so just so he wouldn't have to go back to that shitty shop. The other part of him dreaded to think how they'd cope without his wage.

He was on a ward with three other blokes, all of them coffin dodgers. There must have been fifty years between himself and the next youngest man. One of them was hogging the telly, watching some antiques shite while the man across the room from him snored horrifically. The third was sat in an armchair, gazing out of the window and farting. On top of all that, Jamie's head was pounding.

He perked up when he saw visiting time had started, people wandering past his room peering through the windows, searching for their loved ones.

'Maw,' he smiled, pushing himself upright when she walked in. 'Charlie.' A blonde vision followed them in and, to his surprise, his heart soared. 'Allegra.'

'Your mum told me about your accident,' she said. 'So I gave her and Charlie a lift in.'

Charlie turned scarlet when she ruffled his hair. He was still getting over the shock of being picked up in her posh motor outside school and then sitting so close behind her in the car.

'That's really good of you,' Jamie told her. 'Thanks.'

'You're welcome.'

The way Allegra smiled at her boy reassured Jackie she still liked him.

'I brought you a bag,' said Jackie, dumping it on the edge of his bed. 'A change of clothes, toiletries, a few magazines and a packet of your favourite choccy biccies.'

'Great, cheers.'

'I also put in a few extra pairs of undies, just in case.'

'Just in case what, Maw? I shite myself?' said Jamie, making Charlie laugh.

'It's good sense to have extra undies. I've always taught you that.'

While Charlie continued to giggle, Jamie looked to Allegra, hoping she wasn't laughing too, but she took the chair beside him and took his hand.

'How are you feeling?' she said.

'No' bad. I've got a headache, but...'

'Jackie told me you were rear-ended.'

'Aye, but I cannae remember much, it's all vague and mixed up.'

Jackie was desperate to talk to him about Craig Lawson but couldn't in front of Allegra and Charlie.

'Have you heard anything about Logan?' Jamie asked his mum.

'No, sorry. I'll try to get hold of Dave and find out.' *And when I do I'll ram something long and pointed right up his arse*, she thought.

'Thanks, Maw.'

'So, will you be released tomorrow?' Allegra asked him.

'Aye, as long as I have a good night.'

'I can give you a lift home, if you want?'

'That would be great, thanks.'

Jackie smiled at the way they looked at each other. Perhaps her son was finally beginning to realise what a great woman Allegra was.

'Can I have some of your biscuits, Jamie?' Charlie asked his brother. 'I'm starving.'

'Oh, I'm sorry, Charlie, sweetheart,' said Jackie. 'You usually have a snack after school. I should have brought you something.'

'I can take him to the shop,' said Allegra. 'It's only down the corridor.'

'I'll take him. You stay and chat with Jamie.' Jackie took Charlie's hand and pulled him to the door before anyone could object. 'Would you like anything?' she asked Jamie and Allegra.

They both shook their heads.

'Won't be long.'

Jamie watched them go with a sinking feeling. He wasn't sure he could cope with Allegra when he wasn't feeling very well. 'So,' he said slowly. 'How have you been?'

'Okay. I'm sorry if I seemed off last night when I dropped you off.'

'It's okay. You seemed a bit... worried?'

She nodded and looked down at her hands.

'Was your da okay when you got home?'

Allegra forced a smile. 'I don't want to talk about him. So, who rear-ended you?'

'No idea, I didn't even see them coming. I heard the roar of an engine then there was blackness. It wasnae you, was it? You have a habit of running into people.'

'No, it wasn't,' she said with a dismissive wave. 'If it was me I'd have come at you head on.'

'Aye, probably,' he said, unable to repress a chuckle.

'Wow, a laugh. I don't think I've heard that before. It seems that bang to the head has done you some good.'

'You make me laugh.' *Jeezo*, he thought. *The concussion must be bad.*

She looked around when the man by the window released a loud fart. 'God, it's depressing in here. Let's hope you get sprung tomorrow or you'll end up slitting your wrists.' Unconsciously she ran her fingers along her left forearm.

'I'll be out tomorrow.'

'Why would anyone run into you from behind?'

'It was probably someone going too fast and couldn't stop. There's a load of arseholes who drive way too fast through the scheme.'

'Have you thought that it might not have been an accident?'

'You mean it was on purpose?'

'Well, that *is* the opposite to an accident,' she said with a knowing smile. 'I'm thinking it was that nasty sod from the pub last night, the one with those freaky green eyes.'

'Craig Lawson,' he glowered.

'Yes, him.'

'Maybe. I need to talk to Logan. Christ, I hope he's okay.'

'I'm sure he will be.' She leaned into him, so her lips were just inches from his. 'You look so down, you need some cheering up.'

'What are you doing?' he said when she got up to draw the curtains around his bed.

She returned to her seat and smiled, her hand disappearing beneath the blanket. 'Cheering you up.'

He gasped, his body going rigid when he felt her hand on his crotch. Despite how rotten he was feeling, he responded immediately.

'See,' she smiled. 'You're feeling better already.'

'Allegra, you can't do that here,' he whispered, making a very feeble attempt at pushing her hand away.

'Why not? The other patients are too old to notice what's going on around them. No one will know.'

'My maw will be back any second… oh, God,' he breathed as pulses of pleasure began to move through him. He stopped fighting. He'd been through an ordeal, he deserved a treat.

'Just lie back and relax,' she said.

When she kissed him, his hand went into her hair and he pulled her close as her hand continued to work its magic.

As voices filtered into the room from the corridor outside she sat bolt upright. 'Jackie and Charlie are coming back.'

To his disappointment she removed her hand.

Her eyes widened when she saw the bulge beneath the blanket. 'They can't see that.'

Frantically she looked around for something to hide it with and grabbed the first thing she saw – his overnight bag. Jamie released a grunt of pain when she dumped it right on his crotch.

'What did you do that for?' he rasped, shoving away the heavy bag, turning onto his side and curling up into the foetal position.

'Hi,' beamed Allegra when Jackie whipped one of the curtains open. 'Did you manage to get what you needed?'

'I got a cheese sandwich,' grinned Charlie, holding it up for her to see.

'Yummy,' she smiled.

'Why were the curtains closed?' said Jackie, eyes flicking between Allegra and Jamie.

'Jamie wanted some privacy from the other patients,' replied Allegra. 'So we could talk.'

'Talk, eh?' she said, knowing dancing in her eyes. She frowned down at Jamie. 'What's up with you?'

'I passed him his overnight bag,' said Allegra, replying for Jamie because he hadn't yet recovered the power of speech. 'Unfortunately, I dumped it on a very sensitive area.'

Jamie frowned up at his mum when she sniggered.

'Oh well, accidents will happen,' said Jackie. 'You okay, Jamie, love?'

'Aye, peachy,' he mumbled into the pillow, wondering how he'd gone from ecstasy to agony in the space of a few seconds. His frown deepened when he saw Allegra slyly squirt some hand sanitiser from the dispenser on the wall onto her hands while his mum and brother's backs were turned and rub it into her skin. Charming.

'Logan's two rooms down the hall from here,' Jackie told her son. 'Again, the nurses wouldn't tell me anything. He was asleep so I didn't go in. I'll pop in before visiting's over, see if I can talk to him.'

'Did he look okay?'

'Apart from a massive plaster over his nose and two black eyes, aye.'

'That's a relief. Was Dave with him?'

Her lips tightened into a thin line. 'No. I'll be having words with him, don't you worry.'

Jamie didn't envy Dave McVitie.

Ten minutes before visiting ended, Jackie took Charlie to see Logan, leaving Allegra and Jamie alone once more.

'Please don't try to cheer me up again,' he told her. 'I haven't recovered from the last time.'

'Sorry about that. I was a bit heavy-handed, wasn't I?'

'Just a bit,' he muttered.

'Go on, admit it. You enjoyed it at first.'

'Aye, I did, until you dumped a ten-ton weight on me.'

'You smiled again, Dangerous.'

'Like I said, you make me laugh, Princess. Not always for the right reasons, though.'

'I'm worried about you. That was no accident. Someone's got it in for you.'

'It's the bloody Lawsons. It's always them, the bad blood has existed between us for years.'

'Why would they ram you in a car though? That's a big leap from a row in a pub.'

The memory of Logan showing him the phone returned to Jamie, hitting him with almost as much force as the car had. 'The phone,' he breathed.

'What phone?'

'Logan's. He was showing me something on it before we were hit.'

'What?'

'I can't remember.'

'You're lying, Jamie.'

'I'm not, it's all hazy.'

'Hmm, I'm not sure I believe you.'

'Go easy on me, Allegra, I've got a concussion and I feel like shit.'

She decided to drop her questioning, for now, anyway. 'Okay, but if you remember then you must let me know. I want to help.'

'That's good of you, doll.'

They were forced to stop the conversation when Jackie and Charlie returned.

'You'll be pleased to know I spoke to Logan,' Jackie told her son with a smile. 'I didn't stay long because the poor love could barely keep his eyes open. Like you he's got concussion but he's hoping to be released tomorrow. Unlike you his nose was smashed across his face, so think yourself lucky.'

'I want to see him.'

'I'm sure the nurses won't mind you popping in after visiting hours, just flash them that charming smile,' she said, pinching his cheek, making him frown. 'Or maybe you could meet up in the day room?'

'Aye, maybe.'

'I can hear a bell ringing,' said Charlie. 'Is there a fire?'

'No, sweetheart,' said Jackie. 'It means visiting time's over.' She dipped her head to kiss Jamie's cheek. 'Have a good night and call me in the morning, let me know how you get on and what time we can pick you up, if that's still okay with you, Allegra?'

'Of course,' she smiled. 'Not a problem. I'll give you both my phone number,' she added, producing a small notepad and pen from her handbag and scribbling it down, handing one slip of paper to Jamie and the other to Charlie. 'Look after that for me, won't you, big man?'

'I will, Allegra,' grinned Charlie, reverently placing it in his trouser pocket.

'Aww, look,' Jackie smiled at her younger son. 'He's taken a beamer.'

'Stop it, Maw,' Charlie mumbled at the floor.

'See you later, Spud,' Jamie told his brother.

'Don't call me Spud,' he said, blushing even more.

As Jackie and Charlie turned to leave, Allegra grabbed Jamie's face in both hands and planted a big kiss on his lips. This time he didn't fight it and as she pulled back slightly to look into those unflinching eyes he actually managed to smile.

'See you tomorrow, Dangerous,' she said.

'Aye, you will, Princess.'

He smiled as he watched her leave. But the memory of that photograph blew away all the good feelings the moment she'd gone.

* * *

Jackie bustled about the kitchen cooking tea for herself, Charlie and Allegra. It was a little sad that her other boy was stuck in hospital but at least he would be home tomorrow. Things could have been so much worse. She'd invited Allegra to stay for something to eat as a thank you for the lifts she was giving them; it was the least she could do. Allegra was such a lovely girl, she was even helping Charlie with his homework, the two of them huddled together at the kitchen table. Thank God Allegra was good at maths because she was dreadful. Jamie always had to help him with that particular subject. Charlie's blushes were finally calming down after being in close proximity to Allegra for the past twenty minutes. On the journey home Jackie had tried to get the girl to open up about herself but she'd been very reluctant to talk. Jackie didn't think it was shyness, that seemed to be the last thing Allegra was. Did that mean she had something to hide? She was certainly an enigma.

They all looked round when the back door opened and Craig Lawson strolled in as casually as if he lived there.

'What the hell do you think you're doing?' demanded Jackie, outrage over this trespass into her home overriding her fear. 'Get out.'

'I'll go, just as soon as I've said my piece.' He looked around the poky but spotless kitchen before his eyes settled on Charlie. 'All right there, wee man?'

Charlie just frowned back at him.

'You'll leave him alone,' retorted Jackie.

'We won't have a problem, Jackie, as long as Jamie keeps his mouth shut.'

'About what?'

'He knows exactly what. Don't bother asking him about it because that wouldn't be healthy for either of your boys.'

Jackie gasped when Craig produced a large knife from inside his jacket.

'I know how afraid you are of these,' he continued. 'I heard all about how you watched your brother die. I bet you'd do anything to stop the same from happening to your sons.'

While Jackie turned white with fear, Allegra shot to her feet and stood protectively before Charlie.

'We meet again, Beautiful,' Craig told her. 'I don't get what you see in this bunch of losers.'

'They don't need to threaten weans with knives to make themselves feel like the big man,' she retorted. 'I bet you've got a tiny worm in your pants.'

'You fucking bitch,' Craig snarled, taking an aggressive step towards her.

Allegra produced a pepper spray from her pocket and held it out before her. 'Just try it. I'll hit you with this before you get anywhere near me. Then I'll take that knife off you and shove it down your throat.' She yelled these last few words, her voice filling the room.

Craig recognised that she wasn't speaking from fear or panic. There was a wildness in her eyes that told him she would do it and enjoy herself at the same time. Rather than be angry, he was even more intrigued by her. 'No need to freak out, doll. I'm not here to cause any harm.' He looked back at Jackie. 'Make sure to pass that message on to Jamie. As long as he takes my advice, there'll be no need for me to come back.'

'I will. Now get out before you get the contents of that pan right in the face,' she said, indicating the pan of hot water bubbling away on the hob.

The corner of Craig's mouth curled into a smile. 'Let's hope Jamie sees sense,' he told her as he headed out the door. 'For all your sakes.'

When he'd gone Jackie slammed the door shut and locked it before running to the front door and locking that too.

'Are you both okay?' she asked when she returned to the kitchen.

'Fine, Maw,' said Charlie casually, not wanting Allegra to see how scared he'd been.

'That is one nasty sod,' said Jackie. 'We shouldn't worry, he'll soon find himself back in prison, it's inevitable. Allegra, sweetheart, you were great.'

'I never go anywhere without my trusty pepper spray,' she said, slipping it into her handbag.

'What did he mean, Maw?' said Charlie. 'Why does Jamie need to keep his mouth shut?'

'I've absolutely no idea.' Jackie forced a smile she didn't feel. 'Don't you worry about it, Jamie will sort it out. He'll be home tomorrow and everything will be okay.'

'I can't wait for him to come home, I miss him,' Charlie said, eyes filling with tears.

While Jackie comforted Charlie, Allegra turned her back to dunk the pasta into the pan of boiling water, knowing he'd be embarrassed if she stood there watching him cry.

No one mentioned Craig and his threats until tea was over and Charlie had gone upstairs to take a bath.

'You're a brave girl, hen,' Jackie told Allegra as she helped her tidy up the kitchen. 'Not many people have the nerve to stand up to Craig Lawson.'

'I was more furious than brave. I couldn't believe he just walked in like he owned the place.'

'He always was an arrogant git but make no mistake, he's not a joke like his younger brother. He's never made an idle threat in his life. I wonder what he was talking about?'

Allegra guessed Jamie knew exactly what he'd been talking about, despite his denial, but it wasn't her place to mention it, so she decided to keep quiet.

* * *

While the nurses were on their break in the staff room at the end of the corridor, Jamie took the opportunity to sneak into Logan's room. He was unsteady on his feet and a bit light-headed, so he practically fell into the chair by his friend's bedside. Logan had struck lucky with his room. Only one of the other three bays was occupied and that was by a man not much older than himself, who was sound asleep, not snoring or farting.

Logan's eyes flickered open and he smiled. 'You okay, pal?'

'I'm better than you. Your nose is a mess.'

'So I believe but my doctor said it should heal straight, thank God. How are you?'

'Just a bit of concussion. I'm being let out tomorrow.'

'Aye, me too, I hope.'

'Good.'

'John Lawson's phone's gone.'

Jamie was jolted in his seat. 'What?'

'I only have my phone now. I don't remember anyone taking it but I was out for the count for a while.'

'Then it was either John or Craig who ran into us.'

'I'm guessing Craig. John doesnae have the balls to pull off a stunt like that.'

'Aye, you're probably right. Bollocks, now we have no proof against them. We've nothing to give to the police.'

Logan wasn't sure if that was a good thing or not. 'Craig won't be finished with us. He'll suspect we made a copy.'

'Probably.'

'He'll be feared we'll dob him in but we can't do anything without proof.'

'So we back down, is that what you're saying? We let him get away
with it?'

'I don't know, I need to think it through.' Logan sighed and
slumped back into his pillows. 'I feel like shit, I cannae think at the
moment.'

'We'll discuss it again when we're out of this place. What about
your car?'

'Totalled. It'll cost more to fix than the bloody thing's worth but at
least the insurance will pay out. We were stopped at the kerb and run
into from behind, so the bastards cannae wriggle out of it. It was old
and knackered, so I've nae idea how much I'll get. I need a car to get to
work.'

'Things will work out, don't fret yourself.'

'Let's hope. Anyway, I'm more worried about Craig Lawson than I
am about that shitey call centre.'

'We'll deal with him.'

'How?'

'Nae idea, but we've no bloody choice.'

When a nurse walked into the room carrying two envelopes, Jamie
shot to his feet so quickly his head spun and he had to grab onto the
chair for support.

'You really shouldn't be in here so late,' the nurse gently
chided him.

'Sorry, but he's my pal,' he replied once his head had cleared. 'I
wanted to make sure he was okay.'

'You were in the car crash together, weren't you?'

'Aye, we were.'

'Well, I can understand you wanting to visit him but it's time to
return to your room. You're Jamie Gray, aren't you?'

He nodded.

'A friend of you both popped by. He said he missed visiting time.'

'Probably Digger or Gary,' said Logan.

'I didn't get his name but he left these for you,' she said, holding an envelope out to each of the boys. 'You can open them together but then you really must return to your bed, Jamie.'

'I will. Promise.'

She nodded and smiled before exiting.

'That's not Digger or Gary's writing,' commented Logan.

'Aye, and neither of the bastards bothered to visit us.'

Logan was more concerned with the contents of the envelope. Reluctantly he opened it and peered inside. 'It's a photo.'

'I've had enough of bloody photos,' said Jamie, opening his own envelope. From it he produced a photo of his mum and Charlie going into their house. Judging by what they were wearing, it had been taken that day.

Logan's photo was of his dad entering his own house carrying a blue poly bag that no doubt contained cans of lager.

The boys looked at each other with wide, shocked eyes. Neither of them spoke. Both understood the threat.

* * *

Only once Allegra had gone home and Charlie was in bed did Jackie allow herself to really think about what Craig had said. He knew all about her fear of knives and had used it ruthlessly against her. He'd implanted a seed of dread that was rapidly growing and entwining her so tightly in its vines she felt like she was suffocating.

She poured herself a glass of white wine and drank it down with a shaking hand, tears shining in her eyes as her brother's death replayed itself over and over in her head. If the threat had come from John Lawson she could have taken it with a pinch of salt but Craig was different. That boy had always been a psychopath, right from being a small boy. Even his own mother was wary of him.

Defiance overtook fear and after another fortifying gulp of wine she slammed the glass down on the coffee table. Her boys were in danger so she was buggered if she was going to sit on her arse, crying.

After asking her friend Maureen who lived next door to babysit Charlie, she stomped over to Dave's house. Rather than hammer on the door like she normally would she gently knocked, not wanting to alert him to the fact that she was his visitor.

'Who's there?' he called through the door.

'It's me, Jenny,' she called back, lightening her voice. Jenny Patterson lived on the next street and Dave had been trying to get into her knickers since high school, to no avail. She knew he'd open up if he thought it was her.

There was the sound of the door being unlocked before it was pulled open by a smiling Dave. The grin dropped when he saw who was actually standing on his doorstep.

Before he could recover from his surprise, Jackie stormed inside and slammed the door shut behind her.

'Me and you are finally gonnae have that wee chat, Davey boy,' she told him. 'And you will tell me the God's honest truth because our boys are in trouble, big trouble.'

He sighed and nodded. 'Aye, I know.'

'Have you had a visit from Craig Lawson too?'

'I have. I kicked the lairy little shit out after he babbled something about warning Logan to keep his mouth shut.'

'Stop swinging your dick about, Dave, it doesn't wash with me. I know you stood there quivering in your boots while he laid down the law with a big knife in his hand.'

Dave sighed, shoulders slumping. 'He came in through the back door. I didn't even know he was there until he walked into my front room.'

'He did the same to me. He said me and Charlie would suffer if Jamie opened his mouth but he didn't say about what.' She took an aggressive step towards him. 'Now, I know you know. It's something to do with that phone of John Lawson's. Did the lads steal it?'

'No, well, I mean... not exactly. You're better off keeping well out of it, Jackie.'

When her foot connected with his genitals he released a groan, eyes bulging as he slumped to his knees.

'You're gonnae tell me all about it, Dave, with none of your usual lies or half-truths. If you try to bullshit me what I'll do to you will make Craig Lawson look like Gandhi.'

'You sure you want to know?' he managed to rasp when he'd recovered the power of speech. 'Once I tell you it can't be taken back.'

'I'm a big girl, Dave.'

'Aye, I've noticed.'

'Just get on with it,' she snapped.

* * *

Jamie was experiencing some unusual new feelings. He was actually looking forward to seeing Allegra. He'd never looked forward to seeing any woman before, especially not one who was off her rocker. But she'd impressed him in the pub with Leanne and then with the Lawsons. Plus there was yesterday, when her hand had snuck beneath his blanket... Those few intimate seconds had been more exciting than all his physical encounters with women in the past put together. Maybe his mum was right and Allegra was good for him? There really was no one else like her. Unlike all the other women he'd met, she wasn't afraid to be herself.

His doctor examined him and proclaimed him well enough to go home. After calling his mum – who seemed a little more subdued than usual – he called Allegra, who was likewise subdued. She said she'd pick up his mum and bring her straight to the hospital. What was going on with the women in his life now? Or was it him? He was recovering from concussion, after all.

After taking a shower he shoved everything into his overnight bag and popped into Logan's room to check on him. His doctor wanted to keep him in another night because he wasn't recovering as fast as they'd hoped.

When Jamie was chucked out by a nurse he returned to his own room and perched on the bed to wait. He'd expected Allegra and his mum to be full of smiles but instead they walked into his hospital room looking tired and washed out.

'What's up with you two?' he said.

'We'll talk in the car,' replied his mum.

'About what?'

'In the car, Jamie.'

He frowned but didn't argue as his mum clearly wasn't in the mood. He glanced at Allegra, who seemed a lot less enthusiastic about being in his presence too. It would be bloody typical for her to go off him just as he decided he liked her.

'How are you feeling, son?' Jackie asked him as they made their way through the hospital to the exit.

'Fine. Just a bit of a headache.'

'Did you get a good night's sleep?'

'Aye, I did, Maw, even though all the other patients in my room snored like trains.'

'Trains don't snore because they don't sleep,' commented Allegra.

'I know that,' he frowned. 'It's just a saying.'

'Well, I've never heard anyone say that before.'

'I just meant they were bloody loud and repetitive, that's all,' he retorted, his earlier good feelings about her being eroded. 'I didnae mean they were actual trains lying in the beds, for Christ's sake.'

'Don't talk to Allegra like that,' Jackie snapped at him. 'She didn't have to come here and pick you up. I'm sure she's got a million better things to do.'

'Yes,' replied Allegra coolly as they exited the hospital and made their way across the car park. 'I had to cancel a nail appointment for this.'

'Oh, I am sorry,' he muttered. 'The Princess must make sure she doesn't have chipped nail varnish.'

Jackie stopped and rounded on him. 'That's quite enough from you.

I didn't raise you to be rude to nice lassies who are only trying to do you a favour.' When a car that was attempting to get past them beeped its horn she rounded on them, hands on her substantial hips. 'Shut it,' she yelled. 'Can't you see we're trying to have a private conversation here?'

Jamie took his mum's arm and escorted her onto a narrow island in the middle of the car park, Allegra following, the driver of the car giving them the finger as he continued on his way.

'What's up with you, Maw?' demanded Jamie. 'This isnae like you.'

'I'll tell you what's up with me, boy,' she snarled in his face. 'Craig Lawson barged his way into our kitchen last night with a knife, threatening us because you and Logan saw an incriminating photo on his brother's phone. Aye, you might turn pale,' she said when all the blood drained from his face. 'Get in the car right now. We need a serious talk.'

Jamie slunk after the two women and hopped into the back, feeling it was safer than sitting up front with one of them, holding his bag on his lap like a shield. Allegra made no move to set off. She turned in her seat to face him, as did his mother.

'I only found out about it literally seconds before the car ran into us,' mumbled Jamie. His eyes widened. 'It was Craig Lawson who ran into us, wasn't it?'

'Aye, it was,' said Jackie. 'All the neighbours saw him but of course no one talks to the police on the Gallowburn, so he'll get away with it. He came into our home and threatened me, Allegra and Charlie. He said we'll suffer if you blab. He didn't give any details but I had a quiet word with Davey boy last night and he told me all about it.'

Jamie's eyes flicked to Allegra. 'Did you...'

'The lassie knows all about it,' snapped Jackie. 'I filled her in after we'd dropped Charlie off at school this morning. She has a right to know why she was threatened.'

He looked to Allegra again, wondering if she was going to run away screaming but she just stared back at him impassively, giving away nothing.

'Dave was a bit vague about who nicked that phone in the first place,' added Jackie.

'It wasn't me,' he blurted out. 'I swear. It was Logan, on Dave's orders.'

'I knew that bastard was something to do with it,' she hissed. 'He was too busy trying to heap blame on you and your friends.'

'I swear to God I didn't know. I thought John had lost the phone and was trying to shift the blame onto us so he wouldn't look like a dick. I thought Logan would be the last person to nick anything.'

The two women frowned at him before looking at each other and nodding.

'All right,' said Jackie. 'We believe you.'

'So you should. This isn't my fault.'

'Craig won't let that stop him. He told me to give you a message.'

'What message?'

'That if you go to the police me, Charlie and Allegra will suffer.'

'Aye, I know,' said Jamie, producing the photo he'd been given in the hospital and handing it to his mother. 'I was given this last night. I didn't see who dropped it off but I reckon it was Craig.'

'This was taken yesterday, after we got back from the hospital,' said Jackie, turning pale. 'I'd no idea anyone was there taking our picture.'

'Logan got a similar photo of his dad,' said Jamie.

'I hope snapping that ugly git broke his camera,' muttered Jackie. 'Christ, what a mess. I want to see that photo.'

'You can't, Maw.'

'I want to see it or so help me God...'

'I mean you can't see it because Logan didn't take any copies. I was about to take a photo of it on my own phone when we were rear-ended and Craig took it off him.'

'So there's no proof anyway. Well that should make Craig feel a bit safer.'

'But he killed someone. We cannae let him get away with it.'

'There'll be no proof to find. He'll have got rid of that phone as soon as he got his hands on it and as far as we know the body's not been found. There's nothing you can do.' She frowned at him. 'You swear to me that you didn't know anything about this?'

'I swear, Maw, not until a few seconds before the car hit us and that's the God's honest truth. Logan was a mess. Keeping this secret has really taken its toll on him. He wanted to come to me and the lads sooner with it but Dave wouldnae let him.'

'Now that I can believe. Well, let's get you home and settled and decide how we're going to handle this mess.'

9

Jamie kept glancing at Allegra the entire journey home. Once again she barely spoke and that worried him. From where he was sitting he had a good view of her profile. Of course he knew she was beautiful, although her beauty could be marred by her craziness. Now he was able to appreciate how truly stunning she was. He'd never seen such flawless skin before. She wore make-up, but why? She certainly didn't need it. Plus, life was just more interesting with her around.

Jackie breathed a sigh of relief when they turned onto their street. 'Thank God for that. I expected the entire Lawson clan to have turned out for your return.'

'They can't know I've been released already,' said Jamie.

'You sure about that? You know you can't keep anything quiet in Gallowburn.'

Allegra parked the car right outside the house and the three of them got out, Jackie pausing to look up and down the street. No one was in sight, apart from a small dog sniffing at the nearest lamppost.

'Let's get inside, quick,' she said, hurrying up the garden path, key already in her hand.

She ushered Jamie and Allegra inside, shut the door behind them and locked it. Jackie hated how afraid Craig Lawson had made her feel. If it had been any of the other lairy little shites who lived on this estate she could have handled it. She would have even given them a crack around the head herself but that lunatic was a totally different kettle of fish. He was always willing to go that one step further than anyone else, using knuckledusters when his opponent had no weapon or a knife against a baseball bat. *Knife.* The thought made her shudder.

'Sit yourselves down and I'll get the kettle on,' Jackie told them. 'Oh, unless you've somewhere to be, Allegra?'

'No,' the girl replied, sitting beside Jamie on the couch. 'Nowhere.'

Jackie nodded and vanished into the kitchen, leaving them alone together.

'Are you okay?' Allegra asked Jamie.

'No' really,' he sighed. 'Why, you wantin' to make me feel better again?'

'Your mother is so worried,' Allegra said as though he hadn't spoken, to his disappointment.

'Aye, I know. I wish Logan had never nicked that bloody phone. How did you know it was him, anyway?'

'He looked so guilty in the pub when everyone was talking about it.'

'I never noticed.'

'Because you assumed it couldn't possibly be him. It took someone on the outside to spot it.'

'Probably. I'm sorry you've been dragged into all this.'

'I knew you were dangerous the moment I saw you, so I understood exactly what I was getting into. You might not have noticed but I enjoy excitement, I always have.'

'Oh, I've noticed all right,' he replied.

He pressed his lips to hers, causing her eyes to widen with surprise.

'What was that for?' she said.

'I was being impulsive, like you.'

'You might have warned me first.'

'Like you warned me, I suppose?'

'I didn't need to warn you.'

'Why not?'

'Because I'm the woman.'

'So?'

'It's different.'

'No it isn't and you were the one who stuck their hand in my underwear while I was in my sick bed,' he said, lowering his voice so his mum wouldn't hear.

'I didn't hear you protest.'

'Course I didn't. It felt good.'

'It did?' she smiled.

'Well... aye.'

'Care for a repeat performance?' she purred, leaning into him, cupping his crotch with her hand.

Immediately he responded.

'My,' she smiled. 'Someone's keen.'

Jamie sprang away from her when his mum walked into the room, making Allegra smile. He hastily pulled a cushion onto his lap to hide the evidence.

Jackie placed a plate piled high with biscuits on the coffee table before returning to the kitchen and closing the door.

'Where were we?' said Allegra, leaning into him again.

'Not now,' he whispered, removing her hand when she replaced it on his crotch. 'Not with my maw here.'

'Later,' she winked.

Once again she'd completely confused him, going from cool to volcanic in a few seconds. He still hadn't worked out yet whether that was just the way she was or if she was winding him up.

'Have you talked to Digger and Gary about all this?' said Jackie, returning to the room with a tray holding three mugs of tea.

'No, not yet,' said Jamie. 'I thought they would have visited me in hospital, though.'

'To be fair to the lads they did call to ask if they could but I said only three people were allowed in at visiting time, so there wouldn't be enough room.'

'Oh,' said Jamie, pacified now he knew his friends did actually care about him.

'Call them, ask them to come round,' said Jackie. 'You're going to need their help.'

'Aye, good idea, Maw,' he said, taking out his phone.

Half an hour later Digger and Gary were also ensconced in the Gray living room drinking tea. Gary was tucking into the biscuits but Digger had given them a body swerve because he'd been to the gym that morning and didn't want to undo all his hard work. As Jamie related the story of Logan and the photo on John's mobile phone, Gary's mouth fell open, treating them all to the sight of half-chewed Jammie Dodgers.

'I cannae believe it,' said Digger when he'd finished explaining. 'So, it was Logan after all?'

Both he and Gary threw Jamie accusing looks. He'd been quick to blame them while defending the person who'd actually been responsible.

Jamie ignored the looks. 'Now Craig Lawson's threatening my maw, Allegra, Charlie and Dave too,' he told the room. 'We have to do something.'

'Let's have a look at this photo then,' said Digger.

'You can't. Craig took the phone.'

'No one took a copy?' he said incredulously.

'That's what I was about to do before Craig ran into the back of us.'

'Bugger,' he muttered. 'That could have been handy.'

'Tell me about it.'

'How do we know this photo's the real deal?' said Gary. 'It could be a joke, you know, photoshop and all that.'

'If it was a joke do you honestly think Craig would drive a car into the back of Logan's just to get it back?' said Jackie. 'And then barge in here with a knife and threaten us?'

'Maybe not.'

'Well, I say we hammer the shite out of Craig,' announced Digger. 'Job done.'

They all rolled their eyes.

'Is that your answer to everything?' said Jackie.

Everyone went rigid at a knock at the door.

'It's the Lawsons,' announced Digger, leaping to his feet. Gary did the same, spilling biscuit crumbs all over the carpet.

'Relax, boys,' said Jackie. 'It's just Dave. I thought he should be part of this conversation seeing how he started all this nonsense.'

Jamie nodded at Digger, who nodded back and followed Jackie to the door. Sure enough she pulled it open to reveal a very sheepish Dave McVitie.

'Come on in,' she said icily, opening the door wider.

Dave snuck inside, regarding her warily, as though expecting her to attack him.

'Park your arse, Dave,' she told him.

He nodded and sat on the opposite end of the couch to Jamie, hanging his head when they all glared at him.

'So,' said Jackie, retaking her seat. 'What have you got to say for yourself, Dave?'

He regarded them all one by one and saw their eyes were devoid of sympathy for the awkward situation he found himself in. 'I didn't know all this was gonnae kick off,' he exclaimed when he was unable to take the glares a second longer. 'I just wanted a couple of numbers off the phone.'

'Aye, and I bet you hounded poor Logan until he gave in and got you what you wanted.'

'What numbers?' said Gary.

'Eh?' replied Dave.

'You heard. What numbers?'

He looked down at the floor and mumbled something.

'Speak up,' Jackie snapped at him.

'The numbers of a couple of contacts John Lawson was going to do a robbery with,' he mumbled.

'What robbery?' said Digger.

'Of a jeweller's in the city.'

'By Christ,' sighed Jackie, rolling her eyes. 'He thinks he's Raffles now.'

'Who?' said Digger and Gary in unison.

'It doesn't matter,' she replied. 'A jeweller's. You silly sod Dave McVitie. You would have ended up getting nicked. Were you going to bring Logan in on this robbery too?'

A heavy sigh. 'Aye.'

Before anyone could stop her, Jackie had shot to her feet and charged across the room at Dave. Jamie managed to intervene before she could punch him full in the face.

'Calm down, Maw,' he told her. 'This isn't helping.'

'You're going to be the death of that poor boy, Dave McVitie,' she snarled at him. 'That accident could have been so much worse. Or Craig could have decided to use a different weapon, one our boys wouldn't have walked away from. When are you going to stop using him? He's your son, for God's sake. If anything bad happens to him it'll be because of you. You're supposed to protect your children, not use them up until there's nothing left. Lisa would be ashamed of you.'

The mention of his dead wife caused Dave to hang his head. For the first time, Jackie saw genuine shame in his eyes.

'I'm calm, Jamie, son,' she said, holding up her hands.

Jamie nodded and released her.

As Jackie retook her seat and Dave continued to hang his head, an awkward silence filled the room.

'Well,' said Jamie, breaking the silence. 'What's done is done. Now we have to decide how we're gonnae handle it.'

'Like I said,' replied Digger. 'Break Craig's knees and elbows. That should do it.'

'That won't stop him,' said Jackie. 'If you do that he'll only break your neck when he's better. No matter what you do to him he will always come back at you harder. Whatever plan you decide on, you need to make sure it stops him permanently and no, Digger, I don't mean you should kill him.'

'Then what?'

'Get him put in prison for life.'

'That photo would do that, if we had it.'

'No, it wouldn't, because he's not in the bloody thing,' she exclaimed.

'I bet if John was nicked he'd soon dob him in,' said Gary.

'I wouldn't put it past Craig to get rid of his own brother to save his own skin,' said Jackie.

'What do you think, Jamie?' said Digger. 'What should we do?'

He sighed when they all looked to him. He had no bloody clue and his head still ached, so it was hard to think clearly.

'You need to find his weakness,' said a voice.

They all looked to Allegra, who had remained conspicuously quiet until now.

'How do you mean?' said Digger.

'You need to find out what he's afraid of and use it against him.'

'That boy's afraid of nothing,' said Jackie.

'Everyone has a fear. If you find out what it is you have power over him.' She looked to Jamie. 'It's a tactic my father uses all the time in business and it's served him very well.'

'Who is your da?' Gary asked her.

'Cameron Abernethy.'

They all stared at her in surprise.

'Bloody hell, I've heard of him,' said Digger. 'He owns most of Glasgow.'

'Yes, he does,' she replied. 'Nearly all of it, in fact.' There was no pride or boasting in her tone, merely a weary resignation.

'So that's how he came to own most of the city, is it?' Jamie asked her. 'He finds out people's fears?'

She nodded. 'Yes. Everyone, no matter how scary or psychotic they are, is afraid of something.'

'We could throw a spider at him,' said Gary. 'He might be afraid of spiders.'

Digger snorted. 'You're a fucking dingbat.'

'He's very afraid of going to prison,' said Jackie. 'That much is obvious.'

'Isn't everyone?' said Digger.

'It tells you something about him.'

'That's a great idea,' Jamie told Allegra. Once again, she'd impressed him. If Gary and Digger had her smarts they could have owned the scheme by now. 'We need to find out everything we can about Craig Lawson,' he told the room. 'Speak to people on the estate. Digger, he used to work for the delivery company your da drives for.'

'Aye, he did. My da said he got sacked for knocking out his supervisor.'

'Ask him about Craig's time there. It could give us a clue. I've got a pal in Barlinnie. I'll pay him a visit, find out what he knows. Gary, speak to Craig's ex-girlfriends. I thought you'd enjoy that,' he said when his friend's eyes lit up.

'He used to go out with Tiffany Bryant. She's bloody gorgeous, she looks like Taylor Swift.'

'Taylor Swift if she smoked thirty a day and had three kids before she was twenty-five,' commented Digger. 'I heard one of those weans is Craig's but he denies it.'

'I'll have a word with my pals,' said Jackie. 'I know Iza has some stories to tell about her boys growing up. If anyone knows a person's weakness, it's their mother.'

'Why are you all looking at me?' said Jamie, when all heads turned his way.

'Can I do anything to help?' said Allegra.

'That's very kind of you, sweetheart, but no,' Jackie told her. 'I don't want you dragged any further into this. In both your visits to Gallowburn you've been threatened and intimidated.'

'I don't know about that,' said Gary. 'She put Leanne on her arse.'

Jackie looked to Dave. 'And what are you going to do to help straighten out this mess? This is all your fault and so far you've said nothing.'

'Because it sounds like you've got everything covered,' he replied.

'Oh, no you don't, you cowardly little worm. You're not getting out of it that easy. You'll pull your weight and do something, for once in your life.'

'Like what?'

'You're a big gossiping old biddy. Ask around the pubs about Craig, see what you can find out.'

'Fine,' he sighed. 'I will.'

'Hopefully, we'll find something that can help us handle him.'

'Are you sure you shouldn't go straight to the police?' said Allegra.

'Without evidence it's useless,' said Jackie. 'And the photo of that body didn't even have Craig in it.'

'If we go to the police,' Jamie told Allegra, 'he'll come straight for you, as well as Maw and Charlie.'

Allegra looked thoughtful and nodded. 'I suppose. There could be another possibility. We could set a trap for him.'

'You're a brave girl,' said Jackie. 'And it seems you've inherited your da's wily brain.'

'That's the only thing of his I inherited,' she murmured, looking down at her hands.

Jackie looked questioningly at Jamie, who shook his head, indicating now wasn't the time. 'Right,' she said. 'We've got a plan. Well, don't just sit there boys, get to it.'

'Can I finish my Jammie Dodger first?' said Gary, holding up the half-eaten biscuit.

'You ate them all, you greedy bastard,' said Digger. 'No one else got a look in.'

'I eat when I'm anxious.'

'You should start coming to the gym with me.'

'No thanks. I don't want to look like a bag of rocks,' said Gary with a wink at Allegra.

'Well, on you go then, boys,' said Jackie. 'Let Jamie know the second you find out anything useful.'

'Will do, Mrs Gray,' said Digger as he and Gary got to their feet. 'When's Logan getting out of hospital?'

They all looked to Dave for a reply but he remained silent, staring down at the floor.

'Hopefully tomorrow morning,' replied Jackie when it became apparent he wasn't going to speak.

'Nice one. You finished your Jammie Dodger?' Digger asked Gary.

He stuffed the last of it into his mouth and nodded. 'Aye.'

'And be careful,' Jackie called after them. 'You'll probably be in Craig's sights too.'

'We will, Mrs Gray,' said Gary before closing the front door behind them.

When they'd gone, Jackie looked to Dave. 'You'd better get to it as well. Don't think you're spending all day moping on my sofa.'

He released a martyred sigh and got to his feet. 'All right Jackie, hen, don't burst a blood vessel. I'll get right on it.'

'And you call me the moment you find out anything useful.'

He nodded and saluted before hurrying out to avoid being given any more orders.

'Idiot,' she hissed through her teeth as the door closed behind him.

Jackie looked to Jamie and Allegra, who were casting each other shy glances. The poor loves hadn't had any alone time together since they'd met and Jackie didn't want this relationship to end before it had got off the ground. Allegra was the first girl her son had dated with a brain in her head, so she decided to give them some space.

'I'm popping next door to see Maureen,' she told them. 'We haven't had a catch up for a bit, so I'll be there quite a while. You know how we like to gossip when we get together.'

Jamie raised an eyebrow at his mum's not very subtle hint.

'There's plenty in the fridge so help yourselves,' she continued. 'I'll grab my dinner at Maureen's. The back door's locked and I'll lock the front door behind me, so you don't need to worry about anyone walking in.'

'Bye, Maw,' said Jamie flatly, as she slipped on her shoes and left. He looked to Allegra. 'Sorry, she's not very...'

Before he could finish Allegra sprang at him, pressing her lips to his, knocking him onto his back on the couch.

'Hey, take it easy,' he said, managing to wrench his mouth from hers.

'You're so exciting,' she said, eyes glittering.

'I am?'

'Since I've met you I've hit someone with my car, got into a fight and been threatened.'

'And you still want to be around me?' That just confirmed she was nuts. Any sane woman would be running for the hills.

'You've no idea how boring my life is – shopping, nail bars, hair-dressers, the gym and dull socialite parties talking to two-dimensional people who've never lived a second in the real world. You've brought me to life, Jamie.'

'I...' He was silenced by her lips pressing against his, smothering any sound. He managed to grab her by the shoulders and hold her at arm's length. Her blue eyes sparkled, her cheeks were flushed and her hair was tousled. She looked like a wild woman, someone who could never be tamed, the expensive clothes and jewellery suddenly seeming out of place on her. She should be running free in remote woodland and bathing in streams, not imprisoned in a grand mansion.

'You're so beautiful, Princess,' he said, running his thumb across her plump pink lips.

She smiled into those astonishing obsidian eyes. 'Right back at you, Dangerous,' she said before kissing him again.

Jamie allowed himself to finally fall into the feel of her, the soft skin, silky hair, the scent of coconut filling his head. Her wildness only increased as she pulled off his jumper. She leaned back to study him, running her fingers down the honed lines of his stomach.

'Impressive,' she said.

'Working in that sodding shop does have some benefits.'

He gasped as she kissed his chest, his hand fisting in her hair as she moved her attentions lower to his stomach. He unfastened the buttons of her blouse, revealing full breasts encased in a lacy turquoise bra and an expanse of smooth flat stomach. When he attempted to pull the shirt down her arms she sat up and wrapped her arms around herself.

'What's wrong?' he said.

'I'm... shy.'

'No, you're no'.'

'I have a thing about my body,' she said uncertainly.

'What thing?'

'I just get self-conscious, okay?'

'Okay. Leave the shirt on if it makes you more comfortable.' He was disappointed, though. He couldn't get that bra off without removing her shirt and he ached to see those beautiful breasts set free.

She smiled and lay on top of him, the two of them frantically kissing. Holding her close, he attempted to roll her onto her back, which was no mean feat on the narrow couch.

'Wait,' she gasped.

'What now?' he sighed.

'I like being on top. Being underneath makes me feel claustrophobic.'

'Anything else I should know before we continue?'

'Don't be like that,' she snapped, sitting upright.

'Like what?'

'Snippy.'

'Snippy?' he said, thinking what a toff term that sounded. 'How am I being snippy?' he said in a plummy accent.

'If you're going to take the piss out of me I'm leaving,' she huffed, buttoning up her shirt.

'Well, you could,' he said, remaining on his back, clasping his hands behind his head. 'But that's a lot less interesting than what we could be doing.'

'Maybe I don't want to do that with a sarky git like you.'

'Aye, ya do.'

She tried to hide her smile at the twinkle in his eyes. She'd never seen that gaze anything but hard before. Allegra was unable to stop her eyes wandering over his slender but extremely strong frame, all the muscles in his stomach standing out as he breathed. To her he was perfect, beautiful, and she ached for more, but she did have her pride.

'If it's any consolation,' he continued, 'I don't like my ribs being touched.'

'You don't?' she frowned, wondering if this was leading up to him taking the piss out of her some more.

'I can't stand it. I cracked a rib once playing football when I was nine. It was agony. Anyone touches my ribs now and I go demented. Are you sure you want to try that?' he said in that dangerous voice of his when her hand hovered over his left side.

'I need to make sure you're not winding me up.'

'I'm not. Ask my maw. She'll tell you I can't stand it.'

This convinced her of his sincerity. She couldn't imagine Jackie Gray telling a lie. 'Anything else you don't like?' she asked him.

'An ex-girlfriend stuck her finger up my arse once when we were in the middle of it. It made me jump so much I nearly went through the ceiling. You're no' gonnae do that, are you?'

'Not my thing,' she said, wrinkling her nose.

'Good, because I had to dump her after that. I felt violated.'

'So I'm not the only one with hang-ups.'

'Nope. Everyone has them.'

Allegra realised he was allowing her to see the other side to his tough nature. He was showing her that underneath was a kind heart.

He let his fingertips wander across her bare stomach, up to the swell of her breasts, slyly flicking open the buttons she'd just fastened. When her shirt fell open he continued higher, stroking the soft skin of her neck. 'So,' he said. 'Do you still want to leave?'

'No,' she breathed, closing her eyes to better enjoy the sensation.

'Then get your gorgeous self back down here, Princess.'

With a grin she leapt on him, the two of them desperately kissing.

'Is this okay?' he breathed as he unfastened her trousers.

'Totally,' she said before thrusting her tongue into his mouth.

He groaned as his hands cupped a backside that felt like a firm peach. In response, she unfastened his jeans and slid her hand inside his underwear to continue with the delights she'd started at the hospital. He pushed her trousers and matching lacy turquoise underwear down, and she kicked them off. Jesus, he'd never seen such long legs before. They were incredible. When his hand found the centre of her, his excitement peaked so much he had to fight himself not to flip her onto her back, which was all his instinct was screaming at him to do, even more so when she said his name in a breathy moan.

Allegra looked down at him as they enjoyed a long deep kiss, taking in how flushed his cheeks were, the sweat popping out all over his body, the intensity in his eyes. His attentions were gentle yet practised, knowledgeable, a combination she'd never found before in her previous lovers, who had either been too rough or too inexperienced. She was a woman who constantly kept up her guard but she found herself falling into the moment, allowing the pleasure to swell up and claim her.

Just as the bliss started to bloom inside her, the sound of ringing filled the air.

'Ignore it,' said Jamie when she went rigid in his arms.

'I can't,' she said, leaping off him, snatching up her handbag and scrabbling for her phone. 'That ringtone means it's my father.'

'So?'

'I can't ignore it,' she replied, starting to panic when she couldn't find it in her bulging bag. 'Thank God,' she breathed when her hand closed around it. She put it to her ear and took a deep, calming breath before saying, 'Hello, Father.' She glanced at Jamie and put a finger to her lips, indicating for him to remain silent.

Jamie turned on his side to listen while attempting to slow his breathing, the pleasure that she'd built up in him for the second time gradually cooling. If he didn't get a release soon he thought his head might explode. He pushed thoughts of his own gratification aside as he hitched up his jeans and listened to Allegra talk to her dad.

'Yes, I cancelled that appointment because I don't need my nails doing,' she said. 'It would be a waste of time and I'm bored with the nail bar.' She went silent as she listened to the voice on the other end.

Jamie couldn't make out the words but he could hear the deep berating bass as her father replied. With each word Allegra appeared to fade. All her sparkle and vivacity paled before being extinguished altogether.

'Just driving around,' she told that angry voice. 'And I went for a walk in the countryside. Now? I'm in a restaurant, I've just ordered lunch. I don't know what it's called but it's on Byres Road, I think, anyway. You know I'm terrible with directions. What? I can't do that. The waiter will think I'm nuts if I ask him to talk to you. Right, fine,' she said when the voice started to shout. 'Give me a second, he's dealing with another table.' She covered the mouthpiece and looked to Jamie. 'Pretend to be the waiter,' she whispered. 'Please.'

Her expression told him things would be very bad for her if he didn't do as she asked, so he nodded. The relief in her frightened eyes was the only thanks he needed.

She removed her hand from the phone. 'Er, excuse me?' she said.

'Yes, madam?' said Jamie in as posh a voice as he could muster.

'Please could you talk to my father?'

'Sorry?'

'Could you tell him that I'm in your restaurant?'

'Er, I suppose, but why?'

'Please, it would really help me out.'

'Well, all right then.' He took the phone from her. 'Hello?'

'Who's this?' said a hard, deep voice.

Jamie's eyes narrowed. So this was the bastard who kept Allegra living in fear. 'My name's Alan. How may I help, sir?'

'What's your special of the day?'

'Wild garlic tagliatelle served with a hazelnut ragu, confit egg yolk and provolone cheese,' he replied, causing Allegra's eyebrows to shoot up with surprise. 'Are you wishing to place an order, sir? We do home delivery.'

'No, I do not. Put my daughter back on.'

'Certainly, sir,' he replied, handing back the phone.

Jamie assumed his charade had worked when Allegra's body relaxed. 'Yes, Father. No, I won't, promise. Okay, bye.' She hung up and stuffed the phone back into her bag.

'Does he check up on you a lot?' Jamie asked her, reverting back to his normal accent.

'All the time,' she sighed.

'He cannae do that, you're a grown woman.'

'I know. It doesn't stop him, though.'

'He's a control freak.'

'That's putting it mildly.'

'You shouldn't have to put up with that. You should tell him to piss off and move out.'

'If I did that he'd kill me.' She regarded him with wide, sad eyes. 'And I mean that literally. He would kill me, like he killed my mum.' She attempted to force a smile but couldn't find it in herself. 'Sorry for putting you on a downer.'

'You shouldn't have to live like this.'

'You get used to it.'

'It's no' right.'

She took his face in her hands and kissed him. 'Forget it. I don't want to think about him right now.'

'Do you have to go?'

'No. He just likes to spring surprise calls on me like that to keep me on my toes. Plus he likes to do a lot of his business from home and he doesn't want me hanging around for that. He prefers it when I'm out during the day.'

'Good,' he smiled.

'Where did you dig up that fancy dish from?'

His grin dropped. 'Oh, I see. Because I'm from a manky scheme I couldn't possibly know about good food.'

'Oh, don't go getting all offended,' she said. 'I didn't mean it like that. I just can't imagine Gerry serving it in one of his baskets.'

This comment brought the smile back to his face. 'Fair enough. My maw loves watching cookery programmes. She watched this really poncey one the other night. That was one of the dishes on it.'

'Well, it worked a treat.' She kissed him. 'You're so clever. Why have you pulled your jeans back up?'

'Because I didn't want to sit there with everything hanging out.'

'You've certainly nothing to be ashamed of.'

'Neither have you,' he said, running a hand up one of her bare legs. 'These are incredible, by the way.'

'Thank you. I'm glad all my hard work at the gym isn't for nothing.'

'It certainly isn't.'

When they kissed he could feel that her father's phone call had doused all her passion. Something else that bastard had taken from her. Well, he wasn't having it.

'What are you doing?' she gasped when he scooped her up in his arms. 'I can't go underneath.'

'I know, I haven't forgotten,' he said, placing her on the couch so she was sat upright. 'But I'm no' letting that tosser ruin anything else for you,' he added, kneeling between her splayed legs.

'Oh, you don't need to bother,' she said as he kissed his way up her inner thigh. 'I don't get anything from that... wow,' she yelled, throwing back her head and arching her spine as his tongue found the centre of her. She fell back into the cushions, cheeks blooming with colour. 'Oh, my God.'

Her hand fisted in his hair as he continued to work his magic. All the passion and fire that had been doused returned with a vengeance and before she knew it her head was spinning and a cry of wild abandon flew from her lips.

Gradually the pleasure ebbed away and her muscles could finally relax. She took in a long deep breath while her heart continued to hammer.

'Where the hell did you learn how to do that?' she breathed.

'I had a fling with an older woman when I was seventeen,' he replied. 'She taught me.'

'She should teach that professionally, she'd make a fortune,' she said, still trying to catch her breath. 'How much older than you was she?'

'She was forty-nine.'

'That's a big difference.'

'She only looked thirty-five, max.'

'You don't need to explain to me.'

'My maw was furious when she found out, she threatened to knock her out.'

Allegra smiled, able to picture that scene. She felt so contented she wanted to curl up in his arms and sleep but that wouldn't be fair. Instead she flung herself at him with her usual enthusiasm, knocking him onto his back on the carpet.

'Your turn,' she said.

'Great,' he grinned up at her.

There was a knock and they both looked towards the front door.

'We are so ignoring that,' he said.

'Too right we are,' she replied, unfastening his jeans.

When the letterbox was flipped open, allowing whoever was on the other side to see right into the living room, Allegra released a squeak, rolled off Jamie and hid behind the couch.

'Jamie, are you in there?' called the visitor. 'If you are, please open up.'

'Logan?' he frowned, getting to his feet and hitching up his jeans. 'I thought you were staying in the hospital until tomorrow?' he told the letterbox.

'I had to get out of there. Please let me in. Craig Lawson's following me.'

'Oh, hell,' he said, rushing to the door. Before he opened it, he glanced back at Allegra, who was frantically pulling on her underwear and trousers.

'Okay,' she said once she'd fastened them up, turning her attention to the buttons on her shirt.

Jamie nodded and pulled open the door.

'Thanks Jamie, I...' began Logan, the massive plaster still covering his nose. He frowned. 'Why don't you have a top on?'

'Just get inside.'

As Logan stepped inside, Jamie peeked his head out and looked down the street. Sure enough, there was Craig Lawson, leaning arrogantly against a lamppost. In that moment he was more furious that the bastard had interrupted them before Allegra could reciprocate than the fact that he'd hospitalised him and his best friend. With a glower he slammed the door shut and locked it.

'Allegra,' said Logan, startled when she leapt up from behind the couch. 'What were you doing down there?' He took in her flushed cheeks and the fact that his friend was bare chested, as well as his irritated frown, and realisation finally struck. 'Sorry for interrupting.'

'Why aren't you still in hospital?' demanded Jamie, not bothering to hide his annoyance.

'I had to get out of there. The Lawsons were stalking me and I don't just mean Craig and John, I mean the lot of them.'

'They were just wandering around the ward, seriously?'

'They came in at visiting time to sit by my bed and just stare at me. It was beyond creepy.'

'Didn't your da turn up for visiting?'

'Course he didn't, he hates hospitals. Even when I took a walk to the hospital shop for a newspaper there were more of the Lawsons there. I knew I had to leave, I felt too vulnerable. So I booked a taxi and discharged myself. The taxi was waiting for me right at the door, so I hopped in and escaped. I got it to drop me off at home but one of Craig's cousins must have tipped him off that I'd left because he was waiting for me at the house, so I told the taxi to drop me off here instead. I thought it would be safer. I'm sorry, I didn't realise you were here with Allegra.'

'It's alright, pal,' said Jamie, patting his shoulder when he saw how shaken he was. 'Sit yourself down. Do you want a brew or something stronger?'

'I'd kill for a can of lager but I'm on painkillers, so I'd better have a brew instead.'

'I'll make it,' said Allegra. 'You two need to talk.'

'Thanks, hen,' said Jamie, with a smile in her direction.

She gave him a wink before sashaying into the kitchen.

'Did I interrupt before you could...' began Logan.

'Aye, you did.'

'Sorry about that. She's a stunner.'

'I know. You should see her legs, man, they're amazing.' He was conscious of the taste of her still on his lips. As nice as that was, he didn't want to talk to his best friend like that. 'Just gie' me a sec,' he told him before pulling on his jumper and rushing upstairs to the bathroom. After washing his face he took a couple of minutes to will away what remained of his erection. Surely all this up and down wasn't good for his health? He could feel the nagging frustration swelling inside him.

Once he felt calmer, he headed back downstairs.

'Right,' he said, sitting down beside Logan. 'This is what we've decided to do so far.'

By the time he'd finished explaining his mum's plan, Allegra had returned to the room with three mugs of tea on a tray along with milk and sugar.

'Cheers, doll,' said Jamie when she handed him his mug.

'Thanks,' said Logan as he accepted his, still feeling sheepish for turning up at an inconvenient moment. 'What can I do while you're all intelligence gathering?'

'Rest and get well,' said Jamie. 'We need you at full strength. Craig is into being a creepy stalker right now, but this will get physical.'

'I can't sit on my arse and do nothing. This is all my fault.'

'Actually, we're blaming your da for it, so don't worry.'

'If only I'd had the guts to stand up to him like you said then this wouldn't have happened.'

'Don't beat yourself up about it,' said Allegra. 'Standing up to your father is easier said than done.'

Logan was stunned when Jamie's eyes filled with tenderness and he took Allegra's hand. Jamie had always made a point of never showing public affection to any of his previous girlfriends. He liked to portray himself as the lone wolf when it came to relationships. Allegra, for her part, smiled back at Jamie with equal tenderness. Perhaps she would be more than just his latest shag? Logan felt even more guilty for interrupting them.

'There's no point going over all that again,' said Jamie. 'We can't change the past. We just have to figure out how to deal with the present.'

'When you've figured out his weaknesses you'll know how,' said Allegra.

'It was her idea,' said Jamie when Logan did a double take.

'It's a good plan, hen,' said Logan.

She nodded in acknowledgement of the compliment.

'Let's see if that creepy bastard's still there,' said Jamie, getting up to peer out of the window. Sure enough, there was Craig, staring right back at him. When he saw Allegra appear beside Jamie he made a lewd gesture that involved pointing at his crotch.

'Bastard,' yelled Jamie.

'What are you doing?' demanded Logan, following him when he ran into the kitchen.

'Sorting that bastard out,' said Jamie, opening up one of the cupboards, delving inside and pulling out the loose back, revealing the hiding place where he stashed his bike chains.

'Think about what you're doing,' said Logan as he ran back to the front door. 'This is what he wants.'

'Aye, it is, and he's gonnae get it too.'

Logan looked to Allegra, hoping she could talk some sense into him, but he was dismayed by the excitement in her eyes.

'Kick his head in, Jamie,' she said.

'I fucking will,' he replied, tearing open the door.

10

Jamie marched outside, a bike chain hanging from each hand. 'Oy, you,' he yelled.

Craig appeared delighted by this turn of events. He straightened up and raced to meet him in the middle of the road.

'You're gonnae get a severe doin',' yelled Jamie, drawing back one of the bike chains. He wasn't in the least bit fazed when Craig pulled a metal bar from inside his jacket.

'Oh, Christ,' said Logan, turning to look over his shoulder at the sound of running footsteps to see John and four of his cousins rushing up to meet them. Craig had drawn Jamie into a trap. In the houses all around them curtains were hastily drawn, distancing the occupants from what was about to happen.

Allegra saw the danger too, ran back into the house, snatched her car keys out of her jacket pocket, raced back outside and leapt into her car.

'Jamie, it's a trap,' Logan yelled at his friend.

Jamie didn't even hear him, so caught up was he in fighting Craig, who was managing to ward off each blow of the bike chains with the bar.

Logan spun back round when an engine was gunned behind him. He saw Allegra tearing down the street in her car – aiming right at John and his friends.

'Bloody hell,' he breathed when she mounted the pavement to hit them. He was actually relieved when they leapt over a garden wall, narrowly avoiding the car.

Allegra drove back onto the road, slammed on the brakes and executed a tight U-turn, only just avoiding hitting a parked car, wheels screaming. John and his friends jumped back over the wall onto the pavement and continued running towards Jamie and Craig. Allegra stomped on the accelerator again and gave chase. Logan couldn't help but laugh at the panic in the eyes of John and his friends, who all knew she had no problem with running them over.

As she had them covered, Logan raced to help Jamie, snatching up a broken pushchair that had been abandoned on the kerb and wielding it like a bat. At the same time the door to Maureen's house was pulled open and Jackie charged out, waving a rolling pin in the air.

'Leave my son alone, you bastard,' she screamed.

Seeing his brother and cousins were still trying to escape Allegra's car, which was swerving wildly in an attempt to hit them, Craig realised that now was the time to retreat. Ducking to avoid a bike chain to the head, he ran off down the street, careful to stay on the opposite side to Allegra's car.

'Are you okay?' Jackie anxiously asked Jamie.

'Fine, Maw. He didnae get near me.'

He looked from her to Allegra's car. She'd almost reached the end of the street before deciding to give up the chase, executing another neat U-turn before heading back, zipping into the space outside Jamie's house.

'That lassie should be a stunt driver,' said Logan. 'She had that lot screaming.'

'She's fucking amazing,' said Jamie.

Jackie watched with her mouth hanging open as Jamie charged

up to Allegra as she got out of the car. He let the bike chains drop, pulled her to him and kissed her, cradling her face between his hands.

'Are you okay?' he asked her.

'I'm fine,' she grinned. 'You?'

'Fine. He didnae touch me.'

'Because he couldn't. God, that was exciting.'

'Aye, it was,' he said before kissing her again.

'It's serious, isn't it?' Jackie asked Logan.

'Do you mean with the Lawsons or Jamie and Allegra?'

'Both.' She shook herself out of it. 'All right, let's get inside before that lot come back.'

Jamie collected his bike chains, took Allegra's hand and led her inside, Jackie following them with a smile. Once they were all inside Jackie locked the door behind them.

'Are you okay?' she asked Logan. 'You're very pale.'

'My nose still aches.'

'You should be in hospital. What are you doing out?'

'Craig and his family were stalking me. I didn't feel safe.'

'This just gets worse. They're never going to leave us alone. They're giving us no choice. We have to go to the police.'

'You know about the photo?' Logan asked her.

'I told her all about it,' said Jamie. 'Sorry, pal, I had to.'

'Who else knows?'

'Allegra, Gary and Digger.'

'Great,' he sighed.

'No, it's good,' said Jackie. 'You can't handle this alone. Has Jamie told you about our plan?'

'To find Craig Lawson's weaknesses, aye. Good luck with that. He cares about nothing and no one.'

'I'm pretty certain he'll do anything to protect the person he loves most,' said Allegra. 'Which is himself.'

'Let's just tell the police about that photo,' said Jackie. 'No one needs to know the information came from us, we can do it anonymously.'

'But we don't have the photo,' said Logan. 'It would just be our word against the Lawsons'. Craig's friends who stalked me in the hospital made it very clear that me and Jamie wouldn't suffer. It'll be you, Allegra, Charlie and my da. Christ knows what they'll do to you if we go to the police.'

'He's right,' said Allegra.

'This is madness,' said Jackie. 'We know the Lawsons have committed a really serious crime and we can't do anything about it. Oh, this mess is all Dave's fault.'

'No, it's not, it's mine,' said Logan, hanging his head. 'Jamie told me no' to listen to him but I couldn't help it.' He regarded her with large puppy dog eyes. 'He's my da.'

'Oh, come here love,' she said, grabbing him and pulling him into her substantial bosom, causing his arms to pinwheel.

'Better let him go, Maw,' said Jamie. 'He looks like a beetroot.'

Jackie released Logan, who stumbled backwards, gasping for breath.

'That's the usual effect I have on men,' she announced, making Allegra grin.

'Shall I stick some dinner on, Maw?' said Jamie. It was almost twelve o'clock and he was starving after all the morning's excitement.

'No thanks, love, I'll do it. You spend some time with Allegra.' She looked to Logan. 'Do you want some dinner too?'

'If that's okay? I'm starving. The food in the hospital was crap.'

'Course it is. Take a seat and try to relax for a bit.'

Jackie disappeared into the kitchen and Logan moved to sit on the couch, changing his mind and taking the armchair instead when Jamie and Allegra curled up on the couch together. Jamie whispered something in Allegra's ear, making her giggle. He took her hand and kissed the tips of her fingers, the way they gazed at one another telling Logan they'd forgotten he was even there.

Feeling like a spare part, he decided to join Jackie in the kitchen.

'Need a hand?' he said.

'Sit yourself down,' she told him. 'You're just out of hospital.'

'I'll sit here instead,' he said, sinking into a chair at the kitchen table. 'I feel like a gooseberry in there.'

'Aye, that seems to be going very well, doesn't it?' she beamed.

'Definitely. I've never seen him like this with a bird before.'

'Me neither. She's a terrific lassie.'

'There's no' many birds who would drive their car at the Lawsons,' he chuckled.

'And that's what worries me.'

'How do you mean?'

'She likes the danger. In a lot of ways she's just like Jamie because he enjoys it too, but he's quiet about it, understated, while she's in-your-face wild.'

'So, they're a good pair.'

'They are, but that wildness could get them into even more trouble and we've enough of that right now.'

* * *

The moment Logan had vanished into the kitchen, Allegra whispered in Jamie's ear, 'Let's go to your room. You didn't get your treat.'

'We cannae do that,' he replied. 'They'll know what we're up to.'

'Fine. Let's stay down here and you don't get your treat.'

That decided him. 'All right, let's go.'

They hurried upstairs together, Jamie pulling her into his room and slamming the door shut. He pressed her up against the door and kissed her, her arms locking around his neck, wrapping one thigh around his waist.

He lifted his head when he heard a loud pop and a hiss from outside.

'What was that?' he said.

'Who cares?'

'Just a sec,' he said, releasing her and heading to the window, which looked out over the front street. He flung it open just in time to see one of the Lawson cousins pelting down the street. Allegra's car was listing to one side.

'The dirty little bastard burst two of your tyres,' exclaimed Jamie.

'What?' she said, rushing to his side. She shrugged. 'It doesn't matter. I have great roadside cover. I'll call them, they'll sort it out.' She pulled the window shut and yanked the curtains closed. 'Get on the bed,' she told him.

'Don't you want to sort out your car?'

'It can wait.'

With a grin he leapt onto the bed and lay down on his back.

'Tease,' he rasped as Allegra unfastened his jeans with excruciating slowness.

'I am,' she winked.

He lifted his hips so she could pull down his jeans and underwear, his heart hammering.

'Someone's ready,' she smiled.

'I've been ready since that moment in the hospital.'

'Then let's not keep you waiting a second longer,' she said, lowering her head as his eyes slid shut in anticipation.

'Dinner's ready,' Jackie yelled up the stairs.

'Jesus,' said Jamie, body jumping. 'Already?'

'Sorry, Casanova,' said Allegra, sitting up. 'Looks like it'll have to wait.'

'Again?' he exclaimed. 'That's four times now. All this starting and stopping is gonnae make me ill.'

'Did you hear me?' yelled Jackie.

'Yes we did,' called back Allegra. 'We're coming.'

'Is that supposed to be some sort of joke?' said Jamie flatly.

'All the anticipation will make it even more exciting.'

'And painful,' he groaned.

She got to her feet and ran her fingers through her hair. 'Aren't you getting up?'

'You go. I'll join you when I can move again.'

'Aye, you can't have dinner with your mum with a big bulge in your trousers. What?' she added when he frowned at her.

'That's the first time I've heard you say *aye*. Normally you say yes, like an English person.'

'My dad doesn't like me using any slang.'

'That's not slang, it's just... Scottish.'

'I agree, but he doesn't like it. He hired a tutor to school the Scottish out of me.'

'But that's shite.'

'I know. He likes me to speak real English – his words, not mine.'

'Is he English?'

'No, he's from Possilpark.'

'Possilpark?' he snorted. 'So how come he's such a snob?'

'He had a bad upbringing and he wanted to erase all trace of it, even in his own children.'

'You mean weans.'

'Aye, weans,' she smiled.

'Jamie, put the girl down,' Jackie bellowed up the stairs.

'We'd better get down there,' said Allegra.

Jamie looked down the length of his body and sighed. 'You'd better give me another minute.'

She planted a kiss on his lips. 'I'll see you down there.'

Allegra happily skipped downstairs. She never felt afraid in this house, even when there were psychos outside on the street. Although it wasn't even a quarter of the size of her own home it was so much nicer.

'There you are, hen,' said Jackie when she walked into the kitchen. 'I hope he wasn't pawing you too much.'

'No, he wasn't,' she smiled, taking her seat. 'He's lovely.'

'That's not a word I've ever associated with Jamie,' grinned Logan. 'And he's my best pal. Brooding, yes, moody, definitely but lovely, nah.'

'Well, he is. Great,' she said, her smile increasing when Jackie placed her plate before her. 'Beans on toast.'

'I know it's only basic, love, but it's quick and we're all hungry.'

'I love beans on toast. It was my favourite growing up.' She didn't add that her dad never let her have it because he thought it was common. 'I'll call the breakdown people when I've finished eating.'

'Oh no,' said Jackie. 'Did your lovely car get damaged chasing after John and his pals?'

'No. One of Craig's friends snuck back and burst a couple of the tyres.'

'The despicable wee shite.'

'It's not a problem. It'll be sorted in half an hour.'

'Maureen has a garage on the back street but she never uses it. You could keep your car in there when you come to visit.' Things were going so well between Allegra and Jamie that Jackie wanted nothing putting her off seeing him. She would even be willing to pay Maureen for that garage if it kept them together.

'That's very kind, thank you, but I don't want you going to any trouble.'

'It's no trouble. After dinner I'll pop round and get the key off her.'

Allegra gave her a sweet smile before tearing into her food. Jamie sauntered in, walking rather slowly.

'Are you okay, sweetheart?' said Jackie, pressing a hand to his forehead. 'You look flushed.'

'I'm just... hot,' he replied.

Logan looked from him to Allegra and was unable to repress a snigger.

'You need something to eat, you're crashing,' Jackie told her son.

He slumped into the chair opposite Allegra and tucked into his food.

'Don't shovel it down like your life depends on it,' Jackie told him. 'Have some manners in front of Allegra.'

'It's food, Maw, so my life does depend on it and she doesn't mind.'

'Course I don't mind,' said Allegra, wiping away the tomato sauce staining her chin with her fingers. 'See?'

After they'd finished eating, Allegra called the breakdown company, who said they'd be there within the hour to sort out her car. Jackie washed up then popped next door to Maureen's for the garage key. Her friend said she could use it and refused to take the ten pound note Jackie attempted to give her as compensation. That was the thing she loved most about Gallowburn – the people on the scheme might not have much but they were willing to share what little they did have and would do anything to help someone out. Not all of them, of course, like anywhere there were wallopers too, but there was a sense of community that had fled most other places. It was one of the last bastions of a real community, something the newer, posher estates seriously lacked, where the residents preferred to hide behind their high walls and thick hedges.

While Allegra was outside overseeing the mechanic who turned up to sort out her tyres, Digger and Gary returned in a state of high excitement.

'I've been doing some research,' said Gary, flushed with the enthusiasm of whatever it was he was about to impart.

'About Craig?' Jamie replied distractedly, standing at the window to keep an eye on Allegra. He didn't want the Lawsons turning up again while she was out there. Plus the mechanic was pretty good looking and he hated the jealousy he was experiencing.

'Naw, about Allegra.'

Jamie fixed him with a furious glare. 'You're no' supposed to be researching her, you're supposed to be finding something about Craig we can use.'

'Aye, we're on with that, but look,' he said, waving his phone in his face.

'I'm no gonnae spy on her on the internet.'

'Jamie's right,' said Jackie. 'That's pretty low.'

'Don't worry,' replied Gary. 'It's all good. You see, I'd heard of her father. She's one of them socialites.'

'What are you banging on about?' said Jamie. He found himself staring at an image online of Allegra looking glorious in a floor length dark blue silk dress, her blonde hair piled on top of her head, smiling at the camera.

'This was taken at a film premiere in Edinburgh,' said Gary. 'There were A-lister stars there. Look, Daniel Craig's in the background.'

'So?'

'What do you mean, so? It's amazing, man. Her da's like one of the wealthiest men in the entire country.'

'Aye, and a complete bastard, too.'

'Are you surprised? People don't get to be incredibly rich by being nice. She's all over the internet attending these society dos and A-lister parties. She's an heiress, too, she stands to inherit a ton of cash if her da dies.'

'Don't be so dramatic,' said Jamie, thinking this was another of his tall tales.

'I'm no' being dramatic. It's all there online.'

'It's true, Jamie,' said Digger. 'I've seen it myself.'

'How much is her da worth?' said Jackie.

'A hundred and fourteen million.'

Shocked silence filled the room.

'So he's no' as rich as that bird who wrote those wizard books,' continued Gary, speaking quickly in his excitement.

'You mean Harry Potter?' said Logan.

'No, that was no' her name,' he replied, making him shake his head. 'But he's got more than some bloke who makes whisky. Just think,' he continued eagerly. 'If you get hitched you could inherit all that.'

'I don't want to talk about her da,' retorted Jamie with such vehemence Gary took a step back. 'He's a fucking bastard who treats her like shit and I won't hear one more word about him. You got it?'

They all stared at him in surprise.

'Aye, all right, Jamie,' replied Gary. 'Whatever you say.'

'Put your phone back in your pocket right now,' he said when he saw the mechanic had finished fixing Allegra's car and she was shaking his hand in thanks, making the man blush. 'No one says a word to her about this. I don't want her thinking we've been checking up on her, and if you ever do anything like this again, Gary, I will ram your phone so far up your arse it'll come out your mouth. Got it?'

Gary frantically nodded. 'Aye, I do, pal.'

'Good,' he snarled before returning his attention to the window just in time to see Allegra walking up the garden path. He smiled when she gave him a cheery wave.

'That's my car sorted,' she told them all, stepping inside and closing the door behind her. 'I'll go and pop it in the garage.'

'I'll come with you,' said Jamie. 'Just in case any Lawsons are lurking about.'

'Not to worry. If they are I'll just run them over.'

'Nice one,' chuckled Digger.

'Hi, boys,' she said, addressing him and Gary. 'Have you found out anything about Craig?'

'Actually, I have,' replied Digger.

'Brilliant. What?'

'Why don't you put your car away first?' Jackie told her. 'Before those sods come right back and vandalise it again.'

'Yes, that's probably a good idea.'

Jamie followed her outside, throwing Gary a warning look as he went.

'What you told us changes nothing,' Jackie told the three boys. 'That lassie is the same sweet Allegra and you will treat her as such. She's sharp as a tack and will notice if we start treating her differently.'

'But I was gonnae ask her for a lend,' said Digger, grin falling when she scowled at him in a way reminiscent of her son. 'Only kidding.'

'Well, don't. My nerves can't take it.'

* * *

'All right, what's up?' Allegra asked Jamie when he got into the passenger seat of her car.

'Nothing's up.'

'Yes, it is. I can practically feel the tension radiating off you.'

'Oh, it was just Gary pissing about, as usual. He doesn't seem to be taking all this shite with the Lawsons seriously at all.'

'Just ignore him, he doesn't mean anything by it.'

'I know, but sometimes he can be such a clown and it pisses me off.'

'My friend Clementine's like that.'

'Clementine?' he said, raising his eyebrows.

'I know. It's almost as bad as my name, isn't it?'

'I like your name.'

'You didn't at first. You took the piss out of it.'

'Aye, well, I can change my mind, can't I?'

'Suppose. Well, where's this garage then?'

'Turn left at the end of the street.'

She nodded and set off.

'So, what about Clementine?' he pressed.

'Oh, yes. Well, she was the same as Gary, constantly joking. Then one day she tried to kill herself.'

'Really?'

'Yep. Slit her wrists in the bath. Fortunately, her sister found her and got her to hospital in time, so she was okay. Turned out all the joking was just a front to hide how unhappy she was.'

'I'm no' surprised, being called Clementine.'

'Be serious. There was a bit more to it than that. She got the help she needed and she's much happier now. The point is, sometimes jokers can hide the deepest pain.'

'Nah, not in Gary's case. He's just a fanny. Turn left again,' he added when they reached the back street. 'It's the last garage on the right.'

'I don't think you mean that,' she replied, following his directions. 'I mean about Gary, not the garage. It's obvious the four of you are really close, although I think the other three are a bit afraid of you. Why is that, Dangerous?'

'Haven't you just answered your own question?'

'I've no doubt you're capable of a lot but something happened once to make them that afraid of you. I'm right, aren't I?' she added when he looked down at his hands. 'What did you do that was so bad you scared three men like them?'

He sighed. 'It was two years ago. I got into a fight with a lad from the south side of the scheme. I lost my temper and I... nearly killed him.'

'With your bike chains?'

'No. With my fists. He got better but he was in hospital for a few weeks. He's fine now. Logan and the others kept trying to pull me off him but they couldn't, I just saw red, totally lost it.'

'Why, what had he done?'

'It had been brewing between us for a while. It started over some daft wee bird then just escalated. He wouldn't let it drop, he kept having a go at me and I snapped. I can't even remember it. Luckily he didn't grass to the police otherwise I'd be locked up now.'

'No one grasses in Gallowburn,' she said.

'Aye, exactly. He never went after revenge.'

'He probably wouldn't dare.'

'I've seen him about a few times. When he sees me coming he goes the opposite way.'

'Understandable,' she said, stopping the car outside the garage he'd directed her to and pulling on the handbrake.

'So,' he said. 'You know the worst about me. Has it put you off?'

'No. Why would it?'

'Because I nearly killed someone.'

'But you didn't.'

'Only because Logan, Digger and Gary managed to drag me off him, eventually. If they hadn't I would have gone all the way. They said I went really weird, like my teeth were chattering and my face went bright red and I was even howling. I felt like shite for a couple of days after, physically I mean. I had no energy left.' Jamie couldn't believe he was telling her this, but he felt he could tell her anything and she would never judge him. There weren't many people he could say that about, not even his mum.

'I've heard about stuff like that before,' she replied. 'There was a documentary on the telly about it. It's called "going berserk", after the berserkers, the Viking warriors, only they think they used hallucinogens to get into that state. Had you taken anything like that?'

'No, nothing. I only smoke a bit of weed, which has the opposite effect. It knocks me out and I hadn't had any that night.'

'Well, you're not alone because it still happens to people today, usually when they're insanely angry. He must have wound you up so much you sort of snapped. Maybe you're related to some ancient Viking berserker warrior who wore bear skins when going into battle?'

'Maybe. There were plenty of Vikings around Scotland.'

'You'd make a great Norse warrior.'

'I'm too skinny.'

'You're not skinny, you're slender.'

'Is there a difference?'

'Oh, yes. Skinny men don't have muscles like yours,' she purred, sliding her hand under his jumper to stroke his stomach. 'Oh hello,' she smiled when a bulge appeared in his trousers.

'No' again,' he breathed, turning red in the face. 'You're killing me.'

She dumped the garage keys in his hand. 'In there looks pretty private,' she said, nodding at the garage.

He grinned, flung off his seatbelt and leapt out of the car. He opened up the door to reveal the garage was empty except for a couple of old bicycles. She drove the car inside. When she'd switched off the engine he hit the light switch and pulled the door shut.

'Oh, no you don't,' he said when she opened the driver's door. 'Get in that bloody backseat.'

'Now you're talking,' she smiled, throwing off her seatbelt.

11

'I don't like it,' said Digger. 'They've been gone too long. They were only going to put her car away.'

'Maybe they want to be alone?' said Logan, thinking how he'd interrupted them earlier. If he was Jamie he'd want to get that started again at the earliest possible opportunity.

'That back street is the perfect site for an ambush.'

Jackie went rigid in her seat. 'Oh, my God, you're right. The Lawsons are going to be raging about what happened earlier. What if they were waiting for them?'

'The Lawsons can't know that Allegra's going to be using Maureen's garage,' reasoned Logan.

'What if one of them was watching the house and saw them drive down there? We have to check it out.'

'Go with her,' Logan told Digger and Gary when she bolted out the back door. He got up to follow but because he was still feeling lousy he couldn't run as quickly.

'It's this one,' panted Jackie, indicating the garage door.

Digger reached it first and began hammering on the door. 'Jamie, Jamie, are you in there?' He pressed his ear to the door. 'I can't hear anyone,' he said, turning to Jackie and Gary when they finally caught up.

Jackie began battering the door with both fists. 'Jamie, Allegra! If you're in there, open up right now.'

They all took a step back when the garage door flew open to reveal an angry-looking Jamie.

'Oh, thank God,' said Jackie, flinging her arms around his neck.

Logan finally caught up with them and glimpsed Allegra in the back of the car, hastily dressing. 'It wasnae my fault this time,' he told his friend.

'We were worried, you were taking so long,' Jackie told her son. When she glimpsed what Logan had seen realisation finally struck. 'Oh. Sorry, son.'

'It's okay,' he said through gritted teeth.

'I'll, er, get back to finding out what I can about Craig,' said Digger, already walking away to escape Jamie's wrathful gaze.

'Me too,' said Gary, hurrying after him.

'Come on Jackie,' said Logan, putting an arm around her shoulders. 'Let's go back to the house.'

'Aye, okay,' she said, casting Jamie an apologetic look before leaving.

Jamie closed the door and returned to Allegra, dismayed to find she was fully dressed.

'It's a good job we were interrupted, actually,' she said.

'Good for who?' he replied. Once again they'd been disturbed before they could reach a satisfactory conclusion – for him, anyway.

'I've got to go to some boring party tonight that's been arranged by a friend of my father's. I have to be there.'

He glanced at his watch. 'It's only two o'clock.'

'I know, but I'm helping organise things. It's to raise money for a cancer charity I set up with a friend, so I have to oversee all the arrangements.'

'Where is this party?'

'Countess Gate in Bothwell. This friend of my father's is a bit of a lunatic but in a good way. He's really over the top and extroverted but kind with it. He's got a life-sized giraffe in his front garden and his hedges are all cut into elephants.'

'Why?'

'He likes elephants.'

'Fair enough.'

'Organising parties is one of the few things I enjoy. I've often thought I'd make a good party planner.'

'Why don't you become one, then?'

'Because my father doesn't want me working. He thinks if I get a job everyone will think he doesn't have enough money to provide for me.'

'But that's bollocks.'

'I know, but he's really old-fashioned. He would have been much more at home in the Victorian era. I can just see him working small children to death in some manky old mill.'

'When will I see you again?'

'Why, are you going to miss me, Dangerous?'

'Yes,' he replied without having to think about it.

She kissed him. 'I'll miss you too. I won't be able to see you until tomorrow, the party will run into the early hours. Our last fundraiser raised seventy thousand for the charity. I'm hoping to top that. We have an auction and I've managed to blag some really special donations.'

'I'm sure you'll do it,' he replied while thinking how far apart their worlds were.

'I usually get my way.'

'I don't doubt it, Princess. So, you're gonnae leave me like this?'

'Sorry, Dangerous. Hopefully tomorrow we'll get some real alone time.'

'Why, are we gonnae catch a flight to the Antarctic? Because that's the only way.'

She gave him a deep, lingering kiss that made him ache all over.

'I've got to go,' she said.

'You're torturing me.'

She smiled. 'I know, I enjoy it. Are you going to open the garage door for me?'

'Aye, go on then, although I'm tempted to lock you in and not let you out until we've finally done what we've been trying to do all bloody day.'

'I like all this stopping and starting. When it finally does happen, it'll be incredible.'

With a smile, she clambered into the driver's seat, ran a hand through her hair and pulled on her seatbelt. 'See you tomorrow, Dangerous.'

'Aye, you will. Enjoy the party.'

'I'll be thinking of you the entire time.'

'Oh, aye, when you're surrounded by all those rich tossers?'

She pulled a face. 'You mean inbred, boring tossers. Most of them don't even have chins.'

This made him laugh and appeased his jealousy a little. He shoved open the door for her to drive out. She winked at him as she went and he watched until she turned the corner and disappeared. He stood there, alone, thinking how colourless the world seemed without her.

'Christ, don't go falling in love with her,' he told himself.

The back street he was standing in seemed to darken now her sunny presence had gone. The houses looked down on him, the empty windows reflecting the grey sky, sending a chill down his spine. He wasn't a superstitious man, but he got the feeling the Gallowburn knew something he didn't, a sense of foreboding washing over him.

Shaking himself out of it, he closed and locked the garage door before returning to the house.

'That was fast,' grinned Logan when Jamie walked into the living room. His smile fell when he saw he was alone. 'Where's Allegra? What did you do to her?'

'Nothing. She had to go, she's arranging some party to raise money for a charity she set up.'

'What sort of charity?'

'Cancer.'

'Well that's very admirable of her,' commented Jackie, who was in the middle of dusting.

They looked at each other when there was the jingle of chimes outside.

'That sounds like Ephraim,' said Logan.

'We could do with a word with him with the Lawsons gunning for us,' replied Jamie.

'You got any cash on you?'

'A bit. You?'

'Some. Back in a minute, Maw,' Jamie told her. 'Lock the door behind us.'

'Be careful,' she replied.

'We will.'

'So, you didn't manage to get all the way with the lovely Allegra again then?' said Logan once they were outside.

'Naw. It's fucking killing me.'

'She seems like the type to enjoy teasing a bloke.'

'It's no' her, it's you lot. Maybe if the world ends and we're the only two survivors we might actually manage to do it.'

'She's really keen on you.'

'You think so?'

'Aye, I do. You can see it when she looks at you. I'd love for a bird to look at me that way.'

'How?'

'What do you mean, how?'

'How does she look at me?'

'You know, like she's all... smitten. If you ask me to do an impression I will punch you.'

Jamie smiled and held up his hands. 'I wouldn't dae that, it would be too disturbing.'

They tagged onto the end of the queue that had already formed at the large pink ice cream van with a smiley face painted on the front and eyelashes on the headlights. This most innocuous of vehicles hid a multitude of sins. While some of the lads in front came away with ice cream cones and ice lollies, some tucked the small plastic packages the man serving behind the counter passed them into their pockets before hurrying away, heads bowed.

Finally it was Jamie and Logan's turn and they found themselves facing a sturdy middle-aged man with a heavily lined face, badly dyed black hair swept back off his prominent forehead. A large crucifix hung around his neck. He planted his tattooed forearms on the counter and leaned towards them, peering at them through his narrow dark eyes. Logan's eyes slipped to the tattoos, all of which were Bible quotes, mainly from the old testament.

'All right there, boys?' growled Ephraim in his deep raspy voice. 'How's your maw, Jamie?'

'Aye, she's good.'

'Is she no' coming oot to see me?'

'She's busy dusting.'

'Shame,' he said, gaze sweeping to the front of Jamie's house.

Jamie resented Ephraim's rather worrying obsession with his mum but not even the Blood Brothers would tackle this lunatic.

'We're after something special,' said Logan.

Ephraim's discomforting gaze swept back to the men standing before him. 'Having some trouble, boys?'

'You could say that,' replied Jamie.

'The Lawsons again? I heard someone drove a car into the back of you both.'

'You heard right.'

'What you wantin' to use to get revenge for that? I cannae fit a tank in here.'

'What have you got?'

Ephraim looked up and down the street before ducking under the counter, straightening up and dumping a jumble of weapons on the counter.

'Jesus, we don't need machetes,' sighed Logan.

Ephraim tugged at one of the arms of his crucifix to produce a small shiv and pointed it at Logan's damaged nose. 'What have I told you about taking our saviour's name in vain, wee man?'

'Sorry,' he replied, eyes wide. 'It was a reflex, I couldnae help myself.'

Ephraim glared at him before replacing the weapon in the necklace. 'Don't let it happen again.'

'Nae danger, pal.'

'Good.'

'Have you anything more subtle?' said Jamie, frowning at the collection of baseball bats, knuckledusters and crowbars.

'Just knives, but I know Jackie would go aff her nut if I gave you anything like that.'

'Aye, she would.'

'You going off your bike chains?'

'No, but I'd like something else as back-up.'

Ephraim thought hard before scooping up all the weapons and replacing them back under the counter. 'There's just one thing,' he said. 'It's small, something you can carry about with you. Best of all, if the police catch you with it they can't do you for it.'

'Sounds perfect.'

He produced an object with a flourish and placed it on the counter.

'It's a hairbrush,' said Logan flatly.

'It looks like a hairbrush but it's a lot more than that,' he said, pulling the plastic casing off the end to reveal a lethal point. 'A shank and it keeps your hair tidy too.'

'It's too similar to a knife,' said Jamie. 'Have you anything that doesn't stab?'

'Aye,' he said, producing a piece of wood with a strip of leather stapled to it. Attached to the leather were four razors. 'A razor whip,' he announced with a smile.

'We're still in knife territory,' said Jamie.

'It's no' a knife,' retorted Ephraim as though he were talking to a five-year-old. 'It slashes, no' stabs.'

'Have you got anything that doesn't slash or stab?'

'You won't want my crossbow made from toothbrushes then?'

'We appreciate the offer but no thanks.'

'I might have something else.' They had to wait while he rummaged around under the counter, meanwhile the queue behind them was building up.

'Hey, are you gonnae hurry up?' called one whiny voice from behind them. 'I've got a pan on the boil.'

Ephraim straightened up clutching a machete, narrow eyes alight with fury, causing the entire queue to leap backwards.

'Which wee fanny said that?' he roared.

No one answered, everyone avoiding his eyes while Jamie and Logan looked on in amusement.

'Anyone else opens their mouth and I'll ram this right down their bastarding throat. You got that, you bunch of pricks?'

They all nodded, keeping their gazes fixed on the ground.

Ephraim took a deep breath that made his entire body shudder as the rage that lived inside him returned to its slumber. 'That's better. We're no' savages.'

Logan thought what an ironic statement that was coming from the man holding the machete.

The horrifying weapon disappeared back into the depths of the van and a long leather object was slapped down on the counter. It was roughly fourteen inches long, rounded at one end.

'What's that?' said Jamie.

'A beaver tail, a slap jack, a jacksap, a slap-stick.' Ephraim rolled his eyes when they looked blank. 'It's a fucking cosh.'

'Oh, I see,' said Jamie, picking it up and testing the weight.

'The rounded end is filled with sand. Easy to carry about. Don't hit anyone in the heid with it if you don't want to cause them some serious damage, it's capable of fracturing a skull. If that's no' right for you then you'll have to ask wee Jenny Lafferty at number seventeen if you can borrow her skipping rope.'

'The beaver tail will do,' said Jamie. 'How much?'

'Fifty quid.'

Jamie pulled some notes out of his pocket and looked to Logan. 'I've only got thirty-five.'

'Jesus,' sighed Ephraim.

'It's okay, I've got the rest,' said Logan.

They pooled their money together and dumped it on the counter. Ephraim scooped it up and carefully counted it. 'All right,' he said, stuffing the notes into the back pocket of his jeans. 'You can take it.'

'Cheers, Ephraim,' said Jamie.

'And remember, it didnae come from me. If you tell anyone it did...'

Aye, we know,' said Jamie. 'You'll hack us to pieces in our beds.' He said it in an almost bored tone as this was the stock threat Ephraim had dished out to his customers for the ten years he'd been trading his illegal homemade weapons.

'And don't forget it. Right, on you go. You're holding up the line.'

Jamie and Logan stepped aside and a nervous individual stepped up, swallowing hard when Ephraim glared down at him like an eagle surveying its prey. Despite the rise and fall of the many gangs on the estate over the years, Ephraim had always been the most feared. His freezers were used for a lot more than just ice lollies.

Jackie leapt on them the second they came through the door. 'What did you get?' she asked Jamie. 'What's that?' she frowned when he held it up. 'It looks like a sex toy.'

'It's a beaver tail,' he replied.

'So I was right,' she smiled.

'No, Maw. It's a cosh filled with sand. No blade.'

'That is a relief. I bet he tried to sell you a blade though, didn't he?'

'Aye, he did, but you know I'd never take one.'

She nodded and patted his hand. 'I do. You're a good boy, Jamie.'

'He was asking after you again, Maw.'

'Urgh, I wish he wouldn't. He makes my skin crawl.' She glanced out of the window and was shocked to see Ephraim staring right back at her from his van with unnerving predatory eyes. When he came onto their street he always parked outside her house. She pulled the curtains closed with a shudder.

'You should take this,' said Jamie, dumping the beaver tail in Logan's hands.

'That's no' fair, you put the most money to it.'

'I have my chains. You don't have anything and you're more vulnerable than me, you're still recovering from the accident.'

'You know I prefer my fists.'

'He's right, Logan,' said Jackie. 'You need some protection. This is Craig Lawson we're dealing with, no' his fud of a brother.'

'All right, you've got a point,' Logan said, taking the weapon from Jamie and gripping it in one hand. It was heavier than it looked.

'I really think you should stay with us until this is over,' Jackie told him. 'Apart, you're much more vulnerable.'

Logan would love nothing better than to move into this neat, tidy house where he wouldn't have to do any housework and all his meals would be cooked for him, but there was a particular fly in the ointment. 'What about my da? I can't leave him alone.'

'How no'? This is all his fault.'

'He's still my da. I'd never forgive myself if anything happened to him, and the Lawsons did threaten him directly.'

The last person Jackie wanted in her home was Dave McVitie but Logan was like a third son to her and she couldn't stand the thought of him getting hurt, even if he often did the wrong thing by trying so hard to do the right thing.

'He can stay, too,' she mumbled.

'What?' said a stunned Jamie.

'I said he can stay too. But I want to make it clear I'm only doing it for you, Logan.'

'We can't impose on you like that,' replied Logan.

'Aye, well, you are and I won't hear a word of an argument. You can pay some board and your da better not think he's going to be waited on hand and foot like he is at home. He'll have to pull his weight.'

'But this is a three-bedroomed house,' said Jamie. 'Where will they sleep?'

'Logan can share with you and Dave can have the couch.'

'Is that okay with you, mate?' Logan asked Jamie.

Jamie had wanted to keep his room free for the next time Allegra came round but the sight of his friend's injured face made him feel guilty about that. 'Aye, course it is. It'll be fun, like sleepovers when we were weans.'

'Only we won't be watching kids' TV and playing with toys,' Logan smiled. This was going to be heaven. Part of him hoped this situation dragged on longer.

'What about Gary and Digger?' said Jamie.

'We don't have room for them too,' said Jackie.

'Digger's alright,' said Logan. 'He's got all his family, they're always at home but Gary's vulnerable on his own in that house.'

'I'll have a word with Digger. His mum will let Gary stay with them.'

'Sounds a good plan,' said Jackie. 'I'd love to have them to stay too but there just isn't space.'

'I need to pop home to get some stuff,' said Logan.

'I'll come with you,' replied Jamie.

'Call Gary and Digger,' said Jackie. 'Get them to go with you.'

'We can handle it,' replied her son.

'You're both just out of hospital and I know Logan's still no' right. Get them to go with you.'

'You're probably right, Maw,' he said, getting on his phone.

In no time at all Digger and Gary arrived at the Gray residence together.

'I found out something really interesting,' announced Gary as he walked through the door.

'I hope you've no' been sticking your nose into Allegra's life again,' Jamie glowered at him.

'No. This is about Craig. I heard it from Debbie Cromarty. She was his girlfriend before he got sent down. The second he was sentenced she started shagging Liam Jones. Liam ended up in hospital last night with a broken leg and a shit ton of bruises. He's saying he fell down the stairs but everyone knows Craig did it.'

'Is that the interesting thing or was there something else?' said Logan.

'Something else. Craig does have a fear – you'll never guess of what.'

'Don't keep us in suspense,' said Jackie when he went silent.

'Clowns.'

'Who isn't afraid of those spooky bastards?' said Digger, colouring slightly when they all looked at him.

'They are creepy,' said Logan.

'Yeah, but this is a full-on fear. She said Craig turned up at the house during her wee brother's birthday party and there was this bloke dressed up as a clown and he was blowing up balloons and Craig freaked out and went for him and he was, like, yelling that the clown was sent by the devil and he punched the clown and the clown fell into the couch and Debbie's wee brother started crying and one wean peed himself when the clown's big red wig fell off because he was baldy underneath and the kid thought Craig had punched the hair right off him.'

He ended this monologue with a long deep breath as he hadn't paused for air once. The others stared at him in astonishment.

'Bollocks,' pronounced Jamie.

'It's true,' he retorted. 'Debbie swore down and that lassie doesnae lie.'

'He's got a point there,' said Logan. 'Debbie's a nice girl. Everyone was really shocked when she started going out with a roaster like Craig.'

'This is great if he really does have a clown phobia,' said an eager Digger. 'All we have to do is dress up like Pennywise and we'll probably run him off the scheme.'

'I've got the horrible feeling it won't be that simple,' said Jamie.

'What if we all do dress up as clowns?' said Logan. 'And end up looking like tits because Debbie was wrong. Maybe the guy dressed as the clown owed Craig money or did something to piss him off?'

'He leapt behind the couch when *Killer Clowns from Outer Space* came on the telly,' said Gary.

'Is that a real film?'

'Aye, it is.'

'Jeezo, they'll make any old shite, won't they?'

'Maybe we can test this fear?' said Jamie thoughtfully. 'Drop wee hints and see how he reacts. He won't want a word about this getting out.'

'That's another idea,' said Digger. 'Ruin his reputation. We could spread it about that he likes sticking avocadoes up his arse or something.'

'I thought that was your hobby?' grinned Gary.

'Cheeky bastard.'

'While you're here, boys,' said Jackie. 'You should know that Logan and Dave are staying with us until this is over. Dave doesn't know it yet but he is.'

'You're letting him stay here, in your home?' said an incredulous Digger.

'Aye, I am, for Logan's sake. Gary, you're too vulnerable in that house on your own.'

'I'd love to stay here, Mrs Gray,' he beamed.

'I wish we had the room, lovely,' she said, patting his face. 'But we don't. I thought you could stay at Digger's?'

'Shouldn't be a problem,' replied Digger. 'My brother moved out last week so we have a spare room.'

'But I like my own space,' frowned Gary.

'I'm doing you a favour, you ungrateful git,' Digger told him. 'And you will have your own space, you'll have your own room.'

'It's only temporary,' Jackie told Gary. 'And if it keeps you safe it's worth it.'

'True,' he replied. 'And your maw's an amazing cook, Digger.'

'Aye, she is.'

'She won't mind?'

'Nah, she loves you to bits. Sometimes I think she likes you more than me.'

'Don't all the birds?' he grinned.

'So that's settled,' said Jackie. 'It makes me feel better knowing you won't all be on your own.'

'Where's the lovely Allegra gone?' said Digger, looking around. 'Did you scare her off, Jamie?'

'She's gone to arrange a party she's throwing tonight for a cancer charity she set up,' he said with a hint of pride.

'The Rebecca Abernethy Foundation,' said Gary. 'She named it after her mother.'

'You really are turning into a stalker,' frowned Jamie.

'It was in one of those articles I tried to show you about her. I haven't looked up anything about her since you told me not to, and I won't, Jamie.'

'Aye, I know,' he said, relenting a little. His friend was only trying to help him, as well as satisfy his curiosity because he was a nosy bastard.

'Was there anything online about her da?' Jamie asked Gary.

'Aye, loads.' Gary dropped back into gossip mode, eyes lighting up with eagerness. 'There was one about shady business dealings, nobbling his rivals and making their businesses fail.'

'What's nobbling?' said Digger. 'Was he sexually harassing them?'

'No, you mad mental. It means sabotaging.'

'That's hardly anything new,' said Jackie. 'All these rich businessmen get up to stuff like that.'

'But not all of them hire people to break kneecaps. He was investigated for inciting someone to assault a rival but the case fell apart before it got to court.'

'I'll bet it did,' said Jackie. 'Anyone with that much cash can sweep anything unpleasant under the carpet.'

'Have you still got that article on your phone?' Jamie asked Gary.

'No, but I can bring it up for you,' he said, taking out his phone and tapping at the screen. 'There you go,' he said, holding it out to him.

'Cheers, pal,' he replied.

It wasn't so much the article he was bothered about. He just wanted to see the face of Allegra's father, the monster who kept her living in fear, the owner of the cold, harsh voice on the other end of the phone. The man looked like a bully – mean piggy eyes, big build, permanent scowl. Allegra must take after her mother because she in no way resembled that sasquatch. He googled the name Rebecca Abernethy and, sure enough, up popped a photo of a beautiful golden-haired woman with large blue eyes. In the photo she was smiling, and the smile was Allegra's. He found a story about her death and read how she'd died after her car had been struck by another vehicle on a quiet country road and rammed into a tree. Rebecca had been crushed in the car, trapped in the cold and dark for hours before succumbing to her horrific injuries. The other vehicle was never traced, so whoever was responsible got away with it. There were rumours that it had been deliberate, but no one was ever questioned and the death was written off as an accident. Poor Allegra. That was a terrible thing to have to live with. She'd been shown that life was fragile, vulnerable, and could be snatched from you at any second. No wonder she lived so much in the moment.

'Cheers,' he said, handing Gary back his phone.

'No worries,' Gary replied with his amiable smile.

'So,' said Digger. 'Should we wind up Craig about clowns the next time we see him?'

'I think it's worth a go,' said Jamie. 'We need to know if it's true but we do it subtly. No dressing up.'

'Aye, okay,' Gary sighed, disappointed.

'We'll go to the pub tonight and try it.'

'Is that wise?' said Jackie. 'You and Logan are just out of hospital.'

'The sooner we get this sorted the sooner it's over and we can get back to normal.'

'Logan might not feel up to it. He doesn't look well.'

'I'm fine, Mrs Gray,' he told her. 'Honestly.'

'Well, okay, but if you don't feel well you come straight back and you come together. No wandering about in the dark on your own.'

He smiled and nodded. 'Yes, General.'

'Cheeky bugger,' she said with a fond smile.

12

Allegra floated about the vast lounge of the home of her father's friend, ensuring all the guests had everything they needed and that they were having a good time. She made easy small talk before swiftly passing onto the next person. The caterers she'd hired were efficient, so she didn't need to keep booting them up the bum. In her experience, some were lazy sods who you needed to keep on top of to ensure they did their jobs properly, but that wasn't an issue she was faced with tonight. The silent auction she'd arranged was going down very well, the prizes including European city breaks, expensive jewellery, three barrels of fifty-year-old single malt, a couple of yachts and a stunt boat used in the last James Bond film. She'd amazed herself with the things she'd managed to wangle. The drink was flowing and the bidding was high and it looked like she was going to beat the record she'd set last year.

'Allegra, sweetheart,' said Tarquin, her father's friend, wrapping an arm around her shoulders. 'You've done your mother proud. She loved arranging these parties.'

'Thanks,' she said, swallowing down the lump that always formed in her throat whenever her beloved mother was mentioned. She smiled up into Tarquin's face, which was flushed from sampling the single malt in one of the auction barrels. Sometimes she wished he'd been her father, which wasn't likely as he was as gay as a sunny day. He was kind, gentle-looking, with his mop of grey hair and soft brown eyes. As usual he was dressed in sombre greys with a vivid slash of colour – a garish pink waistcoat covered in tiny hand embroidered elephants. Although he was a badass in a boardroom he did have a good heart and had given away a considerable amount of his fortune to charity, unlike her father, who clung onto every penny. Still, Tarquin had kept enough back to enjoy a lavish lifestyle, and why shouldn't he? He'd worked hard for it.

'I meant to ask,' she said. 'Why elephants?'

'Well, they're just so noble, don't you think? So majestic. I was invited to Gordon's house,' he added, nodding at a grossly overweight man guzzling down champagne as though his life depended on it. 'He lives three houses down. He went on safari and killed one of those beautiful beings.' Tears formed in Tarquin's eyes. 'The cowardly savage. I threatened to punch him. How dare he destroy something so beautiful, so pure.'

Allegra wished he was her dad even more. 'That's terrible.'

'I want to go to Thailand and open an elephant sanctuary. It's my dream.'

'That's a lovely dream,' she said, even though she wasn't sure whether this was the drink talking or not.

'I wondered if you could organise the fundraiser for me?'

'I'd love to.'

'Good, but don't invite that backwards brute Gordon McGee.'

'I won't, promise,' she smiled, patting his arm.

Her heart sank when her dad stormed up to her, resembling a thundercloud as usual. Even at a party the man never smiled.

'Allegra,' he told her. 'Stuart Thomson's been here a full hour and you've not spoken to him once. I've been watching you. Every time he tries to approach you, you find a reason to scurry away.'

'Oh, be reasonable,' said Tarquin. 'Stuart's a greasy wee worm. You can't expect our glorious Allegra to waste her time on a creep like that.'

'Stuart's family is one of the richest in the country and I don't just mean Scotland but the entire UK. It's a good match.'

'Dear God, Cameron, we've gone beyond the days of ladies marrying for land and wealth, thankfully. Let the girl be. This is her night, and what a success she's making of it too.'

'How many children do you have, Tarquin?' her father hissed at him through gritted teeth.

'Well, none.'

'Precisely. You know nothing, so keep your beak out of it.'

'It is my business. She's my goddaughter and as her godfather I say she relaxes and enjoys her triumph without having to deal with oily wee squits like Stuart Thomson. I mean, the boy's repellent. Imagine having to eat across from him every day. Why would you want to have a family member who is less attractive than the food?'

Allegra was unable to stifle a snigger and looked down at her very expensive high heels when her father glared at her.

'Besides, I've got a business proposition that might interest you, Cam,' continued Tarquin, putting an arm around his shoulders and leading him away.

'Really?' said Cameron, the prospect of making even more money driving thoughts of Stuart Thomson right out of his head.

'Yes. It's virtually risk-free with a two hundred percent return.'

'I'm listening.'

Tarquin turned to wink at Allegra over his shoulder, who beamed back at him. He'd given her a reprieve, but it would only be temporary. She was itching to speak to Jamie, so she determined to find somewhere quiet to call him from. She had been tempted to sneak him in, perhaps as one of the waiters, but she didn't dare risk her father finding out. Plus she could imagine Jamie taking umbrage at being dressed up as a waiter, especially as he'd already had to pretend to be one.

She turned for the door and was dismayed to see her older brother Fenston walk through it. He'd told her he didn't know if he'd be able to make it and she'd hoped he would be too caught up at work to come, but sadly here he was, striding through the guests towards her with that intolerable smirk on his face. While she took after their mother, he was all their father, although slimmer, and his face hadn't had the chance to take on all the angry lines that scored Cameron's visage.

'Allegra,' he said, air kissing her on one cheek. 'Another triumph, I see.'

Like herself he'd had the Scottish tutored right out of him, although he'd taken it to the extreme and sounded like he'd be more at home at a royal garden party.

'Yes, it's going well,' she replied. 'Thank you for coming.'

The two siblings didn't like each other and had never been close. Fenston had always worshipped at their father's feet while she'd doted on their mother, which had set them at odds against each other at a young age. Plus, Fenston was cold and cruel and his sole purpose in life was making money. Daddy's little monster.

'I wouldn't miss this,' he told her. 'I want one of those whisky barrels for a party I'm hosting next week,' he said with his usual self-satisfied air.

'You hate parties.'

'I do, but I'm trying to sweet-talk a business associate into signing a deal.'

Allegra had no doubt that deal would only benefit Fenston and not his associate. 'Well, feel free to circulate and enjoy the canapés. They're amazing, by the way. You might want to consider the caterers for your own party.'

'I just might. Thank you for the recommendation.'

This was how they always spoke to each other, coldly polite. There was zero emotion between them, and that made Allegra sad. If he'd cared about her she could have confided in him about their father's unnerving interest in her. At least she had Jamie. The thought of him warmed her inside. She had to talk to him, she was missing him.

'Well, if you'll excuse me I need to nip to the loo,' she said.

'Before you go I want to introduce you to another associate of mine,' he replied, turning to indicate the man standing behind him wearing a very expensive suit. 'Meet Craig Lawson.'

Allegra's stomach dropped as she stared into the face of the man who had been fighting in the street with Jamie only earlier that day.

'Craig, this is my sister, Allegra,' added Fenston.

'Nice to meet you, Allegra,' Craig said, holding his hand out to her.

Her hand automatically went out to shake his, after all, she was an impeccably polite hostess. 'You too, Craig,' she heard herself say even though she thought her jaw had been glued shut with surprise. His suit looked tailored and the watch on his wrist was Tag Heuer. Where had he got the money for all that? Then it struck her. 'He's your new security, isn't he?' she asked her brother. He always liked his security to dress as well as he did, as he thought it reflected well on him, so he outfitted them himself.

'Yes, he is,' replied Fenston. 'I got fed up with my last one, he became far too full of himself.'

'Where did you find this one?'

'Through a friend,' was her brother's evasive reply, snatching a canapé from the tray of a very pretty passing waitress. Fenston smiled at the woman, licking his lips suggestively before sliding the entire canapé into his mouth in one go. The woman's lip curled with disgust before she hastily moved on.

While he was distracted, Allegra glanced at Craig, wondering if he'd told her brother about her relationship with Jamie. Craig must have seen the worry in her eyes but he just gave her an enigmatic smile. No, she thought, perhaps he hadn't. If he had, Fenston would have gone straight to their father about it. After all, he'd enjoyed getting her into trouble ever since they were children and Craig seemed like the type who relished wielding power over people. But she couldn't be certain. She had to speak to Jamie.

'Please join in the party, Craig,' she said as politely as she could. 'Help yourself to drinks and nibbles. I'll talk to you later, Fenston,' she said but he'd already been distracted by some business acquaintance of his. He didn't have friends.

Allegra hurried upstairs, locked herself in one of the five bathrooms and took out her phone.

'Jamie,' she breathed when he answered, delighted to hear his voice.

'Allegra,' he replied, sounding equally pleased. 'How's the party?'

'It was going well until a particular guest turned up.'

'Who?'

'Craig Lawson.'

'How the hell did he get in?'

'He's my brother Fenston's bodyguard.'

There was a beat of surprised silence. 'Your brother's called Fenston?'

'Yes, but that's not the point. Craig's working for him and when I asked where they met he was really evasive in his response.'

'Has he told your brother about us?'

'I can't be a hundred per cent certain but I don't think so. Fenston was too relaxed. I'm sure he would have dropped a snide hint and then run straight to my father about it.'

'Are you okay? Do you need me to come over there?'

'I would love for you to come but I think it would make everything worse, especially if something kicked off between you and Craig.'

'He's dangerous.'

'Yes, he is, but there's plenty of people at the party and we're in my godfather's house, who's a good man. I'm safe.'

'Good. I can't believe this. Craig, working for your brother. It doesnae make sense.'

'I know.'

'Does your brother know he's just got out of prison?'

'Undoubtedly. He carefully vets everyone he hires. The idiot prob-ably thinks he's in safe hands being guarded by someone who was locked up for GBH.'

'We found out Craig's weakness, by the way.'

'I knew he had one. What is it?'

'Clowns. That's the rumour, anyway. I havenae been able to test it yet.'

Allegra's natural wildness surged through her. 'Just leave that with me. I've got an idea.'

'Are you gonnae spring a wee surprise on him, doll?'

'Aye, I am.'

'I wish I could be there to see it.'

'If I play my cards right I might be able to record it for you.'

'You are so sexy.'

'Right back at you. I'd much rather be with you than stuck here.'

'Will I still see you tomorrow?'

'I'll come round tomorrow morning. Not too early, though, because I won't get to bed until late.'

'I can't wait to see you,' he replied in a hesitant way that indicated he wasn't used to saying those words.

'Me too. I've got to go before I'm missed. See you tomorrow.'

'Bye, gorgeous,' Jamie replied.

Allegra hung up with a smile, feeling better just for talking to him. She'd messed around with quite a few men off some of the local dodgy estates but he was the only one who had meant anything to her. In fact, she was surprised by just how quickly her feelings for him were growing – she had thought herself incapable of emotion. Yes, he was dark and brooding, sexy and dangerous, which was what she liked, but he was also kind, tender and fun. She liked being with him. He'd also given her the best orgasm of her life, which was a bonus. The others she'd been with had just been meatheads with little interest outside drinking and fighting. If only Jamie had been born into a wealthy family they wouldn't have to keep their relationship secret, her father would have approved, but he was incapable of seeing the worth of anyone beyond their bank account.

Allegra shoved all those thoughts on the back burner, for now. First she had to get through this night, which had been going so well. She grinned wickedly as she got on her phone. She had a last-minute auction to arrange.

After making her call she exited the bathroom and almost walked straight into Craig.

'Hello, beautiful,' he smiled down at her.

'What do you want?'

'To get to know you better,' he replied, planting his hands against the wall either side of her head, penning her in.

'Well, I don't want to get to know you,' she said, attempting to shove away his arm and failing.

'Surely a tosser like Jamie Gray can't satisfy a woman like you?'

'That is not your business.'

'So he doesn't then?' He smirked. 'Or has he not even done the business yet? The fucking poof,' he chuckled.

She shoved him in the chest as hard as she could, causing him to take a couple of steps back, but she knew that was only because he'd chosen to move.

'You know nothing about it,' she said. 'And do you think you have the right to talk to me like this because you work for my brother now? You're not his friend, you know, Fenston doesn't have friends. You're a lacky, a serf, the paid help. Nothing more.'

He shrugged. 'If you're trying to insult me, it won't work. He's paying me a fucking good whack, that's all that matters. Why would I want to be friends with a complete tosspot like him?'

'You're right, he is a tosspot. Now, if you'll excuse me...' She sighed when she tried to move past him and he stepped in front of her, blocking her way. 'What now?' she snapped.

'I just wanted to let you know that your secret's safe with me. I won't tell your brother about Jamie.'

'Why?' she said suspiciously.

'I like having power over you both, as well as knowing something about you that Fenston doesn't.'

'Why am I not surprised? You're as much of a control freak as he is. But know this – if my brother and father do find out then the police will receive an anonymous tip-off about a dead body.'

His green eyes sharpened and narrowed. 'That would be very dangerous for you, sweetheart, as well as Jackie and Charlie. I'm sure you don't want them getting hurt.'

'You keep my secret and I'll keep yours.'

'There is another way to ensure my silence.'

'What?'

'Get back in that bathroom, hitch up that dress and bend over.'

'You're disgusting.'

'And very, very good,' he breathed, leaning into her. 'Looking for your pepper spray?' he said when she rummaged around in her handbag. His eyes widened when she pulled a small knife from the bag and pressed it to his crotch. His green eyes connected with her blue ones, which were filled with the wildness he'd seen before.

'One more word,' she said. 'And your balls will be rolling down the stairs.'

'I like you, Allegra. We'd make a great pair. Together we could take over this city.'

'No, thanks. I'm not into weak little bullies. Or murderers,' she hissed.

He growled, his hand going to her throat.

'I wouldn't do that if I were you,' she said, increasing the pressure on his crotch with the knife, causing him to retract his hand. 'You know how reckless I am. Don't think I won't do it. My father's so rich and influential he'd easily cover it up. He hates any hint of a scandal. After all, what are you? Nothing.'

'I'm more than Jamie will ever be,' Craig spat.

'I don't think so. He's special. There's thousands of pathetic, inadequate creatures like you. You're on borrowed time. Soon you'll be back in prison.'

Craig experienced the overwhelming urge to throttle the bitch but the blade between his legs forced him to rein it in.

'Is that how you did it, Craig?' she pressed. 'Did you kill that poor sod in the photo with a knife? Did you stab him over and over? Did you enjoy it?'

Danger ignited in his eyes, lips drawing back over his teeth. 'Keep asking, bitch, and you'll find out.' His lips twisted into a disturbing smile, green eyes tapering to reptilian slits. 'You're enjoying this, aren't you?' he hissed. 'You like danger. That's why you're asking a killer if he enjoyed the kill.' A deep laugh rumbled in the back of his throat when she failed to reply, telling him he was right.

At the sound of footsteps on the stairs, Allegra kicked him in the shin, causing him to hop backwards and she pelted downstairs, shoving the knife into her clutch bag as she went, politely dodging around the two women coming up the stairs. At the bottom she took a moment to gather herself, heart hammering. One day her love of danger would get her into serious trouble. She glanced back up the stairs and saw a murderer glaring down at her. Perhaps it already had?

One of the caterers told her there was a delivery waiting at the back door. She smiled. Time to test Jamie's information.

She hurried through to the huge kitchen where a large package six feet square waited, wrapped in brown paper.

'Take the paper off and cover it with a dust sheet before carrying it through to the main room,' she told one of the caterers. 'I want the guests to get the full effect of the reveal.'

It took two caterers to manoeuvre it into the main room where they placed it on a waiting easel. As they worked she slyly took her mobile phone out of her bag, propped it up against a vase on a table so it was pointed at the room, and pressed record.

'Ladies and gentlemen,' she announced. 'If I could have your attention, please.'

Everyone turned to look at her. Allegra wasn't the type to get nervous with a hundred pairs of eyes looking her way and she continued, undaunted. 'There's been a last-minute addition to the silent auction.' Glancing around she saw Craig was back in the room, standing politely just behind Fenston's shoulder on guard duty. Everyone's eyes were riveted on the dust sheet anyway, wondering what could be underneath. 'A painting by a famous local artist of Pennywise the Clown from the recent film *IT*.'

As the caterers removed the dust sheet with a dramatic flourish, Allegra – being careful to keep the phone low – pointed it at Craig. His jaw dropped and all the blood drained from his face, but he wasn't the only one who looked shocked. The painting was pretty terrifying, which was why she'd initially rejected it when it had been offered to her for the auction by the rather disturbed artist. The horror of it went beyond even the movie version of Pennywise; the figure crouched, ready to spring, face tilted slightly down, pointed teeth bared, raging for blood and violence. It looked like he could leap out of the frame at any moment.

'I think he's rather marvellous,' said one elegantly attired woman. She waved her wine glass in the air, slopping a few drops down her arm. 'Luke, bid on him.'

The aforementioned Luke appeared to be rather reluctant to do so. However, the woman's comment broke the ice and some of the other guests began to appreciate the excellent execution of the painting. Allegra's attention was fixed on Craig, who had suddenly found the floor very interesting. He ran a hand through his hair; she was pleased to see it was shaking and he appeared to be taking deep breaths.

She told the caterers to place the painting in the back room with the rest of the auction items, the ones that could fit in the house, anyway, as it was making several of the guests distinctly nervous. With a smile she retreated into the kitchen to forward the video to Jamie.

* * *

Jamie and Logan had decided to have a quiet night in. After the day's excitement they were feeling a little under the weather. Jamie was experiencing a lot of tension, the majority of which he didn't think was due to the threat they were facing from the Lawsons. He was slumped on the couch, staring at the television, not seeing the film he was supposedly watching with Logan, thinking of Allegra. When he realised what he was doing he shook himself out of it. Jamie Gray didn't fall in love.

Jackie returned to the living room after putting Charlie to bed. 'Want a lager, boys?' she asked them.

As they both had headaches, they shook their heads.

'Tea it is, then,' she said. 'Have you heard from your da, Logan?'

'Aye, he called when you were upstairs. He's staying at his pal Jimmy's house.'

'Can't say I'm surprised,' she replied, although she was relieved.

'I'll take the couch so Jamie still has his space.'

'As you like. It's a comfy couch.'

'Aye, it'll be smashing,' he replied, looking forward to a few days of being pampered.

Jamie snatched up his phone when it pinged, indicating he had a message. 'It's Allegra,' he beamed.

'Someone's keen,' smiled Logan.

'Only because I want to see if she managed to get that footage of Craig,' he replied.

'Aye, right,' said Logan, glancing at Jackie, who was also smiling.

'She did it,' said Jamie. 'She's sent a video.'

Jackie and Logan sat either side of Jamie on the couch to watch the video.

'Bloody hell, that's a posh drum,' commented Logan. 'Big, too.'

'It belongs to her godfather,' said Jamie.

'Look at that dress,' said Jackie, indicating one woman in a floor length red gown. 'So elegant,' she sighed wistfully.

'There's Craig,' said Logan. 'Where'd he get that suit? He cannae afford gear like that.'

'He's working for Allegra's brother,' said Jamie. 'He probably bought it for him.'

They could hear Allegra's voice making the grand announcement. The shocked looks on the faces of the guests were priceless.

'I'd love to see that painting,' said Logan.

'I don't think I would,' said Jackie.

'Look at Craig. He looks like he's gonnae faint.'

'It seems Gary's information was right.'

'Great,' said Jamie. 'We can have a lot of fun with this.'

'The lassie's done good,' replied Jackie.

'Aye, she did,' he said with a fond smile, wiping it off his face when they both grinned at him.

* * *

When Allegra arrived on Jamie's street at eleven o'clock the following morning she saw one of Craig's friends keeping lookout at the end of the block. When she gunned the engine he turned tail and fled, not wanting to be chased along the pavement again. Before driving around the corner to the garage she called Jamie and asked him to meet her there. After her encounter with Craig she didn't want to risk an ambush, so she drove around to the garage, locked her car doors and waited inside. She smiled when she saw the four Blood Brothers emerge from around the corner, Jamie leading the way, all of them looking serious and strong, even Gary, the joker of the pack. Somehow Logan, too, had an air of fierceness about him, even with the large plaster across his nose. They seemed such nice, amiable men but when they went into war mode they were a sight to behold.

She got out of the car and chucked Digger the keys to the garage while Jamie swept her to him and kissed her. Gary and Digger, who hadn't seen this public display of affection before, stared open-mouthed.

'Get the door open before the Lawsons come along,' Logan told Digger.

'Aye,' he replied, snapping himself out of his surprise. 'On it.'

He raised the garage door and Jamie released Allegra so she could park the car inside.

Once the car was safely tucked away, Jamie slung an arm around her shoulders as they headed back to the Gray home.

'That was great footage you took last night, Allegra,' said Gary. 'We've watched it about ten times and we still piss ourselves each time at how scared Craig looked, the big poof.'

'Glad you enjoyed it, boys,' she smiled.

'Aye, you pulled a blinder, hen,' said Logan.

'Thanks. The creep cornered me when I came out of the bathroom.'

Jamie stopped dead in the street and turned to face her. 'What?' he positively snarled.

'He killed that man in the photo you saw, he practically confessed to me. I only wished I'd managed to record him but he took me by surprise.'

'Did he hurt you?'

'No, because I held a knife to his balls.'

'What?' they all spluttered in unison.

'It's a small one I carry at all times.'

'No one mentions that to my maw,' Jamie told his friends.

All three men nodded seriously.

'Anyway,' continued Allegra. 'He didn't really do anything except try to act the big man.'

'Did he speak to you again last night?'

'Nah. My brother left shortly after that video was taken, he never stays long at these events, so Craig went with him. He looked pretty shaken up, too, he was pale and a bit sweaty.'

'Good,' said Digger as Jamie slid his arm back around Allegra and they all continued back to the house. 'Let's hire clown outfits, shit the bastard right up.'

'What was this painting like?' Gary asked her.

'Terrifying,' she replied. 'I turned it down for the auction at first because I thought it was so creepy. I took a photo of it for you.'

She brought it up and they all recoiled from the image.

'Jesus,' gasped Gary.

'I'm so tired of shocking photos on phones,' mumbled Logan, massaging his temples.

'Someone bought it,' said Allegra. 'For fifteen grand.'

'For that freakshow?' exclaimed Digger.

'They were pretty drunk. They'll have a shock when it's delivered this morning.'

'Did you beat your record for funds raised?' Jamie asked her.

'Aye, thanks to that painting,' she grinned.

They entered the Gray house through the back door where Jackie was waiting for them.

'Allegra, hen,' she said, embracing her. 'You did smashing.'

'You mean the video?'

'Aye, I do. You're one clever lassie.'

'Thanks,' Allegra beamed.

'Now we know we can proper torture that bastard Craig Lawson with his clown phobia,' said Gary.

'Let's go into town and get costumes,' said an eager Digger.

'Do they make them for people made of rocks?' Gary grinned at him, wincing when Digger slapped him around the back of the head.

'We'll look like dicks going around dressed like clowns,' said Jamie. 'We're better hiring someone to do it for us.'

'You mean like a kissogram?' said Logan.

'Aww, that's pure brilliant man,' said Gary. 'We'll hire one to snog him in the pub in front of everyone. He'll scream like a wee lassie.'

'Or he'll punch their wig off their heid,' replied Digger, making him snigger.

'I know just the company we could hire to do it,' said Allegra. 'I've used them several times for parties I've arranged.'

'Is it wise winding Craig up even more?' said Jackie. 'Aren't things bad enough?'

'If we ruin his rep he'll become the local joke,' said Logan. 'And that will make him weak. No one will be feared of him any more.'

'Or it might make him angrier,' she replied. 'And he might think it a coincidence that he's accosted by a clown in the pub after seeing that painting at Allegra's party. He might take it out on her.'

'I can handle it,' said Allegra.

'No offence, hen,' replied Jackie. 'You're strong and smart but I don't think you understand what Craig Lawson is really capable of. Keep poking a bear with a stick and it will bite your hand off.'

Once again, they all looked to Jamie to lead the way.

'What do you think?' Gary asked him.

'I'm not taking any chances with anyone's safety,' he replied. 'We need to come at this from a different angle.'

'The longer we piss about, the longer this lasts and the more danger everyone's in,' Gary countered.

'Let's think through all our options carefully. We must be able to come up with something better than a kissogram.' He looked back at Allegra. 'What hours does he work for your brother?'

'He'll go everywhere he goes.'

'Why does your brother need a bodyguard?' said Digger. 'Is someone after him?'

'No. It just makes him feel important. He likes someone standing guard at his shoulder during business meetings, he thinks it intimidates his rivals.'

'Does it?'

'It depends on who he's dealing with, but Fenston will keep him busy.'

'Wait a minute,' said Gary. 'Your brother's called Fenston?'

She nodded.

He and Digger looked at each other and burst out laughing.

'Nae offence, doll,' Gary managed to gasp through his laughter.

'None taken,' she replied. 'I think it's stupid, myself. It was my dad's idea, he thought it sounded upper class.'

'It sounds wanky,' he grinned.

'That's appropriate because he is a wanker.'

'Well, this is good news,' said Jackie. 'That means he's going to be too busy to bother us.'

'He's still got his little spies,' said Jamie. 'One of them was hanging around the end of our street.'

'Maybe this will blow over and they'll get bored?'

'I don't think it'll be that easy,' said Logan.

'Have there been any reports of a body being found in the area yet?'

'Nah,' said Gary. 'I've been keeping a close eye on the news. Nothing.'

'Maybe they hid it too well?' said Jamie.

'Perhaps,' said Jackie. She glanced at the clock on the kitchen wall. 'Right, does anyone want an early dinner?'

They all nodded their assent and she shooed them into the front room so she could cook in peace. Gary switched on the television and slumped down in front of it with Logan and Digger.

Jamie took Allegra's hand and nodded to the stairs. She smiled and nodded back. Without a word the two of them hurried upstairs.

'He's one lucky bugger,' commented Gary. Digger and Logan nodded in agreement.

Gary flicked to the news and they all went rigid when the newsreader announced a body had been found in the countryside just outside the village of Thorntonhall, six miles south of Glasgow. A photo was shown on the screen of a man in his early thirties named Ben Wilson.

'That's him,' breathed Logan. 'That's the man in the photo.' He leapt to his feet and raced to the bottom of the stairs. 'Jamie, get your arse down here, pronto.'

There was an angry shout from upstairs followed a few seconds later by the thunder of Jamie's footsteps charging down the stairs. He tore into the room red-faced, hair all over the place.

'What the fuck is it now?' he bellowed.

'Look,' said Logan, pointing to the television.

Jamie's anger melted out of him when he saw an image of the murdered man staring back at him from the television screen. 'Holy crap, it's him.'

'What's going on?' said Allegra, walking into the room, fastening a button on her shirt. At the same time, the kitchen door was pulled open by Jackie, who asked the same question.

'It's him,' said Jamie. 'The dead man in the photo.'

'I know him,' said Allegra, staring at the screen in shock. 'He's my father's accountant.'

They all stared at her in surprise before sitting down to listen to the rest of the report. Ben had been beaten and stabbed twenty-four times. It went on to say that he was married with two children.

At the mention of kids, Jackie got to her feet. 'That's it,' she announced. 'We're going to the police.'

'If we do, Craig might do the same to you or Charlie or Allegra,' countered Jamie.

'We've no choice. That man had weans, Jamie. Imagine how they'll be feeling right now, not to mention his poor wife. This has gone beyond us.'

They all looked at each other. It had been easier when the man in the photo had been nameless. That news report had turned him into a real person.

'You're right, Jackie,' said Allegra. 'We can't sit on this any longer.'

'We've known about the photo for days,' said Jamie. 'We've already become accessories.'

'We could find a way around that,' replied Jackie. 'Maybe send an anonymous tip?'

Jamie looked to Allegra. 'What do you know about this Ben Wilson?' he asked her.

'He's worked for my father for six or seven years and my brother for a couple of years, as well as a lot of other rich people. He's a financial genius, apparently, and is good at helping people hide their money.'

'Looks like he pissed someone off,' said Digger.

'Did your da have any trouble with him?' Jamie asked her.

'Not that I'm aware of. I did hear, though, that he cooked the books for a lot of dangerous people and by that I mean gangsters. A lot of his work wasn't legitimate.'

'But we know Craig Lawson killed him,' said Jackie.

'And Craig works for my brother,' replied an unflinching Allegra. 'But I don't think Fenston would have the balls to order someone's death, which means...'

'It was your da,' said Jamie.

'He would certainly have the balls to do it.' Her thoughts turned to her mother and pain lanced through her. 'It wouldn't be the first time.'

'Now let's not jump to conclusions,' said Jackie. 'Craig's been involved with a lot of dodgy people over the years who could have ordered Ben's murder. Or he could have money of his own he wanted to hide, money that could get him sent back to prison if the police found out about it and he decided to kill the only other person who knew about it. We can't assume anyone else is involved yet.'

'Aye, that's a good point, Maw,' said Jamie.

Logan took a deep breath. 'This is all my fault, I nicked that phone. I'll go to the police and explain. I'll make sure you're kept out of it.'

'That's very brave,' said Jackie. 'But the Lawsons will make sure to drop us all in it anyway.'

'Aye,' said Digger. 'And they'd probably make out we knew a lot more about it than we do.'

'Oh, that's a bloody good point,' said Gary. 'They'll twist things to make it look like we did it.'

'But there's DNA and forensics and stuff like that these days,' said Jamie. 'They'd know it wasnae us.'

'It doesn't always work like that,' said Jackie.

'Maybe we won't have to do anything?' said Digger. 'They might find a strand of Craig's hair on the body or John's fingerprints or something and nick them?'

'Aye, maybe,' said Gary, looking more cheerful.

'What if they don't?' said Jamie, his darkening gaze flicking across them all.

'I think our best bet,' said Jackie, 'is to give the police an anonymous tip about who they should be looking for and we take our chances with the Lawsons.'

'I agree,' said Allegra. 'It's the only thing we can do.'

'And how do we do that?' said Gary. 'They'd trace any call we made.'

'Send an email?' said Digger.

'People can be traced through their email accounts and IP addresses on whichever device they use,' said Logan.

'We use a public computer then,' said Digger. 'The internet café or the library.'

'You have to use your library card to get on the computer there, dickhead,' retorted Gary.

'And there will probably be cameras covering the computers at the café,' said Allegra.

'We need someone who can get around all that,' said Jamie. 'What about Mark?' he asked Logan.

'I don't want to involve him,' he replied. 'I reckon he's the one who dobbed me in to Craig in the first place.'

'So, we're stuck,' sighed Jackie, throwing her hands in the air. 'Well,

I'll speak to the police and make something up about how I know it was the Lawsons.'

'We cannae let you do that, Maw,' said Jamie.

'Then it's a good job I'm giving you no choice, isn't it?'

'You could get into trouble with the police, Mrs G,' said Digger.

'That's preferable to that poor man's family sitting at home wondering who killed their loved one.'

'Let's discuss our options a bit more before doing anything rash,' said Allegra.

'I'm hungry,' announced Gary.

'I'm shocked,' said Digger.

Gary ignored him. 'How about I make my famous macaroni cheese for us all? It'll help us think.'

'Sounds lovely,' smiled Allegra. 'I've heard you're a wonderful cook.'

'One of the best in Gallowburn,' he smiled back. 'Do you have the ingredients in, Mrs G?'

'Aye, I think so,' she sighed. 'Let me check.'

Jamie nodded his gratitude at Gary for distracting her, albeit only temporarily.

Once Gary had everything he needed and was absorbed putting together his creation, Jackie returned to the living room to find the others still discussing their dilemma.

'Whatever we're gonnae do we need to do it quick,' said Logan. 'Now the body's found, Craig will be even more desperate. God knows what he'll do.'

Jackie's mobile phone started to ring.

'Oh, what now?' she sighed, snatching it up off the coffee table. 'It's the school,' she added. 'I hope Charlie's not got into any bother, not with everything that's going on.' She put the phone to her ear. 'Hello?'

They all looked to her when she gasped and turned pale.

'What do you mean, you don't know where he is?' Jackie yelled into the phone. 'You're supposed to be taking care of him. You're a primary school, you're not supposed to let weans wander off. If one hair on his head is hurt I'll sue your backsides off.'

'What's going on?' said Gary, returning to the living room, wiping his hands on a tea towel.

'It's Charlie,' Jackie told them all, dialling her younger son's number with shaking hands. 'He's vanished from school.'

'Vanished?' said Jamie. 'How can that happen?'

'They don't know because they're fucking useless. Come on, son, pick up. Please.' She released a small gasp of fear. 'He's not answering.' She hung up and stuffed the phone into her pocket. 'I have to find him.'

'I'll drive you,' said Allegra.

Logan leapt up. 'We'll come with you.'

'Aye, we will,' said Gary, hurrying back into the kitchen. 'Just let me turn the oven off first.'

'No,' said Jamie. 'Me and Digger will go with my maw and Allegra. You two stay here in case Charlie comes back.'

'Okay, pal,' said Logan. 'Whatever you need, we're here.'

Jamie nodded his thanks, his dark eyes turbulent.

'What if it's Craig?' said Jackie, tears in her eyes as she pulled on her shoes. 'What if he's taken him?'

'Let's not jump to conclusions,' said Jamie. 'You remember us at primary school? We were always sneaking out.'

'That's not Charlie, he wouldn't do that. He enjoys school and things are different now. They're not allowed out of the grounds until home time. If he's left the school he didn't do it by choice.'

'I'll get the car out of the garage,' said Allegra, pulling on her coat and snatching up her handbag.

'Digger, go with her,' said Jamie.

He nodded and the two of them ran out of the house through the back door.

13

Jamie and Jackie waited on the street for Allegra and Digger. Jackie was fighting tears, the worry tearing her apart. Jamie spotted a Lawson spy at the far end of the street, who vanished when he realised he'd been seen. Jamie was tempted to run after him, grab the little shit and make him tell him what he knew, but he'd probably be long gone by now. He was better off trying to find Charlie himself.

There was the roar of an engine and Allegra's car raced down the street towards them, Digger in the back seat. Jamie leapt in the front with her while Jackie climbed in the back with Digger. Once they were all in, Allegra sped off down the road with her usual enthusiasm. She had them at the school in under five minutes. Jamie and Jackie ran inside while Allegra and Digger waited in the car. They found the headmistress, the deputy head, Charlie's teacher and the receptionist all gathered together.

'Where's my boy?' Jackie demanded of them, forcing back tears.

'We've searched the school and grounds and there's no sign of him,' said the headmistress. 'He must have sneaked out.'

'That's not Charlie and you know it. And how the hell did he sneak out? You keep the gates locked.'

'The visitor gate is kept unlocked,' she replied.

'I last saw him at break time,' said his teacher, a sweet young woman with big doe eyes. She appeared to be genuinely distressed. 'He was playing with his friends. I only realised he'd gone when they lined up to go back inside. He's usually at the front of the line with a big smile.' A tear rolled down her cheek. 'I'm so sorry.'

'What did his friends say?'

'Tommy saw him in the allotment. Charlie loves the allotment, he's always in there checking on the cabbages and carrots.'

'The allotment's next to the fence, isn't it?'

'Yes.'

'Is there any way through that fence into the playground?'

'There's a gate but it's kept locked.'

'I want to see the gate.'

'This way,' said the headmistress.

They all hurried into the playground, the confident look on the headmistress's face falling when she saw the gate was partly open.

'How did this happen?' she said.

Jackie rounded on her. 'You tell us.'

Her mouth opened and closed.

'Call the police,' Jackie told her. 'Come on, Jamie, we'll look for him.'

They rushed back to the car and got in.

'He's not there and they've no idea where he's gone,' said Jackie. 'The gate at the back of the playground was open when it should have been locked. Charlie wouldn't sneak out. Someone took him.'

'What if it was Craig?' said Jamie.

'Kidnapping a wean would make things even worse for him.'

'I can find out where Craig is,' said Allegra.

'How?' said Jamie.

'I'll call my brother.' She took out her phone and dialled his number. 'Fenston,' she said. 'I need a favour. You know that bodyguard you introduced me to last night?' She scowled. 'No, I do not. Stop being disgusting. I've got a little problem I think he might be able to help me with. Is he there?' She sighed. 'I'll explain later. Is he there, Fenston? Right, okay. Thanks.' She hung up. 'Craig's not with him. Fenston's spending the day at home, so he doesn't need him.'

'So, it could be him,' said Digger.

'It must be,' said Jackie. 'Charlie wouldn't do this by choice.'

Jamie took out his phone when it rang.

'Is it Charlie?' demanded Jackie.

'No. I don't recognise the number,' he replied before answering. 'Hello?'

'Jamie,' said Craig's smug voice. 'I've got something you've lost.'

'You son of a bitch,' he snarled into the handset.

'Don't worry, he's safe. In fact, I'm dropping him off outside your house right now.'

'What the fuck are you doing, Craig?' he bellowed.

'Just a wee warning about what will happen if you go to the police with what you know. I wasn't even the one who took him. It was a friend of mine, a friend who's willing to do even worse if anything should happen to me. He's not the only one either. I have many friends, Jamie. You've seen how easily I can get to your wee brother. You go to the police and he'll be the first to suffer and next time he won't be coming home. I can get to any of you at any time. Just you remember that.'

'Craig,' yelled Jamie when the line went dead. Immediately he dialled Logan's number.

'He's got him, hasn't he?' said Jackie, white-faced.

'Yes, but he's okay. He said he was dropping him off at home. Logan,' he said when his friend answered. 'Is Charlie... oh, thank Christ.' He looked to the others. 'He's home, he's fine. A wee bit upset but that's it.'

'Thank you, God,' breathed Jackie, tears rolling down her face. Digger put his arm around her and she buried her face in his shoulder.

'Let's get back there,' said Allegra, starting the engine.

'What did Craig say?' Jackie asked her son as Allegra drove.

'Taking Charlie was a warning to keep our mouths shut. He wanted to prove that he can get to any of us at any time and Charlie will be the first to suffer if we go to the police. He said he wasn't even the one who took him, it was a friend. He said he has plenty of friends who can get to us whenever they want.' He wondered if he should tell her this after all she'd been through today, but she needed to know the danger. 'He said next time Charlie won't come home.'

'Oh, God,' she said. 'We can't go to the police now. Lord knows I want to help that poor man's family get justice, but I am not risking my baby to do it. He won't be safe anywhere he goes.'

'Let's just twat the fucker,' exploded Digger. 'If he's laid up in hospital with all his limbs broken he won't be able to hurt Charlie. Then we can tell the police what we know, he'll get banged up, job done.'

'You don't get it, Digger,' said Jackie. 'Craig isn't a thug and a bully like the rest of his family. He's evil and he has equally evil friends. He was in prison for nearly five years, don't forget. Just imagine the people he knows, people who won't think twice about hurting a ten-year-old boy. I'm not taking any chances.' Even though her boy was home she was still terrified for his safety. Memories of her brother lying dead in the street returned, his sightless eyes staring up at the sky. She couldn't bear for one of her boys to be found that way.

'Maw's right,' said Jamie. 'Craig said if anything happens to him, his friends will come for us and they won't go for me or you first. They'll go for Maw and Charlie.'

'Jesus Christ, this is a nightmare,' said Digger.

They returned to the Gray home in worried silence.

'I'll come with you to put your car away,' Jamie told Allegra as she pulled up at the kerb.

'I'll go with her,' said Digger. 'Go and see your brother.'

'Thanks, pal,' he replied, patting his arm before racing inside.

'Charlie,' breathed Jackie, gathering the sobbing boy into her arms. 'Are you okay, sweetheart?'

'I'm sorry, Maw,' he hiccuped between sobs. 'I didn't want to leave school but he made me. Is Miss Armstrong angry?'

'Of course she isn't. She was as worried about you as we were. You are not in any trouble, I promise.'

'Really?' he said, calming down a bit.

'Promise. What happened?'

'I was in the allotment looking at the carrots. I planted some myself and I check on them every day, they'll be ready to dig up soon. I heard someone at the gate calling my name, so I went over. Then the gate opened and I was pulled out. I tried to call for Miss Armstrong but he put his hand over my mouth.'

'Who did, sweetheart?' Even though Craig had said a friend of his had taken Charlie she wanted to be sure. She didn't trust a word that came out of that snake's mouth.

'I don't know, I've never seen him before but he was big and scary and he had a scar on his face. He put me in his car and another man was there.'

'What man? Did you recognise him?'

He nodded. 'It was Craig, Patrick's big brother.'

'Patrick Lawson in the year above you at school?'

Another nod.

'What happened next?'

'We just drove around. Craig told me to stay quiet and everything would be okay. I told him I wanted to go back to school, my teacher would be angry but he wouldn't let me. Then he said he was taking me home.'

'Did they hurt you?'

'Craig shouted at me, he was so mean,' he frowned. 'The man with the scar didn't say anything.'

'So they didn't hit you or anything like that?'

'No.'

'Thank God,' she breathed, cuddling him tighter. She leaned back to regard him, cradling his face in her hands. 'I need you to listen to me, Charlie.'

He nodded seriously.

'We can't tell the school who really took you. Craig's a bad man and if he gets into trouble he might do something even worse. We have to tell the school that the gate was already open and you wandered out.'

'But that's lying. I can't lie to Miss Armstrong.'

'I know I'm always telling you not to lie, baby, and usually I wouldn't but this is very serious. The men who took you said they'd hurt us all if we say anything. They're very bad men who've done terrible things. This is a white lie to protect us all.'

'So it wouldn't be wrong then?'

Jackie had no idea how she'd raised such a moral boy on this estate but there really was something different about Charlie. He had such a strong sense of what was right and wrong and it was difficult for him to go against that. 'No, it wouldn't,' she told him. 'Sometimes lies are necessary to protect ourselves.'

'But they'll be angry with me, I'll get detention.'

'No, you won't, I swear. They'll just be happy you're safe. Miss Armstrong and the headmistress were so worried about you.'

'They were?' he said with wonder.

'Aye. Now I need to call them to let them know you're home. Do you want anything?'

'Am I going back to school?'

'No, you've had a shock. Take today off.'

'Can I have some ice cream?'

'Of course you can.'

'I'll get it,' said Jamie, heading into the kitchen.

Jackie gave Charlie another hug before switching on the television for him. She smiled as he settled himself on the couch beside Gary.

'What do you want to watch, wee man?' Gary asked him. 'Cartoons?'

'Yay, I love cartoons.'

He grinned down at him. 'Me too.'

Soothed by the sound of his cartoons, Charlie picked up his drawing pad and crayons off the coffee table.

'What are you doing, fella?' Gary asked him.

'Drawing what I saw today.'

'Good plan,' he replied before he was distracted by a bird dropping an anvil on a dog's head.

'You okay, Maw?' Jamie asked her when she entered the kitchen and buried her face in her hands.

'Aye, son, I'm just so relieved.'

'Me too,' he replied, scooping ice cream into a bowl.

'Now I need to lie to the school,' she said, dialling. The school were so pleased Charlie was safe and relieved that Jackie wasn't going to sue them that they questioned nothing and told her they'd let the police know. She felt bad about lying to them, they were good people, but she'd lie to Jesus Christ himself if it kept her children safe.

Allegra and Digger came in through the back door.

'How's Charlie?' said Allegra.

'Fine,' replied Jamie. 'They didnae lay a finger on him. He'll be fine. Hopefully he'll forget about it soon. He was more upset he missed school.'

'There's a couple of the Lawsons hanging about on the back street,' said Digger. 'But they didn't do anything.'

'They're spying on us,' said Jamie. 'Keeping Craig informed.'

'Somehow I don't think they'll get bored and go away. We can't go to the police, so we have to end this ourselves.'

'But how?' said Jackie. 'If we do anything they'll target Charlie again.'

'I don't know, Maw,' said Jamie. 'But we'll figure it out.'

Allegra and Digger followed Jamie into the living room when he took Charlie's ice cream through.

'Allegra,' beamed Charlie.

'Hello, big man,' she said, sitting beside him and giving him a cuddle. 'How are you doing?'

'Fine,' he replied, putting on a nonchalant front. 'They didn't scare me.'

'I bet they didn't. You're so tough.'

Jackie could have kissed Allegra when the sparkle returned to her younger son's eyes. Kids were so resilient.

'Here's your ice cream,' said Jamie, handing Charlie the bowl and spoon.

'Thanks,' he said, disappointed when Allegra released him. 'Do you want some, Allegra?'

'No thanks, sweetie. You have it all, you've earned it.'

He grinned at her before tucking in.

Allegra spotted Charlie's drawing pad, which had been discarded on the coffee table.

'What's wrong?' said Jamie when she paled.

She picked up the drawing pad and stared in astonishment at the sketch of the scarred, shaven-headed man. When Charlie looked at her questioningly, she forced a smile. 'You're a great artist, Charlie.'

'Thanks,' he beamed, ice cream smeared around his mouth.

She replaced the pad on the coffee table and nodded at the others to join her in the kitchen. Only Gary remained in the living room, lost in the cartoons, oblivious to the world around him.

'That face Charlie drew,' she said. 'I know him.'

'You sure?' frowned Digger. 'It looked like Mr Potato Head.'

'That scar's unmistakeable. He's called Neil Burrows. He's worked for my father for years.'

'Doing what?' said Jamie.

'He calls him his odd-job man,' she replied.

'I get the feeling this odd-job man doesn't mean he changes light bulbs or mows the lawn,' said Jackie.

'No. He's my father's bully boy who threatens people into doing what he wants. I have even known him to break kneecaps and elbows. Because my dad's so influential he never gets into trouble.'

Jackie closed the kitchen door so Charlie wouldn't overhear and looked to Allegra. 'First we find out that deid body is a man who worked for your da and now the man who abducted Charlie also works for him. I hate to ask this, but is it possible Ben's murder is linked to your da?'

Allegra swallowed hard and nodded. 'Yes, very possible. He had my mother killed, I know he did, so if he could do it to her he could do it to anybody.'

Jamie wrapped a comforting arm around her and she leaned into him.

'It's too much of a coincidence that Craig used this Neil to help snatch Charlie to threaten us into keeping quiet about this body,' said Jamie. 'Craig wouldn't want to risk anyone else finding out about it, which means Neil was in on Ben's murder.'

'Perhaps,' said Logan. 'Or maybe he's just a sadist who likes doing bad things and was happy to help?'

'No,' said Jamie, shaking his head. 'Everything Craig has done so far is to stop word from spreading. Why would he drag someone else into it now?'

'Good point,' replied his friend.

'Maybe I can find something out?' said Allegra. 'Ask around some of the people who work for my father and find out if he had any recent fallings out with Ben?'

'Don't go putting yourself in harm's way, okay?' Jamie told her. 'Leave it to the police.'

'Okay,' she replied, pleased with his concern.

'The ice cream van,' came Charlie's voice from the living room at the sound of chimes from outside. 'Maw, can I have an ice lolly?'

'He's ice cream daft is that boy,' said Jackie with fondness in her eyes. She walked back into the living room. 'You've just had a bowl full of the stuff,' she told him.

'That was ice cream,' he said slyly. 'This is an ice lolly.'

She smiled at his hopeful little face. How could she refuse after what he'd been through? 'Aye, course you can, but you're no' to go out there alone,' she said, afraid he'd step out the door and be snatched again.

'I'll take him,' said Jamie.

'Thanks, sweetheart,' breathed Jackie, relieved she wouldn't have to face Ephraim.

'I'll come too,' said Allegra. 'I could just go an ice lolly.'

'I like strawberry splits,' said Charlie. 'Do you like strawberry splits, Allegra?'

'I love them.'

She took his hand and they left the house, followed by Jamie and Digger, who stalked behind them like bodyguards.

Ephraim's eyes widened at the sight of the vision approaching his van. 'Now, who is this divine angel I see before me?'

'I'm Charlie Gray,' said the boy.

'No' you, ya wee fanny,' he retorted. He nodded at Allegra. 'I mean her.'

'She's Allegra,' he replied, taking no offence at the insult. 'She's a good friend of my brother's.'

'You're with him?' he frowned, pointing at Jamie.

'I am,' she smiled back. 'Do you have any strawberry splits?'

'Aye.'

'Two, please.' She looked over her shoulder at Jamie and Digger. 'Do you want anything, boys?'

'I'd pure love a ninety-nine,' said Digger.

'Jamie?'

'I'm good, thanks.'

She turned back to Ephraim. 'And a ninety-nine,' she said, placing some money on the counter.

'Hey, Charlie,' called a voice. 'Why aren't you in school?'

Charlie whimpered with fear and hid behind Allegra.

'You bastard,' yelled Jamie, racing up to meet Craig.

'Don't, Jamie,' called Allegra. 'That's what he wants.'

She had hoped Digger would intervene but, on the contrary, it looked like he was as keen as his friend was for a fight and he raced after Jamie. Craig just stood there, grinning as John and another five Lawsons rushed to his side.

Jackie, who had been anxiously keeping watch from the window, terrified her youngest son would vanish again, raced out the front door and down the garden path.

'Jamie, stop,' she screamed.

'Still being told what to do by your maw at your age,' goaded Craig.

Jamie came to a halt, fighting with himself. He was very conscious of all the neighbours peering out of the windows and coming out of their houses to watch. If he backed down then the Blood Brothers' reputations would be ruined, but he didn't want to put Charlie at risk again. His rage won out and he continued pelting down the street towards the Lawsons.

'Stop right there, ya wee fuds.'

They all stopped in their tracks at the sound of Ephraim's snarl. They turned to see him standing on the pavement, one of his home-made toothbrush crossbows in his hands, the bow drawn back, a lethal dart waiting to be fired. Incensed by the fear in Jackie's eyes, he'd leapt to her defence.

'Back off you lot,' he said, aiming the weapon at Craig's chest. 'Unless you want to be used as target practice.'

'You taking their side now, Ephraim?' retorted Craig.

'I don't take sides but you're putting off all my nice customers from buying something. And you upset Jackie. No one upsets Jackie.'

The mania that lit up his eyes persuaded them all that Ephraim was not in the mood to be messed with.

Craig looked back at Jamie. 'We'll see you around.'

'You bet you will, you fucking wanker,' roared Digger.

Jamie pressed a hand to his friend's chest to prevent him from charging full tilt at the Lawsons.

Everyone lost interest when the Lawsons sauntered away, throwing glares back over their shoulders, and Jamie and Digger returned to the ice cream van.

'You okay, Jackie, hen?' Ephraim asked her, lowering the crossbow.

'Aye,' she replied. 'Thanks. I appreciate what you did.'

'Anytime for you,' he said adoringly. 'Do you want an icey?'

'Er, aye, thanks,' she replied, feeling it would be rude to just go straight back into the house.

'Great,' he grinned, eagerly clambering back inside the van. 'What can I get you, doll?'

'I'll have an oyster shell with vanilla ice cream, please, Ephraim.'

'And we still need our strawberry splits,' piped up Charlie.

'Coming right up, wee man,' said Ephraim. 'Hey, you lot,' he yelled at a group of teenagers hanging about the van, waiting to be served. 'Get your arses in a proper line before I lop your spotty heids right off.'

The boys hurriedly arranged themselves into a tidy line that didn't offend Ephraim's sense of aesthetics. He dumped two strawberry splits on the counter before turning his attention to Jackie's order, putting it together with a flourish before lovingly scattering chocolate sprinkles all over it. As a finishing touch he swaddled it tenderly in a serviette as though it were a newborn babe.

'Here you go, hen,' he said, passing it to her.

'Thanks, it looks lovely,' she replied, taking it from him. 'How much do I owe you?'

'On the house, and if you have any more trouble with the Lawsons you just let me know.'

'I will. You've been very kind.'

Jackie went rigid when his hand came out of the van and clamped down on her arm. 'I'm always here for you, Jackie,' he told her. 'Always.'

'Aye, that's great,' she said, backing away, forcing him to release her. She looked to her eldest son. 'Get inside, right now. You too, Digger.'

The pair of them slinked into the house along with Allegra and Charlie. Jackie was last, able to feel Ephraim's eyes burning into her back. At least for once his crush had paid off.

'What did we just say?' Jackie yelled at Jamie and Digger the second she'd closed the door behind them.

'What were we supposed to do?' retorted Jamie. 'They were challenging us in front of everyone. We couldn't back down.'

'Jamie's right, Mrs Gray,' said Digger. 'They're trying to use this to destroy the Blood Brothers. If they manage that then we're definitely finished. Our reps protect us all.'

'We have to be more sensible about this than brawling in the street,' she said. 'Allegra, sweetheart, take Jamie out somewhere, will you? He needs to let off some steam before he does something stupid.'

Allegra was delighted by this request. 'No problem.'

'Can I go too?' said Charlie, not wanting to be separated from Allegra.

'No, baby,' replied Jackie more gently. 'They need some privacy.'

'Aww,' he pouted.

'Stay with them, will you?' Jamie asked his friends.

All three nodded.

'Come on,' said Allegra, grabbing his hand and practically dragging him to the door.

Before he could utter a single word, he found himself being pulled outside the kitchen door into the backyard.

'We can't leave them,' said Jamie. 'What if the Lawsons come back?'

'They won't, not for a wee while anyway,' she replied, pushing open the gate and hauling him into the back street. 'Not after Ephraim threatened them with a crossbow.'

'You said wee,' he smiled.

'You're bringing out the Scottish in me,' she grinned back. 'Did you see that crossbow? It was made out of toothbrushes.'

'I did.'

'Did he make it himself?'

'Yeah. He's made weapons himself for years.'

'He must be so smart.'

'You don't fancy him, do you?'

'God, no,' she laughed. 'But I do admire his creativity.'

Jamie opened the garage door, allowing Allegra to steer the car out. He closed the door and hopped into the front passenger seat.

'So where do you want to go?' he asked her.

'I know the perfect place,' she replied, setting off.

'Where? Knowing you it'll be a missile testing site or a zombie apocalypse experience.'

'Neither of those. Somewhere much quieter and more intimate.'

They drove out of Gallowburn and onto the motorway. They'd been on it for less than five minutes when she pulled off again.

'Where are we going?' he asked her.

'Like I said, somewhere private.'

'Don't tell me, you've got your own personal dungeon.'

'You sound nervous, Dangerous.'

'I don't get nervous,' Jamie replied with his best glower.

'I promise you're not about to be tied up and whipped.'

'That's a relief.'

'Is that not your thing, then?'

'No. Why, is it yours?'

'God, no.'

Jamie was secretly relieved about that. 'So, where are we going?' he pressed.

'I don't want to spoil the surprise.'

He wondered if they were going somewhere they could finally cement their relationship, or if she was taking him on another of her weird adventures. Perhaps even a combination of the two?

'We're going to West Maryston?' he said when they passed a sign.

'We are.'

'There's nothing there but grass and trees.'

'I know. We won't be disturbed.'

'Great,' he smiled. 'Although I wouldnae be surprised if Logan or my maw turned up because something else happened.'

She looked up at the sky. 'The weather's a bit iffy, there's some cloud moving in.'

'It'll be fine,' he said with more hope than certainty. 'My gran and granddad lived at West Maryston before it was demolished. Then they were moved onto the Gallowburn.'

'Think of it as a trip through your family history.'

'I wouldnae want my gran seeing what I'm hoping to do with you out there.'

'I'll bet.'

After driving along a narrow winding road, they found a pull-in point where they could park up.

'Come on,' she said, hopping out and setting off at a vigorous pace.

'How do you walk so fast in those heels?' he said, rushing to catch up.

'Practice.'

He glanced up at the sky, not liking the gathering clouds.

'Here we go,' she said, pulling him into the trees.

His worries about the weather were eradicated when she kissed him. With a groan he pushed her up against a tree, sliding his hand up her thigh when she wrapped one leg around his waist.

'No more foreplay and messing about,' she panted, already unfastening his jeans. 'We've waited long enough for this.'

'Too right,' he said, pushing her skirt up to her waist. His entire body ached with anticipation, he'd never wanted a woman so much in his life. 'Christ, I don't believe it,' he yelled when the heavens finally opened and drenched them in icy rain, so cold it took their breath away.

'Oh, that is so not sexy,' she winced.

'Definitely not.'

'Let's get back to the car,' she said, tugging down her skirt.

Holding hands, they hurried back down the track, relieved when they saw the car up ahead. Allegra unlocked it with the key fob.

'Nope,' she said, grabbing the back of his jacket when he moved to get into the front. 'In the back,' she told him.

'You are freakishly strong,' he told her when he found himself shoved towards the back door.

He held it open for her to get in, intending to be a gentleman for the first time in his life, but he was pushed inside, falling onto his back. Allegra jumped in after him, landing on top of him, pulling the door shut behind her.

'Now this is cosy,' she smiled down at him, her wet hair dripping tiny cold drops onto his face.

'We can't do it here,' he said when she unzipped his jeans. 'We're right next to a road.'

'The windows are tinted. No one can see in.'

'What if someone drives past?'

'Who's mad enough to come up here in this weather?'

'Apart from us?'

She unbuttoned her shirt, revealing her breasts, encased in a plum-coloured satin bra. 'I can always take you home if you prefer?'

'Come here,' he said, pulling her down to him and kissing her while pushing up her skirt.

She moved like a whirlwind. The next thing he knew her underwear was gone. His own underwear, along with his jeans, were down his ankles and he was inside her, finally. Allegra moaned and tossed back her head, the ends of her wet hair tickling his bare legs. The sweat poured off him as the temperature in the car skyrocketed, despite the furiously pounding rain bashing against the car. Once again, she'd made him feel disorientated and overwhelmed. He'd been Allegra'd and it was fantastic.

She bucked and cried out, fingers creating smear marks through the steam masking one of the windows while he clung onto her bare thighs as she lifted him higher than he'd ever gone before. Everything reached a crescendo, her cries echoing in his ears, mingling with his own, the scent of coconut filling his head, his body going rigid as the orgasm gripped him. Then he could breathe again, and she flopped forward onto him, resting her head on his chest. He wrapped his arms around her and kissed the top of her head.

'Well, that's a relief,' he said, making her laugh.

She raised her head to look into his eyes. 'Finally. I've wondered what that would feel like ever since I first saw you through the shop window.'

'And?'

'It was even better than I imagined.'

'Good,' he said, kissing her.

'What is it?' she said when his eyes widened.

'We didn't think about protection.'

'Relax, I'm on the Pill. Don't worry.'

He breathed a sigh of relief. His maw had repeatedly told him she wasn't ready to be a grandma and he'd always told her he wouldn't be so stupid, but he'd forgotten about protection because he'd been so overwhelmed with lust.

The couple curled up together in the back of the car, Allegra enjoying being cradled in Jamie's arms. He made her feel so safe and cared for. She closed her eyes, enjoying the feel of his fingers playing through her hair. When they gently kissed he attempted once again to push her shirt off her shoulders.

'Sorry,' he said when she sat up and pulled it back around her. 'I forgot but you don't need to be paranoid about your body. You're gorgeous.'

'Thanks, but... I'm not ready for that.'

'That's okay.' His ran his hand across her bra. 'I'm aching to see you without this on, though.'

'That can be arranged,' she said, unhooking the bra at the back, sliding the straps down under the shirt and whipping it off.

Desire surged through him again and he pulled her to him and kissed her, pulling off his own t-shirt so he could enjoy the feel of her bare skin against his.

'Sorry,' he said again when he tried to roll her onto her side.

'Sit up,' she told him.

He obeyed and she straddled him.

'You're insatiable, Dangerous,' she said, releasing a gasp when he slid inside her.

'I am with you, Princess,' he breathed shakily. 'I can't get enough of you.' He touched her face with his fingertips. 'You're perfect.'

Too late. He was falling in love.

14

Jamie felt much more able to face up to the mess with the Lawson family after his and Allegra's time alone. Jackie smiled at how relaxed he looked when they walked through the door together holding hands.

'Did you have a nice time?' she asked them.

'Aye, we did,' said Jamie, he and Allegra smiling at each other. 'We thought we'd go to the pub for a drink.'

'Is that wise? The Lawsons might be there.'

'So what? I'm no' hiding away. Anyone else up for it?'

'Aye,' said Digger, leaping to his feet.

'Me too,' said Gary. 'I'm gagging for a pint.'

'I'll come too,' said Logan. His nose was aching, he didn't really feel like a pint, but he refused to let his friends down again.

'Maybe you should stay here with my maw and Charlie?' Jamie told him, recognising Logan wasn't feeling very well.

'If you insist,' he replied, flopping back onto the couch.

'Are you sure you want to go?' Jackie asked Allegra. 'It might get rough.'

Her eyes sparkled. 'Good.'

'Have you got your pepper spray?'

'Always.'

'Are you sure about this?'

'We have to show everyone that we won't let the Lawsons intimidate us,' replied Jamie.

'Okay, I see that, but please be careful and stick together. Don't go anywhere alone.'

'Aye, Maw,' sighed Jamie, not liking being spoken to as though he were five years old in front of Allegra.

The four of them left, Allegra and Jamie leading the way, his arm around her shoulders, the pair of them smiling at each other while Digger and Gary followed, still a little startled by how quickly their usually strong, distant leader was falling for this woman.

'Where you off to, Jamie?' Ephraim, who was chatting to a couple of pals at his van, called after him.

'To the pub,' he replied.

'Is your maw going?'

'Nah, she's looking after Charlie.'

'Oh,' he said, looking back to the house, hoping to catch a glimpse of his crush, but she'd closed the curtains.

Digger led the way into The Bonnie Brae, slapping the door open aggressively with his palm.

'Oh,' he said, coming to a halt. 'The Lawsons aren't here.'

'Get your big rocky body out the way,' Gary told him, pushing him in the back. 'I'm gagging for a pint.'

Digger side-stepped, allowing them all to enter and they approached the bar.

'Well, this looks to be going well,' said Deirdre, smiling at Jamie and Allegra.

'Aye, it is,' he grinned.

'Sit yourselves down. I'll bring your drinks over.'

'Thanks, Deirdre,' he replied.

The four of them took a seat, Jamie and Allegra curling up into one of the booths together.

'Oy,' said Gary when they started to kiss. 'Do you mind?'

'Mind what?' said Jamie.

'You're making us feel like gooseberries.'

'I'm no' surprised you feel like one,' Digger told him. 'You look like one and all.'

'You're not sexually repressed, are you?' Allegra asked Gary.

He turned crimson. 'No, I'm bloody not. It's just not much fun sitting here watching you two going at it when I've no' had a girlfriend for three months.'

'Maybe we can find someone for you?' Allegra said, looking around the pub, spotting a group of four women Gary's age chatting at a table in the corner. 'Look, they're pretty,' she said. 'Well, two of them are. Do you want me to have a word with them for you?'

'Aye,' grinned Digger. 'Beg one of them to shag him because he hasnae had his hole in months.'

'I wouldn't put it like that,' she replied, unaware he was cracking a joke. 'I'd be subtle.'

'Please don't,' said Gary, by now so red he looked like he was about to keel over from a heart attack. It was made worse by Deirdre arriving at the table with their drinks on a tray, doing her best not to laugh.

'You're a good catch, Gary,' said Allegra, getting to her feet. 'It's lack of confidence, that's all.'

'The lassie's right,' said Deirdre, placing his pint before him, eyes dancing with amusement. 'I'm sure she can hook you up with a nice wee woman.'

Gary had never been pleased to see the Lawsons before but when Craig, John and three more of them walked through the door and Allegra retook her seat, he wanted to throw his arms around them in gratitude.

'Oy,' Deirdre told them. 'I'll have no trouble in here. You want to start a rammy, you do it outside.'

Craig held up his hands. 'We're just here for a pint, that's all.'

'You'd better be telling the truth, Craig Lawson.'

'I swear I am.'

'That'll be a first.' She stalked back behind the bar. She was serving on her own because this time of day was usually pretty quiet and her husband was at the dentist. 'What will it be, boys?' she asked the Lawsons.

They ordered pints all round and as she poured Craig turned his attention to Jamie and his friends. 'So, you're still with him, are you, doll?' he asked Allegra.

'Yes,' she said, taking Jamie's hand.

'I didn't used to get why you were with him. Now I know.'

Allegra turned cold when she realised one of the men accompanying Craig was an ex-boyfriend of hers. She'd once found the blonde-haired, blue-eyed man standing beside Craig physically attractive, but now he just looked like a particularly malevolent rat.

'You must remember Isaac,' continued Craig. 'He's my cousin. He lives on the Easterhouse scheme.'

'Why should she know that walloper?' glowered Jamie.

'Allegra knows Isaac very well. They spent a lot of time together, didn't you, Isaac?' he said, turning to his cousin, who leered more than smiled.

'Bollocks,' said Jamie.

'Is it?' Craig looked to Isaac. 'What are the names of Allegra's other special friends?'

'There's Leo Miller,' he replied. 'He lives in Possilpark and Danny Barker in Barlanark.' His face split into an unnerving grin. 'And Noah Anderson. He lives in Keppochhill. He's just been sent down for fourteen years for attempted murder. Still, he'll have nice memories of you to get him through, eh, sweetheart?' he winked at Allegra.

Jamie shot to his feet. 'You lying bastard.'

Allegra rose too and stood in front of him when Jamie attempted to make a move on the grinning Isaac. 'I do know those men,' she said quietly, not wanting anyone else to overhear.

All the anger drained out of him, replaced by pain. 'What?'

'He's telling the truth,' she whispered.

'Looks like you've got yourself a posh bird after a bit of rough,' said Craig, casually leaning against the bar. 'That's all you are to her, Jamie. She wanted to slum it and you were the perfect candidate.'

'Aye, she pure loves us trash,' grinned Isaac. 'Me and Leo and Danny enjoyed comparing notes about her. I'm sure Noah will share his very pleasant memories of her with his new pals in Barlinnie.'

'You piece of shit,' yelled Digger, shooting to his feet.

'Oy, no fighting,' screeched Deirdre, running around from behind the bar with one of Ephraim's razor whips. 'Aye, that stopped you in your tracks, didn't it?' she told Digger, brandishing it threateningly. 'The first bastard who makes a move is gonnae get this right in his trouble-making face, do you hear me?' she said, looking from the Blood Brothers to the Lawsons.

'Like I said,' replied Craig. 'We're just here for a quiet pint.'

'Don't lie to me,' she retorted.

'Jamie has the right to know the truth about his new girlfriend,' said Craig, green cat's eyes narrowing. 'I'm trying to do him a favour.'

'I know exactly what you're trying to do. He's got something nice in his life and you want to spoil it. Don't let him spoil it for you, Jamie.'

But Jamie couldn't hear her; his attention was riveted on Allegra. Digger and Gary looked to him to tell them how to handle the situation, but he'd forgotten the rest of the pub existed.

'Is it true?' Jamie asked her.

The hurt in his eyes brought a lump to her throat. 'I hung around with them but I never slept with them and that's the truth.'

'Don't tell me you've forgotten about all the time we spent in the back of your wee blue car, going at it like knives,' said Isaac, thrusting his pelvis back and forth.

Jamie's instinct was to pulverise the arsehole into the floor, but he was struggling with feelings that were entirely new to him, a deep well of pain opening up inside him that he'd never known before. So instead of tearing into Isaac as he was longing to do, he turned and hurried towards the door at the back of the pub before anyone saw that pain and used it against him. The door led towards the toilets but he walked past them and through the door at the end of the passage that led outside.

'Jamie, wait,' called Allegra, hurrying after him.

Digger and Gary made a move towards the Lawsons, intent on defending their friends, but Deirdre cracked the razor whip with the skill of Indiana Jones, forcing the two groups to keep their distance, so they had to content themselves with standing at opposing sides of the room, glaring at each other.

* * *

'Jamie, hold on,' called Allegra, rushing after him.

'Why?' he retorted over his shoulder. 'You wantin' to humiliate me some more?'

'If you'd just let me explain.'

'What's to explain? You wanted a bit of rough and you got it. Where's next on the agenda, Princess, Govan?'

'That's not fair,' she retorted, having to break into a run to catch up. She grabbed him by the arm, forcing him to stop. 'At least give me the chance to defend myself before condemning me.'

He rounded on her, eyes blazing with hurt. 'Get on with it, then,' he snapped.

'I know those men, I even messed around a bit with them but Isaac was lying. I never slept with him. I never slept with any of them. Just you.'

'You expect me to believe that?'

'It's the truth. I admit, I enjoyed the excitement. Their lives were so different to mine and I was curious, but they were wallopers.'

The word sounded so strange coming from her lips that he couldn't help but smile. He immediately crushed it with his pain and hurt. 'How can I believe that?'

'Because I do not sleep with every man I meet. You're special, Jamie. They weren't.'

'It's funny Isaac just happened to mention having sex with you in your car when that's exactly what we did today.'

'Well, it's hardly a stretch of the imagination, is it? He knows my car but the only person I have ever done that with in my car is you.'

There was something so straightforward and brutally honest about Allegra that it was hard to imagine she was lying. But Jamie's pride had been hurt, he'd been humiliated in front of his friends, as well as half a dozen people in the pub.

He gazed at this stunning, unique woman with her expensive clothes, immaculately styled hair and nail extensions. She was like something from another realm, out of place on the unkempt streets of Gallowburn, a discarded crisp packet fluttering around her designer shoes in the breeze, the pair of them surrounded by the grim Gallow-burn houses. Once again, that strange superstitious fear gripped him as he felt the estate could swallow her whole as it had so many others. Letting her go might be the right thing to do for her but inwardly he rebelled against the thought.

'Please, Jamie,' Allegra said, reaching out to take his hand. 'This is going so well. Don't let them spoil it.'

He didn't want to let her go, he hadn't felt this good in a long time, but he refused to be taken for a ride.

'I'll prove how much you mean to me,' she said when it appeared he was going to turn his back on her. 'I'll show you something I've never shown anyone else.'

'It seems most of Glasgow's seen everything you've got to offer.' He felt ashamed when her blue eyes filled with tears. 'What the hell are you doing?' he said when she dumped her handbag on the pavement and tore off her jacket.

'You wanted to know why I won't take off my shirt. Well, I'm going to show you.'

He watched as she rolled up her sleeves. 'Oh my God,' he breathed when he saw the patchwork of angry red scars crisscrossing her forearms. Some looked old and healed, others were fresher.

'I've been self-harming since my mother died,' she replied, a tear sliding down her cheek. 'I have a special knife in my bedside table that I use to do it. When I feel the pain and see the blood it makes me feel better, like some of the pressure's been released. No one, not even my father, brother and best friend know that. Only you. Does that prove how much you mean to me?'

He stared back at her, lost for words. She looked so strong and proud, standing tall, head tilted back, eyes full of unshed tears and vulnerability.

'Come on,' he said.

'Where are we going?' she replied, scooping up her bag and jacket before following him back the way they'd come, pulling her sleeves back down her arms.

'Back to the pub,' he replied. 'Let's give Isaac a wee test.'

They walked into The Bonnie Brae to find Digger and Gary hurling insults at the Lawsons, who were hurling them right back, except for Craig, who was leaning against the bar drinking his pint, looking very pleased with himself. Deirdre was still in the middle of them all, screeching that she'd slash their faces open if they started a rammy. They all went silent when Jamie and Allegra walked in.

'There you are,' grinned Isaac. 'My wee firecracker.'

'Are you talking to me?' Jamie asked him, once again putting Allegra in mind of De Niro. He stood right before Isaac, who was a little unnerved by those challenging dark eyes.

'If you slept with her,' said Jamie. 'Tell me about her.'

'You cannae do that,' exclaimed Gary.

'Gary's right,' said Deirdre. 'That's out of order, Jamie.'

He ignored them, gaze riveted on Isaac while Allegra stood beside him doing a magnificent job of maintaining her dignity.

'Tell me,' Jamie told Isaac.

'You sure you want to know?' replied Isaac.

'Aye, I do.'

'Fine. She was all over me in the back of the car. She's a wild one, too, she stripped everything off. She wanted me to see all of her, you see. Those tits, wow. The best I've ever seen.'

'What tattoo has she got on her right inner thigh?'

Jamie already knew he was lying, no way would Allegra have stripped naked for anyone, but he wanted some extra confirmation, which he got when Isaac's eyes danced with panic. 'Er, a wee swallow.'

'You never slept with her and you've never seen her naked, you lying twat,' he said before slamming his forehead into Isaac's face.

Isaac groaned and crumpled to the floor.

'I warned you what would happen to the person who struck the first blow,' screeched Deirdre, drawing back the razor whip. She went silent when Jamie snatched it from her hand and rounded on Craig.

'You really are getting desperate, aren't you, you fucking dick?' Jamie snarled in his face.

'And for anyone who thinks that little weasel was telling the truth,' Allegra announced to the room. 'Here's proof he was lying.'

The eyes of every man bulged when she pulled up her skirt to reveal a substantial amount of thigh.

'See, no tattoo,' she said before pulling her skirt back down again.

Jamie slung his arm around Allegra. 'Let's get out of here,' he smiled at her.

She grinned and wrapped her arms around his waist, resting her head on his shoulder.

Jamie dumped the razor whip on the bar. 'You want to be careful with that,' he told Deirdre. 'You might hurt yourself.'

Gary and Digger followed them out, Digger pausing to kick Isaac in the stomach as he passed him by, making him grunt. The other Lawsons looked to Craig to lead the way but instead Craig dragged Isaac up by the back of his T-shirt and propelled him out the door.

'You stupid lying bastard,' he snarled, ramming his fist into his stomach with such violence Isaac vomited a violent spray of lager against the wall.

He was dragged upright by his neck and slammed back against the wall.

'Get the fuck out of my sight,' thundered Craig. 'If I ever see you on this scheme again you're fucking dead.'

With a disgusted snarl he threw him to the ground. Isaac hauled himself to his feet and stumbled off down the street, arms wrapped around his belly. Craig turned to watch Jamie walking away, laughing and joking with his friends, and the urge to commit murder rose inside him again.

* * *

'You're back early,' said Jackie the moment they came through the door. 'What happened?'

'Craig got one of his pals to tell a load of lies about Allegra,' replied Jamie. 'But we sorted it out.'

'How did you sort it out? Please tell me there wasn't any violence.'

'It's fine, Maw, don't worry.'

'God, I hope so.'

'Did anything happen while we were out?'

'Ephraim chapped the door to ask if I wanted to go to the cinema with him. I told him I couldn't because I was ill with female problems and had to see the doctor. That scared him off, for now.'

'You sure you don't want to gie' him a chance, Mrs Gray?' said Digger. 'He's pretty minted.'

'He could be a billionaire and I'd still gie' the creepy sod a body swerve.'

'Where's Charlie?' said Jamie.

'Playing in his room. Right, none of us got our dinner so I'm going to try cooking something again. Hopefully we'll get to eat it this time.'

'My macaroni cheese is still in the oven,' said Gary, following her into the kitchen.

'Can I talk to you?' Allegra asked Jamie. 'In private?'

'Aye, we'll go upstairs.'

They headed up to his bedroom and sat on the bed together to talk.

'So, we're okay?' she asked him.

'Aye, we are,' he said. 'This is too good to gie' up.'

'Aye, it is,' she smiled. Seriousness filled her eyes. 'But there is something else that worries me.'

'If it's Craig don't worry, I can handle him.'

'No, it's not him. It's my father.'

'What about him?'

'I should have told you this before but I didn't want to ruin things. Have you any idea what he'd do if he found out about us?'

'He wouldn't approve? Not good enough, am I?' he glowered.

'You are to me but he's such a snobby bastard, he always has been.' She took his hand. 'You've no idea how dangerous he is. He found out about Danny Barker in Barlanark and had him hospitalised. He was jumped by three men and had the shit beaten out of him. That's what he did to a man who meant nothing to me, who I'd had a drink with a few times. That's as far as it ever went. Imagine what he'd do to the man I love.'

It took him a few moments to process what she'd said. 'You what?'

'I said imagine what he'd do to the man...' She paused to take a deep, nervous breath. 'I love.'

His face cracked into a grin. 'You love me?'

She nodded. 'I've never said that before to anyone, except my mother. She's the only person I've ever loved.'

'I still don't get what you see in me. You could have anyone you wanted.'

'Because I like myself when I'm with you. You make me feel like I'm worth something. When I'm around you, I don't want to hurt myself. When I met you, it felt like my life finally started.'

'Well, it's lucky because I love you, too.'

Allegra smiled as he kissed her and pressed her back onto the bed.

'Sorry,' he said, sitting up. 'I forgot again.'

'No,' she replied, pulling him back down to her. 'It's okay.'

Jamie rested his weight on one elbow so he wouldn't squash her. 'Why does that freak you out? Allegra?' he pressed when she bit her lip and looked away.

'I don't want to tell you.'

'Why not?'

'The cuts on the arms weren't enough to scare you off but this might be.'

'Try me.'

'Okay.' She looked straight into his eyes as she spoke. She refused to let her dignity be taken from her. 'My father's cornered me a couple of times.'

'Cornered you?'

'One night a few months ago I was woken by... a weight on me. I opened my eyes. It was him... lying on top of me.'

Jamie sat upright. 'Jesus Christ.'

She sat up with him. 'He didn't say or do anything, he just stared at me. He's a huge man, tall with massive shoulders and it felt like I was suffocating under his weight. He'd been drinking too, he reeked of whisky. Something told me that if I kept calm everything would be okay. So I asked him what he was doing. He didn't say anything, he just got up and left the room.'

'Has it happened since?'

'Twice more. Each time he never says anything, he just stares at me, like he's fighting with himself. After that my self-harming got worse.'

'I'm no' surprised.' Jamie shot to his feet. 'I'll fucking kill him.'

Allegra leapt up after him. 'No Jamie, you can't.'

'I fucking can,' he said, flinging open his wardrobe doors and delving inside. 'Rich fuds like him think they can do what they like but their bones break like everyone else's.'

'What are those?' she said when he straightened up with what appeared to be two chair legs tied together with a torn strip of sheet.

'Nunchucks,' he replied. 'Ephraim made them.'

She grabbed his arm when he charged for the door. 'You can't.'

'Why the hell not?'

'Because he'll destroy you. That's what he does, it's what he excels at. That's how he made so much money. He'll take everything from you – your home, your possessions. He'll make sure you and Jackie can never get a job. He could even get Charlie put in care.'

'No one can do that.'

'He can, he's done it to plenty of other people.' Tenderly she cupped his face in her hands. 'He might do it anyway if he finds out about us. You think Craig Lawson's dangerous but he's nothing compared to my dad. Craig physically hurts people, beats them up, even kills them, but my dad, he… he obliterates them.'

'But you can't live like this. One day he'll go too far.'

'I know. I keep praying he has a heart attack or gets hit by a bus but it never happens.'

'Can't you go to the police?'

'He has a lot of good friends in the police, the higher ranks, anyway. Last week we had the Deputy Chief Constable round for dinner. The only thing I can do is go somewhere far away, and by far away I mean abroad. Even then I don't know if it would work. He has people who are good at tracking people down. They can find anyone, but it's my only chance. I've been saving for two years, I've got a good amount of cash put by plus all my jewellery.'

'You're really going to leave?' he said, crestfallen.

'I have to, before he…'

Jamie pulled her into his arms when she started to cry. 'I can't even imagine how scared you've been,' he said.

'It's because I look so much like my mother,' she murmured into his shoulder, clinging onto him. 'He thinks I should replace her.'

'The dirty bastard.'

'So you see, I've no choice.' She raised her head to look into his eyes. 'Come with me.'

'What? You want me to go halfway across the world with you?'

'Yes, I do, more than anything. I was thinking Switzerland. It's an amazing country, so beautiful.'

'Switzerland? I've never been further than Ardrossan.'

'You'll love it. We can hire a nice little lodge, make love in front of the fire then go skiing.'

'I cannae ski,' he exclaimed.

'I'll teach you, I'm a very good teacher. We could have a wonderful life out there.'

'But we've not even known each other a week.'

'So what? I know this is right and so do you.'

'What if you go aff me and chuck me out and I'm stuck in Switzerland with no cash, no digs and unable to speak the language.'

'That won't happen. I love you, Jamie. There's a whole world outside Gallowburn. We can explore it together.'

The prospect was a very appealing one. If it worked out between him and Allegra they could have an amazing life together, travelling the world, finding work where they could because he refused to live off someone else. But there was a fly in the ointment. 'What about my maw and Charlie?'

Her enthusiastic smile faltered. 'They could come out to visit.'

'They rely on me to protect them.'

'I'm sure Logan and the others would look out for them.'

'And they need the wage I bring in.'

'We can send them money each month. We'll easily find work.'

'I'd miss them so much.'

She took his hands. 'I have to leave, Jamie. If I don't... well, I don't want to think about what would happen. I want you to come with me but you should know that when I'm gone I'm never coming back. I intend to disappear.'

Jamie sucked in air sharply and dragged his hands through his hair. What the hell should he do?

'Dinner's ready,' Jackie yelled up the stairs.

'Coming,' he yelled back.

'Just think it over, okay?' Allegra told him.

'When are you going?'

'Three months. By then I'll have all the money I need.'

'So soon,' he said sadly.

'At least it gives you time to think about it.' She threaded her fingers through his. 'I hope you do come with me though, Jamie. I don't want to say goodbye.'

'Me neither,' he said, touching her face.

'Jamie,' screeched his mum. 'Dinner.'

He rolled his eyes. 'Coming,' he yelled so loudly Allegra winced. He looked back at her. 'I'll really think about it, but it's such a big decision.'

'I know. But if my father finds out about us God knows what he'll do and Craig knows that. It would be a good way for Craig to get his own back.'

'The hold we have over him is bigger than the hold he has over us, but I think it's time me and Craig had a chat, just me and him.'

'That's risky.'

'I can handle him, don't worry.' He took her hand. 'Let's get something to eat, I cannae think on an empty stomach.'

They headed downstairs to find Jackie standing at the bottom, frowning.

'About bloody time,' she said.

'Sorry,' he replied, wondering if he could leave her and Charlie behind. He looked to Allegra, wondering how he could let her go.

Jesus, what should he do?

* * *

While they ate, everyone chatted about mundane things, wanting to forget about the Lawsons and Ben Wilson, just for a little while. Allegra and Jackie discussed who they could set Gary up with, to his mortification, while Digger and Logan cracked jokes. Jackie kept one eye on Charlie, relieved when he tucked into Gary's macaroni cheese with gusto even though he'd had an ice lolly and ice cream.

Only Jamie remained silent, picking at his food, lost in his own world.

'I'm going to talk to Craig Lawson alone,' he announced.

They all went silent and turned to look at him.

'You can't do that,' spluttered Jackie. 'He'd set a trap for you.'

'No, he won't. Anything happens to me there's all you lot to tell the police what you know. This has to end and this is the only way.'

'I don't like this at all,' said Jackie. 'How can you possibly convince him to let all this drop?'

He glanced at Allegra, amusement dancing in his eyes. 'I'll make him an offer he can't refuse.'

She beamed back at him. He was so De Niro.

'Where are you going?' said Jackie when he got to his feet.

'To talk to his wee spy at the end of the street. He can pass on a message. No, you lot stay here,' he told Logan, Gary and Digger when they rose too. 'I don't want to scare him off.'

'We'll stand at the door and keep an eye out,' said Logan. 'And that isn't up for debate.'

'Fine,' said Jamie before stalking out, leaving his friends to gather anxiously on the step to keep watch.

Sure enough, a solitary Lawson was hanging around the end of the block, kicking a pebble and puffing on a cigarette. When he saw Jamie approaching, he broke into a run.

'Wait,' called Jamie. 'I want you to pass on a message to Craig.'

The boy, who couldn't have been more than sixteen, halted in his tracks and turned to look at him. 'Wit message?'

'Tell him to meet me at the Gallows at six o'clock tomorrow

evening. Tell him to come alone. I'll be there alone too so he doesnae need to worry. I just want to talk. We need to sort this out.'

'Aye, I'll tell him,' the boy replied before sprinting away.

When he'd vanished from view, Jamie returned to the house.

'You sure you don't want us there?' said Logan. 'This could go bad.'

'Sure. Craig will want this put to bed as much as us,' he replied as he walked back into the house.

He was confronted by his mum, whose lips were pursed with disapproval, arms folded across her substantial bosom.

'I hope to God you know what you're doing,' said Jackie.

'I do, Maw, trust me. After this meeting we won't need to worry about the Lawsons again.'

'I doubt it'll be that easy. That family lives for trouble.'

'They're about to change their ways,' he said, dark eyes narrowing.

15

Jamie arrived at the Gallows for his meeting with Craig Lawson ten minutes early. No one else was there. Before the site had been used for executions it would have been a very pleasant spot, with a bubbling stream running through woodland. But the ancient forest had been cleared to make way for the estate and the trees had been replaced by a flat expanse of grass. A plaque had been erected to mark the site of the gallows. The last public hanging at Gallowburn had been in 1868, although hanging in Scotland didn't end until 1963. Henry John Winterburn had been the last man to die on this spot for the murder of a merchant seaman. His hanging had gone badly. The poor sod's neck hadn't snapped on the drop, so he'd slowly strangled to death. Jamie's grandfather had taken a great interest in the local history and had told him in lurid detail how the cheers of the crowd had turned into appalled cries for mercy as Henry's eyes had popped right out of his head and his tongue had protruded like a bloated leech.

Jamie shivered and pushed the thoughts away. It was a lonely, desolate spot, despite the fact that it was slap bang in the middle of the estate, marking the boundary between north and south, as though the developers had sensed there was something wrong about it and decided to leave it be. Or maybe they'd thought no one would want to live in a house built on a site where so many people had met a grisly end. The local historical society had insisted it was preserved, and consequently the nearest houses were a good six hundred metres away. Because the ground was flat these houses were clearly visible, but the Gallows still felt isolated. The hanging tree, which had been used to execute criminals for decades before the permanent gallows had been erected, still stood. It was a massive tentacled thing that cast its twisted shadow over the rest of the trees, all of which grew a safe distance from it. No one knew how many had died dangling from its thick limbs. A small ringed fence had been placed around it for protection, but as it was only waist high it kept no one out. After one teen had almost died when a branch had fallen on his head while he was in the process of carving his initials into its trunk with a knife, a superstitious dread had built up around it, and now no one, not even the lairiest of teenagers, dared disrespect it. Consequently, it was the only spot on the Gallowburn that hadn't been defaced.

It had been instinct on Jamie's part to select this spot for the confrontation with Craig. This place of so much death had felt the right place to bury dark secrets. No one could sneak up on him, there was no tree cover and no hillocks to hide behind, so if Craig did come mob-handed Jamie would have plenty of notice and could make his escape.

At two minutes to six he saw the familiar figure of Craig Lawson making his way across the grass towards him. He was alone, but Jamie would stay alert because he wouldn't put it past Craig to set an ambush.

Craig came to a halt about ten feet from him, refusing to get any closer, sharp green eyes scanning the area.

'Thanks for coming,' said Jamie. It only just occurred to him that he was standing in an area where so many people had been brutally killed with a murderer. This time he managed to stifle the shiver wanting to creep down his spine.

'What's this about, Jamie?'

'This feud between our families has to end.'

'I'm no' sure that's possible. Too much bad blood.'

'It is possible because we both have holds over each other – I know what you did to Ben Wilson and you know about my relationship with Allegra.'

'What you know about me is much worse than what I know about you.'

'No, it's not. I take it you've met Allegra's da?'

'Aye, I have.'

'Then you'll understand the consequences of him finding out about my relationship with his daughter.'

Craig's green eyes were sly. 'He'd kill you and probably her too.'

'Aye, he would. So, I want to do a deal – me and my family will keep quiet about what you did to Ben and you keep quiet about my relationship with Allegra.'

Craig appeared thoughtful and Jamie got the impression he liked the sound of this deal. It would certainly take the pressure off.

'How can I trust your word?' said Craig.

'Because Allegra means more to me than Ben Wilson.'

'Cold.'

'Maybe, but that's how it is.'

'What about Jackie and your pals? Will they go grassing to the police?'

'No, they won't because not only does grassing go against everything they believe in, but we want this over with as much as you. We want to know our families will be safe and that we can go for a pint without a rammy. I bet you're as sick of it as we are?'

Craig nodded.

'Let's put it all behind us and get on with our lives. The secrets we hold about each other will guarantee the peace. You stick to the south side of the scheme and we'll stick to the north. The pub is no man's land, so we can all go there but no trouble kicks off. I reckon if we start another rammy in there Deirdre will snap and bar us all.'

Craig's eyes scanned the area again, attempting to spot a trap and finding none. 'All right, Jamie, you've got a deal.'

'Good,' Jamie said, hiding his relief well. He held out his hand to Craig.

Craig shifted from foot to foot as he pondered whether it would be wise to accept it. Not wanting to look the lesser man, he shook Jamie's extended hand. The two men nodded at each other.

'Nice one,' said Jamie. 'See you around, Craig.'

'See you,' Craig replied.

Both men headed off in different directions, casting mistrustful glances over their shoulders. Suspicion would always exist between them, but Jamie got the strong sense they had just brokered a genuine peace.

As soon as he stepped back onto the north side of the estate, Logan, Allegra, Digger and Gary leapt out at him.

'Jesus,' he breathed. 'You scared the shite out of me.'

'How did it go?' said Allegra.

'It worked. We've got a truce. We even shook on it.'

'And you believed him?' said Logan.

'Aye, I did. Now we can get on with our lives.'

Allegra smiled and flung her arms around his neck. 'I knew you could do it.'

'Let's hope the truce holds,' said Jamie. 'If you see a Lawson in the street you do not start anything. You ignore them and carry on your way. No name-calling and no fights. I'm looking at you, Digger.'

'Me?' Digger replied, pointing at himself. 'What have I done?'

'You love a good fight the most out of us all. You're gonnae have to take it easy. There's a lot more at stake than scrapping over turf.'

'Aye, I've got it,' he mumbled, kicking an empty can across the road.

'Good. Let's go to the pub to celebrate.'

'Will Deirdre let you in after you took her razor whip from her?' said Allegra.

'I think so. We're good customers.'

She smiled and wrapped her arms around his waist as they headed down the street together.

* * *

To the surprise of everyone in Gallowburn, the truce between the Blood Brothers and the Lawsons did indeed hold, both sides sticking to their respective territories. When they encountered each other in the pub, glares were still thrown – there was too much bad blood between them for that not to happen – but no violence ensued.

Although Jackie was relieved that her sons were safe, she was unable to ignore the guilt she felt every time another news report popped up about Ben Wilson's murder. The police had no suspects. Jackie was now certain Allegra's father had ordered his death and she wondered what the man had done to bring that down on his head. It made sense, going off what she'd learnt about Cameron from Allegra. What she couldn't understand, though, was why John Lawson had been involved. Surely Craig and this Neil Burrows who did all Cameron's dirty work would have been perfectly capable of committing the murder between them. Why take along a turnip like John? Jackie had the distinct feeling they were missing part of the story. The worst thing was watching the appeal by Ben's widow, a pretty blonde who sobbed her way through the press conference, begging for any information that could lead to her husband's killers. That distraught face haunted Jackie's dreams but every time she considered picking up the phone and calling the police she was hit by the full force of the fear she'd experienced when Charlie had gone missing. This, combined with the fear of what Cameron Abernethy would do to Jamie if he found out about his relationship with his daughter, was enough to stay her hand.

* * *

Three months after Jamie had negotiated the truce with Craig Lawson, Allegra made the announcement he'd been dreading. She turned up at the shop a few minutes before his lunchbreak. Malcolm had given him a week off to recover from the car accident. The break had been blissful and it had been difficult going back to a job he loathed but they needed the money. However, having Allegra in his life made things easier to bear. Malcolm had been appalled when he'd realised his only employee was dating the woman who had abused him in his own shop but Allegra had apologised so sweetly, fluttering her eyelashes and sticking out her chest, that Malcolm had forgiven her. She'd charmed him so much he didn't even mind when she turned up to see Jamie while he was working.

'Hi, Malcolm,' she said, breezing into the shop.

Despite her usual big smile, Jamie could immediately tell that something was wrong. Her skin was pale and there were shadows around her eyes, which she'd failed to conceal with make-up.

'Allegra,' smiled Malcolm. 'How lovely to see you. I take it you're here to see Jamie and no' me?'

'I come in to see you both,' she winked. 'You know that, Malcolm.'

Malcolm beamed at her. One thing Jamie had noticed about Allegra was that she always knew what to say to make people feel good about themselves. It was a rare and beautiful gift that charmed everyone she met.

'It's not Jamie's lunchbreak for another five minutes but he's worked hard today,' said Malcolm. 'So he can take it early.'

'You're a star, Malcolm,' she smiled.

Malcolm blushed and cleared his throat. 'Right, I need to rearrange the toilet brushes.'

'Have fun,' she said, walking to the door with Jamie.

'He's been so much easier to work for since you came along,' Jamie told her, taking her hand as they walked down the street together.

'He's all right, is Malcolm,' she replied. 'For a llama.'

Jamie chuckled. 'Where do you want to eat?'

'The Buttercup Café.'

'Again?'

'I love their paninis.'

Jamie smiled. Despite its whimsical name, the Buttercup Café was a greasy spoon with surly staff and chairs so hard and uncompromising your spine was jarred every time you sat down, but for some reason he couldn't fathom Allegra loved it.

'Okay, the Buttercup Café it is,' he replied.

After they'd found a table and placed their orders, she dropped the bombshell.

'I've finally got enough cash,' she told him. 'I'm leaving.'

His stomach dropped. 'When?'

'In two weeks. I've booked the flight to Switzerland – two tickets, one in your name. Both are one-way. It's there if you want it and I hope you do.'

'Jesus,' he breathed, dragging his hands through his hair.

'Have you decided what you want to do?'

'I want to go with you Allegra, Christ, I do, but I don't want to leave my family and friends.'

'I understand,' she said, looking down at her hands.

'Your da's done something else, hasn't he?'

She nodded and pulled down the scarf wrapped around her neck to reveal a couple of bruises at her throat. 'I woke up with him on top of me again and he did this.'

Anger surged through Jamie so fast and hard he felt capable of ripping apart the café with his bare hands.

'Take it easy, Dangerous,' she told him, seeing the anger ignite in his eyes.

'Just let me and the lads go at him with baseball bats,' he whispered. 'We'll break his fucking legs. We'll wear balaclavas, he won't know it's us.'

'Maybe not at first, but he will find out, he always does, and when he does he'll get some very bad people to do a lot worse to you. There's no option but to escape from the monster's shadow.' She covered his hand with her own. 'Come with me, Jamie, please. We can have such an amazing life together.'

'I looked up Switzerland on the internet,' he told her. 'It looks incredible, and I do love Toblerone,' he added, making her smile. 'Plus, I've always wanted to travel.'

'This is your perfect opportunity.' Allegra's eyes filled with tears. 'I love you, Jamie, and I don't want to go without you, but I've no choice. Come with me, please.'

'Cheese panini,' said a reedy voice.

They looked up to see a young waitress standing by their table chewing gum, two plates lazily clasped in her hands. One plate was tilted so much that the panini was in danger of sliding off.

'That's mine, thanks,' said Allegra, hastily taking it from her before her lunch was spilt onto the sticky floor.

The waitress dumped Jamie's plate before him and sauntered off, picking at one of her ears.

'I've lost my appetite,' he frowned, pushing away the plate. 'What would we do when we got there?'

'I've already rented a lovely little apartment in Zurich, not far from the Arosa ski resort. We'll be so cosy.'

'I've been saving but I've not managed to save much, just what I have left over from my wage after the bills are paid. Combined with what I already had saved it's just over a grand.'

'You don't need to worry about money, I've got plenty.'

'But I don't want to live off you. I want my own money.'

'And you will, you can get a job.'

'I can't speak French or German.'

'You'll pick it up. Anyway, we don't have to stay in Switzerland. It's just a starting point. From there we can go on to Greece or Spain, somewhere touristy where you don't need to speak the local lingo. There's always jobs for British workers out there. My friend Alice spent six months travelling around Greece working in bars and restaurants.'

'She did?' he said. Now this was more like it.

'Yes, and we don't have to stop there. We can go wherever we want, see whatever we want. We'll have total freedom, no one telling us what to do.'

That sounded like heaven. No more toiling in a boring shop or living on a manky estate strewn with litter and dog shite. It would be hot sun and sandy beaches, making love with Allegra in exotic places.

'You actually look excited about it,' she smiled.

'I am.'

'Do you have a passport?'

'Aye. I ordered one when you first mentioned leaving, just in case. I'm just afraid you'll get sick of me and I'll be left stranded in a strange place.'

'I could never get sick of you, but if it makes you feel better I'll do you a deal – you take the grand with you that you've saved but you keep it. That way, if things don't work out you know you'll always have the money to get home.'

'I don't want to live off you,' he replied. 'It's no' me.'

'It'll only be temporary, until we can find jobs, and we will.'

'How much are you taking? What if it doesn't last us until we can find work?'

'Eighty grand.'

'What?' he said, eyebrows shooting up.

'I've got eighty grand to take. I think that'll do us for a while.'

'Where did you get eighty grand from?' It wasn't the ridiculous question it sounded because she'd told him her father only gave her a bit of spending money. Neither would he let her work.

'My mother left it to me in her will,' she replied. 'When I turned twenty-one it was turned over to me.' She'd celebrated her twenty-first birthday just last month. 'She knew my father would have contested it, so she made my godfather executor, knowing he was strong and powerful enough to make sure my father didn't get his hands on it. He put it in an offshore account only I know about for safety. Just before we go I'll sell my car, too, that'll be another twenty grand in the pot.'

He gaped at her. They'd be going with a hundred grand. That was a sum of money he could only dream about. 'So, we'll be okay for a while then?' he murmured.

'Aye, we will. So, what do you say?'

'I need to talk it over with my maw.'

Allegra didn't like anyone else knowing her plans but she knew Jackie Gray could be trusted to keep it to herself. 'Well, all right, but please don't tell anyone else. I can't risk word getting back to my father.'

'It won't.'

'How do you fancy staying over at my house tomorrow night?'

'What?' he said, lips spreading into a slow smile. They'd never had the chance to spend a full night together as her father always insisted on her being home each night.

'My father's going to Aberdeen for a couple of nights on business, so I'll have the house to myself.'

'Christ, yes,' he grinned. 'You sure you want me in your home?'

'It is just a house you know.'

'Aye, a bloody big one.'

'So, what do you say?'

'Try and stop me.'

'Great. I'll pick you up at seven. He'll be gone by then and we can discuss Switzerland some more. It might help you come to a decision.'

He took both her hands in his, the limp paninis on their plates forgotten. His granddad had told him that you might only get one big chance in life to truly live, to do something remarkable. Jamie got the strong feeling that this was his chance.

* * *

Jamie caught the bus home after work, the enthusiasm he'd felt talking to Allegra in the café only increasing as he stared out of the window at the Gallowburn. The estate seemed to get mankier every day. Litter was still scattered along the streets. A gang of kids no more than twelve years old was gathered on a street corner, smoking. Ephraim was flogging his dodgy wares from his van. If he stayed he knew there was a good chance he'd never escape and he could become the drunken old sod in the stained clothes stumbling down the street, getting pissed day after day to escape the awful reality of his life. Perhaps that drunk had once been given his big chance and had rejected it out of fear and now he was tormented by his regrets, only able to escape his demons through a bottle. Determination filled him. That would not be him. But the Gallowburn didn't like to let people go. It was a dead end that was difficult to escape, like sinking into quicksand. But he had Allegra to help him break free.

Jamie got off the bus and walked the rest of the way home. His resolve started to waver, however, when he saw his front door, beyond which were his mother and little brother. He'd miss them so much it would hurt – Digger, Logan and Gary, too. They'd grown up together, been there for each other. Being without their friendship and back-up would be like losing a limb. But would that pain be worse than letting Allegra go? He might never find love like that again. That would be another regret to destroy him.

'All right, sweetheart,' smiled Jackie when he walked through the door. As usual she was busy dusting, the sight filling him with fondness. 'Something wrong?' she added.

'No. Why would it be?'

'Because you're standing there with this weird sentimental look in your eyes.'

'I need to talk to you, Maw. Is Charlie in his room?'

'No. He's down the street playing with Tommy.' It had taken her a few weeks to feel confident enough to let her younger son out of her sight but things were so quiet with the Lawsons now she felt it was safe. 'I get the feeling this is serious?'

'It is.'

He sat on the couch and she sat beside him.

'You've no' knocked up Allegra, have you?' she said.

'No, it's nothing like that, although it does involve her.'

'What is it, sweetheart? You know you can tell me anything.'

'Allegra's leaving Scotland. She's already booked the tickets and she wants me to go with her.'

'Where is she going? Down south?'

'No, she's leaving the country. Switzerland, to be precise, and from there maybe Greece or Spain.'

'You mean a holiday? Well, that's wonderful, you should go with her.'

'No, Maw, not a holiday. She's leaving permanently and she's never coming back.'

'That sounds a bit drastic.'

'She has to get away from her da before he does something really bad to her.'

'Bad? I know he's a nasty piece of work but what would he do to his own daughter?'

Jackie turned ashen as Jamie explained Cameron Abernethy's night-time forays into his daughter's bedroom.

'Bloody hell,' she breathed. 'That's sick.'

'I know and she's terrified. She cannae take it any longer, she has to get away. If she stays in the country he will find her, which is why she's going abroad.'

'But...' she began, struggling to take in this information. 'When is she going?'

'Two weeks.'

'So soon? She can't drop this bombshell on you and expect you to decide so quickly.'

'She didn't. She told me three months ago.'

'Three months? And you're only mentioning it now?'

'I've been trying to make up my mind. I don't know what to do, Maw.'

'Why the hell don't you know what to do?'

He sighed. 'It's all right, Maw, I'll stay.'

'Have you lost your mind? You'll go with her.'

'Eh?'

'Why wouldn't you want to travel around the world with a beautiful woman who you love and who loves you back?'

'What about you and Charlie and my friends?'

'We'll still be here if it doesn't work out.'

'But I'd miss you all so much. I don't want to leave you behind.'

'How many people in Gallowburn get an opportunity like this? I'm pretty sure you're the first. I could never afford to take you to Switzerland. I couldn't afford to take you to Blackpool. If it was me I'd be off like a shot.'

'But what about you and Charlie? Who'll look out for you?'

'Sweetheart, I managed for years raising you and Charlie alone. I can manage again. You've got to take this chance, Jamie. What's the option? Living on this sink estate, working in a job you hate for peanuts.'

'But I'd miss you.'

'We'll miss you too but, like I said, we'll still be here. Grab this chance, Jamie, with both hands. Even if it doesn't work out and you only go for a few months, at least you tried and you knew how it worked out. As you get older you don't regret the things you did, you regret the things you didn't do. Don't become that bitter, angry person. That lassie loves the bones of you and you her. Go and live a happy life and don't look back.'

'But I'd worry about you, Maw.'

'Don't. Logan's not happy living back with his da. I'll ask him to move in. He can pay board and there'd be a man in the house to look out for me and Charlie. Would that make you feel better?'

'Aye, a lot better.'

'Then that's what I'll do. Just make sure you send me a postcard from every place you visit, okay?' she said, eyes filling with tears.

'Promise,' he rasped, hugging her.

Everyone on the Gallowburn estate would have been surprised to see Jamie Gray crying on his mum's shoulder.

* * *

'Oh my God, this place is amazing,' said Jamie as he walked through Allegra's front door.

'It's all right, I suppose,' she replied.

'All right? It's a bloody palace. How many bedrooms has it got?'

'Six.'

'Wow.'

She took his hand and pulled him towards the stairs. 'Come on, I'll show you mine.'

They enjoyed rolling around on the super king size bed together, the space a revelation to them. Before they'd had to content themselves with Allegra's car and attempting to make silent love in Jamie's bed. Now they could throw themselves about with wild abandon and cry out as much as they liked.

They fell back onto the bed together, breathing hard.

'Wow,' gasped Jamie.

'I know,' smiled Allegra, snuggling up to him. All her hang-ups about her body had gone, thanks to him. Now she had no problem with being completely naked in front of him or letting him go on top. 'It felt so free, didn't it?'

'Aye, it did.'

'Imagine what that would be like in front of a log fire in a Swiss chalet or under the Spanish sun.'

'Let's go and find out.'

She leapt on top of him, brushing her long hair out of her face. 'You mean you're coming?'

'Too right, I am.'

'Fantastic,' she grinned. 'You won't regret it, I promise.'

'I know.'

'What made up your mind?'

'I talked to my maw. She was the one who told me to go, that I'd regret if it I didn't. She said if it was her she'd leap at the chance.'

'Jackie's a very wise woman.'

'Aye, she is. She's gonnae ask Logan to move in with her when I've gone, which made me feel a lot better about leaving her and Charlie.'

'You do understand that I can't ever come back, not until my father's dead anyway?'

'I do, but you never know your luck. Hopefully something nasty will happen to him in Aberdeen and you'll never see him again.'

'I can only hope. Or perhaps he'll choke on one of the many steaks he loves shoving down his throat, the fat greedy bastard.'

'I spent a bit of the money I saved today,' he told her.

'What did you do that for? We're going to need every penny.'

'It's for a good reason,' he said, picking up his jeans off the floor. He pulled out a small gift-wrapped package and placed it in her hands. 'I got you a present for the trip.'

'You didn't need to do that.'

'I wanted to. Open it.'

She untied the red ribbon wrapped around the gold paper, which fell off to reveal a small black box. Opening it up, she beamed when she saw a thin gold band with a single stone.

'I thought,' he began, 'that we could get married either in the Swiss snow or the Spanish sun. Whichever would be easier. I don't know if there might be a language barrier. Spain might be better...'

'Jamie, you're babbling.'

'Aye,' he said, taking a deep breath to slow his thudding heart. 'I babble when I'm nervous. Kind of a new experience for me because I don't get nervous but right now I'm bloody terrified.'

'Why?'

'Because I don't want you to say no.'

'A man like you is good at weighing up the odds. You wouldn't have asked me if you thought I'd turn you down.'

'I thought there was a good chance you'd say yes. Eighty-twenty odds. The ring's not from some fancy jeweller's, though. I got it from a pawn shop but I saw it and I thought it was pretty, like you. I wanted to get you a solid gold one with an expensive diamond but...'

'You're babbling again.'

'Sorry.'

'Don't you want to hear my answer?'

'Aye, please put me out of my misery.'

She took the ring out of the box and slid it onto her finger. 'Yes, Jamie, I will marry you. Or should I say, aye, I will.'

He took her face in his hands and pulled her down to him for a kiss.

'Allegra Gray,' she smiled. 'I like that.'

'It's got a nice ring to it.'

'Did you ever think when I was in your shop shoving vape refills into my bag that you'd end up proposing to me?'

'God, no, but I did think I'd end up calling the police,' he grinned.

'I knew you were different, Dangerous, from the moment I saw you. I never thought it would come to this, though.'

'You sure you don't want to trade me in for an inbred chinless wonder?'

'No way. I like a man who hits people with bike chains and keeps homemade nunchucks in his wardrobe. Now let's cement our engagement in the swimming pool.'

'You have a pool?' he exclaimed as she took his hand and encouraged him up off the bed.

'Aye, we do,' she smiled. 'And a sauna.'

He gazed at her in awe as she led him out of the room but it wasn't the house or the swimming pool that was the source of his wonder. She looked more otherworldly than real, her blonde hair cascading down her bare back, sparkling blue eyes bursting with life, the moonlight cast through the hallway window painting her skin silver. Was she truly his future wife or an elusive phantom, something that could slip through his fingers as easily as water?

16

Jackie returned to the house after having dinner at Tricia's house. It had been very hard not confiding in her friend about her son's imminent departure. In one week Jamie would be leaving Scotland, perhaps permanently, and it was tearing her heart in two but she didn't dare tell anyone for fear of it getting back to Cameron Abernethy. She and Jamie had agreed to keep it from Charlie until the day before he was due to leave in case the boy, in his innocence, spilled the beans. He was in the same school as a couple of the Lawson children, so they couldn't take the chance. Logan was the only member of the Blood Brothers who knew about Jamie's departure, as he wasn't as prone to gossiping as Digger and Gary. The pain of knowing he might never see his best friend again was soothed a little by the fact that he'd agreed to move into the Gray home when Jamie had left. But Gallowburn would never be the same without Jamie; he'd certainly made his mark on it.

Jackie had only been home five minutes when there was a knock at the door.

'What do you want?' she frowned at Craig Lawson, preparing to slam the door shut in his face.

'I come in peace,' he said, holding up his hands. 'You need to get an urgent message to Jamie.'

'What message?'

'I don't know the exact details but Cameron Abernethy knows about what he's up to with his daughter.'

'You mean their relationship?'

'Aye, but it's more than that. Something about Switzerland.'

Jackie could see Craig had no idea what Jamie and Allegra had planned because he was regarding her curiously, hoping for some clue, which she was determined not to give him. 'How do you know?' she said.

'Cameron called me into his office. He was raging about Jamie, asking me what I knew about him. I told him our families have been rivals a long time but that was it. It was Neil who filled me in about Switzerland.'

'Neil Burrows?' she said, paling.

Craig nodded. 'You have to warn Jamie.'

'Why are you telling me this?'

'Because I don't want your family thinking this is down to me. Cameron planted microphones in Allegra's bedroom.'

'Oh, my God.'

'Just remember,' he said as he headed back down the garden path. 'I kept your secret.'

'I won't forget,' she replied before slamming the door shut. She glanced at the clock on the mantlepiece. Jamie would be on his lunch-break and not in the safety of the shop. He always went out for his dinner to escape for a while.

Jackie snatched up her phone and dialled. 'Come on, son, pick up, please. Jamie,' she gasped with relief when he answered.

'All right, Maw? I've just picked up some clothes for the trip. Simpsons is having a sale...'

'Never mind all that and listen – Cameron Abernethy knows about you and Allegra, he planted microphones in her bedroom. He also knows you're planning to leave together for Switzerland.'

'How do you know this?'

'Craig Lawson told me.'

'Him? Then it's probably bollocks.'

'Why would he lie about this? And if he is lying how does he know about Switzerland? Only me, you, Allegra and Logan know about that.'

'Nae idea, but it's a trick.'

'I'm sure he was being honest. Get back to the shop right now, you'll be safe there.'

'All right, I will if it makes you feel better...'

'Jamie?' she said when he broke off.

On the other end of the line she heard the roar of an engine followed by Jamie's yell of panic. There was a loud thud of something hitting metal, the sound making her feel sick, accompanied by screams in the background and a clatter and the cracking of plastic, she assumed because the phone had been dropped.

'Jamie?' she whispered, throat so constricted by fear she could barely speak. 'Jamie?'

When the line went dead she screamed her son's name into the phone as her terror erupted out of her. When she tried calling him back the phone refused to connect.

With tears streaming down her face Jackie pulled on her shoes and jacket and tore out of the house, feeling disorientated and a little dizzy, trying to think how to get to the street where he worked as fast as possible. Dozens of possibilities whizzed through her mind but she was in such a state they evaporated the moment she attempted to cling onto them. So upset was she that she ran through the garden gate and smacked into someone on the pavement.

'Woah, where's the fire, hen?' said a deep voice. Strong hands gently took her by the shoulders to keep her upright.

Jackie found herself staring up into Ephraim's concerned face. She was so distraught she didn't even pause to consider what he was doing outside her house.

'Jamie,' she gasped. 'He's been hit by a car, I think. I was on the phone to him when it happened... I have to go to him.'

'Jesus. Where is he?'

'Simpsons, the clothes shop near where he works.'

'Aye, I know it. My van's just doon the road. I'll take you.'

'Thank you so much.'

Ephraim's big pink van waited at the end of the street for them. They leapt inside and he gunned the engine. As they sped away from the kerb he started up the chimes as though they were a police siren. It was the most surreal and frightening journey of Jackie's life, clinging onto the door as Ephraim drove them at high speed through the streets of Gallowburn with his chimes blaring. His aggressive driving style combined with the threats he hurled at other drivers by sticking his head out of the window ensured they arrived in double-quick time.

The street had been cordoned off by the police. One uniformed officer stepped out before them, hand raised, preventing them from going any further. For one awful moment Jackie thought Ephraim was going to drive right over him. Instead he slammed on the brakes.

'Oh, God, there's an ambulance,' said Jackie, flinging off her seat-belt and leaping out.

'I'm sorry, Madam,' said the police officer, barring her way. 'You can't go down there. There's been an accident.'

'I know, it's my son,' she cried. 'I was on the phone to him when it happened. It sounded like he was hit by a car.'

The officer's eyes softened. 'What's your son's name, madam?'

'Jamie,' she replied, clinging onto her composure by her fingernails. 'Jamie Gray.'

He nodded and beckoned over one of his colleagues. 'Take her through. She's the victim's maw.'

The female officer nodded. 'This way, madam.'

'Is he okay?' Jackie asked the officer as she was led through the gawping crowd gathered at the police cordon.

'The paramedics are with him. Beyond that I'm afraid I don't know.'

Jackie nodded. That was good. Why would they need paramedics if he was dead? 'Have you got who did it?'

'No, I'm sorry,' she replied. 'It was a hit and run but we have plenty of witnesses and CCTV. We'll find them.'

Ephraim approached the officer on guard duty after parking the van. 'Let me through, I'm... the lad's da. Mr Gray.'

'Of course, sir,' he replied, standing aside to let him pass.

As the crowd parted, Jackie was afraid to look. Memories of her brother lying dead on the pavement returned. If she had to watch another person she loved dearly die on the street she wasn't sure she would survive it. After what Cameron Abernethy had done to his own wife she was almost convinced she was going to find Jamie dead. Tears of relief poured down her face when she saw Jamie was still breathing, an oxygen mask over his face. He lay on a stretcher, two paramedics attending to him. His left leg had been packed in some sort of brace, as had his neck. His face was badly cut and bruised, his left eye massively swollen. A carrier bag with the Simpsons logo emblazoned on the side lay on the pavement beside him, the contents spilled out. The sight made her cry harder because it represented broken dreams. How could he travel to Switzerland now?

'Jamie,' she said, kneeling by his side.

His eyes flickered open but he was unable to speak, reaching out a hand to her, which she took and cradled between her own.

'It's all right, sweetheart,' she said. 'Everything will be okay, don't you worry.' She looked to the paramedics. 'How is he?'

'You're a relative?'

'I'm his maw.'

'He's stable but his left leg's broken in two places, he's got some broken ribs, whiplash and several lacerations. He could also have a fractured pelvis but we can't be certain about that until he's had an X-ray.'

'So, he'll be okay?'

'We'll know more at the hospital.'

'Please, can't you give me a straight answer?'

'He's stable. That's good.'

That was the best she was going to get so she decided to stop hassling them and let them do their jobs. 'Can I go with him to the hospital?'

'Of course. You're just in time, we're preparing to move him.'

She stood back when they gently loaded Jamie onto a trolley and wheeled him to the ambulance. It was only then she realised Ephraim was standing right behind her.

'Jesus,' she said, physically jumping.

'Sorry, hen. What do you need me to do? I want to help.'

'Could you pick up Charlie from school and take him to the hospital?'

'Aye, nae problem. Which hospital?'

'Oh, I don't know. Which hospital are you taking him to?' she asked the paramedics.

'Glasgow Royal,' one of them replied.

Jackie looked back at Ephraim. 'I'll call the school to let them know you're on your way.'

'On it,' he replied, giving her hand a gentle squeeze before sprinting back to his van.

Jackie climbed into the back of the ambulance with Jamie, relieved when the doors were closed, blocking out the sight of the ghoulish bystanders. She talked to Jamie during the mad dash to the hospital, the siren screaming, but he didn't seem to hear her, although his eyes did flicker open a few times and attempt to focus on her face before sliding shut. After calling the school to let them know Ephraim was on his way to collect Charlie, she called Allegra but there was no reply.

That wasn't like her and she was afraid for the lassie. If Cameron had done this to Jamie what would he do to her?

* * *

Allegra was lying on her bed at home. The stereo in the corner of the room was blaring out Snow Patrol, her favourite group. Her father was out at some meeting so she was free to relax.

She stared at the magazine in her hands but she hadn't taken in a single word from the article about the latest Paris fashions, she was too busy dreaming about her future with Jamie and the adventures they would have. Suddenly things like the latest trends, shoes and clothes seemed unimportant. Her hand went to the engagement ring he'd given her, which she wore on a chain around her neck, hidden beneath her clothes so her father wouldn't see it. She'd resolved that as soon as they were on the plane she was taking it off the chain and putting it on her finger, where she would wear it forever.

When the door swung open to reveal her hulking brute of a father, she gasped with surprise and sat up. He kicked the door shut, stomped over to the stereo and slammed his fist down on it, silencing it with a smash of plastic.

'Sorry, was that too loud?' she said, attempting to keep her cool. 'I thought it would be okay because you were out at a meeting.'

They both glanced at her phone when it started to ring on the bed beside her. Allegra was relieved when Jackie's name popped up on the screen. If it had been Jamie her father would have questioned her about it and it wouldn't have been pleasant.

'You thought I was at a meeting because that's what I wanted you to think,' he retorted. 'I control your life at all times. Surely you've realised that by now?'

Allegra got up off the bed when her father advanced on her, attempting to keep it between them like a barrier. He was furious, that much was obvious. When he was angry the rage made his already powerful body swell until he seemed to fill the entire room, taking up every corner, suffocating her.

'I know all about you and that piece of scum off the Gallowburn estate,' he added.

'I've no idea what you're talking about,' she replied, not daring to take her eyes off him for a single second.

'Then let me refresh your memory – Jamie Gray. Mother Jackie, brother Charlie. He works in some shitty shop in Baillieston.'

'Father, I've seriously no idea who you're talking about.'

'Don't lie to me,' he roared. 'I know everything about him, including the fact that you're planning to run away with him to Switzerland.' His lip curled with disgust. 'You even lowered yourself to agree to marry him. How dare you degrade me like that?'

Allegra's heart thudded with panic. 'I really don't know where you've got this from. Someone's having you on.'

He held up his phone and pressed a button. She thought she would throw up when her own voice played out loud and clear, followed by Jamie's as they discussed their escape.

'Condemned by your own words,' he said, stopping the recording and slipping the phone back into his trouser pocket.

'You actually planted a listening device in my room?' she exclaimed.

'Yes, and I heard every single disgusting sound, you fucking whore.'

'I'm your daughter, you can't talk to me like that.'

'I feed you, clothe you, I do everything for you, so I'll treat you any fucking way I like. I had a feeling you'd taken up with another scummy ned, so I made up that trip to Aberdeen knowing you'd invite him to stay over when in fact I never left the city. I heard you discussing your plans as well as you agreeing to marry him.' His hands curled into fists. 'I heard it all.'

Allegra wasn't sure whether she wanted to cry, throw up or scream with the madness of it all. His meaning was clear – he'd also listened to them having sex.

'You thought you could make a fool of me,' he continued. 'You thought you could leave me. No one leaves me.' Slyness filled his eyes. 'Your mother thought she could leave me too but I showed her how wrong she was.'

'I knew it.' Tears filled her eyes. 'You killed her.'

'That's what happens to disgusting slags, as you're about to find out.'

Sadness filled Allegra, a tear sliding down her cheek as her thoughts turned to Jamie. Finally, her father had confessed to what he'd done to her mother, which could only mean one thing – he was going to kill her too. Her relationship with Jamie he could have handled. He still would have punished her but it wouldn't have come to this. It was the fact that she was leaving that he couldn't deal with. He'd rather kill her than let her go. But she refused to go down without a fight, her future was worth fighting for.

Allegra sped for the door, intent on reaching her handbag containing her pepper spray and knife, which was downstairs in the kitchen, but her father grabbed her by the waist and dragged her back into the room. She screamed but there was no one to hear her, the house was too big and they were alone. He grabbed a handful of her hair and bashed her head off the wall. She groaned and crumpled to the floor.

Before she could recover he yanked her head back by her hair and shoved his phone under her nose.

'Before you get what's coming to you,' he said. 'I want you to see what I did to that fucking loser you've been debasing yourself with.'

Allegra's eyes widened with horror as she watched the car mount the pavement and slam into Jamie, sending him flying through the air. He hit the concrete hard, where he lay unmoving, his left leg bent at an unnatural angle.

'No, Jamie,' she wailed before bursting into tears.

'He's dead,' he hissed in her ear. 'Smashed to bits and left to rot on the pavement like the trash he is.' As Allegra continued to sob he wrapped his hand around her throat, pushed her to the floor and drew a knife from the back of his trousers. Her eyes widened when she saw it was the knife she used to cut herself.

'I thought you'd recognise it,' he said, revelling in his triumph as well as the sheer power he had over her.

His twisted smile screamed *look how clever I am.*

'I know all about your self-harming,' he continued. 'I have for a long time.' His lip curled. 'You're so weak and pathetic. I can't believe you have my blood in your veins. Well, lover boy's been dealt with. Now it's your turn.'

Allegra screamed, helplessly pinned to the floor by his massive hand around her throat as he raised the knife.

* * *

'Why isn't she picking up?' Jackie asked Logan, who'd arrived at the hospital after she'd called him to let him know what had happened.

Jackie had called Digger and Gary too and they were on their way. Ephraim was still hanging about but he'd popped down to the canteen to get them all a brew and a snack. The hospital staff thought he was Jamie's father, and Jackie strongly suspected he'd put that notion in their heads himself, but she was letting it slide because he was being so helpful. Now she was on the ward just outside Jamie's room so she could make her call.

'You mean Allegra?' Logan asked her.

'Aye,' she replied, looking troubled. 'It's no' like the lassie, her phone's usually welded to her hand.'

'She's probably at the hairdressers or getting her nails done.'

'The police stopped by earlier but Jamie was still being treated by the doctors. They told me witnesses said the car hit him on purpose. It actually mounted the pavement to do it, so it definitely wasn't an accident. I don't think it's a coincidence this happens just as Craig Lawson tells me Allegra's da knows about her and Jamie.'

'Jesus, you're right. Allegra said her da killed her maw.'

'And if he did that, what do you think he'd do to Allegra?'

'You have to tell the police.'

'What if Craig was lying and Cameron knows nothing about them? If I go to the police Cameron will find out about them, if he doesn't already know, of course, and that could cause even more trouble.'

'And what if Cameron Abernethy did this to Jamie and he's done something equally bad or even worse to Allegra? The man's a psychopath.'

She sighed. 'I've no choice, have I?'

'No, I don't think so.'

'One of the police left their card,' she told him, producing it from her pocket.

Before she could dial, the door to Jamie's room was opened by Charlie.

'He's awake,' he told them.

'Jamie,' said Jackie rushing into his room and taking his hand. 'It's your maw. Logan and Charlie are here too.'

Jamie pulled the oxygen mask off his face with a weak hand, attempting to talk. 'Neil,' he breathed.

'Neil?' said Logan. 'You mean Neil Burrows who works for Allegra's da? Did he do this to you?'

'Aye,' he murmured, fighting to stay awake.

'That's it,' said Jackie. 'I'm calling the police.' She looked to Jamie to gauge his reaction to this statement but he'd already drifted back off.

'Jamie?' said Charlie, welling up.

'He's fine, baby,' Jackie told him, replacing the oxygen mask on Jamie's face. 'He's just really tired, that's all. Don't worry.'

'I'll stay with them if you want to make the call,' Logan told Jackie.

'Thanks, love,' she said, exiting the room.

She took a deep breath before dialling. Going to the police went against everything she'd been taught on the Gallowburn but sometimes there was no choice.

* * *

DI Ross was a balding, slightly overweight man in a shirt that was one size too small and his tie was askew. He looked like a man who was fed up of the shite life continually threw at him and who was on the verge of burnout. This first impression didn't fill Jackie with confidence. However, the seriousness with which he obviously took his job and the thoroughness of his questioning made her feel ashamed of her earlier snap judgement.

As Jamie was still asleep when he arrived and his doctor had firmly stated he was in no fit state to be interviewed, it was left to Jackie to explain everything. Not wanting to discuss it in front of Charlie, she and the inspector talked in the relatives' room. She decided to leave out any reference to Craig Lawson. The last thing she wanted was to stir up that hornet's nest again; things had been so peaceful on the Gallowburn for the last three months. Neither did she want to admit that she'd been hiding the identity of a murderer.

'How can you be sure this is anything to do with Cameron Abernethy?' said Ross.

'Jamie woke up and told us he was run over by a man called Neil Burrows. He does all Cameron's nasty jobs for him. Allegra thinks he's the one who killed her mother, on Cameron's orders.' She frowned when Ross just nodded before looking thoughtful. 'You know the name Neil Burrows, don't you?'

'He has come to my attention before. I was the senior investigating officer into Rebecca Abernethy's death.'

'And I bet you found yourself stonewalled at every turn.'

Although DI Ross didn't admit it, she could see the truth in his eyes.

'You have to find Allegra,' she pressed. 'If Cameron hurt Jamie, he's hurt her too.'

He flipped his notebook shut and got to his feet. 'Thank you, Mrs Gray. I'll find Allegra and check on her wellbeing.'

'Thank you,' she breathed with relief.

'I'd be obliged if you could let me know when Jamie's ready to talk.'

'I will.'

'How's he doing?'

'Well, his pelvic X-ray showed no fractures, thank God, but his entire body's black and blue and he's got a broken leg that's being held together with pins, as well as whiplash, concussion and cracked ribs. His doctor said he got off pretty lightly, but he was hit by the corner of the car, not full-on, which lessened the possible damage.'

'He's a lucky man.'

Jackie frowned. Was there a hint of suspicion in his tone?

As Ross walked away, already talking on his phone, issuing orders, she prayed he was a man of his word. She also hoped he wasn't one of Cameron Abernethy's minions. Perhaps that was why the mystery of Rebecca Abernethy's death had never been solved?

* * *

Jamie wasn't fully alert until the next morning. Jackie hadn't been permitted to stay the night with him but the ward didn't have set visiting hours, so she was free to come and go as she pleased. She decided to keep Charlie off school as he was so upset and because it just made life easier.

Not only was she worried for her son, but she was also afraid for Allegra. She'd lost count of the number of times she'd tried calling her. At first her calls had just rung out. Now every time she tried, a robotic voice on the other end said the call couldn't be connected, which bloody terrified her.

Digger and Gary were predictably raging and plotting how they could get at Cameron Abernethy. Jackie told them in no uncertain terms to leave it well alone. Even a sheepish Dave turned up at the hospital. He'd stayed well out of Jackie's way ever since he and Logan had returned to their home after the truce Jamie had brokered with

Craig Lawson. For once, she wasn't angry at him. This wasn't his fault, which made a rare change and she appreciated the effort he made for her son. Luckily for him, Jackie Gray's heart was big.

Dave was there when Jamie repeatedly asked for Allegra, as were Digger, Gary and Charlie. Logan was at work. Jackie had kept fobbing her son off with excuses for her absence, not wanting to upset him when he was still so fragile but he was becoming so distressed she was left with little choice. She looked to Dave for help.

'You have to tell him,' he said.

'Tell me what, Maw?' said Jamie. 'What are you hiding from me?'

'I've been trying to get hold of Allegra,' she told him. 'But she's not answering her phone. I'll keep trying for you, though.'

'He's hurt her,' he gasped, attempting to sit up and failing. 'Her da's done something to her.'

'What do you mean, Jamie?' said Charlie, his lower lip starting to wobble.

But Jamie didn't even hear him. 'You have to tell the police, Maw. Cameron tried to kill me and he'll do the same to her.'

'Jamie, you have to calm down,' said Jackie, pulling a sobbing, bewildered Charlie to her. 'I've already told them. They're looking for her.'

Jamie pressed his hands to his eyes, wincing when he compressed his swollen black eye. 'Allegra,' he breathed, starting to cry.

Digger and Gary glanced at each other, no idea how to handle the situation. They'd never seen Jamie cry before. Even when they were kids and he'd fallen and hurt himself or his drunken dad had beaten him he'd always refused to cry.

'The police will find her, sweetheart,' said Jackie.

'They're too late,' he replied.

'You don't know that.'

'If she was okay she would have answered her phone. She always answers.'

'What do you need us to do?'

'I want to be on my own.'

'I don't think that's a good idea.'

'Please,' he said, the word more of an order than a request.

'Okay, if that's what you want. Come on,' she told the others.

When they'd gone, Jamie sobbed into his hands. The bastard had finally done what Allegra had always been afraid of.

He'd killed her.

* * *

DI Ross turned up at Jamie's room to find his mother, brother and friends sat on plastic chairs in the corridor outside the door.

'Why aren't you inside?' he asked them.

It was left to Jackie to be the spokesperson. 'Jamie got upset that we can't get hold of Allegra. He's convinced it's something to do with her da.' The look in Ross's eyes turned her insides to water. 'Gary,' she said. 'Will you take Charlie for something to eat? He didn't get any breakfast.'

'No problem, Mrs G,' he replied, getting to his feet and taking Charlie's hand. 'Come on, wee man.'

But Charlie refused to be moved. 'Do you know where Allegra is?' he asked the inspector.

'No' yet,' replied Ross. 'But I'm working on it.'

'Will you tell me when you find her?'

'Course I will.'

'Thanks,' the boy replied before leaving with Gary, glancing back over his shoulder at Ross, as though he was certain he knew more than he was saying.

'Are you Jamie's father?' Ross asked Dave.

'You must be joking,' retorted Jackie. 'As if I'd ever go with that.'

'Charming as always, Jackie,' frowned Dave.

'He's the da of one of Jamie's best friends,' she added.

'I see.' Ross looked to Digger. 'And you?'

'I'm one of his best pals.'

'One of the Blood Brothers?'

'Aye.'

'And is the lad who just left with Charlie a Blood Brother too?'

They all nodded.

'Where's the fourth member of your wee posse?'

'At work,' said Digger.

'Where does he work?'

'In a call centre.' He frowned when the corner of Ross's mouth lifted in amusement.

'I need to ask you both to leave,' said Ross. 'What I have to say is for Mrs Gray's ears only.'

'If this is about Jamie I want to know,' announced Digger. 'We practically grew up together, he's more like my brother than my pal.'

Ross's eyes narrowed. 'Go away.'

'Do as he says, Digger,' said Jackie gently. 'It's okay.'

Dave got to his feet. 'Come on, let's grab a brew.'

Eventually he managed to encourage Digger away. Digger strutted arrogantly down the corridor, throwing Ross scowls over his shoulder as he went.

'All right,' Jackie asked Ross. 'What do you know?'

'I want to discuss it with Jamie,' he replied. 'I still haven't interviewed him. He may have vital information.'

'What did his doctor say about that?'

'That he's fit to be interviewed.'

'Okay.'

They entered Jamie's room to find him staring miserably out of the window, eyes red from crying. He hastily wiped his face, erasing the tears that stained his cheeks.

'Who are you?' he asked Ross.

The inspector took out his warrant card. 'DI Ross, Glasgow North East. I'm investigating the hit and run.'

'Have you found Allegra?' he said hopefully.

'Not yet, I'm afraid.'

'Jesus,' he breathed. 'Have you spoken to her da, Cameron Abernethy? He's hurt her, I know it. He found out about our relationship and that we were going to Switzerland together and he killed her for it. He's a fucking psycho.'

'Please calm down, Mr Gray.'

'I'll be calm when you find Allegra. Have you caught Neil Burrows? He's the one who did this to me.'

'So your mother's already informed me.'

'Allegra told me Neil drove the car that killed her maw. Find him and you'll find out what happened to Allegra.'

'Please, Mr Gray,' said Ross, taking the seat by his bedside. 'Or may I call you Jamie?'

Jamie nodded, totally indifferent to what the inspector called him.

'I have some information to share,' continued Ross. 'I also need to take your statement.'

'Let the man do his job, Jamie,' said Jackie.

Jamie sighed and nodded. 'Get on with it, then.'

'Thank you,' said Ross, Jamie's bad mood failing to affect him. 'Cameron Abernethy himself gave Neil Burrows an alibi. He said he couldn't possibly have been on Main Street running you over because he was with him at his home.'

'The lying twat.'

'Mr Abernethy's son Fenston corroborated his alibi. He said the three of them were together all afternoon.'

'Surely you have CCTV and witnesses?' exclaimed Jackie.

'There was only one camera positioned to capture the driver of the car and the footage is far too grainy to make a positive ID. I've got someone on with trying to clean it up but I don't hold out much hope. The witnesses' descriptions differ too much. Most of them saw the car from the rear or the side. Only Jamie had a view from the front.'

'Aye, I did, and it was him,' said Jamie. 'The bastard was smiling, he enjoyed it.'

'That fits in with what I know of his sadistic personality.'

'Isn't that enough to arrest him?' said Jackie.

'I'm afraid not,' replied Ross. 'It would just be Jamie's word against Burrows'. I did question him, but he denies all knowledge.'

'This is insane,' said Jackie. 'Jamie saw his attacker's face, he tells you who he is and you can't do anything about it.'

'What about Allegra?' said Jamie, more concerned with her than the attack on himself.

'Me and my team have been unable to track her down. I spoke to her father and he told me she's gone away for a few days.'

'Bollocks,' he exclaimed.

'I'm inclined to agree.'

'You are?'

'Her car's gone, as are a few of her personal belongings – handbag, passport and some clothes. But there's been no activity on her credit card, debit cards or her passport and she hasn't popped up on any CCTV or facial recognition.'

'If Allegra was okay she'd be here by my son's side,' said Jackie. 'They're crazy about each other.'

'Cameron has scratches to his face, indicating he was in a struggle,' added Ross.

'Allegra has long nails,' said Jamie. 'She could easily have done that to him. Oh my God, I'm right, aren't I? He attacked her.'

'How did he explain the scratches?' Jackie asked the inspector.

'He gave some vague excuse about a stray dog. He seemed surprised he was even being questioned.'

'I'll bet. The arrogant git thinks he's above the law.'

'I did ask Mr Abernethy if I could search Allegra's room, which is standard procedure, but he refused. He said it was ridiculous I was even worried because she was always going off on unplanned trips.'

'He's lying,' snarled Jamie. 'She daren't go anywhere because she's so afraid of him. She can't spend a single night away from home because he always insists she's there.'

'I've arranged to talk to Allegra's best friend Veronica Hughes this afternoon. Hopefully she'll be able to give me a clearer picture.'

'Can't you just get a search warrant for the house?' demanded Jackie.

'It's not that easy, Mrs Gray. First, I have to establish that Allegra is indeed missing before any judge will grant me a warrant.'

'Well, of course she's missing. Are your lot all stupid or something?'

'They'll be afraid of upsetting that murdering twat,' hissed Jamie, his bruised hands forming into fists. 'He's gonnae get away with it again because everyone's so feared of him.'

'You should know,' said Ross, 'that I was senior investigating officer into Rebecca Abernethy's death.'

'Oh, great,' he snarled. 'So you're gonnae do nothing about this just like you did about her mother's death.'

'I'll do no such fucking thing,' Ross snarled back, surprising Jamie into silence. He took a deep breath and attempted to straighten his crooked tie, skewing it even more. 'I apologise. That case, well, it still haunts me. If I tell you both something, can you keep it to yourselves? I could get the sack for what I'm about to tell you but it's only right. It's time someone knew.'

'You can trust us,' said Jackie.

He nodded. 'Aye, all right. I did my best with the Rebecca Abernethy case. I knew someone had purposefully run that poor woman off the road and I knew her husband was responsible. Cameron didn't do it personally, he got one of his paid lackeys to do it, probably Neil Burrows but I couldn't prove it. Not only was there no evidence but I was pressured to let it drop. I put my all into that case. I saw what was done to Rebecca, she suffered a lot before she died. I interviewed Cameron several times until he threatened to sue me for harassment. I spoke to him one time off the record when I turned up at his home and the bastard practically admitted what he'd done. You see, I found evidence Rebecca was planning to leave him and she was going to take Allegra with her. Cameron had a very strong motive, but I just couldn't get anything concrete to pin on him. Now his daughter goes missing when she's about to leave for Switzerland. That is one coincidence I can't ignore. I managed to track down the booking for two tickets under her name. When I confronted Cameron with that, he denied all knowledge.'

'But he did know,' said Jackie. 'He planted a listening device in Allegra's room, he heard her and Jamie discussing their plans.'

'And you're certain you didn't recognise the mystery informant who told you that?'

'Absolutely. I'd never seen him before.'

She returned the detective's suspicious stare. It was obvious he didn't believe her but he couldn't prove anything. Let him think what he liked.

'This is my chance to correct my first failure,' continued Ross. 'I don't care if it kills my career, I'm bringing the bastard down. Perhaps, if I'd been successful the first time, you wouldn't be lying in a hospital bed and Allegra wouldn't be missing,' he said sadly.

The misery in his eyes caused Jackie's big heart to open right up. 'I'm sure you will,' she said kindly. 'You seem very dedicated.'

DI Ross nodded. 'Thanks. I've put an alert out for Allegra's car and every officer in Glasgow is on the lookout for her. I don't care what her father says. We'll find her, don't worry.'

'There's something else you should know,' said Jamie uncertainly.

'Yes?' replied Ross.

'Allegra wouldn't want me to tell anyone this but I think you need to know, then you'll understand the danger she's in.'

'You can trust me to be discreet, Jamie.'

'All right. She told me she's woken up a few times in bed to find her da lying on top of her. He didn't do or say anything, she said he seemed to be fighting with himself. Then he got up and left. The last time he did it, he grabbed her by the throat – she showed me the bruises on her neck.'

'That poor lassie,' said Jackie, eyes filling with tears.

'I must say I'm shocked,' said Ross. 'I didn't think even Cameron Abernethy capable of that.'

'That's why Allegra's so desperate to leave,' said Jamie. 'She's afraid of what will happen if she stays. She said her da seemed to think she should take her mother's place because she looks just like her.'

'There is a striking resemblance between Allegra and Rebecca.' Ross really hoped he wasn't going to come across the daughter's mangled body too. The thought filled him with sadness. 'Excuse me,' he said when his phone rang. 'I need to take this.'

'I feel sick,' said Jackie, sinking into the chair by Jamie's bed as Ross left the room.

'I wish I was out there looking for her,' said Jamie. He gestured to his leg. 'But I'm fucking useless.'

'The best thing you can do for Allegra is get well,' replied Jackie. 'That lassie needs you fit and strong.'

'We're no' going to Switzerland now, are we?'

'No, sorry, sweetheart, but it doesn't mean you never will.'

They looked round when the door opened and Ross returned.

'I've got to go,' he told them. 'Allegra's car's been found at Cathkin Braes Country Park.'

'Is she there?' said Jamie hopefully.

'No,' he replied. 'But it could lead us to her whereabouts. Does Cathkin Braes hold any special significance to her?'

'Not that I know of,' replied Jamie. 'She wouldn't just abandon her car. She told me she had a buyer lined up for it to give us more money to go away with.'

Ross nodded, looking troubled. 'I'll keep you informed,' was all he said before leaving.

'If Cameron's done anything to her I'm going to fucking kill him,' spat Jamie. 'I'm going to get well, get this cast off my leg and I'm going for the bastard.'

'Leave it be, Jamie. Let the police do their job.'

'Seriously? You heard Ross. Cameron got away with it before and he thinks he's gonnae get away with it again. Well, I won't let him.'

'Ross seemed determined. If there's something to find he'll find it.'

'Or he could be on Cameron's payroll and he just said that to make us think he'll go all out.'

'Give him a chance. You're in no fit state to do anything anyway.'

'I can't just lie around here while she's in trouble. Christ,' he said, burying his face in his hands when tears threatened again.

Jackie wrapped her arms around him, and he clung onto her as he cried.

'It's all right, sweetheart,' she said. 'Everything will be okay. You'll see.'

She knew it was a lie. Nothing would ever be the same again.

17

Ross surveyed Allegra's car with dismay. This didn't look good. Cathkin Braes was a massive 493 acres. At 200 metres above sea level it was the highest point in Glasgow, but he was unable to enjoy the amazing view over the city because of his fear that Cameron Abernethy had killed someone else. It wasn't just family members he was keen on bumping off – disgruntled employees, business rivals. Cameron had managed to wriggle out of every tight spot he'd found himself in thanks to his team of greasy lawyers, powerful friends and enormous wealth.

'What have you found?' Ross asked one of the scene examiners going over the car. Other officers might think he was being a bit over the top, after all Allegra hadn't even officially been reported missing, but his gut was telling him this was the right way to go.

'We've got blood in the boot,' replied the woman grimly.

'How much?' he said.

'Enough to make me look further, unless she had a very heavy nosebleed.'

'Who has a nosebleed in the boot?' Ross frowned.

'That's what I thought. I also found several long blonde hairs with the follicles attached. In my opinion they were torn out.'

'So, you think she was actually in the boot?'

'That's what the evidence suggests. Plus, I can smell coconut and, according to her best friend, Allegra always wore coconut-scented perfume.'

'Then where did she go?'

'Or where was she put?'

'You think that's what happened?'

'Unless she enjoys lying in her own boot while bleeding and tearing out her hair, I'd say so. Due to the amount of blood, I'd say you need to find her pretty quickly.'

'We don't know that blood is hers.'

'I'll run a DNA comparison on the blood and hair. I'll push it through quickly, so you'll have the results in about four hours, but I've been doing this job for fifteen years. It's hers, I'm sure. I'd stake my reputation on it.'

'Thank you,' Ross said sincerely. The evidence had given him what he needed to start a search. 'I'll call in a dog team,' he said, getting on his phone. 'They're going to be our best bet.'

* * *

Jamie was irritable. He felt bad about snapping at the hospital staff, who were only trying to do their best for him, as well as his family and friends, but he couldn't help it. He was tormented with fear for Allegra and he could do nothing to help her. As his leg was elevated he couldn't even get out of bed. Fortunately, the strong painkillers he was on made him drowsy, blocking out a little of the anxiety. He was tortured by bizarre dreams where he was chasing Allegra but she always remained just out of reach. Hideous slobbering beasts that obviously represented her father snatched her away from him before he could get near her. Her high-pitched screams echoed in his head, causing him to jump awake.

'DI Ross,' he breathed as the inspector came through the door, a buff folder tucked under one arm.

'Are you okay?' said Ross. 'You're sweating.'

'Bad dreams,' he replied, running a hand down his face. Jamie squinted at the clock on the wall. 'It's almost midnight. What are you doing here so late?' His visitors had left hours ago, so he was alone. Jamie swallowed hard. 'Have you found her?'

'Not as such.'

'What does that mean?'

'It was her car at Cathkin Braes.' Ross broke off, wondering how he could phrase what he had to say. In all the years he'd been doing this job, he'd never got used to breaking bad news.

'What did you find?' demanded Jamie, barely able to cling onto his calm.

'We found blood and hair in the boot. Tests confirmed they belong to Allegra.'

'Is she still alive?' he whispered.

'We called in a dog handling team. They traced Allegra's scent from the car to Cathkin Marshes, where the trail stopped.'

'Y... you mean she went in the marsh?'

'We can't know for sure.'

'But if she hadn't then the dogs would have followed her scent.'

'Possibly. There's been no rain or bad weather and we came across the car pretty quickly, but there are plenty of footpaths through the marshes and there are a lot of tributary streams into them which might have confused the dogs.'

'Would the dogs have picked up her scent if she'd gone along one of the paths?'

'Perhaps. Nothing is one hundred per cent certain.'

'So, there's still hope?'

'Yes, I'd say so. As soon as it's daylight a team will start searching the marsh.'

'You mean you'll be looking for her body?'

'To discount the possibility that she's in there, that's all.'

'Don't treat me like an idiot. You think she's in there, don't you? Please tell me the truth.'

'I'd say it's a strong possibility,' Ross mumbled.

'Christ,' said Jamie, burying his face in his hands. He raised his head as an idea came to him. 'Can't you track her through her phone?'

'We've tried that but we couldn't find a signal, meaning it's probably switched off.'

'Which is why it keeps going to voicemail when I try calling her.'

'The last time it pinged a mobile phone mast the data indicates she was at home. After that, nothing. A formal missing person's report hasn't been filed yet, her father refused to do it, which isn't helping my investigation.'

'You need someone to file one? I'll bloody do it.'

'Thank you. Let's do the formalities now, if you're feeling up to it?'

'Too right, I am,' replied Jamie, glad to be able to do something useful.

'Thank you,' said Ross, taking a seat and opening the buff folder he carried.

Ross filled out the relevant paperwork, feeling better now that formality had been taken care of. It would be harder for anyone to shut down his investigation. He flipped the folder shut and got to his feet. 'I'll let you know how we get on tomorrow.'

Jamie nodded, breathing deeply to try and keep calm.

Ross hesitated at the door. 'Don't give up yet. This could still end well.'

'When have you ever known anything involving Cameron Abernethy to end well?'

'Something else you should know – the media have got hold of the story. They also know about your relationship with Allegra.'

'Oh, great. So they're gonnae start bandying it about like entertainment?'

'Aye, that's usually the way it goes, so brace yourself.'

Ross left, leaving Jamie to wonder how life had gone from being so amazing to so incredibly shitty.

* * *

Media interest in Allegra Abernethy's disappearance was intense. It had everything the press liked in a story – a rich heiress, a father with a chequered history, rumours of murder, an illicit relationship. Jamie was astonished the next morning when his mum brought him several newspapers – nationals, not just locals – detailing his relationship with Allegra. The majority of the stuff they'd written was over-romanticised nonsense. Fortunately, opinion did seem to be on his side and they'd painted him as a tragic Romeo figure rather than a ned off a sink estate, who had almost been killed attempting to rescue an innocent girl from her brute of a father. They also lapped up the fact that he belonged to a gang called the Blood Brothers. Jamie wondered what all the journalists would say if they knew the first time he met Allegra she'd stolen from his shop then dragged him into another shop to steal from there too. Rebecca Abernethy's death was resurrected as well, with hints that her husband could have been behind it. None of the reporters were daft enough to come right out and say it for fear of being sued, but the undertone made it perfectly clear what they were saying. It seemed everyone thought there was something distinctly suspicious about a man whose wife dies in mysterious circumstances and whose daughter then goes missing. A few journalists attempted to come onto the ward to talk to Jamie but they were fended off by the staff, who zealously guarded their patient.

* * *

The rest of the Blood Brothers were fuming and wanted to do something. Logan learnt that Cameron was holding a press conference outside an office block he owned in the city centre so they headed down there. They managed to mingle with the throng of reporters and found a spot not far from where Cameron stood with his lawyer at his side, a man who resembled a hyper-alert Doberman.

'He makes me fucking sick,' muttered Logan as Cameron lamented about how worried he was about his daughter. Unable to contain himself, Logan shouted out, 'Oy, you!'

Cameron's massive bull head scanned the crowd, his fiery gaze settling on him. 'Yes?'

'If you're so worried about Allegra, why didn't you file a missing person's report?'

'Because I assumed she'd gone off on one of her trips. She enjoys travelling.'

'Bollocks,' Logan retorted. 'She was too scared to leave the city because she knew you'd punish her for it. You're a control freak and you controlled her.'

'Aye, ya did,' piped up Gary. 'Allegra told us all about it. She's pure feared of you. Twenty-one years old and she couldnae even have a night away from the hoose because you insisted on her being home.'

'Because I wanted to keep her safe,' Cameron replied smoothly.

'That's shite,' said Digger. 'You hurt that lassie. If she was fine she'd be by Jamie's bedside because they're madly in love.'

The journalists started talking excitedly amongst themselves as they realised three of the four Blood Brothers were present.

Cameron's lawyer looked to the single police officer present. 'I insist you remove these men.'

'We're on a public pavement,' said Logan. 'We cannae be removed.'

'Well?' the lawyer demanded of the police officer.

'He's right,' he replied. 'They're on a public pavement and they've not done anything wrong.'

'They're disrupting proceedings.'

'Your client's disrupted them by lying through his teeth,' said Logan. He looked to the journalists. 'We'll give you an interview and we'll give you the truth, unlike that lying pair.'

Logan's eyes widened when the journalists surged towards them, all shouting out their questions at once.

'What my friend didn't add,' called out Gary. 'Was that we'll give you our stories for the right price.'

Cameron stood there impotently, fury clearly building inside him. It seemed the journalists had forgotten all about him. They were even ignoring his lawyer's demands for their attention. His chance to put forward his own side of the story had been lost. His hands balled into fists when the three Blood Brothers smirked at him. The little bastards were smarter than he'd thought.

* * *

Jamie sighed at the phone in his hand. He'd repeatedly tried Allegra's number and even though each call refused to connect, he resolved never to give up trying. If he was the one who'd disappeared she wouldn't give up on him. He also called Ross to see how the search of the marshes was going but was just told that it was ongoing and they'd let him know if they found anything. The thought of that beautiful vivacious woman lying dead at the bottom of a cold bleak marsh nearly drove Jamie insane and he tried not to think about it.

All he had left of Allegra were the photos he'd taken of her on his phone, but looking at them was like stabbing himself in the chest. If this was love he didn't want it any more, it hurt too much. Jamie resolved that if the worst did happen and she never came back, he would never fall in love again.

* * *

Ross sipped coffee from a flask his wife had made up for him as he watched the team he'd put together search the marshland. He stood on the boardwalk, a wooden platform stretching out across the deep, grey marsh water, so he could oversee everything without getting his feet wet. On a warm sunny day he imagined this would be a very pleasant spot, but today it was grey and overcast, a chill wind blowing across the reeds, and it felt quite desolate. Christ, he hoped the girl wasn't in there. That was not how he wanted this to end. The dog handlers were still at work, but the task was impossible because the marsh was criss-crossed with inlets from different sources, which confused the dogs. At least they'd indicated that Allegra had come up to the marshes and, as far as they could tell, she'd never left, but the team couldn't rely on the tracking dogs to confirm that. Some parts of the marshes were simply too dangerous to take the dogs through.

There was a whine overhead and Ross looked up to see the drone he'd drafted in sweeping across the marsh, giving them a bird's eye view while the police divers searched what part of the marsh they could. In parts it was so deep and intensely cold and murky that visibility was reduced to zero.

'I've found something,' yelled a voice.

Ross tutted when he saw it was the fucking nerd in charge of piloting the drone. With his jam jar glasses, overbite and balding scalp he looked like he should be at a sci-fi convention rather than a crime scene. He was also one of the most patronising tossers Ross had ever met, and he couldn't stand him. Sadly, he was the best drone pilot they had.

'Where?' Ross snapped at him.

'Quadrant seven, sector fourteen...'

'Never mind all that bollocks, just point.'

'There, by the group of meadowsweet,' he sighed, as though he were talking to a particularly backwards child, extending his arm out to the marsh.

'The what?'

'That patch of tall pretty white wild flowers.'

'Don't patronise me. What has your wee plane seen?'

The tech rolled his eyes. 'The *drone* has spotted something colourful, like a piece of clothing or a shoe, but it's in a bit of a dodgy spot. The ground isn't solid.'

'Can't you lower your plane so we can get a better look?'

'I don't want to risk my *drone* getting wet, unless you're going to pay the hundreds of pounds it would cost to repair it?'

'Let me look at the screen.'

The tech turned the screen for him to see and Ross spotted a small blue object lying amid the meadowsweet.

'Tell the divers,' Ross told the tech. 'They're the best equipped to reach whatever it is. If it turns out to be a crisp packet you're for it.'

'I never make a mistake,' he sniffed before rushing off to speak to the divers.

'What a wee bawbag,' muttered Ross, pouring himself a fresh cup of coffee from his flask. One of the uniformed constables assisting in the search, his nose bright red with cold, stared at the steaming cup with longing in his eyes.

'Piss off,' retorted Ross. 'You should have brought your own.'

'You're all heart, sir.'

'Be quiet or I'll give you to the nerd to use as his personal slave.'

Ross turned his attention from the miserable constable to the divers, who were fighting their way through the reeds to reach whatever it was, the drone tech barking orders at them about which way to go. The look the lead diver gave him said he wished they were allowed to carry harpoon guns. Ross hoped the object in the meadowsweet was a crisp packet because that would mean perhaps Allegra wasn't in there after all and the tech would get savaged by a bunch of irate divers.

Finally, the object was carefully placed into a clear plastic evidence bag by one of the divers, who then made slow progress with it towards the boardwalk Ross was standing on.

'What have you got?' Ross called to the diver while he was still about fifteen feet away, unable to wait any longer.

The diver didn't reply, contenting himself with a glower as he fought through the reeds to reach him.

The dripping wet bag was dumped at his feet, the diver holding onto the boardwalk to catch his breath.

'You okay?' Ross asked him.

'Aye,' he breathed. 'It's like trying to swim through mud in here.'

Ross scooped up the bag. Inside was a single dark blue leather shoe. He didn't know much about women's shoes but it looked expensive to him.

'Hold this,' he told the miserable constable, holding the bag out to him.

The man took the bag in his hands, wincing as the cold water that dripped from it soaked into his sleeve. Ross tugged the list of what Allegra had last been seen wearing out of his jacket pocket.

'Royal blue Saint Laurent leather shoes. Size six.'

The constable studied the bottom of the sole. 'They're size six, sir.'

'Damn,' he sighed.

'We've found something,' yelled the team searching the bird hide at the end of the boardwalk.

Ross rushed over, followed by the constable, who still clutched the bag containing the shoe.

'What is it?' he demanded of the scene examiners inside who wore white paper suits, stopping at the entrance to the hide so he wouldn't trample any evidence.

'It's okay, you can come in,' said one of them, beckoning him in with a gloved hand. 'Just stand outside the tape we've put down.'

'Okay,' he replied, gingerly stepping inside. 'Not you,' he frowned at the constable holding the shoe when he moved to follow.

'We've got fingernails and more blood,' said one of the scene examiners.

Ross saw the remnants of three blood red nails embedded in the wooden floor at the base of three deep gouge marks, along with drops of blood.

'Jesus,' he breathed.

'They're false nails,' explained the scene examiner. 'But a hell of a struggle must have taken place for them to be embedded in the wood like that. There's also a few long blonde hairs back here.'

'Bag it all and be extra careful with the nails,' said Ross. 'If Cameron Abernethy's blood and DNA is on them then we've got the bastard.'

* * *

It was with a great sense of triumph that Ross knocked on Cameron Abernethy's front door, accompanied by a team of scene examiners, detectives and uniformed constables. They'd made a big show of turning up with sirens blaring and a train of official vehicles. The bastard's mask was slipping and DI Ross was going to enjoy tearing it right off his face.

It was Cameron's slippery lawyer who opened the door. 'Well, look at this circus,' he said, eyes flashing with malice. 'Mr Abernethy's been very patient but this is now harassment. I insist you leave. If you go immediately, we might not take your job from you.'

Ross held up the piece of paper in his hand. 'We have a search warrant for this house in connection with the disappearance of Allegra Abernethy.' He enjoyed the way the git's face fell. 'Out of the way, unless you want me to nick you for obstruction, which I have absolutely no problem with. Well?' he added when he failed to reply. 'What will it be?'

The lawyer sighed and stood aside, allowing them to enter.

'What the hell's going on?' demanded Cameron as they all steamed into the house.

'Concentrate the search in Allegra's bedroom,' Ross told his officers as they split up and headed in different directions.

'Get the fuck out of my house right now before I throw you through a fucking wall,' bellowed Cameron.

'We have every right to be here,' said Ross. 'As your solicitor will tell you.'

'You're mad,' Cameron told them. 'You've got a vendetta against me. You tried to blame me for my wife's accident and now you're trying to blame me for this.'

'I take it by "this" you mean the disappearance of your daughter?'

'You should look closer at the manky scrag-end from that scummy estate she was sleeping with. If anyone's dodgy, it's him.'

'Are you referring to Mr Gray who is currently in hospital after being hit by a car that he alleges was driven into him by an employee of yours?'

'You're as mad as he is. Neil never went near him, I know that for a fact.'

'Allegra was last seen entering this house.'

'Did the scrag-end tell you that?' he sneered.

'No, one of your neighbours. Here was the last place she was seen. Surely you want her found safely, Mr Abernethy?'

'Yes, well... of course I do.'

'Then surely you should be helping our investigation rather than hindering it?'

'Mr Abernethy is happy to help in any way he can,' his lawyer smoothly interjected.

'Good. Then you'll both wait outside nice and quietly with my colleague DC Morton while we search the house and you will not interfere.'

'You ba—' began Cameron before his lawyer put a restraining hand on his arm.

'Mr Abernethy agrees,' said the lawyer.

'Excellent,' smiled Ross. 'If you need me, I'll be in Allegra's room.' God this felt good.

Ross headed upstairs and stood on sentry duty at the door to her bedroom. He wouldn't put it past Cameron to bully his way in and tamper with their investigation. He didn't trust any of his people to stand up to him.

'There's evidence of a clean-up,' said the lead scene examiner after studying the room.

'Where?' demanded Ross from the door.

'Here, near the foot of the bed. We've got blood. I can still smell the chemicals used to clean it but there's traces of blood left. They're not visible to the naked eye.'

'There's a dent in the wall too,' said another investigator, pointing to a dink in the wall just a few inches off the floor. 'Looks like it was done by someone kicking it with a heel.'

'A woman's heel?'

'From the position of it, she'd have to have been lying on her back to put it there.'

'How does that fit in with the blood?'

'Allegra could have been lying on her back and kicked the wall. If that was the case the blood we found would have come from her head, neck or possibly her upper arm or shoulder. From the description we were given, Allegra is five feet eight inches tall.'

'How fresh is that blood?'

'No older than forty-eight hours.'

'Ruling out Jamie Gray. He was at work in Baillieston and then he was hit by a car.'

'We've got more blood,' said another investigator, peering behind a set of shelves propped against the wall just a foot away from the blood they'd already found. 'Looks like quite a bit of spatter. The shelves have been cleaned very recently but whoever did it was in a hurry and failed to realise some of the spatter had gone behind the shelves too.'

'There's more over here,' said a female scene examiner, who was studying the area around Allegra's bed. 'There's minute traces of it on the bedside cabinet and in the drawer but it's definitely older.'

'What does that mean?'

'I'm not sure yet, I need more time.'

'Get all these samples tested for Allegra's DNA as soon as possible,' Ross told them.

He felt ashamed of himself when excitement rose inside him. Cameron Abernethy could finally be about to get what he deserved, but his daughter might have to have died for that to happen. There was no doubt in his mind any more.

Allegra Abernethy was dead.

* * *

'You should have seen it, man,' said Digger as they told Jamie all about their encounter with Cameron Abernethy at the press conference. 'He shite himself.'

'Aye,' grinned Gary. 'He was gonnae come out with a load of crap to make himself look the big man but he couldn't. The journos were more interested in us than him. He wasnae impressed.'

Jamie tried to find some enthusiasm, after all they'd done a very good thing, but he couldn't find it in himself. He didn't think he'd ever smile again.

'Hey, look,' said Logan, gesturing to the television mounted on the wall, which Jamie kept switched on at all times. He wanted to be kept up to date on every single scrap of news.

They watched Cameron Abernethy being led out of his home, DI Ross gripping onto his arm as though he was afraid he'd do a runner. Ross wasn't a small man but beside his monstrous prisoner he looked tiny.

'Cameron Abernethy has been taken in for questioning in relation to the disappearance of his daughter Allegra, which police are now treating as a murder inquiry,' said the reporter outside the Abernethy home.

All the blood drained from Jamie's face. 'Murder? Have they found her? Ross promised to tell me first if they found her but he didn't.'

'Take it easy, man,' said Logan, patting his arm. 'The journo's probably just guessing. They've only just nicked him. I doubt the first thing the police did was run outside to tell the reporters.'

'Aye, Logan's right,' said Digger. 'They're just making it up.'

Jamie anxiously twisted the sheet that was pulled up to his waist. 'He killed her. She's dead, isn't she?'

He regarded them all with tear-filled eyes. None of them knew what to say.

18

Ross wanted Cameron writhing in discomfort, stammering pathetic excuses and tripping himself up with his own lies, but on the contrary the accused was cool and calm, letting his slimy git lawyer do all the talking. Ross had hammered him with questions about how Allegra's car had got to the marshes, why no one had seen her since she'd walked through the gates of her home and now he was confronting him with the evidence of blood spatter in her bedroom. He was saving everything they'd found at the marshes until last.

'This is ridiculous,' said the lawyer. 'You've still no evidence that anything has happened to Allegra.'

'If she's alive and well, why hasn't she come forward to let us know?' countered Ross. 'It can't be because she's left the country as there's been no movement on her passport.'

'Allegra was a very highly-strung girl,' replied Cameron. 'Always has been. She's probably too afraid to come forward because of the media circus that you, Detective Inspector, have been personally responsible for stirring up.'

'Her fiancé's in hospital with very serious injuries. You don't think that would be enough to drag her out of hiding?'

'He wasn't her fiancé,' Cameron snarled, eyes blazing. 'He's just a bit of rough she was using.'

Ross was quick to spot that Cameron referred to his daughter in the past tense. 'That's not what Mr Gray and his family and friends assert.'

'They're all fucking liars,' Cameron yelled, slamming his fist down on the table. 'Gold diggers, the lot of them.'

Ross's smile was sly. He'd found the right nerve to prod. 'Is that what happened, Mr Abernethy? Did you get angry about her relationship with Mr Gray? Your families are poles apart. Did you feel a union with their family would degrade you, humiliate you?' He smiled at how red Cameron's face had gone, his massive chest heaving. 'I know how much you prize your reputation, which would be damaged in the eyes of your wealthy, powerful friends if you were connected to a family from the infamous Gallowburn scheme. Did you argue with Allegra over her relationship? Did you get angry?'

Cameron shot to his feet to bellow, 'She'll never marry that fucking loser.'

'Mr Abernethy,' said the lawyer. 'I suggest you sit down...'

'Shut it, you fucking prick,' Cameron yelled at him, dropping back into his strong native Glaswegian accent.

'That's quite a temper you have, Mr Abernethy,' said Ross as Cameron's dark hellish eyes were turned back on him. 'Is that what happened to your daughter? Did she refuse to give up her fiancé and you got angry? Did you attack her?'

'DI Ross,' spluttered the lawyer. 'You're out of line.'

Ross ignored him, gaze fixed on the beast looming over him. 'Is that how you got those scratches on your face?'

'Mr Abernethy has already explained those were from a dog attack,' interjected the lawyer.

'A dog we've never managed to trace.'

'Because it ran off. Dog's run off. Mr Abernethy, please sit down.'

Cameron slammed himself back down in his chair so hard the plastic threatened to crack.

'That's better,' said Ross. 'Do you still refuse to allow our doctor to take a look at those scratches to ascertain where they came from?'

'Yes, I fucking do,' spat Cameron. 'You're wasting time questioning me when you could be doing your job and finding my daughter.'

'I will, just as soon as you explain the blood spatter we found in Allegra's bedroom.'

To Ross's consternation, Cameron leaned back in his seat and smiled. 'Gladly. Allegra's been self-harming for a number of years.'

'What?' the detective said, thrown by this admission.

'She thinks I don't know but a father always knows. She has a knife she keeps in her bedside cabinet that she uses to cut her arms.'

'We found no knife in her room.' Although he did think that explained the older traces of blood found in and around her bedside cabinet.

'Perhaps she moved it? Or perhaps she didn't need it any more since she met...' He swallowed hard, as though he was attempting to stop himself from vomiting. 'Jamie.'

'That's a quick turnabout. You've gone from calling him a gold digger to suggesting he stopped your daughter from self-harming. If he did indeed help her stop then surely you should be welcoming him into your family with open arms.'

'I don't know for a fact that he did. Anyway, the point is that my daughter is a very disturbed girl.'

'Is there anyone who can corroborate that she was self-harming?'

'Yes,' he smiled smugly. 'She saw several counsellors. Sadly, none were able to help her with her problem.'

'I want the names and addresses of these counsellors.'

'Not a problem.'

Ross forced himself not to panic. He hadn't played his trump card yet.

'So you see, Inspector,' continued Cameron. 'You should stop wasting your time with me and find her before she hurts herself. Ever since her mother's death, she's not been able to cope with her loss. The two of them were very close. I'm so afraid that you found her car at the marsh because it just got too much for her.'

Cameron's look challenged him to dare suggest he was responsible for his wife's death with his solicitor present. Despite how much he wanted to, Ross forced himself not to walk into his trap. Instead, the inspector decided it was time to wipe the insincerity off his face.

'We found something else at the marshes,' he said. 'In the bird hide at the end of the boardwalk. Are you familiar with the layout of the marshes, Mr Abernethy?'

'What are you alluding to, Inspector?' said the solicitor.

'Nothing. Cathkin Braes is a popular local beauty spot. It would help Mr Abernethy get a better picture if he's already been there on an innocent day trip.' His smile was insincere. 'That's all.'

'No,' muttered Cameron. 'I've never been there.'

'In the bird hide we found strands of blonde hair.'

'They could belong to anyone,' said Cameron dismissively. 'Or maybe some randy teenagers used it to have a shag.'

Ross resisted the urge to punch him. The man wasn't even trying to act the worried father any more. He had all the confidence of someone who thought he'd got away with it. 'We found something else. Three gouges in the wood. Funnily enough, the gouges resemble the scratches on your face.'

'A dog probably scratched at the wood too. Dogs enjoy scratching things,' Cameron said with an amused smile at his solicitor.

'There were fingernails embedded in the wood, as well as several spots of blood. The hair, blood and nails all belong to Allegra. And before you ask, yes, we've confirmed that with DNA testing. Feeling unwell, Mr Abernethy?' he said when he paled.

'No,' he replied. 'I'm totally fine.'

'I'm very glad to hear it. I'd like those scratches on your face compared to the nails we found. I'd also like to get a sample of your DNA to compare to the skin we found under those nails. Then we can officially eliminate you from our enquiries and move the investigation along, just like you said you wished we'd do.'

'I'll do no such thing. You're trying to pin this on me, and I won't let you.'

'I won't do the examination personally, it'll be done by an impartial examiner, I can promise you, Mr Abernethy.'

'Absolutely not.'

'If you won't consent to the examination voluntarily then I'll be forced to arrest you.'

Cameron shot to his feet. 'You can't do that,' he bellowed so loudly that Ross, the solicitor and the sergeant guarding the door all winced.

'Can I see your forearms, Mr Abernethy?'

Cameron was thrown and he frowned suspiciously. 'You what?'

'Your forearms. I'd like to see them.'

'What for, you fucking poof?'

'I want to know if there are any scratches on your arms. Then we can definitely rule out that you've been in a struggle.'

'You're not seeing my arms. Oh, I'm done with this,' Cameron said striding for the door, glaring at the uniformed sergeant on guard duty when he placed himself in his way.

'I wouldn't do that if I were you, Mr Abernethy,' said Ross. 'It won't help your case.'

'What case? This is all bollocks.' He looked back at the sergeant, who returned his steady glare. Cameron was used to inspiring fear but when he failed to find it in the sergeant's eyes he was enraged. How dare this cretin not be afraid of him?

Ross smiled. He'd picked this particular sergeant as he was the hardest bastard in the entire station. Ex-army, qualified in several martial arts. No one got through him, not even a monster like Cameron Abernethy.

'Just show me your forearms,' said Ross reasonably. 'The sooner you do it the sooner this can all be put to bed.'

'Show the inspector your forearms, Cameron,' said the solicitor casually. 'Prove to the world that he's making a fool of himself.'

'No,' retorted Cameron.

The solicitor frowned, for the first time not looking so confident about his client's innocence.

'Why don't you want to show me your forearms, Mr Abernethy?' said Ross. 'Is it possible there's something on them you don't want me to see? Scratches, for instance?'

'You're not getting any sample from me,' thundered Cameron. 'Knowing you, you'll plant it somewhere.'

'I won't handle the sample personally, we have technicians to do that and I resent the slur to my reputation. I'm a respected police officer with an unblemished record.'

'You have no right to take any DNA sample from my client,' said the solicitor. 'He hasn't been charged with anything.'

'I can if he's detained on suspicion of committing an offence, which I am perfectly willing to do. I would prefer not to do that and risk tarnishing Mr Abernethy's reputation, so if he would give the sample voluntarily it would make everyone's lives easier.'

'It would be reasonable to expect my client's DNA to be found under his daughter's fingernails. They live together, parents and children hug.'

'I don't know about you, but I've never scratched my children when I've hugged them and they've certainly never had my blood under their nails.' He looked back at Cameron. 'When was the last time you hugged your daughter, Mr Abernethy?'

With a furious roar, Cameron hurled himself at Ross, who sat awaiting the inevitable fist to the face. But the rock-hard sergeant was too fast, and pinned Cameron to the table, twisting his arms up his back before he could strike. Ross was a little disappointed, he would have loved to throw a charge of assault on a police officer at him, that way he would definitely have been able to fling him in a cell.

'Cameron, calm down,' exclaimed his solicitor, who'd been forced to leap out of the way to avoid getting caught up in the onslaught.

'Cameron Abernethy,' said Ross, getting to his feet to make his grand pronouncement. 'I am arresting you on suspicion of the murder of Allegra Abernethy...'

'This is ridiculous,' exclaimed the solicitor. 'You don't even have a body.'

'Under Scottish Law we don't need one,' replied Ross, who had to assist the sergeant in holding Cameron down while he snapped on the cuffs. He continued reading Cameron his rights, his sense of triumph growing with each word. Once their prisoner was restrained, Ross rolled up Cameron's right sleeve to reveal several scratches cutting through his skin, almost hidden by the forest of thick black hair.

'What's this, Cameron?' said Ross. 'Did a dog do that, too?'

'Fuck you, you fucking twat,' bellowed Cameron, shaking his whole body in an effort to throw off the officers.

'I'm going to fight this,' exclaimed the solicitor.

'Good for you,' retorted Ross.

He and the sergeant dragged Cameron to his feet. 'Get that DNA sample off him,' he told the sergeant, who nodded, hauling his prisoner away, a constable rushing to assist him as Cameron struggled every step of the way.

'You won't get away with this, Inspector,' said the solicitor. 'Make the most of your job because you won't have it for much longer, I promise you that.'

'Piss off, you slimy prick,' Ross told him.

The solicitor harrumphed before snatching up his briefcase and stalking out.

* * *

'Jamie, you can't leave,' said Jackie. 'You can't even walk on that leg.'

He'd thrown the covers aside and was sat up in bed. Unfortunately, that was as far as he'd managed to get because of the thigh-high cast on his left leg, which was held in a sling to keep the limb elevated.

'I'll manage,' he retorted. 'I can use crutches.' He looked to the two nurses and the doctor gathered in his room. 'Get this thing off me,' he yelled at them, indicating the sling.

'We can't,' replied the doctor. 'It will cause irreparable damage to the limb.'

'I don't give a shite about that. I have to find Allegra, I have to find out what's going on.' He glared at the medical staff with hard eyes. 'Get the fuck on with it, then.'

'Jamie Gray, do not speak to them like that,' Jackie told him. 'I did not raise you to be rude to good people who are only trying to help you.' He was so distressed she'd had to send Charlie away with Gary and Digger.

'I have to find out about Allegra,' he replied. 'Ross is telling me nothing and the news said she's dead.'

'That is not definite. You can't trust the news, it's full of shite.' She breathed a sigh of relief when Ross walked through the door. 'About bloody time. Jamie's going demented here.'

'Sorry I haven't come sooner,' the detective replied. 'But it's been full tilt on the investigation.'

'What's going on?' demanded Jamie. 'Why have you arrested Cameron?'

Ross looked to the medical staff. 'I need to talk to Jamie in private.'

They were only too happy to oblige and hurried out of the room, closing the door behind them.

'Is she dead?' said Jamie. 'Have you found her?'

'No, we haven't.'

'But the news said you've arrested Cameron for her murder.'

'We have,' said Ross as gently as he could. Even he was touched when Jamie's eyes welled up, a single tear rolling down his cheek.

'But if you haven't found her…'

'We've enough evidence to suggest that she was killed.'

'What evidence?'

Ross went on to relate the hair, blood and fingernails they'd found, as well as the fact that they could find no trace of her anywhere.

'DNA testing confirmed it was Cameron's blood and skin they found under her nails. The nails we found match the scratches to his face. We also found his hair where the nails were discovered. Physical examination revealed a small patch of hair had been torn out of the top of his head, most probably in a fight, as well as a large bruise to the back of his head. Three hours ago, the team searching the marshes found a knife covered in Cameron's fingerprints. Allegra's blood was on the blade. It looked like an attempt had been made to throw the weapon into the water but it got stuck in a patch of reeds, preserving it from the water.'

Jamie turned ashen. 'That's how he did it? With... with a knife?'

Jackie shuddered and turned her back, softly crying.

'Yes, we think so,' said Ross as gently as he could. 'This persuaded the procurator fiscal that the evidence threshold had been reached to formally charge him.'

'She could still be alive, though, couldn't she? He might have injured her, she could have got away and she's hiding somewhere hurt, scared to come out in case he attacks her again.'

'I really hope that's the case, Jamie, but I've been a police officer a long time and sadly I don't think so. It's all over the news about his arrest. If she was hiding she'd know it was safe to return. All her money and credit cards were in her handbag, which we found in the car or in bank accounts that haven't been touched and we found her mobile phone in the water not far from the knife. How has she managed to survive with no money or a way to contact anyone?'

'She has eighty grand in an offshore account,' Jamie said excitedly. 'Her mother left it to her in her will. Her godfather put it in there to protect it from Cameron, she could have been using that...'

'We know about that account and it's not been touched either,' Ross said gently.

Jamie frantically hunted around for another explanation, one that would mean she was still alive and that his worst fears weren't coming true but all his hopes were being smashed with each word. 'She could be staying with a friend,' he said lamely.

'My son has a point,' said Jackie, her body shaking with suppressed sobs. 'Until a body's found there's always hope.'

'There certainly is,' said Ross, forcing himself to say what he knew in his heart wasn't true. 'We're going to keep searching the marshes and if we don't find anything there we'll extend the search to the rest of Cathkin Braes. One way or another, we will bring her home.'

Jamie looked down at his hands, in a state of shock.

'Jamie,' said Ross softly. 'Did you know Allegra was self-harming?'

He nodded.

'What?' said a stunned Jackie. 'You never said.'

'I was afraid if I did the police would think she'd vanished because she'd done something to herself. They wouldn't have gone near Cameron Abernethy.'

'That's how he explained the blood we found in her room,' said Ross. 'He said it was because she cut herself.'

'He knew?' he frowned. 'She told me no one knew, that I was the only one she told.'

'That's probably true. I think Cameron knew a lot more about her life than she realised. He mentioned the counsellors she saw. I spoke to those counsellors. One in particular was very squirrelly. I got the impression Cameron had bribed her for information about his daughter, but I can't prove it. We think the knife we found was the one she used to self-harm because some of the blood on it was old.'

'So that could mean she is alive, then?' he said, hope surging through him again.

'Perhaps, but the majority of the blood we found on the blade was fresh.'

'Oh,' murmured Jamie, looking down at his hands, another tear sliding off his cheek and landing on his knuckles.

He looked so devastated that DI Ross was desperate to give him some tiny ray of positivity. 'Our techs managed to retrieve an audio file off Cameron's mobile phone that he'd deleted. It was the recording he'd taken of you and Allegra talking about your trip to Switzerland. If it's any consolation, she sounded so happy.'

Jamie swallowed hard, more tears spilling down his cheeks.

'What will happen to that evil sod?' demanded Jackie. 'Will he be thrown in prison?'

'He's being held at the station overnight until he can be transferred to the magistrate's court tomorrow morning. They will more than likely send him to prison to await trial.'

'What do you mean more than likely? Could he be released on bail?'

'Due to the seriousness of the crime, probably not.'

'But he's rich and connected, so he might get bail.'

'You have to prepare yourself for that possibility.' Ross sighed when his phone rang. 'Sorry, I need to get that.'

Jamie just nodded, attempting to wrap his head around everything he'd just been told. An ashen Jackie stood by his bedside in a state of shock.

'Okay, thanks,' said Ross before hanging up. He looked to Jamie and Jackie. 'That was one of my sergeants. We've got Cameron on CCTV heading towards Cathkin Braes driving Allegra's car the day she disappeared. The footage shows no one else in the car with him, which means...' He trailed off, attempting to figure out how to break this fresh shock.

'Are you saying he had Allegra in the boot?' rasped Jackie.

Ross nodded. 'It's a distinct possibility. We found her blood and hair in there.'

Jackie flung open the door of the small bathroom in Jamie's room and ran inside. The sound of vomiting followed, replaced by quiet sobs.

Ross could see how much love the Gray family had for Allegra. It was so sad her own father had never felt the same.

* * *

Digger and Gary returned with Charlie to Jamie's room half an hour after Ross had left.

'We took the wee man to the park for a kick about,' announced Digger. 'It was fun, wasn't it?'

Charlie nodded, bright-eyed, the exercise taking his mind off his woes for a short time. 'Aye, it was fun.'

The three of them frowned at Jamie and Jackie's pale faces and red-rimmed eyes.

'What's happened?' said Gary.

'Cameron's been arrested and charged with Allegra's murder,' murmured Jamie.

'What?' exclaimed Charlie, starting to cry. 'No, she's not dead, she's not dead.'

Gary pulled the boy to him and he sobbed into his chest.

'So, it's true?' said a stunned Digger. 'He really... did that to her?'

'Aye, the sick bastard,' said Jackie, dabbing at her eyes with a tissue.

'She's gone,' he breathed, sinking into a chair, swallowing back his own tears, surprised by how hard this news was hitting him. Of course, he'd liked Allegra, but it was only just striking him how much she'd touched all their lives. He'd only known her a few months but it felt so much longer.

Jamie didn't speak for the rest of the day. He retreated in on himself, cutting himself off from the world. He spent all of his time on his phone, flicking through the photos he had of Allegra, while obsessively monitoring the news.

As their home was being staked out by reporters, Jackie and Charlie spent most of their time at the hospital, at friends' houses or out at the park, anything to get away from the commotion. Jackie feared her oldest son would pull away from them so much he'd never come back. The first time he'd fallen in love and his fiancée had been murdered by her own father.

When it got too late to hang around the hospital or go to the park and Charlie was complaining about being exhausted she was forced to return to Gallowburn. Logan picked them up in his new car – a nine-year-old silver Honda Civic that he got after the insurance company finally paid out on the old car – and took them back to the scheme. Tricia offered them a bed for the night because their house was still surrounded by reporters.

Allegra's relationship with Jamie had really stirred something in the public consciousness and everyone was desperate to hear the story from Jamie's own lips, but so far he was refusing to comment.

* * *

On arrival at the hospital the next morning with Logan, Digger and Gary in tow, Jackie had hoped to find Jamie in a more stable frame of mind, but if anything he looked even worse and was barely communicative. Jackie was relieved she had left Charlie with Tricia because she thought he could use a break from the darkness that was gathering around his older brother.

'Did you get any sleep, sweetheart?' Jackie asked Jamie, kissing his forehead.

'Not much,' he mumbled. 'I tried to stay awake. When I fall asleep I have bad dreams.'

'You need your rest. You won't heal properly without it.'

'What does it matter now?'

'I hope you haven't forgotten that you have family and friends who love you and want you home?'

He saw the hurt in her eyes and was ashamed. 'Sorry, Maw. I promise I'll try to sleep more.'

'Good lad.'

'No, don't,' he exclaimed when she switched off the television.

'Having that thing on constantly won't help you rest.'

'I keep the sound turned off, it's just so I can keep an eye on the news,' he said, switching it back on with the remote control on his bed.

'DI Ross will contact you when there's more news and he'll know before any journalist.'

'Your maw's right,' said Logan. 'You'll drive yourself crazy watching all that shite.'

Jamie didn't hear him because the footage flicked to the outside of the magistrate's court. Cameron was striding out of the front of it not in handcuffs and surrounded by police but with a smug smile and his solicitor by his side. The caption 'Cameron Abernethy released on bail' appeared at the bottom of the screen.

'What the fuck?' exclaimed Jamie, causing them all to turn to the television.

Gary turned up the volume.

'Mr Abernethy wishes to state how distraught he is about being arrested for his daughter's disappearance,' announced his solicitor to the assembled press. 'The investigation is being led by a police officer with an axe to grind who persecuted my client for his wife's accidental death. The evidence is flimsy, to say the least. DI Ross hasn't even been able to confirm that Allegra is deceased.'

'How do you explain the fact you were caught on CCTV driving Allegra's car, Mr Abernethy?' called out one journalist. 'And that her hair and blood were found in the boot?'

'My client isn't going to lower himself to explaining away evidence provided by a police officer with a vendetta,' said the solicitor. 'The judge recognised how weak the evidence is, which is why he released my client on bail.'

'Seven hundred and fifty thousand pound bail,' retorted another journalist.

'A sum the judge knew my client could easily pay, which goes to show how little faith he has in this case.'

'He was also ordered to surrender his passport.'

'Which is standard procedure, nothing more. Now, if you'll excuse us, Mr Abernethy is very upset about his daughter's disappearance and wishes to return home as soon as possible so he's there when she turns up, which she will.'

The journalists shouted out more questions but Cameron and his solicitor got in the black limo waiting at the kerb and drove off.

Jackie turned the television off in disgust.

'I don't believe it,' said Jamie. 'They let him out. How could they let him out after what he did?'

'At least he can't go anywhere,' said Logan. 'Not without his passport.'

'He only got bail because he's rich and connected,' said Gary. 'If he'd been off the Gallowburn they'd have thrown him in Barlinnie.'

'You're not wrong there, Gary,' sighed Jackie.

'He'll get away with it, won't he?' said Jamie. 'He killed her and the court will let him off because he's a fucking millionaire. Well, I'm not having it. I'm going to see him pay.'

'You'll leave it to Ross,' said Jackie. 'He'll get justice for Allegra.'

'He didn't get it for her maw,' Jamie retorted. 'But I swear Abernethy's not gonnae escape it this time.'

Jackie didn't like the look in her son's eyes, which, since Allegra's disappearance, had become harder and darker than ever.

'You're not to go near him, do you hear me Jamie?' Jackie said. 'You'll end up getting put in prison and he's not worth it.'

Jamie didn't hear her as he'd retreated into a cold, dark place full of hate and pain. 'I'm gonnae get better and I'm gonnae kill the fucker.'

'Don't talk like this. If you go anywhere near Cameron Abernethy you'll be arrested.'

'I won't need to go to him. He'll come for me.'

'He won't be stupid enough to do that.'

'Oh, yes he will. He won't be able to let it go. He blames me for taking his daughter from him and he thinks he can get away with anything.'

'You might have a point there, Jamie,' said Logan. 'He got away with killing his wife and thanks to him being released on bail he thinks he'll get away with what he did to Allegra too, so right now he must be feeling invincible. Men like that think they can just throw cash at a situation, grease the right palms and they can do whatever they like.'

'I don't like this talk, Logan,' said Jackie.

'Sorry, Mrs G, but Jamie's right,' said Gary. 'Cameron tried to kill Jamie and he failed. He might try again.'

She looked to Digger. 'I suppose you agree with them?'

'Aye, I do. The guy's a control freak. His ego won't allow him to leave Jamie alone. He already sent Neil Burrows after him once. He's no gonnae gie' up, he'll just wait until he's let out of here where there's no' so many people around.'

'Let him come for me,' said Jamie, eyes narrowing. 'I'll be fucking waiting.'

'Well, I'm not giving up hope that Allegra is still out there some-where,' announced Jackie.

The silence that greeted her said she was the only one with any hope left.

19

'Is he still there?' said Cameron.

Fenston peered out of the lounge window. 'Yes, he is, the persistent little ferret.'

Cameron sighed and joined his son at the window. Sure enough, there was Jamie Gray standing on the pavement opposite the Abernethy home, giving him a good view straight down the drive to the front of the house.

'That's four hours he's been there now,' said Cameron.

It was Saturday and Jamie Gray had stood in the same spot since Monday for several hours each day. He'd been discharged from hospital six weeks ago and he'd dropped off the radar. He'd assumed the lad had realised he couldn't possibly go up against him and was hiding out in that scummy rat's nest of a scheme. Cameron had even dropped his plans to send someone in to quietly kill him while making it look like suicide. It would be one less person to give evidence against him in court. His trial wasn't due to start for another four months and he had plenty of people working hard to disprove all the evidence against him. He was growing confident that he could survive this particular crisis. If it went according to plan, all the charges would be dropped before he even set foot inside a courtroom.

Then Jamie Gray had shown up, his injuries healed, walking about as though that car had never driven into him. Although he'd only seen him from a distance, he could tell there was something harder about the boy, something stonier. It was in that unwavering gaze that stared back at him right into his own home, his sanctuary. Jamie Gray had changed, and Cameron got the feeling he was now a dangerous opponent. So he'd revived his plans to have him removed before he caused him any more problems. He just wished he'd stop standing there, staring at him. The sooner the little prick was gone the better.

'That's it,' snarled Cameron. 'I'll make the sod leave.'

'Father, don't,' said Fenston, rushing to put himself before the front door, blocking his way. 'Don't give Ross an excuse to persecute you some more.'

'Well, this is intolerable. Who the fuck does he think he is?' He'd called the police but they'd refused to do anything as Jamie had the right to stand on a public pavement. So he'd tried having a word with the neighbour whose house the little runt was standing outside, thinking if two of them made a complaint the police would be forced to take action but the git had refused, saying the lad wasn't doing him any harm. The bastard had always hated him, just because he'd used his influence to block an extension he'd wanted to put on his house. The extension wouldn't have affected him in any way, but the neighbour had only been a resident on their exclusive street a few months and Cameron had wanted to show him who was king around here.

Cameron's temper got the better of him. No one treated him like this.

'Father, don't,' said Fenston when he stormed back to the door.

With a grunt Cameron shoved him aside and pelted up the drive and onto the pavement. Jamie stood across the road, glaring at him with that incessant stare. For fuck's sake, did the boy never blink?

'What do you want?' Cameron bellowed at him, forced to wait on the opposite side of the road as a car was coming along it.

'Where is she?' Jamie called back.

'I don't know.'

'Aye, ya do, you lying bastard. Is she in that marsh?'

'I've nae... I mean no idea,' snarled Cameron, turning purple.

Jamie's lip curled into a grim smile. 'Part of the real you slipped out then. Dae you think your big hoose and posh cars make you better than me? Well, they don't. You'll always be estate trash, just like me.'

Cameron raced across the road, but he was shocked when Jamie aggressively stepped forward to meet him. He wasn't used to this, he was used to people being afraid of him. Jamie wasn't stupid enough to throw out any threats that Cameron could use to report him. He just stood there silently goading him, which for Cameron was even worse.

Fenston pelted up the drive after him. 'Father, don't,' he called.

'Fucking stay there,' Cameron yelled at him over his shoulder.

Fenston, who had never dared disobey his father in his entire life, remained at the top of the drive, hopping from foot to foot with anxiety.

Cameron turned his attention back to Jamie. 'You'll never see her again,' he told him.

'Is she in Cathkin Braes?'

'You'll never know.' He dropped his voice to a whisper. 'I've separated you forever. You'll never see her again – dead or alive.'

'You fucking bastard,' spat Jamie.

'Come on, attack me. I know you want to. I've heard about your reputation and you're not someone to be taken lightly in a fight. Have you got those famous bike chains of yours? I'm sure you could cause me some real damage with them.' He smiled when Jamie continued to glare at him, making no move to attack. 'Disappointing. Maybe you don't love my daughter as much as I thought you did?'

'I'm just no' stupid. I'm no' gonnae attack you but I promise you one thing – I will find her and bring her home.'

'She's mine,' Cameron hissed through clenched teeth. 'Only I know where she is and that's the way it's going to stay. Let the police stumble about up at Cathkin Braes like the fucking pricks they are. They'll never find her.' It was incredibly satisfying to see the panic ignite in Jamie's eyes.

'Do you mean they're searching in the wrong place?' Jamie demanded.

It was Cameron's turn to smile. 'That is something you will never know. Now piss off, you're not good enough for this street.'

With that he turned and ambled back across the road, confident in his victory.

'Where is she?' Jamie yelled after him, desperation in his tone. 'Tell me.'

Cameron just threw him a smirk over his shoulder before following a relieved Fenston back to the house.

Jamie turned and stomped down the road, deciding to get out of there before he did something stupid and attacked Cameron. He'd been winning, beating down that beast with his silent vigil but the bastard had completely turned the situation on its head. Had he put Allegra somewhere else, after all? Was everything the police had found at Cathkin Braes a blind? Perhaps Cameron had assumed he couldn't possibly be tried for murder without a body, failing to realise that wasn't the case.

Jamie was forced to slow his pace when his left lower leg started aching. He'd worked bloody hard to get back on his feet as fast as possible. In fact, he was in better shape than ever. His body felt stronger, harder, but his leg still wasn't one hundred per cent.

Finally, he reached the bus stop and sat down on the small plastic bench. He pulled the hood of his jacket up when someone driving past glanced his way and pointed. Hounded wasn't the word for how the press had treated him. When he'd left the hospital, they'd been waiting for him and they'd surrounded his home for days. It had felt like they'd been under siege. His maw had got so sick of it she'd stormed into the garden swinging a frying pan. The harassment had only let up when Ephraim had freaked the journalists out so much with his natural creepiness that they'd decided to back off, although that hadn't stopped the bombardment of emails and phone calls. Jamie had refused to give a single interview, which might have got them off his back, but he didn't want them bandying about the most intense and beautiful relationship of his entire life as entertainment. He couldn't stand the thought of people devouring details of what he'd had with Allegra over their breakfast then gossiping about it with their friends. It would have sullied everything they'd shared. Although the thousands of pounds he was offered for his story would have come in very handy, he'd told them all where to stick their offers. Fortunately, his maw had been in total agreement, so she hadn't pressured him to accept any of the offers. Logan, Gary and Digger had all earned from selling their stories to the newspapers but they'd only given very minimal details about his relationship with Allegra. Most of it had been about Allegra herself, nice things about how kind and warm-hearted she'd been and how she'd touched the lives of everyone she'd met. They'd painted her in a beautiful light, cancelling out the smear stories that had been leaked to the press, which Jamie had the feeling had come from her own father.

Over the last couple of weeks, things had quietened down much more but he was still recognised in the street, which he hated. Still, as Ross had said, one day that would stop. Jamie wasn't sure he wanted it to though because the day it stopped was the day everyone forgot about Allegra. It seemed they'd already forgotten about Ben Wilson, there hadn't been any mention of his murder for weeks, unless the investigation had stalled. But he would never stop looking for her. Even if the police called off their search, he would never give up.

* * *

'Da, what are you doing?' Fenston asked his father. He swallowed hard when Cameron scowled at him. 'I mean Father,' he hastily added.

'I'm making a call that you don't want to be a part of. Now piss off.'

'You're angry. Please don't make any rash moves. You don't want to compromise your trial.'

'Are you stupid, boy? I won't get to trial, the case will have collapsed by then, I promise you that.'

'But... how?'

'Get out,' he snarled, shoving him through the kitchen door and slamming it shut behind him. 'Fucking useless,' he muttered. 'No, not you,' he told the voice on the other end when they answered. 'I've got a job for you.' He didn't dare use Neil for anything any more, not after how much police interest there had been in him. Fortunately, he had other people willing to get their hands dirty on his behalf. After today he wouldn't need to worry about Jamie Gray.

* * *

'Jamie, are you okay?' Jackie asked him when he came through the front door.

'Fine, Maw,' he said, sinking onto the couch with a grimace.

'You're sweating.'

'My leg's aching.'

'Where have you been?' She frowned. 'Don't tell me you've been hanging around outside Cameron Abernethy's house again? You have, haven't you?'

He nodded.

'What have I told you about that? You'll get into trouble.'

'I was just standing on the pavement not doing any harm. He came out of the house this time.'

'Please don't tell me you got into a fight?'

'Naw, but he said Allegra's not at Cathkin Braes. He made out it was a blind and he said I'd never find her.'

'He admitted it, then?'

'Not in so many words but as good as.'

'He's the devil himself is that one.'

'Aye, he went as red as him too. I pushed him to his limit today. Soon he'll make his move.'

'Don't talk like that, Jamie.'

'It's true.'

'I hope to God you're not offering yourself up as bait?'

'No, but he will try something, I know it.'

'That's why you've been standing outside his house all this time, isn't it? You've been purposefully winding him up to attack you.'

'He was gonnae do it anyway. At least this way I'll face him on my own terms.'

'Do you think it's wise winding up a man who's had God knows how many people killed?'

'It's the only way to stop him, and make no mistake, Maw, he will come for me and soon.'

Jackie stifled a shudder and turned to the window. 'You got back just in time. It's started raining.' She looked back at her son, who was shifting on the couch, attempting to get comfortable. 'Do you want your painkillers?'

'No, thanks,' he replied.

'As you wish,' she said. It was hard seeing him in pain but she was also proud of the fact that he'd refused to rely on the painkillers, only taking them when the pain got unbearable.

Jamie fell asleep on the couch. Since he'd been hit by the car things did take it out of him more than they'd used to, but his doctor had assured him it was only temporary. It would take him a few more months to get back to normal, physically anyway. Inside he was permanently changed.

He was roused by the sound of his phone ringing over an hour later. It was just going dark outside. At least he felt refreshed and the ache in his leg had gone.

'Hello?' he yawned into the phone.

Jackie, who was sat in the armchair watching the television, frowned when he sat bolt upright.

'How many?' he said. 'Aye, do it, just like we planned. I'll be right there.'

'What's going on?' she said when he leapt to his feet.

'It's the Lawsons,' he replied. 'They're coming onto the north side with a load of their friends.'

'Don't panic, they could just be going for a walk.'

'They've got baseball bats, hammers and other weapons.'

'Knives?' she said, turning pale.

'Wee Kenny Mitchell didn't mention any knives,' he replied. 'He's been keeping watch for them coming onto the north side, I had a feeling this would happen.'

'Is Craig with them?'

'No.'

'Then he might not know about this, he was the one who agreed the truce.'

'Of course he knows. Craig works for Cameron, he always has.'

'But I thought he worked for Fen... whatever his name is.'

'Cameron used him to spy on his own son. He trusts no one, not even his own family. His wee lapdog Neil met Craig through a mutual friend in Barlinnie. My pal in the prison told me Craig was busy making connections he could use on the outside. Craig killed Ben Wilson on Cameron's orders, I don't know why, though. Neil took John Lawson to the body and took a photo of him with it to use as leverage to keep Craig in line. It was the only way Cameron could control a man like that.'

'How do you know all this?'

His chest heaved. 'Allegra worked it out. You need to get to Tricia's. Take Charlie with you. Cameron's coming for me and he might come here. I don't want you and Charlie here when he arrives.'

'Oh, my God,' Jackie said, leaping to her feet. She tore upstairs, yelling her younger son's name.

Jamie got on his phone to call Logan, who said he'd call Digger while Jamie phoned Gary.

A minute later Jackie tore back downstairs with Charlie.

'Please take care,' said Jackie, hugging Jamie.

'I will. Now go.'

'Maw, what's going on?' said Charlie as he was dragged out the door.

Jamie watched them go to make sure they got to Tricia's safely. Only once they were inside and the door had closed behind them did he jog down the street. It had stopped raining and the night air was warm and slightly humid.

'Kenny,' said Jamie, getting back on his phone. 'Have they reached the Gallows yet?'

'Naw, not quite. They've just reached the end of the south side.'

'Why aren't I seeing any smoke?'

'Any second now, mate... aww quality, look at that.'

Jamie gaped at the column of smoke and flame that shot up into the sky, so vast he was able to see it from the north side of the estate. 'I told you to light up a car. What the hell did you use, Semtex?'

'Naw, but I can get hold of some if you want?'

'Jesus Christ, no. What are the Lawsons doing?'

'Some of them shat themselves and ran back onto the south side. It was pure funny.'

'How many are left?'

'About fifteen, twenty of the bastards.'

'Can't you be more specific?'

'It's dark and I'm shite at counting.'

'Jesus,' sighed Jamie. 'However many it is, it's still too many. Okay, Kenny, get your pals. It's onto stage two. Steer them towards the Gallows.'

Jamie tore up the street and turned the corner just as Logan came around it in his car.

Logan flung open the passenger side door for him. 'Was that bang a nuclear missile being detonated or the car going up?' he asked Jamie.

'The car,' Jamie replied, leaping inside and slamming the door shut, Logan setting off with wheels spinning. 'I don't know what the lompers used on it and I don't want to know.'

As they reached the road running along the top of the Gallows, Logan pulled the car up at the kerb and slammed on the brakes, when they saw the mass of Lawsons coming down the street, led by John.

'There's closer to thirty of them,' said Jamie as they leapt out of the car. He took out his phone and dialled. 'Bloody Kenny, useless as always. All right, Stevie,' he added when the voice on the other end answered. 'Do it.'

The men at the front of the Lawson clan released surprised cries and toppled forward when a thick chain that had been stretched across the road between two lampposts snapped up into the air about two feet off the ground, knocking them off their feet.

'Argh, my fucking knee,' cried John Lawson, rolling about on the ground clutching his leg, while the other half dozen men the heavy chain had taken down grumbled about various other injuries.

But their friends simply stepped over them, breaking into a run when they saw two of the Blood Brothers at the end of the street.

'You bastards,' yelled a voice behind Jamie and Logan.

They turned to see Digger racing up the road towards them in full-on battle mode, a baseball bat clutched in his hands, eyes wild with fury and excitement. Gary followed, puffing and panting behind him, wielding a hammer.

Gary looked back over his shoulder, eyes widening when he saw another twelve Lawsons turn the corner, penning the Blood Brothers in between the two approaching groups.

Digger was stunned when Gary actually managed to outsprint him, racing by him with a speed no one realised he was capable of.

He was so surprised he slowed his pace, watching him go with confusion.

'Run, you dumb bag of rocks,' Gary yelled at him.

Digger looked over his shoulder, spotted the danger and ran harder, catching up with Gary, meeting with Logan and Jamie in the middle of the street.

'The bastards have blocked us in,' panted Gary, doubling over to catch his breath. 'I knew the tricky bastards would do something like this.'

'Not to worry,' said Jamie, putting the phone to his ear. The four of them had come up with this plan between them. If it failed, they would be dead. Fortunately, it wasn't just the Blood Brothers fighting this battle. Every lad over the age of twelve on the north side of the scheme had wanted to help. 'Debbie,' he said when his call was answered. 'You're up.'

There was a rallying cry and shadows darted out of the gardens of the surrounding houses dragging six large metal bins along with them. They dumped the bins in the middle of the street before retreating back into the gardens. The four Blood Brothers threw themselves behind a garden wall, peering over the top to watch the action.

The two groups of Lawsons reeled backwards when fireworks exploded out of the bins and shot into the sky. One went rogue and blasted straight into the group of Lawsons approaching them from the left, sending them all scattering.

'Aww, that's fucking brilliant, man,' laughed Digger. 'Look, Sammy Lawson's pants are on fire.'

He and Gary roared with laughter as Sammy flapped about in a panic before he was shoved to the ground by one of his friends, who used their jacket to put out the flames.

Jamie dialled another of his allies. 'Alex, are you ready? Good. Go for it.'

A car drove down from either end of the street, aiming for the two groups of Lawsons, who were now in complete disarray. The cars didn't actually run anyone over, Jamie had told them he wanted as few people injured as possible. In fact, this part of the plan was in honour of Allegra, who would have loved to have participated. The cars managed to speed down the street without hitting anyone, passing each other in the middle but they succeeded in dividing the Lawson forces even more, splitting them into small groups.

While the Lawsons were still recovering from this latest assault, Jamie yelled, 'Get them.'

The four Blood Brothers leapt over the wall, Jamie pulling his bike chains from his pockets and Logan drawing the beaver tail. The four of them barrelled into the Lawsons, many of whom had just managed to get back to their feet, knocking them back over.

Digger raised his baseball bat in the air. 'Come on, you bastards.'

The Lawsons – the ones who still felt up to it after all the shocks – turned to face them, grinning when they saw there were only four of them.

As the Lawsons ran at them, the Blood Brothers outnumbered four to one, a cry let up from the surrounding houses and a dozen men, ages ranging from late teens to early twenties ran out of them, wielding either Ephraim's nunchucks or his beaver tails.

The Lawsons found themselves assaulted not just from the men attacking them from all sides but from the inside too by the Blood Brothers, who battered every Lawson out of the way.

The next few minutes were a confusion of war cries, dull thuds, snapping bones and cries of pain as the two sides brutally fought.

Jamie grabbed one Lawson cousin, who he'd whacked in the face with a bike chain, and hauled him towards him. 'Where's Craig?' he snarled in his face.

'I... I don't know,' stammered the man, his face cut and bruised.

Jamie shoved him to the ground and paused to assess the situation. The street was still full of furiously fighting bodies. Word had got back to other men from the south side of the scheme, who were running to assist their friends while the north side numbers were equally bolstered and the battle was showing no sign of slowing. Night had drawn in fully and someone had smashed one of the streetlights, making it even harder to see.

Logan was in full-on war mode, which always surprised those who only knew the serious, calm side of him. His curly hair sprang from his head, his eyes were feral, and he was savagely throwing himself into the fight. Jamie thought that was how his friend maintained his calm so well, because he got all his rage out in fights. He was using the beaver tail to ruthless effect, although he was careful to take Ephraim's advice and not hit anyone on the head with it. He wanted to maim, not murder.

When Jamie saw a Lawson sneaking up on his friend from behind with a hammer, he moved to intercept but the man went staggering forward from a punch to the back.

'Don't touch my son,' yelled Dave, kicking the man in the stomach while he was down.

'Thanks,' Logan nodded at his dad, his lower lip cut. He was drenched in sweat and panting for breath.

'Nae worries, son. Let's hammer these bastards,' Dave roared before launching himself at a big bruiser with a droopy moustache.

Ephraim leapt into the fray, a machete in one hand and a pair of his homemade nunchucks in the other. Several members of both the north and south sides scattered at the mere sight of him as he unleashed a roar, the tendons popping out in his neck. One man was too slow and received the full force of his nunchucks right in his face.

While Jamie was distracted assessing the situation, one Lawson tried to sneak up on him and kick him in his weak left leg. He managed to dodge the kick and punched him in the face.

As his opponent fell to the ground, a rope was thrown over Jamie's head. He just managed to get his hand between the rope and his throat before it was pulled tight around his neck, causing him to drop one of his bike chains, although he managed to keep hold of the one in his left hand.

Jamie found himself being dragged away from the battle and across the ground towards the Gallows, struggling all the way while ensuring his hand stayed between the rope and his neck. His friends didn't notice, everyone was too involved in the fight. The sound of the battle retreated, the darkness moving in as he was inexorably dragged away from the main road onto the lonely waste ground.

When they reached the burn, he was kicked to his knees, pain shooting through his left leg as he fell into the shadow of the hanging tree. Jamie slumped onto his backside to take the pressure off his leg and managed to crane his neck to see Craig Lawson staring down at him pitilessly. Craig kept a tight hold of the rope, ensuring Jamie couldn't wriggle free.

'You're not the only one who can set a trap,' smiled Craig, green eyes glittering with cunning.

Jamie sighed. The Lawson clan charging into the north side had all been a distraction and he'd fallen for it, allowing himself to be separated from his friends.

When a huge pair of feet appeared before him, Jamie looked up to see Cameron Abernethy glaring down at him, massive barrel chest heaving with suppressed rage. Jamie returned his glare with one filled with equal hate.

Cameron knelt before him and smiled. 'My daughter got what she deserved and now it's your turn.' He nodded up at the hanging tree. 'You're so distraught over Allegra that you can't go on without her. Look,' he said, holding up a piece of paper with a gloved hand. 'You've even written a suicide note.'

Jamie's eyes widened as he found himself staring at a letter that did indeed look to be written in his own hand. How the hell had he managed that?

Cameron pinned the note to his jumper. 'So sad. I wonder how your mother will manage on the estate without you? She might be forced into prostitution.' A humourless grin split his face. 'I'll be the first in the queue there, I can tell you.' Cameron's smile widened when

Jamie grunted and attempted to lash out at him but Craig had him held too tightly.

'All right, string the little bastard up,' said Cameron.

Jamie furiously struggled as Craig dragged him towards the tree, grimacing as his knuckles were pushed into his throat.

'Don't throttle him before we've hanged him,' said Cameron when Jamie began to grunt, lips drawing back over his teeth, eyes rolling about in his head.

'I'm not,' said Craig, coming to a halt.

'Is he having some sort of fit? The git's not dying before I can kill him.'

Cameron recoiled when Jamie's eyes snapped open and glared at him in a way that was more animal than human.

Jamie rammed his elbow into Craig's crotch. His eyes bulged and he sank to his knees in agony. When Jamie threw back his head, he caught him on the bridge of his nose, knocking him off his feet.

Jamie rose to his feet, pulling the rope off over his head and casting it aside, glowering eyes locked on Cameron, a growl rumbling in the back of his throat. The way Jamie held himself made him resemble a predator preparing to spring. The most disturbing thing was the way he puffed air in and out of his lungs and that God-awful grunting noise.

Cameron backed away when he advanced on him, swinging his bike chain, head lowered, feral gaze fixed on him. With a cry of rage Jamie ran at Cameron and lashed out with the chain, hitting him on the side of the left arm. Cameron cried out with pain and backed away. Then his ego reasserted control. He was Cameron fucking Abernethy. He was afraid of no one, especially not methed-up little scheme rats. He'd already decided drugs were the only logical reason for this bizarre display. He dodged another blow from the chain and grabbed Jamie around his already tender neck, squeezing before tossing him aside. Jamie rolled and leapt back to his feet with astonishing agility.

Even his sore leg seemed to have recovered because it certainly didn't slow him down as he ran at his opponent.

Deciding his best advantage was his superior size and weight, Cameron ran at Jamie and the two men met with a bang. Jamie was knocked to the ground and Cameron succeeded in pinning him beneath him. He attempted to lock his hands around Jamie's throat but he couldn't get a grip because the boy was writhing so much.

'Stay still, you little bastard,' he snarled.

Jamie knocked his hands away from his neck and slammed his forehead into the other man's face. While Cameron was reeling from that blow Jamie continued to headbutt him again and again, all the while roaring and growling with rage, the sound bestial. Cameron felt his nose being turned to pulp and still Jamie didn't let up, grabbing him by the front of the shirt and pulling him down to him better to smash his forehead into his face.

Jamie kicked the stunned Cameron off him, the man flopping onto his side like a stranded whale, and leapt to his feet while drawing back his bike chain. Before he could strike a blow his right arm was twisted up his back, forcing him to drop the chain. Howling with rage, Jamie looked over his shoulder into Craig's bloodied face.

'You're dying tonight,' hissed Craig, wrapping the rope back around his neck.

Jamie threw himself backwards, knocking Craig off his feet and landing on top of him. Jamie leapt up and Craig rolled, dodging Jamie's foot when he attempted to stamp on his face. He grabbed Jamie's injured leg and punched him in the back of the knee. Jamie just looked down at him impassively, causing Craig's eyes to widen with shock, before Jamie kicked him in the side of the face, snapping Craig's head sideways, blood spraying from his mouth.

Jamie coldly watched Craig groaning on the ground, eyes rolling back in his head as he attempted to cling onto consciousness. Satisfied he was staying down, Jamie pulled the rope off over his head and tossed it contemptuously to the ground before turning his attention back to Cameron, who had managed to push himself up to his knees, face a bloodied, swollen mess.

'No,' said Cameron, holding up his hands. 'Please.'

Jamie kicked him onto his front and wrapped the bike chain around his neck, pulling so hard Cameron's chest was lifted off the ground.

'Where is she?' Jamie roared in his ear.

Cameron's response was a gurgle, fingers frantically scrabbling at the chain.

'Where is she?' bellowed Jamie in the same inhuman roar.

'Jamie, stop,' yelled a voice. 'You're gonnae kill him.'

Jamie's head snapped sideways to see the rest of the Blood Brothers tearing their way towards him, Dave puffing and panting a few feet behind them, attempting to keep up.

'Oh, Christ,' said Gary when pitch black eyes were turned his way, the scene made more nightmarish by the blood splattered across Jamie's face from headbutting Cameron. 'He's gone all freaky again.'

Jamie spat and snarled when the three of them grabbed him and dragged him off Cameron, who gasped with relief and fell facedown to the ground.

'Where is she? Where is she?' yelled Jamie, fighting to get back at him.

'Take it easy, pal,' said Logan. 'Do you want to go to prison for that jobby?'

Jamie's response was a growl, hands clawing at the air as he fought to free himself.

'Jeezo,' exclaimed Dave when he finally caught up. 'What's wrong with him?'

No one replied.

'Sorry, pal,' Digger told Jamie. 'I've no choice.'

He punched Jamie in the face. He stumbled slightly and shook his head. Digger kept his fists raised, ready to defend himself. He was relieved when the eyes that looked back at him contained his friend.

'Did it happen again?' murmured Jamie, feeling disorientated and a little dizzy.

'Aye, it did,' said Logan while his dad looked on in bewilderment. 'You okay?'

'I think so.' Jamie looked to Digger, who swallowed nervously. 'Thanks, pal.'

He breathed a sigh of relief and lowered his fists. 'You're welcome.'

They turned their attention to Cameron and Craig, who were sprawled on the ground, bleeding and groaning.

'You proper kicked the shite out of those dobbers,' grinned Gary.

Jamie turned to the line of trees. 'Did you get all that?' he yelled.

Two teenage boys, no more than sixteen, emerged from the trees. One of them held a mobile phone. They looked to be very wary of Jamie, not surprising after what they'd just witnessed him do.

'Aye, Jamie,' mumbled one of them. 'We got it.'

'Nice one, lads,' he said, holding his bloodied hand out for the phone.

The boy dumped it in his hand before hastily retreating a few paces.

'Just in time, too,' said Jamie as the sound of sirens filled the air.

'What is going on?' said Dave.

Once again no one replied.

'Don't move, you fucking wankers,' someone yelled.

They all turned to see John Lawson brandishing an enormous machete. His face was bruised and sweaty, eyes wild.

'Now just take it easy, eh, John?' said Logan.

'Take it easy? What have you done to my brother?'

'He deserved it,' said Jamie. 'He was the one who killed Ben Wilson, wasn't he?'

John's eyes flickered. 'Shut the fuck up. Finally, Jamie Gray, you're gonnae get what you de—'

There was a loud clang and he groaned and toppled forward to reveal Jackie wielding her trusty frying pan.

'Maw!' exclaimed Jamie.

'Oh, that's pure funny,' grinned Gary. 'He got twatted by a woman again.'

'I hate blades,' screamed Jackie before kicking the machete away from John's limp hand. 'Oh my God,' she said when she looked back at Jamie. 'Your face is covered in blood.'

'Don't worry,' he replied. 'It's no' mine.'

They all watched as he snatched up John's dropped machete and returned to Cameron's side. He lay on the ground gasping for breath, having to breathe through his mouth because of his ruined nose.

'Jamie, take it easy,' said Jackie.

'I'm under control, Maw,' he replied before kicking Cameron onto his back. He knelt before him, thinking how pathetic he suddenly looked. In this moment his money and power meant nothing. 'Where is she?' said Jamie, waving the machete before his face.

Cameron released a weak chuckle. 'She's my secret. You'll never get her back. She's all mine, she always will be.'

'Is she at Cathkin Braes?'

'Go fuck yourself, scrag-end.'

Jamie grabbed Cameron's hand and stretched it out across the grass, holding it steady and lining the blade of the machete up with his wrist.

Jackie urged the three Blood Brothers to move closer so they could intercept if Jamie went too far. Dave remained where he was, not wanting to get too close to the vicious weapon.

'One last chance, Cameron,' said Jamie. 'Where is she?'

'Take my hand off, I don't care. I'll gladly pay the price. Only I know where she is, lying cold and alone. I separated you forever and whenever you think of her you'll think of me. Finally, I've got between you and I'll always be there.'

'No, Jamie,' cried Jackie when he raised the machete.

His friends leapt forward to intercept but they were too slow. They all breathed a sigh of relief when the blade embedded itself in the grass one inch from the tips of Cameron's fingers.

'I knew you didn't have the balls, you fucking runt,' said Cameron.

'I could happily take your head right off but I'm no' getting banged up for a jobby like you. I'm staying on the outside and I'm gonnae find her.'

'You'll never find her.' His lips drew back over his teeth, eyes blazing. 'I win.'

Jamie kicked him in the side of the head, knocking him out.

Next he turned his attention to John Lawson, who was just coming round.

'What are you going to do to him?' said Jackie.

'I just want to talk to him, Maw, don't worry.' He looked down at John. 'Neil forced you to have your photo taken with Ben Wilson's body, didn't he?'

He sighed and nodded, grimacing at the pain in his head. 'Aye, as leverage over my brother. He said he'd kill me and my maw if I didn't go with him and have that photo taken. He had a gun,' he added, eyes wide.

'Allegra was right.'

'Neil sent me that photo minutes before we started the rammy with you. Are you gonnae tell the police?' he said in a defeated voice.

'No one grasses on the Gallowburn.'

John's eyes filled with gratitude and he nodded, although he couldn't bring himself to thank him with words.

Blue lights strobed across the ground as a team of police cars screeched to a halt. The officers leapt out, the majority of them racing to deal with the battle still raging on the street while four of them ran towards the Gallows, Digger and Gary laughing when two officers fell into the stream, unable to see it in the dark. Jamie was relieved that one of the officers was Ross. With an agility Jamie hadn't thought him capable of, Ross hurdled the burn, slowing to a halt as he surveyed the carnage before him.

'What are you doing here?' Jamie asked him.

'I was at the station when a call came through about a rammy on the Gallowburn. I knew you'd be involved somehow.' He frowned at Cameron Abernethy lying injured on the ground. 'What the bloody hell happened here?'

'Craig Lawson got his family to start a fight to cause a distraction so he and Cameron could kill me,' replied Jamie. 'They were gonnae hang me from the hanging tree to make it look like I topped myself.'

'What?' screamed Jackie. 'You bastards, I'll kill you.'

When she aimed a kick at Cameron's head, Jamie pulled her back.

'Don't, Maw, he's no' worth it.'

'They deserve it, they're pieces of shit.'

'Aye, and they're gonnae get what's coming to them.' Jamie realised the forged suicide note was still pinned to his jumper, albeit creased and smeared with dirt and blood. Carefully he removed it and held it out to Ross, who pulled on nitrile gloves he took out of his pocket before accepting it. 'They forged this note. I don't know how they copied my handwriting, but they've done a good job.'

Ross held it in the air when Jackie attempted to snatch it from his hands.

'Please, Mrs Gray,' he told her. 'You could destroy important evidence.'

She scowled and folded her arms across her chest.

'Who's Craig Lawson?' he said.

They all pointed at him, lying unconscious on the ground.

'He works for that disgusting beast,' said Jackie, nodding at Cameron.

'Who knocked him out?' said Ross.

'I did,' said Jamie.

'Who did that to Cameron?'

'That was me as well.'

'Remind me never to get on the wrong side of you, Jamie.'

Jamie dumped the phone in Ross's hand. 'It's all on there. Fortunately, these two lads recorded everything. It's a good job they were passing by when Craig dragged me down here.'

Ross looked to the two boys Jamie indicated. 'They just happened to be here when the attack took place and recorded everything on this phone, is that what you're saying?'

'Aye. Lucky, eh?'

Ross's look was knowing. 'Very.'

'Cameron wouldn't tell me where Allegra is. He just said she'd never be found.'

Jamie looked so miserable Ross patted his shoulder. 'We're still searching for her. We won't give up. Looks like he's awake,' he added when there was a groan from Cameron's direction. 'Get the cuffs on him.'

'Get off me,' mumbled Cameron, shrugging off one of the constables when he attempted to snap on the handcuffs. 'You so much as touch me and I'll have your fucking job.' His voice was pinched and nasal thanks to his shattered nose.

'We wouldn't be able to find a uniform big enough,' commented Ross wryly as he watched the footage that had been recorded.

'You cheeky fucker. You're done too, Ross, do you hear me? Done.'

'Nah, I don't think so but you are, Abernethy, finally.' He turned the phone so he could show him the video the boys had recorded. 'You're on here saying you were going to kill Mr Gray by hanging him from a tree as well as admitting that you know where Allegra's body is.' He smiled when Cameron stared at the phone in astonishment. 'It looks like you finally met your match.'

'Aye,' said Jamie. 'A scheme rat brought down the great Cameron Abernethy.'

'One of our techs also pulled footage off your mobile phone of Mr Gray being run over,' Ross told Cameron. 'It was sent by an associate of yours – Neil Burrows, the very man you and your son alibied. We arrested him and he's already dropped you right in it. We spoke to your son, who was also very quick to tell us that you forced him to alibi Neil

Burrows. I don't know what to charge you with first, Mr Abernethy – conspiracy to commit murder, grievous bodily harm, perverting the course of justice, the list is endless.' He smiled, revelling in his victory. 'I anticipate you're going away for a very long time.'

Cameron's grin was more gurning than sly thanks to his injuries. 'You know that won't happen. I'll get off and when I'm free I'll obliterate the lot of you.'

'Whatever. Cuff him. Now.'

Cameron's ferocious gaze constantly flicked between Jamie and Ross as his hands were pulled behind his back and the cuffs snapped on.

'You're both dead,' he yelled as he was led away. 'I'll finish you, I swear. I never lose.'

'Make sure Mr Abernethy gets seen by the paramedics,' Ross called after the officers escorting his prisoner. 'We don't want his big fat body wriggling off the hook because of a technicality.'

A torrent of abuse poured from Cameron's lips as he was inexorably dragged away, screaming about how powerful he was and how no one could ever bring him down.

'Will you listen to him?' said Jackie. 'I bet he's got a tiny wee boaby.'

Gary and Digger both sniggered.

'Get the cuffs on him, too,' Ross told his two remaining detectives, gesturing to the unconscious Craig. 'He also tried to kill Mr Gray.'

'He killed Ben Wilson on Cameron's orders,' said Jamie.

'What?' exclaimed Ross, thrown by this turn of events.

'Allegra worked it out just before she vanished, although she wasn't sure why they murdered Ben.' He decided to make no mention of the photo. No way was he going to drop himself, his mother and his friends right in it, not when everything was working out in their favour.

'Have you any proof?'

'He's no' doing all your job for you,' commented Digger.

'What about him?' said Ross, gesturing to John, who was slumped on the ground, the essence of misery.

'He's just a fud,' replied Jamie.

'Fair enough.'

As the officers moved to cuff Craig, his eyes snapped open and he leapt up, drawing a knife from the back of his jeans. 'I'm not going back to prison, you ba—'

There was a loud clang and Craig toppled forward, landing face down in the grass.

'Thank you, Mrs Gray,' said Ross.

She frowned at her frying pan. 'Great, it's dented. I'll have to buy a new one, now.'

'Well, get him restrained quickly before he leaps up again,' Ross barked at his officers. 'Mrs Gray's frying pan is on its last legs.'

Jamie swallowed hard when Ross's intense gaze was turned his way. He probably knew there was a bit more going on than he'd been told and Jamie just prayed he was so pleased with his arrests he didn't press the issue.

'You look tired, Jamie. Get yourself checked out with the paramedics and then get yourself home. You can come into the station in the morning to give your statement.'

It was the permission he wanted, and he nodded. 'I will. Thanks.'

'How many more have you lifted?' Gary asked Ross.

'I don't know but probably not many,' replied Ross. 'As soon as they heard the sirens everyone scarpered. Not to worry, I've got what I came for. Now I suggest you all go home. No more wandering the streets tonight, you hear me? My officers will be patrolling the estate just to make sure there's no more trouble.'

'We will,' said Digger with an innocent smile that didn't fool the grizzled inspector for a moment.

Jamie sighed with relief when the police finally left.

'Thank God that's over,' said Jackie. She looked up at the hanging tree and tears sprang in her eyes when she thought how close her son had come to dangling from it, his body kicking and spasming as his eyes and tongue bulged from his face...

She hugged him, dropping the frying pan, which finally gave up the ghost, the handle falling off it.

'I'm okay, Maw,' he said when he felt her body tremble with suppressed tears. 'Let's go home.'

'Aye, all right, but you'll see the paramedics first. I'm taking no chances.'

'Okay, Maw, whatever you say.'

Jamie wrapped his arm around her, limping as they all headed back to the road. Now the adrenaline had worn off the pain had started up. He looked back over his shoulder at the hanging tree that had been cheated of one final victim, its crooked branches standing out starkly against the moonlit sky. For the briefest moment he'd considered letting Cameron and Craig hang him. At least then he'd be back with Allegra.

But now she was gone and he was stuck here.

The Gallowburn had won.

It always won.

20

A month later, Allegra's body still hadn't been found and Cameron was refusing to say where she was. He'd dropped several hints but none had panned out, sending the police on half a dozen wild goose chases. As he'd been remanded to Barlinnie Prison until his trial after his repeated assaults on Jamie, the whereabouts of his daughter's body was the last thing he could control and he jealously hung onto his secret, using it to taunt the police as well as those who'd loved Allegra.

Her best friend Veronica had arranged a memorial for Allegra at a country club they'd been fond of frequenting together. Everyone thought Fenston should have arranged it but when it became obvious he wasn't about to, Veronica had taken it upon herself.

The function room she'd hired for the event was bursting with roses of all colours, Allegra's favourite flower. As it was a warm sunny day, the doors had been left open to allow in a gentle breeze. A huge photograph of Allegra had been placed on an easel at the head of the room and a slide show of images of her flicked by on a screen behind Veronica, who was in the middle of an impassioned speech about her closest friend, tears rolling down her face. Jamie sat on the front row with his mother and Charlie, his friends in the row behind. The Blood

Brothers had proved to be very popular with all the pretty rich girls in attendance. In fact, they seemed to find them quite fascinating, especially after they'd heard about the Battle of Gallowburn, as the newspapers had termed it. That event had done their reputation no end of good and Logan, Digger and Gary had all collected the phone numbers of several of the women present.

Allegra had certainly made her mark in Gallowburn because in attendance were Deirdre and Eric, a very emotional Gerry, and Ephraim, who'd insisted on sitting by Jackie's side, patting her arm intermittently to comfort her. Allegra's godfather Tarquin was present, the man she'd told Jamie she would have liked to have as a father, who was crying into his pink silk handkerchief at Veronica's moving words. Before the memorial had started, he'd shaken Jamie's hand heartily and thanked him for the joy he'd given Allegra in the last months of her life. Broken by what had happened, he'd told Jamie he was in the process of selling his businesses and retiring to Thailand to open an elephant sanctuary, of all things, which he intended to call Allegra's Reservation. Jamie thought Allegra would have liked that.

Despite the fact there was no body, they were all here to say goodbye. They'd finally accepted that she was never coming home.

The only one who didn't seem particularly moved was Fenston, who sat at the end of the row on the opposite side of the room to Jamie, the two men casting each other mistrustful glares. Fenston had opened proceedings by giving a rather lacklustre speech about Allegra, attempting to say nice things about someone he'd never felt anything for. The end of his speech had been greeted with stony silence and he'd scurried back to his seat, head bowed. He'd narrowly escaped a prison sentence for perverting the course of justice by telling the police everything they wanted to know. He was now running the Abernethy empire and was revelling in having complete control. Already he was fermenting plans to have his father completely ousted.

The only thing Fenston hadn't been able to tell them was why Ben Wilson had been murdered. Neil had confessed to the crime to get a reduced sentence, implicating Craig and Cameron, but he didn't know why either. Ross suspected Ben had stolen from Cameron – being his accountant he'd be in the perfect position – but so far no evidence had been found confirming that. Cameron was still protesting his innocence in Ben's murder and the only thing linking him to it was Neil's statement, so it was possible he wouldn't get sent down for it. But he was being done for attempting to kill Jamie as well as Allegra's murder so he was looking at a very long stretch.

Finally, the memorial was over. Drinks and nibbles had been laid on, but Jamie made straight for the door.

'Where are you going?' Jackie asked him.

'Outside. I need some air.'

'Okay, sweetheart,' she said, patting his hand.

Jamie managed to sneak out before anyone noticed and loped across the vast lawn of the country club towards the sunken garden he'd spotted on his way in. To his relief no one was there, and he sank onto a bench and buried his face in his hands.

When he sensed someone sit beside him he looked up to see a dark-haired woman dressed all in black. Feeling she was a bit too close for comfort, he inched up towards the edge of the bench. To his consternation she followed until her side was practically pressing against his and he was trapped between her and the arm of the bench. Oh, great, one of the posh tarts from the memorial was trying to hit on him.

'Er, excuse me,' he said. 'You're invading my personal space.'

'It never bothered you before, Dangerous,' she replied.

Every muscle in Jamie's body froze, his mouth opening and closing as he tried to form the word wanting to burst out of his chest. His jaw fell open as the woman turned to face him, but rather than blue eyes he found himself looking into a pair of soft green eyes. But he'd recognise that face anywhere. The word came up from the pit of his stomach, through his tightening chest, past his frantically beating heart and into his throat before erupting out of him.

'Allegra,' he spluttered so loudly a pair of starlings pecking at the ground took off into the air. 'But... but...'

'I guess I've a lot of explaining to do,' she smiled.

But he didn't want explanations, not yet. He wanted to feel her in his arms, to know this wasn't some phantom created by his tortured brain. He pulled her to him, clinging onto her for dear life.

'I can't believe it,' he rasped, tears sliding down his face. 'I can't believe it.' Her arms went around his neck, her fingers playing through his hair warm and real. This was no dream.

'I'm so sorry,' she murmured in his ear. 'I can only imagine what I've put you through.'

He wanted to get angry at her and demand to know what the hell she was playing at, but the relief that she was alive and well was too overwhelming. He pressed his lips to hers and the passion with which she kissed him back told him she'd missed him as much as he'd missed her.

She leaned back slightly and took his face in her hands, her smile sad and gentle. 'I'm sorry for hurting you. I didn't want to, but I had no choice.'

His relief and delight morphed into anger. All that pain and heartache for nothing. 'You've put me through absolute hell,' he told her. 'As well as your friends and my maw and Charlie. Poor Tarquin's broken, he's moving to Thailand to open an elephant sanctuary. He's naming it after you.'

'An elephant?' she frowned.

'No, the whole sanctuary.'

'Aww, that's sweet. I'm glad he's finally going to live his dream.'

'What the hell have you been playing at? Why didn't you let us know you were okay?'

'Because I couldn't.'

'Why the hell not?'

'I'll explain, but no one else can know.'

'Why?'

'Please, let me explain and you'll understand, I hope.'

He took a deep, calming breath and nodded. She was alive and safe, that was what was important. 'Okay.'

They gripped onto each other's hands as she started to talk.

'My father attacked me in my bedroom,' she began, voice trembling at the traumatic memory. 'He told me he knew about us and that we were planning to leave together. He showed me footage of you getting hit by that car.' A tear slid down her cheek. 'He told me you were dead. He slashed my arm with the knife I used to cut myself with and strangled me. He thought he'd killed me but I was only unconscious. I think he panicked because he put me in the boot of my own car. I woke up in there, trapped in the dark, my arm bleeding. I couldn't shout for help because my throat hurt so much from being strangled. I only realised where I was when I found the bag I'd packed to take on our trip. I didn't have my phone so I couldn't call anyone. At first I decided not to do anything and just let him get rid of me because I thought you were dead. I couldn't imagine life without you. But then I got angry. The bastard had already got away with killing my mother. I wasn't going to let him get away with killing you, too.

'When he opened the boot, I played dead. He leaned in to lift me out and I whacked him on the back of the head with the wheel wrench. The shock on his face was priceless. There was panic there too, like he realised he wasn't going to be able to control a situation, for the first time in his life. I managed to knock him out and he fell like a big fat tree. I got out of the boot and saw he'd taken me to Coulter's Wood at Cathkin Braes. I reckon if I hadn't knocked him out I could have ended up being buried in there. I had minutes to decide what I was going to do. I knew his attacks on us wouldn't be enough to get him imprisoned for life. He'd got away with killing my mother and it was possible he'd get away with killing you. But I thought he might get sent down for killing me.'

As she uttered this last sentence everything became clear and Jamie fell in love with her even more.

'I parked the car not far from the marshes. I couldn't risk anyone seeing me alive in the area. He'd put my handbag in the back seat with my phone in and packed an overnight bag with some clothes. It was obvious he was trying to make it look like I'd gone away. Fortunately I'd left the bag containing my passport, cash, the flight tickets, a change of clothes and the disguise I intended to wear to leave the country in the boot so he wouldn't find it in the house.'

'But the police found your passport and the tickets...'

'I'll get to that later.'

'Okay.'

'I pulled on the long black wig and slipped in the contact lenses. I also changed clothes. Then I went to the marshes and threw one of the shoes I'd been wearing when he attacked me into the water. I knew that wouldn't be enough to arouse suspicion so I threw my phone in too, taking the SIM card out first and the knife he slashed me with. He'd put that in the car as well. Then I went into the bird hide and pulled out some of my hair. That wasn't hard as there were a lot of loose strands from where he'd grabbed my hair back at the house. My arm was still bleeding so that took care of that evidence. Gouging those marks in the wood bloody hurt, though. I ripped out three of my nail extensions,' she said, showing him her right hand to reveal the index, middle and ring fingernails were damaged and split. 'I was scared and so angry that he'd killed you as well as my mother that I determined to do it. I wanted to leave something nasty for the police to find that would definitely put him in prison.

'I couldn't risk going back to the house to plant evidence there but after the fight I put up I figured there might be enough left there anyway. After bandaging my arm with a piece of my old blouse I walked to the nearest bus stop, caught a bus to the train station, got the train to Dover and then the ferry over to Calais. I got my arm sorted out over there so there wouldn't be any hospital records in this country. It needed twelve stitches. I'll always have the scar. From France I travelled through Spain into Portugal. From there I thought it would be wise to get out of Europe for a while, so I flew to Morocco, I'd always wanted to go there. After a couple of weeks, I flew to Italy. I went to an English bar in Milan to catch up on the UK news. I wanted to see if my father was being investigated for killing me. It was then I found out you were still alive. I couldn't believe it. If I'd known I never would have run, so I decided to chance it and come back, I had to see you to explain.'

Jamie stared at her with his mouth hanging open.

'Questions?' she said with her sweet smile.

'But... but...'

'Oh yes, you wanted to know about the passport and tickets. The passport I used to get to France was false. I got it off a bloke in Possilpark who I met through Leo Miller.'

'That's why you were hanging around with those creeps,' he said. 'You were planning your escape even then and you thought they might know people who could help.'

'Yep. I thought I was going to throw up the first time I had to use the false passport. It must be good because I've travelled all over the world on it and no one's batted an eyelid. I never intended us to fly out to Switzerland, that was a decoy to stop my father from tracking us. I bought tickets to Athens under the name on my false passport. I was going to tell you the day before we went.'

'You didn't trust me not to tell anyone?'

'Of course I trusted you. It was to protect your mum and friends, so they couldn't tell my father where we really were if he came calling, which he undoubtedly would have done.'

'But your dad practically told me that he'd killed you. He's told the police where you're buried. Of course they never found anything but why would he do that? Why not tell them he's innocent?'

'Simple. He's a control freak and like all control freaks he can't bear to admit that he'd lost control and hadn't the first clue where I was. Perhaps he thought he'd injured me so badly I'd wandered off somewhere and died and that I'd turn up in time.'

'Maybe. He did enjoy using it to torment me and the police.'

'That's typical of him.'

'And you set him up too well. There was so much evidence everyone thought he'd killed you.' Jamie sighed and sank back into the bench as he processed all this information.

'Are you okay?' she said when he'd been silent for a full minute.

'I should have known something more was going on, especially when the police couldn't find you. You always surprise me, but this takes the bloody biscuit,' he snapped.

'You're not angry, are you?'

'Angry? I'm fucking furious. You've no idea what I've gone through and not just me but my maw, Charlie, your godfather and all your friends. They're all in there in bits,' he spat, pointing back to the hotel.

'I'm so sorry, but it was the only way to stop my father. He had to pay for what he did to my mother and to us, and don't forget, I thought you were dead. At the time I think he thought you were too.' Tears filled her eyes. 'It's been so hard for me travelling around these strange places on my own, aching to have you beside me and thinking you were gone. You mourned me, yes, but I mourned you too. If only I'd checked the UK news earlier but I couldn't bear to. I couldn't stand to see reports about your death or photos of your funeral and I didn't want to find out that my father had got away with it *again*.'

Allegra broke off, her lower lip trembling indignantly, those green eyes that seemed so strange to him filled with tears.

He looked round at the sound of voices coming from the direction of the hotel and took her hand. 'Come on.'

Together they ran up the steps leading out of the sunken garden and into the woodland that circled the hotel, not stopping until they'd reached a particularly dense, dark patch, well out of sight of any passers-by.

Jamie pulled her to him. 'So, what happens now?'

'Now I have to go away again,' she replied.

'But you've only just come back.'

'If anyone finds out what I did I'll go to prison for a long time and my father will be released to hurt people again.'

'I don't want you to go.'

'It's just for a few years, until everything dies down. Then we can be together.'

'Years?' he exclaimed.

'The world has grown small. If anyone saw us together everything would come out and it might look suspicious, you leaving the country so soon. Let me disappear from everyone's memories. It'll be safer that way. Then you can come out to me, we can still travel like we planned.'

'You're never coming back, are you?'

'I can't. It was a risk coming back now but I had to see you. When I realised you were still alive... I can't describe how happy I was.'

'I'm getting a good idea of how you felt right now,' Jamie said with a gentle smile.

Allegra beamed back at him and slid her arms around his neck. 'You don't hate me, do you?'

'I could never hate you,' he said, cupping her face in his hands.

Her fingers brushed his throat. 'It said on the news my father tried to hang you from the Gallowburn hanging tree.'

'Aye, but I kicked the shite out of him and Craig Lawson. I went berserker on them.'

'I bet that terrified them.'

'Too right it did. Your da was on the ground, squealing like a wee lassie.'

'Good,' she spat. 'I hope you hurt him a lot.'

'Well, his nose will never look the same. How will I contact you?'

'You can't. If the police get suspicious and check your phone...'

'They won't.'

'I don't know how well I covered my tracks. Something might turn up. We need to be patient.'

He sighed and nodded. 'Suppose.'

'We will see each other again, I promise. I love you, Jamie.'

'I love you, too.'

She produced the ring he'd given her, which she still wore on a chain around her neck. 'Do you want this back?'

He nodded.

'Oh, right,' she said, pain filling her as she removed the chain and dumped the ring in his waiting hand.

He took her left hand and slid the ring onto her engagement finger.

'You had me going then,' she breathed.

'I know,' he said with a mischievous smile. 'Wear it there always. One day I will marry you.'

'I got you something,' she said, producing a gold band from her pocket. 'I picked it up in Milan when I heard you were still alive. I swore I'd come back and give it to you to prove how serious I am that I still want us to be together.'

When she looked at him questioningly, he nodded, and she placed the ring on his left ring finger.

'You didn't nick it, did you?' he said playfully.

'No,' she smiled. 'It's bought and paid for.'

'But what have you been living off? Tarquin told the police about the eighty grand in that offshore account. I think he was hoping you were alive and well, living it up somewhere, but it hasn't been touched.'

'I know. That's because I've got another seventy-five grand that was stolen from my father.'

He blinked at her. 'What?'

'Ben Wilson.'

Jamie's eyes widened. 'That's why he was killed, because he stole from Cameron?'

'A lot of my father's wealth has come from money laundering, which Ben Wilson was in charge of. Some of the companies in the Abernethy empire are dummy companies he uses to launder the money through. I overheard my father telling Neil he thought Ben was skimming off the top. Naturally, he couldn't go to the police with his suspicions, so he had to leave it in the hands of that animal. I liked Ben, he was a nice, quiet, gentle man who loved his family, so I warned him, I told him to get away before Neil caught up with him. Ben had a hundred and fifty grand in cash he'd stolen from my father, so he gave it to me to look after in case Neil came calling and decided to search his home or office. He knew he could trust me with it and besides, he had no choice. I told him to do a runner, I knew my father was planning to do something bad to him, but he said Neil would give him a beating at most. He thought he was too valuable to my father because the entire money laundering operation was stored in his head, but my father must have been so furious he'd been duped that he couldn't let him live. When I saw the report of his body being found when I was at your house I was shocked but not surprised. I was just sad that Ben hadn't listened to me. I sent half the cash anonymously to Ben's wife. She knew what sort of business her husband was in, so she was smart enough to keep quiet about it, and I kept the other half for my escape.'

'Bloody hell,' he breathed. 'Why didn't you tell me?'

'Because you could have got into trouble by association. I didn't want you or your family dragged into it. I did intend to tell you once we'd left the country.'

'But his family have to know why he was killed, it's only fair.'

'I'm working on that. I will find a way to let them know, perhaps with an anonymous tip-off. Don't worry, I'll make sure it's sorted. I think his wife has probably guessed by now who's responsible, especially after everything that's happened.'

'So, you've got enough to live on then?'

'Plenty. Don't worry about me. I'm very resourceful.'

'So I see,' he smiled. 'It must be hard knowing you've got eighty grand and you can't touch it.'

'I will be able to in seven years.'

'Why seven years?' he frowned.

'After you proposed to me I made a will in your favour and filed it with a solicitor, one with no connection to my father.'

'What?'

'It made sense seeing how you were going to be my husband. If we'd married it would have gone to you anyway, but I wanted something set in stone in case anything happened to me. I wouldn't put it past my father to interfere. So, in seven years' time, I'll be officially declared dead and you'll inherit everything of mine, including the eighty grand, which will be a lot more by then because of the interest.'

He stared at her in astonishment, attempting to wrap his head around how smart she was. He'd assumed she got her intelligence from her father, but he was wrong. She was way smarter than he was. 'You're amazing.'

'I know,' she smiled.

They kissed, Jamie pressing her up against a tree.

'Jamie,' yelled a voice not far from the tree line.

'Oh, hell,' he muttered. 'I think it's my maw.'

'I have to go before anyone sees me,' said Allegra.

'No, please don't go,' he said, keeping a tight hold of her.

'No one can see me. I am not going to prison for that piece of shit.'

Jamie nodded, took a deep breath and forced himself to release her.

'Jamie,' repeated Jackie.

'You can't tell her that I'm still alive,' said Allegra. 'You can't tell anyone.'

'I won't, promise.'

'Don't forget to hide that,' she added, indicating the ring on his finger.

'Oh aye,' he replied, taking it off and sliding it into his trouser pocket.

'Jamie,' repeated Jackie.

'Coming,' he yelled back, making Allegra smile as she was reminded of the times she'd spent at his house.

'When the time's right I will contact you, I swear,' Allegra told him. She grabbed his face in both hands and kissed him before taking a few reluctant steps back. 'I love you, Dangerous,' she said as she retreated further into the trees, her dark clothes melding with the shadows.

'Love you too, Princess,' he tenderly replied.

He watched until she'd vanished from view.

'Jamie,' yelled Jackie again.

'For God's sake,' he muttered before sprinting back the way he'd come.

'Thank God,' breathed Jackie when her son emerged from the trees. 'What were you doing in there?'

'I needed some privacy. The memorial was hard for me,' Jamie replied, feeling like a hypocrite. 'Don't worry, I wasn't going to top myself.' For some reason, after Cameron had forged that note in his handwriting, Jackie had become paranoid that he was going to harm himself. Admittedly, the thought had crossed his mind a few times but never again. The future now felt like something to look forward to.

'Are you okay sweetheart?' Jackie asked him. 'You look a bit... dazed.'

'I feel it,' he murmured. Once again he'd been Allegra'd.

'Do you want to go home?'

'Aye, please,' he replied, unable to face all the mourners inside, knowing their suffering was for nothing. At least Cameron Abernethy was finally behind bars where he belonged.

'We'll collect Charlie and make our excuses,' Jackie said, linking her arm through his as they headed back to the hotel. 'Has the memorial helped? Maybe now you can start to move on.'

'Aye, it has,' he said, thinking what an understatement that was. 'I feel a little better.'

'That's good. She was a beautiful lassie who we were lucky to have in our lives. It's best to remember her that way.'

Jamie slid his hand into his pocket to touch the gold band nestled there, just to reassure himself that it had all been real. He glanced over his shoulder at the trees, just able to see a dark-haired figure dressed in black watching them before she melded into the foliage and vanished.

'Aye,' he smiled, voice barely a murmur. 'Beautiful.'

MORE FROM HEATHER ATKINSON

We hope you enjoyed reading *Blood Brothers*. If you did, please leave a review.

If you'd like to gift a copy, this book is also available as an ebook, digital audio download and audiobook CD.

Sign up to Heather Atkinson's mailing list for news, competitions and updates on future books.

http://bit.ly/HeatherAtkinsonNewsletter

ABOUT THE AUTHOR

Heather Atkinson is the author of over fifty books - predominantly in the crime fiction genre. Although Lancashire born and bred she now lives with her family, including twin teenage daughters, on the beautiful west coast of Scotland. Her new gangland series for Boldwood, set on the fictional Gallowburn estate in Glasgow begins with *Blood Brothers* which will be published in December 2020.

Visit Heather's website: https://www.heatheratkinsonbooks.com/

Follow Heather on social media:

twitter.com/HeatherAtkinsoɪ
instagram.com/heathercrimeauthor
bookbub.com/authors/heather-atkinson
facebook.com/booksofheatheratkinson

ABOUT BOLDWOOD BOOKS

Boldwood Books is a fiction publishing company seeking out the best stories from around the world.

Find out more at www.boldwoodbooks.com

Sign up to the Book and Tonic newsletter for news, offers and competitions from Boldwood Books!

http://www.bit.ly/bookandtonic

We'd love to hear from you, follow us on social media:

facebook.com/BookandTonic

twitter.com/BoldwoodBooks

instagram.com/BookandTonic

Printed in Great Britain
by Amazon